Mrs Israel Hall
Toledo

THE HEEDLESS EXPOSURE.

VILLAGE LIFE IN THE WEST.

BEYOND THE BREAKERS.

A STORY OF THE PRESENT DAY.

BY

ROBERT DALE OWEN.

"From seeming evil still educing good,
And better yet again and better still,
In infinite progression."

THOMSON.

PHILADELPHIA
J. B. LIPPINCOTT & CO.
1870.

LIPPINCOTT'S PRESS,
PHILADELPHIA.

TO AN EXCELLENT FRIEND,

IN WHOSE LIBRARY THE FIRST OF THE FOLLOWING CHAPTERS WAS WRITTEN,

FERDINAND J. DREER, OF PHILADELPHIA,

THIS STORY

IS INSCRIBED.

BEYOND THE BREAKERS.

"From seeming evil still educing good;
And better thence again, and better still,
In infinite progression." THOMSON.

CHAPTER I.

THE ACCUSATION.

IT was in the old days, now almost forgotten, when bits of gold and silver passed current among us as money. As we mortals reckon time, it was some twelve or fourteen years ago, but if one estimates by thick-crowding events and revolutions, social and political, there has passed a generation since the incidents that are to be related occurred in the sober Quaker State of Pennsylvania.

One cold, rainy evening, late in the spring, there sauntered into a tavern kept in Water street, Philadelphia, a man not beyond middle age and somewhat shabbily dressed. It was a tavern, not only in the strict old sense of the term—to wit, a resort of the thirsty, where wines and sundry hot potations might be had at retail, as eighteen hundred years ago they were in the *thermopolia* of Pompeii (whose marble *tabulæ* are cup-stained still)—but also taken according to the modernized American phraseology; for its hearty, bright-eyed owner furnished to the emigrant and to the chance traveler board and lodging, as well as grog and punch. Terence O'Reilly was an Irishman, every inch of him: one saw that at a glance. The high cheek-bones, the ruddy color, the touch of the brogue, came unmistakably from the Green Island. The world had gone well with Terence. He liked it: he thoroughly enjoyed life, and sought to make it as pleasant to others as to himself. He had selected a sorry mode of doing so, it is true, not being satisfied to dispense Cowper's cups that "cheer but not inebriate." I dare say he had not heard Gough lecture, and probably had never taken a serious thought as to whether the world was the better or the worse for the gin and the whisky that are made in it. He had imbibed, with his hardy mother's milk, her careless, thoughtless, hopeful temperament. His father, hail-fellow-well-met with every one, had not improved his son's habits by suffering him, when he had outgrown the maternal beverage, occasionally to taste a little of the *potheen* that had the sweetness of stolen waters about it, being manufactured of nights in a small underground still, of which the masked entrance could be reached only through the intricacies of an Irish bog, and so had escaped, for years, the argus-eyed revenue officers. The lad grew up light-hearted, jovial, but not intemperate, nor yet without a wholesome ambition to better his condition, and attain the respectability which he saw that money was wont to bring.

His first step in life had been as hostler in a country inn. There the hard-working fellow served faithfully, finally attracting the attention of a young officer in the Guards, the eldest son of the Honorable Patrick Halloran, a wealthy landed proprietor, on whose property Terence's father lived. Captain Halloran, pleased with the lad's spirit and good-humor, took him into his service as groom, promoting him, in gay livery, to a seat behind his stylish curricle when he drove that fine-stepping pair of black-limbed bays of his in Hyde Park. It was not a situation to improve the young groom's morals; for those of his master were none of the best, especially in his relations with women; and the white-cravatted, black-clothed valet whom the Captain had picked up in Paris, and who stood high in his confidence, pandered to vices from which the scoundrel well knew how to profit. But here again, as in the article of *potheen*, Terence escaped any serious contamination. This happened partly because of the fact that though the young man's ideas on ethics were of the vaguest sort, he had a sturdy, rude-fashioned sense of the fair and the honorable; partly because he had an inborn dislike of anything French, and barely tolerated his fellow-servant, who, on his part, looked down with supreme contempt on the rough young Irishman.

Had Terence been less of a favorite with Captain Halloran, this mutual aversion would probably have cost him his place within the first few months; but Louis Villemont — so the valet was called—was a man to bide his time, and let his revenge sleep till the moment came when it could be safely indulged. He was rewarded for his patience after enduring Terence nearly a year and a half. Reckless self-indulgence, long continued, readily hardens into vice when the tempter is at hand to encourage and facilitate. So it was with Captain Halloran. Aided and prompted by Louis, he committed an act of villainy from which, in the early part of his career as a young man of fashion, he would have shrunk with abhorrence. His victim, an interesting and accomplished young girl, fled, one night, in an agony of despair, no one knew whither. Terence, getting to know the main facts, and stirred by that spirit of rude chivalry which is not unfrequently found in his class and nation, broke forth upon Louis, calling him names which caused the Frenchman's dark eyes to flash with fury; and not satisfied with that, his indignation once fairly roused, he proceeded to denounce the master himself in no measured terms. Thereupon Louis' wrath subsided into a sinister smile. "Tu me le payeras," he muttered under his breath, as his master's bell rung. Half an hour later he returned, and, with a civil leer, handed the groom his wages to date, with a handsome gratuity and a message from Captain Halloran that he had no further occasion for his services. Terence found himself possessor of a sum sufficient to pay a steerage passage to New York, and leave him a hundred and fifty dollars to begin life with in the New World. Nor, up to this stormy May evening, had he ever once had cause to repent his change of country.

The shabby stranger sat by the stove, leaning forward, drying himself; his white hands (for they *were* white) resting on his knees, and gleaming through the dull steam that rose from his wet clothes. Handsome, most people would have called him; yet it was a bad countenance, furtive and gloomy. The large gray eyes were well formed, but they seemed not to look straight at any one; the features well cut; brown curling hair and whiskers of the same color. One could see, however, that there was power about the man. Though the forehead was low, it was a fair-sized head, fully developed above the eyes and behind the large ears, of which one was somewhat disfigured by a purple line across it, as from an old wound. The features bore the stamp of self-indulgence and something of the flush of dissipation. A sullen frown passed over them from time to time, prompted, it was evident, by thoughts that were anything but pleasant.

After a time he rose and approached the bar. "A glass of grog, landlord," he said: "I want it stiff. A hell of a wet night I've had of it!"

"In a minute," replied the other: then to a man with whom he had been conversing: "You haven't got that last sack of potatoes down: how much is the bill, altogether?"

"Seventeen dollars and a half, Terence; but I don't want the money now if it isn't just handy."

"Never handier," said Terence. "I don't buy till I have the cash ready." And producing from an inner breast-pocket a stout linen bag, he poured on the counter its entire contents, consisting of a number of eagles, together with a few half-eagles and bank-bills. "Is it gold you'll be wanting?"

"Well," said the other, "city bills are good enough, but I'm going South to-morrow, and you may as well give me a couple of those half-eagles."

"Heartily welcome," said Terence, paying him, and taking a receipt in return.

If the two men who happened at the moment to be the only occupants of the bar-room except the stranger, had chanced to notice the eager, sidelong, persistent look which the latter cast on the gold that still lay scattered on the counter, it might have been interpreted to his discredit; yet one ought not to think hard of the hungry vagrant who, as he passes the brilliantly-lighted window of a pastry cook's shop, casts wistful glances at tart and cheese-cake.

As it was, Terence was scarcely conscious of the man's presence, until the latter repeated his request for a glass of brandy and water.

"Faith, an' I clane forgot ye," he said, pouring out a liberal portion, as if to atone for the delay.

The man tossed off the potent dram with a relish.

Several lodgers came in. Then he asked: "Can I put up with you, Mr. O'Reilly, to-night?"

Terence stopped in the act of closing the bag whence he had poured the gold, looked hard at the questioner, and hesitated. The man spoke, as if in answer to the hesitation:

"You wouldn't be turning a poor man, and a countryman of your own, out in a stormy night like this? I'm from Tipperary."

"What's your name?"

"My name? — Byron — Byron Cassiday."

"Well, Bryan—"

"It's Byron, not Bryan, I told you," retorted the other, more sharply than the occasion seemed to call for.

"Well, Byron, then: ye needn't flare up. Bryan's a better Irish name, any way."

"If you're afraid of the pay, there's my watch," pulling a silver one from his fob.

"Who said I was afraid? Put up your watch. It's an ugly night, and I'll not turn you from the door," pushing the register toward him, in which the man entered his name, with the address, "Port Richmond," and the remark: "I've been working in the country, but I came last from Port Richmond."

"He can write, any how," said the landlord to himself, glancing at the name: "maybe he's dacent;" and he led the way to a small bed-room, setting a candlestick on the washstand.

Left alone, Cassiday sat down on a straight-backed, rush-bottomed chair, tilted it back against the bed, and sank into moody thought. Half an hour passed ere he stirred. At last, muttering, "A man must do something for a living: nothing venture, nothing have," he rose and examined the fastenings of the bed-room door. There was a lock, with the key inside. It locked readily, but that did not seem to satisfy him. Unlocking it, he wrenched the key forcibly to the left. Something snapped. Then he tried repeatedly to lock the door again, but failed each time. The lock was evidently spoilt. Finally he relinquished all effort to secure the door, took the candlestick from the washstand and placed it on the floor of the passage outside, undressed partially, and, after tossing restlessly for an hour or two, and gazing occasionally around the room, dropped into a heavy sleep.

Next morning, after breakfast, he was again in the bar-room, where he sat watching the demeanor of his landlord. Terence was behind the counter, exchanging jest and banter with two or three early customers, and his bold cheery voice rung out from a happy and careless heart. The embodiment of good-humor, he was, notwithstanding, a man whom it might be dangerous to irritate. There was a flash in his laughing eye, and his broad shoulders and brawny, large-fisted arms would not have disgraced the prize-ring.

Cassiday eyed him closely, seeming about to address him ; then, as if he had thought better of it, sauntered around the room, examining various marvels of art with which it was adorned. In the centre of the principal wall was "Washington's Deathbed," the garments and the countenances of the attendants alike lugubrious ; and this was flanked, on the one side, by a portrait of the wonderful horse with white legs—the pride of the English race-course—that was foaled during the great eclipse, taking his name from his birth-day ; and on the other by a print setting forth, in startling colors, the fight between Crib and Molineux—that Crib, as the landlord delighted in relating, who at the close of a fair stand-up fight, in which he had battered in three ribs of the black giant that was pitted against him, turned a standing somerset on the ground, in proof that wind and pluck were alike untouched by the exertions of the terrible contest.

Finally, when he had sufficiently admired these ambitious productions of fancy, and when all the customers had departed, the stranger slowly approached the counter.

"I wish I had stayed in the country," he began.

"I didn't ax ye to leave it," said Terence. "What's the matter?"

"Matter enough! Bad luck to your city taverns!"

"Ye're uncivil, stranger: ye had a clean bed and a good breakfast," his color rising. "If the accommodations don't suit you, pay for what ye've had and be off with ye."

"I've paid pretty dearly for them already."

"What does that mean?"

"It means that when I went up to your bed-room last night I had a hundred and seventy dollars in my pocket, and that I came down this morning with just ten cents to pay for my night's lodging."

Terence flushed scarlet, but he restrained himself:

"Oh, that's the dodge, is it? I thought the chance was a poor one, but ye looked tired and wet. Well, it's only a half dollar thrown away. A hundred and seventy dollars, and ye wanted to pledge your watch! Why, man, ye should make one part o' your story tally wi' the rest."

"It tallies well enough. Do you think I was going to show my hand before all your lodgers? It wasn't quite safe, it seems, to let them know there was a hundred and seventy dollars to be had in my bed-room for the fetching of it."

"Look ye here, Mister Cassiday," said the landlord, "you'd best be gone while the play's good. I ought to send for a police officer and have ye taken up for a swindler; and I will, if you say another word about my lodgers. I expect the next thing will be, you'll be telling me I stole it myself."

"Likelier-looking men than you have done the same before now. I advise you to bridle your tongue, or maybe you may make acquaintance with the police yourself, sooner than you think for."

Terence just touched the counter with his left hand, and was over in a single bound. With the right he throttled his man, forced him back, as though he had but a child in his grasp, to the street door, which he flung open, and there released him, at the same moment dealing him a hearty kick, which sent him staggering down the steps, over the sidewalk and half-way across the street, where he fell prostrate, but where, luckily for him, no vehicle was just then passing. The whole transpired in less time than it has taken to relate it.

CHAPTER II.

THE ARREST.

AN hour and a half had elapsed; and Terence, the scuffle of the morning already forgotten, was standing at the street door, somewhat anxiously awaiting the arrival of the owner of the house he occupied, with whom he hoped, that morning, to conclude a purchase of the premises, when a police officer stopped before the door. A cloth cap, turned up with gray fur, which the young man wore, seemed to attract the attention of the officer, who, after eyeing him for a few moments, said: "Is this Terence O'Reilly?"

"At your service." Then, as the other hesitated, he added, cheerily, "It's sort o' chilly, if it is 'most summer. Come in and warm yourself."

The officer entered: Terence drew a chair for him before the stove, and they sat down together.

"I'm sorry," the policeman said, after a pause—"I think there must be some mistake—but—I have a warrant for your arrest."

"A warrant!" Then, with a smile: "Oh, for 'sault and battery. So the rascal bears malice, does he? Well, if he didn't deserve the kick I gave him, nobody ever did."

"I wish it were nothing else," said the officer, gravely; "but it's on a charge of larceny. The man lodged information at our station that you robbed him last night of a hundred and seventy dollars."

For a moment the poor man was utterly confounded. But he rallied: "It's me lodgers he charges it on. But a man isn't a thief because money's stolen in his house."

"He didn't say a word about your lodgers. He swore, point-blank, that you came into his room in the middle of the night and took his money, and that he saw you and knew you."

"The Lord above!"

"I'll have to take you before the mayor."

Terence sprung from his chair. The officer also started up and stood between the door and his prisoner, but the latter did not even notice the action. He had turned to a lad who was tending bar for him:

"Pat, d'ye like my service?"

"Is it your service, Mister O'Reilly? And don't ye know I do? I'd go through fire and water for ye."

"I'll never forgive ye the longest day I live—I'll send ye packing afore the day's out—if you say one word o' this to Norah. It would kill the lassie." Then to the officer: "At your service."

They walked some distance in silence. At last O'Reilly asked:

"Can they send a man to prison for a thief, that never did a dishonest thing since the day his mother bore him?"

The question was a deeper one than the young man thought for. The officer evaded it: "A man that's accused of larceny need not go to prison till he's tried and convicted. This is a preliminary investigation, and they'll take bail."

"They must prove it on him, then?"

"Certainly."

Terence stepped out more freely—almost with unconcern. But at the mayor's office there was delay till several petty charges were disposed of; and these, with their sordid details, somewhat sunk the poor fellow's spirits again. He felt the humiliation of the associations into which, for the first time, he had been brought, and he looked somewhat dispirited when placed at the bar.

"Is this the charge of larceny?" said the mayor.

"Yes, your honor."

"Has the prisoner been searched?"

"No." The officer proceeded to search him, and the bag of money with which we are already familiar was taken from an inner pocket.

Cassiday was then called as witness. Terence started as the man came forward; then involuntarily drew up first one sleeve and then the other, exposing, as he did so, a ring of white on each wrist above the large, tanned hands. The mayor's quick eye detected the movement, and he turned to the officer apparently to give an order; then glancing again at the prisoner, from whose face the flush of anger was fading, he seemed to think better of it, and merely said to the witness, "Go on."

Cassiday deposed that, the previous night, he had lodged in No. 36, a small front hall bed-room on the third floor of the house kept by the prisoner; that in the middle of the night he had been awakened by the sound of some one moving about in his room; that he recognized the prisoner by his general appearance, but especially by his cloth cap trimmed with fur; that at the moment he first saw him the prisoner was stooping over a chair, just beyond the washstand, where he (the deponent) had laid his coat before going to bed; that he (the prisoner) remained for some time in this stooping position, as if searching for something, then turned to the washstand, so that he (the deponent) could distinctly see his side face, took up a candlestick which was standing there, and passed out of the room on tiptoe; that in the inside pocket of the coat he (the deponent) had a hundred and seventy dollars in a stout linen sack, and all in gold eagles, which, on rising afterward to search his coat, he found was gone.

Terence sat like one in a stupor, till awakened by a question of the mayor addressed to the witness:

"Did you lock your door before going to rest?"

"No; I tried to, but I found the lock wouldn't work."

"That's a lie!" burst forth Terence. "Divil a lock out of order in my house from garret to cellar!"

"Wait your turn, prisoner," said the mayor, a little sternly: "you shall be heard in defence." Then to the witness:

"You say you saw the prisoner. Had you left your candle burning? There was no moon last night, I think."

"No, your honor, but there was a lamp in the street just opposite, and there was no curtain to the window; so I could see well enough."

"Why did not you stop him and raise the alarm at once?"

"I was scared, just waking up, and I was afraid he might murder me if I stirred."

The contempt on the prisoner's bold, frank face was something refreshing to see. "The chicken-sowled, perjured villain!" he muttered, under his breath.

"Look at that money-bag," said the mayor to the witness: "is it the one you had?"

After what seemed a careful examination the man answered "No."

"Officer, see what it contains."

Seventeen gold eagles, ten half-eagles and twenty-two dollars in bank-notes—two hundred and forty-two dollars in all—were the contents.

"Prisoner, where did you get these seventeen eagles?"

"A peddler paid me fifteen of them, to-morrow will be a week."

"For what?"

"For a gold watch and chain and some jewelry."

"How came you to have a watch and jewelry for sale?"

"Sure, an' I took them from one of me boarders, for a debt of two hundred and twenty dollars, bein' I could get nothin' else."

"And you have kept the money in that bag in your pocket ever since?"

"Till this blessed day, yer honor."

"Was any one present when you traded with the peddler?"

"I disremember exactly, but I think not."

"What was his name!"

"I never axed him."

The mayor reflected, then made a few memoranda in pencil and handed them to the police officer: "Bring me word whether the lock in room 36 of the house occupied by the prisoner works well or not. Observe whether the window of that room has a curtain, and whether it is opposite to a street lamp. Then ask the chambermaid of the house if she found a candlestick in No. 36 when she went to make the bed. Prisoner, we shall have to detain you till the officer returns. In any event, the offence you are charged with is bailable, and you may send by him for any of your friends in case bail is required."

In an hour the police officer returned, reporting that the lock of No. 36 would not work, that the window of that room was uncurtained, that there was a street-lamp just opposite to it, and that the chambermaid declared that when she went, after breakfast, to do up the room, instead of finding the candlestick there, as she expected, it was on the floor of the passage outside.

After listening to this report, the mayor again called up the case, asked the prisoner what he had to say for himself, listened patiently to his vague, incoherent protestations of innocence, and then ordered that he find bail for his appearance to stand trial at the next term for larceny, and that the money-bag and its contents be meanwhile retained. Two of his associates, whom he had reluctantly sent for, came eagerly forward with the requisite bail, and Terence was released.

Among his friends once more, Terence soon regained, in a measure, the habitual flow of high spirits which had contributed to make him the general favorite he was.

"Norah," he said to his wife, from whom it had been impossible to conceal the transaction—"Norah, me darlint, is it cryin' ye are? Hold up your head. Ye know yer husband isn't a thief. Ye would swear to that any day, wouldn't ye, mavourneen?"

The young wife threw her arms about his neck, hid her face on his shoulder and sobbed out: "Afore the throne o' God, Terence—afore the throne o' God!"

"Then she's the true grit," said her husband, kissing her. "Now hearken to what I tell ye: I axed that officer—he was a dacent man, Norah, and a civil-spoken, if he was a policeman—I axed him could they put the darbies on and make a prison-bird o' me—me that never stole a red cent in me life. And he said, says he, 'No, SIR, they can't; they dar'n't touch a hair of yer head till they prove it on ye.' Them was his very words. An' sure ye know, Norah, that they can't prove what never was. Could they prove that I wasn't yer lagel husband, acushla, or that them two children ye bore me wasn't mine? Tell me that!"

That was putting the case strongly, but the wife's lingering fears suggested a contingency:

"What if that bad man swears a lie to get yer money?"

"And isn't there the judge sittin' on the bench, with his gown and his larnin'?" (Terence's ideas of judicial dignity were somewhat old-country-fashioned.) "D'ye think a low, lyin' scoundrel like that can chate *him* out o' the face?"

So Norah dried her eyes and was comforted. For didn't Terence know best?

Six weeks later the trial came on before Judge Oswald Thomas. He wore neither wig nor gown, but, as he turned to look at the prisoner who had just taken his place in the dock, Terence's heart was lightened of a load: it was an honest, kind-hearted face. "It's all right," was his thought, and that helped him to bear up under the infliction of the public gaze.

The usual question as to whether he was guilty or not guilty was repeated twice before Terence had collected his senses to answer: "Is it whether I stole the money? The rascal knows I never did."

A smile passed over the audience as the clerk recorded the plea "Not Guilty."

"Who is your counsel, prisoner?" said the district attorney.

"Me counsel?" with a vacant stare.

"Yes: what lawyer have you engaged to defend you?"

"Is it a lawyer ye're axing after? I'll leave it all to his honor, there. It's only a thief that needs a lawyer, and do ye take me for a thief?"

"This is a very grave charge," said the prosecutor, addressing the court: "the prisoner ought surely to have counsel."

"Have you no money with which to pay a lawyer, prisoner?" said the judge to Terence.

"They took me bag with more'n two hundred dollars, but I've four hundred in the bank yet."

"Then you had better take a part of that four hundred and get a lawyer to attend to your case?"

"Does your honor think I'm a thief, too?"

"Never mind what I think. Take my advice: it's kindly meant. The court gives you three days for preparation. Call the next case."

CHAPTER III.

THE TRIAL.

"I was interrupted in the heyday of this soliloquy with a voice which I took to be that of a child, which complained 'it could not get out.' I looked up and down the passage, and seeing neither man nor woman nor child, I went out without further attention. In my return back through the passage, I heard the same words repeated twice over; and, looking up, I saw it was a starling, hung in a little cage. 'I can't get out, I can't get out!' said the starling."—STERNE'S *Sentimental Journey.*

TERENCE fell into good hands. Carrol Bagster was an upright man and an earnest, eloquent advocate. He ran his eye rapidly over the notes of the case. "Terence, my good fellow," said he, "this is a bad scrape. Three days only, and the court will probably adjourn in two days more. Look here! I should have to charge you a hundred dollars: it will take every hour of my time till the trial comes on; and its only throwing good money after bad. Plead guilty: then the sentence will be light—maybe three or four months only. It's your best chance."

"Does *everybody* think I'm a thief?"

"I didn't say I thought you took the money. The evidence is strong against you, but I've known it to be stronger against an innocent man. And I've seen more than one such convicted in my day. I advise you to plead guilty."

"You want me to say I'm a thief?"

"Well, do as you think right. I only tell you how I believe you can shorten the term of your service if it goes against you."

"And Norah is to be a thief's wife! And the blessed young ones are to be a thief's childher! And the ould man there in Connaught, that used to nurse me on his knee, and was just beginnin' to be proud of his son—"

Here the poor young fellow fairly broke down, and he sobbed till his sturdy frame shook like a child's. The lawyer looked at him compassionately and with a mingling of curiosity till the gust was over. Then he said:

"I do believe you never touched the money, Terence."

"The Lord in heaven reward you for that blessed word! Then ye don't want me to be after telling the lie and making a thief of myself?"

"No: I'll stand by you and do my best to show that you told the truth when you pleaded not guilty."

"It was a lucky day for me when Lawyer Hartman wouldn't look at me case."

"Ah! you applied to him?"

"Yes, and he told me to go to the divil, and so I came straight to your honor."

"Much obliged to you for the compliment."

"Sorro' a bit! It's little me and Norah—that's me wife—can ever do for the likes of you, but we'll never darken the door of the church without prayin' for you and yours. Maybe it'll help a bit up yonder."

Bagster smiled. "Wait till you see what I can do for you. But now to business."

Terence, questioned by the lawyer as to whether Cassidy knew he had the money by him, related what happened the evening before the arrest. He remembered to whom he had paid the seventeen dollars and a half—the only witness to the heedless exposure of the gold—but the man had gone South: no clue could be obtained to his address, and it was uncertain whether he would return. The peddler, too, who had paid the fifteen eagles to Terence for jewelry, had left the city, and all trace of him was lost. So of the lodger who had given the jewelry in payment of his board-bill.

Nor were the efforts to obtain some knowledge of Cassiday's antecedents any more successful in their results. It was on the ninth of May that he slept at Terence's tavern. He had recorded Port Richmond as the last place he came from. No one there knew anything of Byron Cassiday. His name was not on the register of any adjacent tavern, nor on that of the police station, which Bagster carefully looked over.

He began to be discouraged. He was good lawyer enough to know that the only reliable defence was one backed by an array of facts rebutting the testimony adduced by the prosecution, or at least explaining away suspicious circumstances. Nearly two days were gone and nothing obtained. "If I had but a week," he said to himself, "it would go hard but I'd get on the rascal's tracks; but with a single day only left, I must trust to general testimonials of good character, a touch on circumstantial evidence, and then a warm appeal to the jury. Weak enough — but what can I do?"

He spent the night before the trial in searching out from the *Causes Célèbres* and other authorities examples in which innocent men had been convicted and suffered imprisonment or death.

On the trial the principal witness, Cassiday, adhered, point for point, to the evidence he had given before the mayor; nor did a searching cross-examination elicit any thing contradictory or suspicious. He never lost his self-possession. Interrogated as to whether he could swear positively to the identity of the prisoner, he replied emphatically in the affirmative, adding that he had a view of his features for as much, he thought, as half a minute, at first in profile — afterward, as he turned to leave the room, his full face; and that he (witness) was absolutely certain he was not mistaken in the man. When asked where he got the hundred and seventy dollars which he alleged to have been stolen from him, he replied that he had worked for two years and three-quarters on the farm of a rich German named Gottlieb Bauerman, living in the western part of Berks county, with whom he had stipulated that the money paid to him should all be in gold; that the hundred and seventy dollars were the savings of these two years and three-quarters; that he had left Mr. Bauerman's on the second day of May last, and had come to Philadelphia to deposit the money in a savings bank. The man's look was not in his favor, but his testimony was given with great clearness and an apparent desire to be strictly exact. His demeanor was far from being that of an illiterate laborer: the Irish accent was readily to be recognized, but his language, with slight exceptions, was correct and to the point.

The policeman gave the same testimony which had been contained in his report to the mayor touching the lock of the room and the street lamp immediately opposite. The chambermaid of the tavern, Arrah O'Neil, an unwilling witness, whose testimony was elicited only by direct questions on the part of the prosecution, testified that she found the candlestick, on the morning after the alleged theft, on the floor of the passage outside; that she did not remember such a thing ever to have happened before in the year and a half she had been in the house; that the lock was found to be out of order when she took the policeman to the room; that, to her knowledge, it worked well two days before; that she had sometimes arranged room No. 36 for a traveler, after night, by the light afforded by the street lamp alone; and, finally, that she had heard her master, on the Sunday morning before his arrest, when conversing with his wife at breakfast, say that his landlord had offered him the house he was living in on very favorable terms, provided he could pay a thousand dollars down within a week; that he told his wife he would jump at the offer if he had or could borrow a couple of hundred dollars more, but where to find that he didn't know. This testimony produced the more effect upon the jury because it was evidently wrung from a witness who was particularly anxious to say nothing that might prejudice the case of the prisoner.

For the defence several tradesmen and others, chiefly Irishmen, were examined as to the general character of the accused. Nothing could be more laudatory than the statements they made, but the effect of these was weakened by the very warmth and transparent zeal with which they volunteered their commendations. Beyond this point of good previous character nothing was proved by the defence.

The prosecuting attorney behaved tolerably well. He pressed his points, indeed, sharply, but not more so than might have been expected from pride of profession in a young man ambitious of distinction, speaking in a large courtroom that was crowded to its utmost capacity. How little men usually consider what a terrible thing it is to set the satisfaction of professional success against a human reputation or a human life! I think that an attorney prosecuting in the people's name fails in duty if he conceals from the jury whatever may have come to his knowledge in extenuation or defence of the accused; since, though this be more especially the province of the prisoner's counsel, or of the judge in delivering his charge, every officer engaged in judicial proceedings ought to feel conscience-bound to aid, to the full extent of his knowledge, in bringing to the surface all facts bearing on the case. Is this a fastidious refinement in morality? So is a slack world wont to regard many other bounden duties in social life.

In the present case the prosecutor probably considered the young Irishman guilty. He reminded the jury that the identity of the prisoner had been most positively sworn to by the witness Cassiday; that no attempt had been made to prove whence the prisoner had obtained the large amount of gold that was found on his person on the morning after the larceny; that the prisoner's occupation, that of retailing ardent spirits, was not one calculated to encourage or preserve a high tone of morality, especially when strong temptation presented itself; and that there evidently was in the prisoner's mind a motive such as might tempt, and had often tempted, to crime even those who had hitherto borne a fair character before the world—namely, a craving desire to become the owner of the house he lived in. Such a desire, he remarked, was often the one absorbing ambition of a man's life, particularly of one born in humble rank in a country where the possession of land, monopolized by the rich, was an almost hopeless prize to persons of his condition. But the points which, to judge by the countenances of the jurors, chiefly told upon them were contained in the closing argument of the prosecutor.

"Gentlemen," he said, "in cases of secret crime, committed under the veiling cloud of night, small incidents, such as are usually called accidental, often expose and convict the most wily criminal. Of this truth two striking proofs present themselves in the present case. The accusing witness lost a sum of money: the exact amount was a hundred and seventy dollars: the exact form in which the witness possessed that sum was in gold-pieces of ten dollars each. Now precisely that amount, in precisely that denomination of gold-pieces—seventeen eagles—was found on the prisoner's person a few hours after the scene by the washstand. Was this chance? What a strange chance! Supposing the witness a perjurer, how could he, an entire stranger to the prisoner, possibly guess that the prisoner had precisely that number of precisely that denomination of pieces of gold in his pocket? What an infinite number of chances against such a coincidence! Was it accidental? Is it not rather to be believed that it was ordained by Providence that the infatuated man should retain on his person this mute witness of his guilt? Nor is the finger of God, which reveals so much of hidden wickedness, less evident in another apparently unimportant accessory to the deed. The prisoner, intending, no doubt, to cloak his retreat from the scene of his iniquity (in case some eye should spy him), picks up the candlestick and carries it from the room; but he does not take it to his own bedchamber, lest it should testify against him. Finding everything quiet in the hall outside, he deposits it on the floor. A trifle light as air in itself, if you will; and yet even such a trifle has ere now brought home to the conscience of the blood-stained criminal the truth of the adage, that 'Murder will out.' The witness O'Neil, the chambermaid, reluctantly confesses that, during the eighteen months she had spent in the prisoner's house, such a thing had not happened. Why should it happen? What imaginable motive could any one have to take that candlestick from the washstand and deposit it on the floor outside?—what imaginable motive save the whisperings of guilt? God moves in a mysterious way in bringing sinners to punishment. The Great and the Small—the revolution that unseats a tyrant, and the veriest act of insignificance which enables us to track crime through the darkness in which it seeks to enshroud itself—are alike of His ordaining whose finger appears in all."

Bagster had uphill work: no witness to prove that Cassiday had seen the gold in Terence's possession—no evidence as to how Terence became possessed of that gold. Then the evident importance that the prisoner should obtain, just at that time, the lacking two hundred dollars to complete the purchase of his house. All this was against his client. Again: though he could suggest, and did ingeniously suggest, explanations which seemed to strip the evidence adduced against the accused of its force, he could not prove these: they remained unsustained suggestions only, offset by direct testimony which he had failed to controvert.

Taken at such disadvantage, however, he made a brilliant defence, the trial lasting two entire days. He brought forward, one after another, an array of cases in which, under what seemed incontrovertible circumstantial evidence, men and women, afterward proved to have been guiltless as Abel was, had suffered obloquy, lingering imprisonment, torture, death. He painted, in colors so vivid as to bring tears to the eyes of more than one juror, the terrible sufferings, mental as well as bodily, of these victims, guiltless of all crime, condemned and punished without even the shadow of offence. He reminded the jury of the fallibility of all human testimony, quoting the opinion of that prince of mathematicians, La Place, that "it may be said, speaking in strictness, that almost all our knowledge consists of probabilities only."* Then he brought the case home to themselves.

"There is not a man among you," he said, "though he be law-abiding to the utmost verge of religious scruple, who may not himself be placed in the same position now occupied by my client. There is not a father or a mother among the hundreds who now hear me that may not find a son or a daughter entangled to-morrow in the like inexorable net; appealing to Heaven for the justice which men on earth refuse to grant; struggling in the meshes which suspicion and abasement have wound around them, till their very consciousness, taken captive, turns traitor and half persuades them that they really are the guilty wretches which the world unites in declaring them to be; fainting, at last, in direst need, and crying out like Him, the chiefest of immaculate sufferers, 'My God! my God! why hast thou forsaken me?' Have you ever heard," he pursued, his voice swelling with emotion, till there fell on the vast audience a stillness that awed himself—"have you ever read the terrible story of the Inevitable Fate—how the poor victim of some tyrant's jealousy was overtaken by a death the details of which humanity shudders to recall?

"Thus, in brief, it befell. He found himself immured in a dungeon, some twelve feet square and as many in height—walls, floor, ceiling all of one material, hard as lava, and so crystal-smooth to the touch that it seemed as if a fly could scarce maintain itself on

* La Place: *Théorie des Probabilités*, Introd., p. 1.

its polished surface. On the floor a straw mattress; no other furniture. When the new-made prisoner, snatched from a life of light and happiness without, awoke from a trance of thought to his condition, it seemed to him but a murky vision of the night. He was not in darkness, however: that was a grain of comfort. On two sides of his dungeon there were small windows near the roof, two on each side, giving a dim, reddish light, reflected from a lamp as it seemed to him, for it did not resemble the light of day.

"But where was the door by which he had been carried in, gagged and muffled? He felt all over the seamless walls of his cell—carefully at first, nervously at last—but neither sight nor touch could detect even the slenderest fissure indicating a possible means of entrance or exit. He listened. Not a sound! Hour passed after hour, and ever the same unbroken stillness. He had cast himself on his pallet and closed his eyes to shut it all out. But his thoughts choked him, and at last, as if motion might shake them off, he sprang to his feet. Just before him, some three feet from the ground, was suspended, by a chain from the ceiling, a metal tray, on which stood food and water. He turned from it in utter disgust, and paced his cell, impatient in his desolation. His steps awoke not the slightest footfall: they had placed on his feet soft, flannel-soled slippers, of which the tread gave back no sound; but he scarcely noticed this at the time. Again he threw himself on his couch, seeking sleep in vain. Whether half an hour or an hour passed he knew not, but when he looked up the tray and its contents had disappeared, though not the slightest noise—not the creak of a wheel, not the clink of a chain—had reached his ears. After a time the light from the windows waned, went out, and he supposed it night. Tumultuous fever-dreams, that could not be called slumber, wore out the hours of darkness. The lurid light gradually reappeared. With it, at last, came the cravings of hunger. He had refused food—would they leave him to starve? When hour passed after hour the terror grew stronger. But as he turned on his pallet, there again, before him, stood the tray and its contents, unannounced by breath of sound. Trembling lest it should rise again before his eyes, he rushed toward it like some famished animal.

"Two days, as the captive reckoned them, passed by—the second like the first: then the third night. As light dawned, he gazed eagerly toward it. It was his one visitor—the single incident that broke the dreary monotony of his days. But what was this? The light shone through three windows only: some shutter or curtain must have darkened the fourth. He thought but little of the matter, and only hoped that such an accident would not happen often, for he needed all the light he had.

"Another day, and still the fourth window seemed veiled. Another night. How! Were his eyes cheating him? *Two* windows only! He sprang up as if some one had stricken him a blow. Could it be? He grasped his mattress, rolled it up as tightly as he could, set it against the wall just under one of the veiled windows, stood upon it on tiptoe. His hands nearly reached the lower line of the windows. His eyes peered eagerly through the dim light. It was no shutter, no curtain that obscured it. *The window itself had disappeared,* leaving not a trace behind!

"Words are weak to picture the prisoner's dismay. One sense had already lost its earthly correspondence. His was an existence without sound—as utterly still as if there were neither life nor motion in the world, or as if the man, breathing still, had been a tenant of the tomb. He had stamped for very rage, but his footsteps fell on that ice-smooth floor as mute as snow-flakes on the sea. Was another sense to be reduced to impotence?

"He gazed around him, a look of entreaty on the upturned face, almost as if he were imploring the lost windows to reappear. In the diminished light his dungeon seemed to be contracting in its dimensions, or was it his senses, thus cruelly abused, that were failing in their office?

"Another morning! Ah! two windows still: he had dreamed there was but one, and awoke with a deep sigh of relief. Yet the illusion remained—nay, gained upon him—that his dungeon was diminishing in size. If his senses began to play him false, would his reason go next?

"The sixth morning came. Was it his dream again? He touched his limbs, he felt his pallet. He was awake. It was reality. The light glimmered from *one* window only! He struggled against belief, closing his eyes and pressing his hands tightly over them, as if thus he could shut out the terrible conviction. Then, ere his eyes unclosed, he turned resolutely from the light. God in heaven! His dungeon *was* closing upon him! His pallet was close on one wall, and yet there before him—not seven or eight feet distant, but almost within his reach—there stood (or *seemed*, at least, to stand) that adamantine surface! *Was* it so close? He must touch it. For a time his limbs, as if smitten with palsy, refused their office. But he forced them to that step—a single step: he was in contact with the dungeon-wall!

"The touch flashed conviction over him. It was all before him now. It burned itself into his brain. Light going, Hope gone! All human effort as vain as against Omnipotence itself! Window after window, inch by inch! He felt—ah how vividly!—what was coming. In utter silence, in brooding darkness, slowly, slowly advancing, a creeping Fate! Was ever death of horror conceived like that!"

The orator paused amid a hush that almost typified the scene his fancy had summoned into existence. The jury sat entranced, as by magnetic glamour, their eyes riveted on the speaker. In lower, more level tones he proceeded: "I pursue the terrible story no farther. But has it no counterpart here, in this nineteenth century, amid our civilization? We have, indeed, no dungeons of adamant, with windows that vanish in succession—no prison-cells of which the walls, impelled by infernal mechanism, close and crush out the victim's life. And yet the parallel may hold. Look at that man, now awaiting, as it were, life or death from your lips. A felon, if all be truth that has been testified before you—an innocent man, if one villain has perjured himself. Is it theft alone to which there may be tempting motive? You know the law. If your verdict convicts my client, seventeen eagles will be paid over to the accusing witness as his property. What proof have you—certainly none in the man's sinister countenance and flushed cheek and cowardly eye—that he is not a penniless vagabond? Is perjury an unheard-of crime? Did no villain, steeped in poverty that was due to an abandoned life, ever swear a false oath to obtain a hundred and seventy dollars—ay, or a tenth part of that sum? Think well of it, I beseech you, jurors! If that man, as thousands have done before him, sold his soul for gold, my client is innocent. If you consign an innocent man for months—for years, who knows?—to the solitude of a Moyamensing cell, though one small window will admit, day after day, the light of Heaven, yet hopes dearer than Heaven's light will go out there, one by one—the hope of a good name, of a happy and contented lot—the hope that his wife may rejoice in his fair fame, that his children may honor his memory. The walls of his solitary cell will remain stationary: he need not fear that they will close upon him: the grated, iron-bound door will continue visible, and will open daily to the under-keeper—now and then to the chaplain. But can the words of jailer or holy man undo what you will have done? Can they persuade him that when, at the close of his term, he shall emerge to the world, it will be the same man who in the time gone by went about his avocations careless and light-hearted, with many to love and to trust him—with none to make him afraid? The man of God may declare to him that if his conscience be void of offence a day will come when the Great Judge of the quick and the dead will reverse the verdict of a fallible earthly tribunal. But what can he assure to him upon earth meanwhile? Here, at this very moment, are hundreds who have seen and noted the accused, and who will recognize him wherever, in after life, they meet him or hear his name. To-morrow the press with its thousand tongues, the magnet-wire with its lightning speed, will bruit that name over the length and breadth of the land. Will the prisoner change his name when he issues from his prison-house? I should not advise him to do that. He *must* live a once-convicted felon; he need *not* live under a perpetual lie—a lie that his associates may, any day, detect. But if he conceal not the Cain-brand that is upon him, whither shall he flee where it may not, some day, show forth? Among strangers he may win back again a fair name, he may build up, once more, a thriving business. But shall not a bird of the air carry the matter? Go where he will, there stand up around him, albeit unseen by stranger eyes, the adamantine walls of public opinion, a perpetual menace. *He* sees them: *he* knows that, under the impulse of an invisible, intangible mechanism, which a breath may set in motion, these mysterious walls may close around him, crushing to fragments honest reputation, bright business prospects, respect of neighbors, trust of friends, honored rank in the community—everything that makes life worth having. Better the tyrant's dungeon of tangible adamant! A single agony, and its victim was at rest for ever!"

Again the speaker paused. His eyes were moist and his voice was tremulous as he resumed: "Terrible must the penalty be regarded, even when the guilt it requites is flagrant as the sun at noonday! But of this I make no complaint. I bow to the majesty of the law. I remember it is written: 'The wicked flee when no man pursueth.' So be it! I but ask that you will not take wickedness for granted. I but entreat you not to mete out to the innocent—no, nor to him who, for aught that appears against him, may be innocent—the doom—worse than Indian Pariah's!—the lifelong doom of outlawry which (that society may obtain protection) a stern code has provided for the guilty."

Very effective, for the moment, was the speech of which these extracts give but an imperfect idea. Had the jury retired as soon as Bagster concluded, the verdict would probably have been of acquittal. But there was interposed the judge's charge; and its calm, dispassionate tones contrasted strangely with the impetuous appeal of the advocate.

"You have been greatly moved," he said to the jury, "and I confess to having shared the emotion. Eloquence is a noble gift, yet it behooves us to be on our guard lest it encroach on the province of reason, and obscure sound judgment. In a case like that before us, one should look rather to the plain, matter-of-fact details than to glittering generalities which apply, in a measure, to all human decisions. Undoubtedly innocent persons, in all ages, have been convicted; but this *must* sometimes occur, so long as judges are men and jurors are fallible creatures. From the very disposition of lawlessness to cloak itself, it often happens that for the worst crimes we can have circumstantial evidence only. Again, certain offences are of such a nature that one witness only *can* be obtained to give direct evidence. Such an offence is that with which the prisoner stands charged. The testimony, positively sworn to by the witness Cassiday, is, that the prisoner entered his bed-chamber in the dead of night and took thence a bag of money. Unless some one had seen the accused enter the room or leave it—and against the happening of such an incident there are extreme improbabilities—what direct testimony except that of the sufferer was possible? But the law never demands impossibilities. It is my duty to tell you that it is not sufficient reason for acquitting the prisoner that one person only was present when the alleged theft was committed. If you see reason to believe that the witness has sworn to a falsehood, of course your verdict should free the prisoner. But you ought not hastily to conclude that he is a perjurer because he has a pecuniary interest in bringing about conviction. In every case where a man has property stolen from him, and that property is found on the thief, the same pecuniary interest exists. You are the judges how far the man's countenance and demeanor are against him; but it is proper I should remind you that the defence was unable, on cross-examination, to break down his evidence, or at all to weaken the same by drawing forth a single contradictory admission."

Then the judge called the jury's attention to the various corroboratory circumstances going to sustain the testimony of the main witness—the unexplained incident of the chamber-door lock, evidently tampered with by some one shortly before the alleged theft; that of the candlestick found in an unusual place; the coincidence between the seventeen eagles found on the person of the prisoner and the sum said to have been stolen by him. This last, however, he said, was not to be taken as evidence of the same grade as that obtained when a specific piece of stolen property is identified. One eagle precisely resembles another: there was no allegation that any of the stolen eagles were marked, nor had any testimony been adduced by the prosecution, beyond the assertion of the man himself, that the witness Cassiday really possessed the money which he swore to having lost. On the other hand, there had been failure, on the part of the defence, to show from whom the prisoner obtained the large amount of gold which he had about him the morning after the alleged larceny. The jury ought to give full weight to the strong testimonials of good character borne in favor of the prisoner. No such testimony had been adduced by the prosecution to sustain the character of the accusing witness, but neither had the defence introduced any witnesses to impeach his character.

Judge Thomas concluded a charge which was regarded as sustaining the high character he bore for judicial impartiality, as follows:

"Do not suffer your feelings to be carried away by that graphic recital of the fate, real or imagined, of some tyrant's victim. The parallel between the self-closing dungeon and a Moyamensing cell is more ingenious than exact. Nor is the question submitted to you whether the punishment prescribed by our laws for larceny is or is not unduly severe. You are not members of the Legislature, with power to decide whether a certain penal law shall or shall not be modified. You are jurors called together to determine a simple matter of fact. Seek to divest yourselves of all considerations not strictly bearing on that one point. If the entire evidence, carefully sifted, leave on your minds a reasonable doubt whether the offence was committed, give the prisoner the benefit of that doubt. If, on the contrary, it produces conviction of his guilt, do not scruple to express this by your verdict, leaving the culprit to be dealt with according to the laws of that country which he has voluntarily selected as his own."

The jury were all night in session. Half an hour after the opening of the court, next morning, they brought in their verdict—GUILTY!

CHAPTER IV.

ASTRAY.

FOLLOW we, for a season, the fortunes of Byron Cassiday—not an interesting character, anything but a good or a moral one; yet of such among others—some much better, a few worse—is this checkered world of ours made up. If we had had the making of it, we should have excluded—should we not?—the Byron Cassidays from our scheme, for is not that an element which could well be spared? To us, in our earthly wisdom, it seems so. I am not willing to go farther in my admission, being, indeed, indisposed to spend much time on that question of questions, that has puzzled men ever since they began to think—the origin of evil. We have not light enough by which to answer it here.

We look at it through a glass, darkly. Had we not better postpone the inquiry?—it need not be for long. By and by the solution may be within our reach. In a short time a Friend—how strange that, because he translates us to a better world, he should have been thought an Enemy!—will usher us into a phase of existence where we shall look over a wider periscope—where we shall enjoy keener perceptions and clearer skies.

Meanwhile, through the glass, dark as it is, we can see *some* of the uses of evil. They are worth noting, for they supply lessons tending to increase the tranquillity and the contentment of our lives.

Then, not without profit perhaps, we may track, for a brief space, a man deceitful in heart through the crooked paths where, in his ignorance, he sought that which in crooked paths is never found.

Owner, for the only time in several years, of a hundred and seventy dollars, Cassiday's first care was to replenish his wardrobe. He appeared, and to some extent he felt, a different man in the neat, well-fitting dress which he had selected. His air was less downcast, his bearing more assured; yet the restless, challenging glance of the gray eyes, and the hard, uneasy, half-defiant lines of the mouth, betrayed, to an eye accustomed to look beneath the surface, that there might be more of swagger than of true courage there. For the rest, a comely person of medium size, with limbs muscular and well knit; the only defect of the figure being a slight outward curve of the legs, caused, probably, by too much riding at an early age.

In his childhood and youth this man, to use a common phrase, had not had a fair chance. The illegitimate son of an Irish peasant-girl, Bridget Cassiday, whose good looks and gay spirits had attracted the attentions of Squire Delorny, the keenest fox-hunter and most eager horse-racer in the county, he had been suffered, by his heedless, reckless mother, to grow up in unchecked willfulness. His father thought he did his duty by the child in giving his mother a few pounds yearly to feed and clothe him, in sending him for two or three years to a country school, where the lad showed quickness and desire to learn; and finally, when he was old enough to sit and rule a horse, in promoting him to be his principal jockey. His youthful years thereafter were chiefly spent in the racing-stable, his bed beside the horses, and his associates the stable-boys and other hangers-on of the place. An idle, exciting, dissolute life, one of its attractions being the handsome gratuities which his father handed him, from time to time, when he chanced to bring in the horse he rode a winner.

At the age of seventeen, finding that the youth had outgrown the proper jockey-weight, the Squire apprenticed him to a neighboring miller. There he might have done well enough, had not his antecedents engendered disgust for any steady occupation. He bore it, in a grumbling way, for two years, then ran off to America.

Here, for several years, he found employment in a livery stable in Philadelphia, his habits, the while, degenerating. During a drunken frolic one night he got into a serious difficulty with the police, from which he was extricated by a young man, a recent acquaintance, formerly articled clerk to a conveyancer, but who had lately set up for himself as attorney-at-law. Better he had been left in the hands of the authorities, for his new acquaintance led him from vice to crime. The legal profession in our country is seldom disgraced, even among its humblest members, by lawless men. But Amos Cranstoun, smooth and plausible in exterior, was one of these. His wages as clerk had been low: he wanted a start in life without working too hard and waiting too long for it. Yet he greatly disliked to incur the penalties of the law: he had no intention of employing hazardous tools except for a season, just to get over the first roughness of poverty. Nay, his natural caution might have deterred him, in default of better motive, from overstepping legal bounds at all, had not a tempting lawsuit, involving a large amount of property, been put into his hands by a young profligate, just as his own small savings, laid up during his clerkship, had nearly run out, while his meagre practice scarcely defrayed office-rent. He saw that his client's case, whether just or not, was hopeless in law as it stood. There was lacking a witness to one of the main points, and no chance whatever that such could be honestly found. Then he cast his eyes on Cassiday, self-possessed, audacious, unscrupulous. Yet it needed all his sophistry to bring over the stable-boy. He had never transgressed the law except by some venial breaches of the peace.

"I don't want you to help out any swindling," Cranstoun said to him: "my client has justice on his side; but a main witness is not forthcoming—dead, no doubt. All I want you to do is to swear what he would have sworn if living."

"But if I know nothing about it, that would be swearing false."

"For a good purpose."

"Maybe!" with a contemptuous smile. Then, his face darkening, he added: "What is your punishment for it?"

"A year or two in the State prison; but do you think I would propose such a thing to you if there were any risk?"

"Humph!"

"Don't you see, man, that I am in the same boat myself?"

"I see that if I get paid for such a piece of work, you'll get far better paid; and so far we are in the same boat. But I'm like to be caught, and you'll be sure to come off free."

"That's a mistake. Suppose it were a false oath: if I procure you to swear it I am guilty of subornation of perjury, and that is a State prison offence. Do you think I would chance a prison cell if I thought there was any risk worth talking of?"

"Can you show me how such a thing may be done without risk, Mr. Cranstoun?"

"Easily." He took from one of the pigeon-holes of his desk a paper, which he read over to Cassiday slowly, repeating several passages. "That's your lesson. You must learn it so that nobody can put you out. When you know it all, I'll cross-examine you."

"Cross-examine me?"

"Yes," taking up another paper. "Here are all the questions the opposite lawyers are the most likely to ask you. If you can stand my cross-examination, you can stand theirs. You'll have it all as pat as the catechism before you go into court."

Cassiday paused, and the other resumed:

"Two hundred and fifty dollars, whether we win or lose. How long will it take you to earn that, rubbing down horses in a livery stable?"

The last question touched Cassiday's weak spot. Not even daily intercourse with the dissolute retainers of his father's racing stable had so demoralized the young man as the large sums he occasionally received when victor in a race. These came so easily, giving him for weeks or months at a time the means of prodigal indulgence. It was as fatal to after content in honest labor as if he had won prize after prize in a lottery. No prizes at the mill where he had been apprenticed; no prizes in a Philadelphia livery stable—nothing but dull, toilsome, tedious work at a dollar a day. He wanted to put into the lottery again, and the old Serpent that cheated Eve gave him a chance—a chance to win two hundred and fifty dollars in little more time than it had taken him to ride a winning horse.

When the suit came on he was perfect in his lesson, impassive under cross-examination, won his prize, and squandered it, ere three months were over, in reckless dissipation.

About the time when Cassiday's purse was exhausted, volunteers were called for to serve in the war against Mexico. Fighting, he thought, was better than working, and he enlisted.

Just according to the motives that prompt a citizen to become a soldier are the results on his character of two or three campaigns. These may make out of an unformed stripling a self-possessed, energetic man; or they may confirm a rogue in a spirit of lawlessness and harden habits of license and excess.

The latter was the result in Cassiday's case. He served under Shields; fought creditably enough; fell, stunned by a sabre-cut from a Mexican dragoon, on the same field on which his commander was shot through the body by an escopette ball; and came home with a heavy bag of Mexican dollars. "To the victors belong the spoils" was his favorite maxim for some time after his return.

The Mexican dollars soon went the usual way of ill-gotten gains. Then came several years of poverty and sordid expedients; so bitter in the recollection that Cassiday, with purse once more filled out of Satan's lottery and with an unwontedly decent coat on his back, began to doubt whether work, if it was not too hard, might not be preferable to his recent struggles against starvation.

Either work or another prize out of the lottery; and that brought his thoughts back to Cranstoun, of whom he had lost sight since he first enlisted. After several days spent in baffled inquiries, he learned that he had settled, eight or nine years before, in Western Ohio, having become a resident of the village of Chiskauga, situated at a short distance from one of the stations on the Riverdale Railway.

In the afternoon of the second day he reached the station; and, leaving his baggage to come on by the stage in the morning, set out to walk to the village—five miles distant, they told him it was.

The road, chiefly through the forest, was bounded, at intervals on either side, by farms—some with comparatively spacious and comfortable dwellings and outhouses; others of more recent date and scantier accommodations.

Soon after leaving the station, as he was ascending a hill, a horseman overtook him, and suffered the animal he rode—a stout hackney—to drop into a walk.

"You are bound for Chiskauga?" he asked.

"Yes, for the first time. Is it a large place?"

"A village of some fifteen hundred people."

"I thought any settlement out here that had reached a thousand inhabitants was above being called anything but a town."

"Ours isn't. It's a village—looks like a village, and has village ways. You'll find the houses, except along part of the main street, set back from the sidewalks, each in a garden — small houses, most of them. We have scarcely any rich people, but very few who are not pretty well-to-do. It's a place that likes pic-nics and strawberry parties and blackberry gatherings, and Fourth-of-July celebrations, and Christmas balls, and theatre-going about New Year's Day."

"Balls, theatres! — out here in the woods!"

"Why not? We're not in such a hurry to get rich that we can't enjoy ourselves as we go along. When the girls have washed up the dishes after dinner, they get up their horses, saddle them and make up riding parties. When the young men get tired selling dry goods, they start out—two afternoons in the week, maybe—for the common across Kinshon Creek, to play base ball."

"And what becomes of the shops in the mean time?"

"Shops, man! Oh, you're from the old country. Why, they're merchants, and they sell ribbons and coffee out of stores, not shops. I don't advise you to call these young gentlemen shopkeepers if you intend to stay here. We have no shops, except maybe tailors' and barbers'—yes, and a blacksmith's or a carpenter's shop—that will pass."

"I'll be careful; but do the stores take care of themselves till the game's ended?"

"No, there's a clerk left, and he sends a boy to the play-ground for the owner, if he's specially wanted. Next day they let the clerk take his turn. Then, on Saturday afternoons, if it's fine, they generally shut up and go boating on the lake."

"Are there no rich men in the place?"

"Yes—Mr. Sydenham: you'll see his

house or the hill, about a mile west of town, on the left as you go in: Rosebank he calls it. You'll know it, for it's the handsomest house in the county, with stables and coach-house, and a barn good enough to live in. He owns seven or eight thousand acres of land round here."

"Are there no other rich people?"

"Well, there's Cranstoun, the lawyer: nobody knows exactly whether he's rich or not."

"Amos Cranstoun? Is he at home?"

"Yes: you know him?"

"Very little. I've seen him in Philadelphia."

"Then you've seen a sharp trader. There's others pretty well off, too. Thomas Hartland lives on the south edge of the village: he goes hunting bugs all the time."

"Bugs! Is the place infested with them?"

"We've plenty in the woods—beetles and caterpillars, butterflies, and all kinds of bugs. And—bless me!—there's his niece: I ought not to forget such a pretty girl as Miss Celia, and an heiress at that! By the way, Cranstoun may be pretty rich one of these days—if he gets her.'"

"You think he's after her?"

"Or after her fortune: they say so. But I did hear that some young fellow—I've forgotten who they said it was—is courting her too."

"Is Mr. Sydenham married?"

"A widower—near on forty, I should think: a good citizen, that has done more for the neighborhood than e'er another man in the country. The village has doubled in size since he settled here."

"You haven't named yourself, stranger, on your list. I think you must be pretty well off. That's a capital roadster."

"I'm Nelson Tyler, owner of Tyler's Mill—that road just before us to the left turns off to it. Yes," patting the horse's neck, "the gelding's not amiss."

"Shoulder fine and high; hips well up; just room for the saddle; thick through the heart; good round barrel, clean limbs and a muzzle that could drink out of a pint cup; a good feeder and a good goer, I'll warrant. Can make his fifty miles a day and never turn a hair."

"Seventy of them, easy, with your weight. I'm rather heavy for him."

The speaker must have been, in his youth, a specimen of rough, manly beauty; of which, though now somewhat stricken in years and a little inclined to corpulency, he still retained traces. His countenance was open and bold, with a clear, spirited eye, well-marked eyebrows, and a forehead which, though not of that capacity which indicates great reasoning power, was well formed, and in its lower portion strongly marked by that projection over the eyebrows which phrenologists set down as indicative of shrewd, practical sense. His round, gladiator-looking head, with its short curling hair, now grizzled by years, was set on a pair of Herculean shoulders. His muscular, well-proportioned limbs and height of six feet set off a frame, it would seem, of unusual power, though its owner lacked but a year or two of sixty. He had a rich, powerful voice, deep and sonorous. He was good-natured, and the commendation of his saddle-horse pleased him.

"You're a good judge of a horse: I can tell that by your eye, Mr. ——"

"Cassiday—Byron Cassiday is my name."

"Well, Mr. Cassiday, if you conclude to stay here, come and see me at the mill. I'm not rich; I work hard for a living, but it's a pretty good living, and something to spare for a friend. Our roads part here. It's less than four miles to the village. Good-evening."

Cassiday walked on, musing: "After an heiress! He'll leave no stone unturned, if some of them *are* pretty deep in the mud. He goes in to win. I'll bet on him if the stakes are only large enough."

Occupied by such thoughts, he reached a point where the road had been cut, with a gradual descent, on one side of a picturesque ravine, the opposite slope, on the left, being covered with a wilderness of blackberry bushes, among which, had he come a month or two sooner, he might have seen women and children busy gathering the fruit.

"Is it far to Chiskauga?" he said to a young girl whom he met, her willow basket filled with tempting cantaloupes.

"It's close by. You can see the place, and ever so far round it, from that hill," pointing to a small eminence on the right, a blue-grass pasture, where sheep were feeding.

"Do they mind people walking there?"

"Walking there!" said the girl, her large blue eyes opening wide with astonishment. "Why should they care about that?" laughing.

Cassiday leaped the post-and-rail-fence, and ascended to the summit. Even his senses, impassive usually to influences of Nature in any of her aspects, were arrested by the beauty of the rural scene that stretched out for miles at his feet.

The rounded knoll on which he stood formed portion of a semi-circular range of undulating hills, rising sixty or seventy feet above the plain below, and sweeping round, about a mile from the village, on its western side. Where these were too steep for ordinary cultivation, they were laid out in vineyards, terraced. Elsewhere they furnished building-spots (each with a charming prospect), gardens, orchards, pasture-fields. On the left, where the range of hills increased in height, and some half a mile or three-quarters north of where Cassiday stood, he noticed, through the trees, a dwelling which he set down as Mr. Sydenham's—a pretty villa built of some dark-reddish stone, standing part of the way up the hillside. It fronted east, with garden and meadow on the slope in front; and beyond there were vineyards, reaching north to a small stream, or creek as it was usually called. A little way up that stream could be seen a rustic bridge, crossing to what seemed a cemetery; for one could discern, here and there, under the evergreens with which it was dotted, small white monuments, shining in the evening sun. Lower down, a light mist or spray seemed to indicate a waterfall. Beyond the creek, the hill-range swept round to the east, half enclosing the village common, the resort of those truant lovers of base-ball to whom the burly owner of Tyler's mill had alluded.

In front, directly east of him, was the village, literally embowered in trees, the rows of black locusts marking the street lines. Several large buildings stood out above the foliage—a produce warehouse, a granary, a mill for the manufacture of dried corn meal, four or five good-sized stores, and the like. There were also two simple churches, and several dwellings bespeaking the easy circumstances of the owners; but three-fourths of the houses were small brick or frame buildings, scarcely distinguishable through the mass of orchard and shade trees which covered up the view.

On the left of the eminence on which Cassiday stood was the main avenue leading into Chiskauga, planted, on each side, with a double row of trees, which sheltered a sidewalk for foot-passengers.

On the right of the village stretched out, four or five miles to the south, a magnificent champaign country, with but slight undulations, and, to judge by the heavy crops that loaded it, having the richest quality of soil. The view in that direction was bounded by a strip of primæval forest. From the centre of the village, and running south through this plain, there was a wide, shaded avenue similar to that above described; and, crossing that at right angles and at regular intervals, other avenues; the shade-trees which bordered these seeming, however, to be of a few years' growth only.

But the most striking feature in that charming landscape was a lake, its blue waters just then rippling under a light southern breeze. It lay immediately beyond the village, to which it had given its Indian name. Chiskauga Water it had been called by the aborigines, doubtless because of the multitude of grasshoppers seen on its banks.* It was approached on the east and connected with the vil-

* *Chiskauga* means, in the Oneida tongue, *grass-hopper.*

lage, by an avenue, usually called the Elm Walk, from the double row of elm trees which bordered it on either side, and which had been planted thirty years before by Mr. Sydenham's father. This picturesque bit of water was some three or four miles in length and a mile and a half or two miles wide. On its south and west shores, its banks, of fine gravel and sand, were low and sloping; but the range of hills which swept round the village common struck the lake on its northern bank, rising into steep cliffs, seventy feet in height, crowned with cedars. Thus, as Cassiday looked at it from his commanding stand-point, he could see that its shores were low and level toward the village, from which it was distant about half a mile, but rocky and precipitous on the left almost to its eastern extremity.

In that hard profligate, who had sent to prison among felons an innocent man whom he had robbed, there must have been, underlying the selfish, reckless, lawless propensities, some dash of good —a little leaven, though the lump, the growth of lax self-indulgence, proved too large for it. It did not amount to much in practice; yet it kept him there, face to face with that peaceful scene, till the shadow of the hill on which he sat had stolen half-way across the fields that separated him from the village; till several white-sailed boats had come slowly to land, and their light-hearted crews were seen sauntering along the Elm Walk toward home; till the villagers' cattle, returning from the scanty herbage of the autumnal forest-range to be milked and fed, straggled, lowing, along the shady road. It held him there, stirring faint thoughts and doubts, and a scruple or two—just stirring them, but with no Bethesdal power of cure. He would have been glad, at the moment, to hear that Terence had escaped from prison, provided he could have been assured that the young fellow would never cross his path again. But to redeem his victim from penal servitude by paying back the sum he had gained by his conviction, and donning his own shabby suit again—that never crossed his mind. He began to wonder whether some of the dwellers in that quiet village might not be living happier lives than himself, even if they did work day by day. But he had no desire to change places with them and try the experiment. He must find a shorter road to a living: perhaps he could, honestly. If not— Then it occurred to him that he was wasting his time when he might already have seen Cranstoun. He rose, shook off his thoughts and strode hastily toward the village.

Two hours later he knocked at Cranstoun's door.

The servant-girl took from a small box hanging against the wall of the entrance-hall a scrap of paper and a pencil, which she handed to Cassiday, saying, "Your name, please, sir."

He wrote it, and followed to the office-door. Hearing Cranstoun's voice repeating, in a tone of inquiry, "Cassiday? Cassiday?" he entered unannounced.

"Yes, an old friend of yours. You mustn't forget his name. You remember me, don't you?"

"Of course, but I thought you were killed at the battle of Cerro Gordo."

"A cut across the ear," pointing to it: "that was all—the scar of honorable service, Mr. Cranstoun. Shall I take a chair?"

"Certainly. I didn't notice you were standing. I'm glad to see you again."

Cranstoun's face, as the other knew by experience, never furnished an index as to the truth or falsehood of such an assertion as that last. So his visitor asked bluntly:

"Do you happen to have anything on hand that I can help in?"

"Nothing—that is, nothing in the old line. It is better we should be frank with each other, Mr.—" glancing at the paper—"Mr. Cassiday. I've done well since you saw me. This house is my own, with three or four more, and a couple of sections of good land beside."

"I'm glad to hear it."

"Now observe! There's a time for everything. The time has passed, years ago, when I thought it worth while to do business at a risk. I never do any such now. I can't afford it."

"Nor I."

"Indeed? What's become of my friend Bryan Delorny?"

"He has disappeared: you won't be troubled with him any more. I've come out respectable."

"You!"

"Why not?"—taking a linen bag from an inside waistcoat pocket and pouring the contents on the table. "I once saw a young fellow show his money like that, and he repented it bitterly afterward. But I'm safe with you, Mr. Cranstoun. We were in the same boat together at a risky time, and we mustn't quarrel," pocketing the gold.

"Why should I quarrel with you?"

"Not one reason why you should, and at least ten very good reasons why you shouldn't. Could not you get me something to do—in the safe line, but not too hard work?"

"What sort?"

"Well, suppose we say—coachman to Mr. Hartland."

Cranstoun, off his guard for a moment, turned sharply on Cassiday, but the latter stood the look without the slightest indication that he noticed it. Then the lawyer asked quietly, "What do you know of him?"

"They were talking in the tavern, at the supper-table, about the match pair of sorrels he bought for his carriage last week. I hate sorrels, they're so hard to keep clean; but a man can't have everything just to his hand. They said a good deal about him, and—" looking at Cranstoun and adding in an indifferent tone—"about some niece of his, I think."

This time Cranstoun was on his guard, and he merely asked, in a tone as indifferent as the other's, "Ah! what did they have to say about her?"

"Well, I didn't take much notice: some rigmarole, I believe, about a young man that was courting her, but I've forgotten the name."

Cranstoun never swore—aloud. And if he did sometimes curse a man in his heart, the spark of profitless, unregulated irritation speedily went out. The tendency of his temperment was not to hate his fellow-creatures, but to use them. And this man before him, who had just turned up so unexpectedly—there were useful points about him, if he *was* impertinent. Here the fellow had probably been but a couple of hours in Chiskauga, and it seemed doubtful whether he hadn't already made some shrewd guesses at matters which he (Cranstoun) had no mind the public should know anything about. A dangerous man, too, to have for an enemy. He turned all this over in his mind, silently, for several minutes, Cassiday, the while, maintaining his look of unconcern, and apparently occupied in critical examination of a portrait of Chief-Justice Marshall over the fireplace. At last Cranstoun said:

"I think you once told me you had been two years apprentice to a miller in the old country."

"Yes, and I never was more sick of anything in my life. Just before I ran away, I went to see a girl I used to care a good deal about, and the hussy sang, right to my face, some old Scotch song about

'Dusty was his coat, and dusty was his siller:
Dusty was the kiss that I gat frae the miller.'

I'd rather take care of the sorrels."

"But Mr. Hartland has somebody else to take care of them, just at present."

"So you want to recommend me as a hand to Nelson Tyler?"

"Hang the fellow!" thought Cranstoun. Then aloud: "When did you get to Chiskauga?"

"Just before supper."

"You've been making good use of your time, it seems. Maybe you know that the miller has a pretty daughter?"

"No, I didn't know he had a daughter at all."

"He has—the best rider, too, in the county. She took the red ribbon at our agricultural fair last year."

"Her father would want me to slave all day in the dirt for a paltry thirty dollars a month, I suppose?"

"He's short of hands, I know: he'll

give you that, at least, if I recommend you as a skilled mill-hand from the old country; and then—hark ye, Cassiday—"

"Well!"

"I'll make it as much more if you'll stay there a month or so, and do a small job for me."

"Ah! But let us understand one another at the start. I've been thinking it must be an infernal ugly thing to be shut up in one of them accursed jail-cages for five or six years. I'm not going to risk it again—not for ten times what you offer me."

"Didn't I tell you, man, that I was out of that line myself ever so long ago? It's a good honest deed I want you to help me in."

"Well, that *is* something new."

"Let us have no sneering. I want to save a poor girl from destruction."

Cassiday looked to see if all this was serious: it seemed so, by Cranstoun's face, as he added:

"There's a young fellow in this village sets himself up for somebody. His name is Mowbray—John Evelyn Mowbray. He gets himself called Evelyn, as if John were not good enough for him." Then, seeing a smile on Cassiday's face, "Maybe you know him, too?"

"No; but—now I think of it—that was the name of the spark they said was making up to Miss Celia."

"Never mind Miss Celia. If you watch this young cock-of-the-walk, as I wish you to do—(don't go and forget his name again—John Mowbray)—if you keep on his tracks a week or two, you'll find out that it's somebody else he cares about—a certain Miss Ellen Tyler, that I saw him help from her saddle last September, when she won that red ribbon."

"You think he wants to marry her?"

"Not I. He does little else, all day, than ride a flea-bitten gray, with Arabian blood in him: the brute's handsome enough, if he were only paid for. Then the fellow brags of the old family he comes of, and is down upon you with his fashionable connections. He marry a miller's daughter!"

"So—that's the game. Well, Mr. Cranstoun, you've made me a liberal offer: thirty dollars a month to look after a pretty girl and her lover. It's light work; that suits me well enough; and they'll have to get up early in the morning if they intend to do much courting without my finding it out. But I can't stand the dust and the meal-bags more than one month. Don't you want some watching done where a man hasn't to carry sacks on his back?—at Mr. Hartland's or any other good place? I took lessons from Rarey after I returned from Mexico, and I have a certificate from him." (Cranstoun made a note of this.) "If I don't understand horses and how to keep them—me that have slept with them for years—I'd like to know who does."

"You're well fitted for the place, and I think I can get it for you. But as to Mowbray and that girl, I must have proofs, Cassiday—evidence that would stand in a court of justice. Her father must be put on his guard. I like the girl: we mustn't have her ruined."

Cassiday was right when he took it for granted that Cranstoun would never have meddled with this matter, nor promised him a single dollar, if he had not had his own ends to subserve by exposing Mowbray. But he was wrong when he concluded that there was nothing but sheer hypocrisy in these last words of his. Cranstoun *did* take a friendly interest in the brave, bright-eyed girl, and did wish her saved, just as Cassiday, sitting on that mound, had wished Terence out of prison. Yet both of these feeble stirrings of benevolence might have served to eke out a certain subterrene pavement. Neither of the men would have put himself specially out of the way, or made any serious sacrifice, to rescue from death the object of his barren well-wishes.

Next morning Cassiday inquired the way to Mr. Hartland's house. He had a curiosity about its inmates, and a vague idea that he might find out something concerning them by reconnoitring the premises. He was directed to a cross street, of which the continuation was the avenue running south through the rich champaign country already described. He passed several pretty houses of humble pretension, but neatly kept and painted; some having ivy stretching up between the green shutters; most of them with porches of trellis-work, overgrown with honeysuckle or other creeper—all suggesting the idea of home-comfort in a modest way. Hartland's residence was on the right, the last house in the street, with a pasture of several acres adjoining. It was a spacious, well-built mansion of bright red brick, surmounted with dormer windows; a nicely kept shrubbery in front, and the entrance by a pillared porch on the side. A light dearborn, to which was harnessed a handsome, good-sized pony, stood before the front gate: there were no sorrels visible.

Cassiday sauntered on the opposite side of the street till two ladies issued from the house and entered the carriage. Just as they were about to start, a young man, whom Cassiday had previously noticed riding up from the direction of the lake, turned into the street. The horse he rode instantly arrested Cassiday's attention—a light gray of splendid action and lofty carriage, with minute mouse-colored spots about the head and neck. The rider, good-looking and well-dressed, saluted the ladies, bowing low; then, after a brief inquiry touching their health, passing on.

Cassiday observed two things—one, that the younger of the two ladies, a girl of much beauty, who held the reins as driver, blushed deeply as the horseman addressed them, at the same time glancing uneasily at the windows of the house; the other, that the elder lady said to the groom who had been holding the pony, "Potter, if any one calls, say we have gone to Mr. Sydenham's, and shall be back in an hour or two." From all which the said Cassiday concluded—

First, That he had seen Mrs. Hartland and her niece Celia.

Second, That the horseman on that showy gray gelding was John Evelyn Mowbray.

Third, That Miss Celia preferred a handsome young man to a middle-aged lawyer.

Fourth (this he gathered from the furtive glance at the window), That the guardian, as guardians will, probably held to a different opinion; and—a corollary from the last deduction—that Cranstoun's influence with Hartland was likely to be considerable. Thence came hopes that he himself might supplant Potter, slipping into a snug, easy place.

Before noon he had delivered Cranstoun's letter at Tyler's mill, and made a satisfactory contract with its owner to begin work with him next day.

He retired that night well satisfied with himself. It was all open to him now, clear as noonday—the rivalry, the revenge and all the rest: he had looked over Cranstoun's hand and seen his cards. This was what Cassiday said to himself. Yet he was premature in his self-gratulation. He *had* made good use of his first twenty-four hours in Chiskauga, no doubt, and had found out more than he could reasonably have expected; but he overrated the measure of his discoveries. Cranstoun had cards in reserve which no human eye had detected.

PART II.

CHAPTER V.

BAVENO.

WHILE Miss Celia Pembroke—for that was the name of Mrs. Hartland's niece—is driving her aunt to Mr. Sydenham's, our readers shall have some information touching the early life of that gentleman.

A Philadelphian, of Quaker family, Franklin Sydenham had left the Society of Friends, respecting them and by them respected. Having devoted a few years to the study of law, he bid fair to do honor to his profession. But, at the age of nineteen, having a handsome fortune left him (consisting chiefly, however, of a large tract of land adjoining the village of Chiskauga), he was tempted to indulge himself in a few years of European travel. In London he met the Selbournes, a delightful English family, who resided chiefly at their country-seat in Devonshire. In that retired and beautiful spot Sydenham became almost domesticated among them, joined with ardor in the field-sports of the sons, and won the heart of the only daughter. Her mother, Imelda Gherardi, of an ancient but decayed Italian family, had become acquainted with Mr. Selbourne at Florence, whither he had been attracted by love of art.

Anna Selbourne was a woman of remarkable idiosyncrasies, alike of mind and body. Her large dark eyes and jet-black hair were a maternal inheritance, while her fresh, bright complexion and ruddy cheeks betokened Northern blood. Her step had the firm, free tread of the English gentlewoman, to whom ten or twelve miles was but a pleasant morning's walk; and her form had the willow-grace of the Italian, to whom comes the poetry of motion as words come to the improvisatrice, spirit-moved. So, also, of mental gifts, strangely mingled. There was the calm good sense, the steady constancy, the unpaltering truth, the modest dignity of her Saxon ancestors, without a particle of their coldness or prudery or reserve. Beneath the habitually quiet bearing there lay—derived from a more genial clime—the generous impulse, the ready-kindling emotion, quick sympathies, noble enthusiasm—Juliet's warmth, Arria's devotion. When she gave her hand to a friend, it was with her heart in it. And when, at the altar, she plighted to the young Philadelphian the love that was already his by ties far stronger than plighted vows, it was a guerdon rich as any which in this sublunary sphere man is permitted to win.

I believe there are few thoughtful men

who have not come to regard as one of the least explicable among the great riddles of the earthly economy the rarity of well-assorted marriages. It might be so different, one cannot help thinking. The adaptations for harmony so wonderful! The elements of happiness so manifold and so rich! Yet how often—how miserably sometimes—it all miscarries! The waters of Paradise turned to fountains of bitterness—the gifts of Heaven perverted to curses upon earth!

I do not mean that there are few unions yielding reasonable comfort, friendly relations, a life free from open quarrel or secret heart-burning; but I speak of very marriage, without flaw or jar—a mating alike of the material, with its intangible affinities and its wondrous magnetisms, and of the immaterial principle within that survives the death-change. I speak of a heart-home pervaded by harmony not only unbroken—immutable as that of the spheres; felt to be so by those whom it blesses, calms, satisfies; a social state to which, when man and woman attain, there remains nothing in the way of earthly need or acquisition, save daily bread, to be coveted or prayed for.

Some think that, in this trial-phase of our existence, no such state of harmony and happiness is to be found. Among the few who do find it none of these skeptics will have place. No entrance into that temple except for those who believe! Without faith in the Good and the Beautiful—the Good that is felt, not seen—the Beautiful that must be conceived before it is realized—a man is shut out from the highest enjoyment. And such a man can do little to meliorate the world or elevate his race.

Sydenham, despite his Quaker origin, was romantic. I remind those who may think slightingly of him on that account that ROMANCE, though a word of indifferent reputation, has some claim to excellent etymology, having been traced by certain philologists to the Welsh *rhamanta*, to rise over, to soar, to reach to a distance. In addition, the young man had an inherent love of excellence. He sought, even in such trifling matters as personal purchases, the best of everything. Whatever he did, trifling or important, his instinct was to strive therein to excel; not from vulgar ambition, but because he found pleasure in the strife. His future brothers-in-law had a touch of aversion to an American alliance, but Sydenham's personal accomplishments overbore the prejudice. A "deuced gentlemanly young fellow," they voted him among themselves: "can ride across country with the best of us, fence like a Frenchman, and then shame us all in the ball-room at night."

But it was something else that attracted the sister. Sydenham was a devout believer in the IDEAL. He had strong faith in his kind. He was a dreamer of what men may do and may become. Every struggle for popular liberty, or what he regarded as such, awoke his warm sympathies. William of Orange, Hampden, Kosciusko, Lamartine, La Fayette, these were his favorite heroes. He had spent a week with the latter at La Grange, the genial old man driving him out, in his own carriage, from Paris, and recounting to him, the while, with charming garrulity, original anecdotes of two Revolutions. One of these, presenting the Father of our Country in a rare aspect, often recurred to Sydenham in after years, vividly recalling as it did the tender eyes and the gracious, loving manner which made the grand old Frenchman the idol of all young people who were fortunate enough to share his friendship.

It was just before the unmasking of the sole traitor who loomed up during our Revolution. Washington had accepted an invitation from Arnold to breakfast with him at West Point on the very day the plot was discovered, but was prevented from keeping his engagement by what men call chance—by the earnest request, namely, of an old officer, near whose station they passed, to spend the night there and inspect some works in the neighborhood. Next day, while Washington, with his staff, including La Fayette, were seated at table at this officer's quarters, a despatch was brought to the American general, which he immediately opened and read and then laid down, without comment. No alteration was visible in his countenance, and he remained perfectly silent. Conversation dropped among his suite; and, after some minutes, the general, beckoning La Fayette to follow him, passed to an inner apartment, turned to his young friend without uttering a syllable, placed the fatal despatch in his hands, and then, giving way to an ungovernable burst of feeling, fell on his neck and sobbed aloud. The effect produced on the young French marquis, accustomed to regard his general (cold and dignified in his usual manner) as devoid of the usual weaknesses of humanity, may be imagined. "I believe," said La Fayette in relating this anecdote, "that this was the only occasion, throughout that long and sometimes hopeless struggle, that Washington ever gave way, even for a moment, under a reverse of fortune; and perhaps I was the only human being who ever witnessed in him an exhibition of feeling so foreign to his temperament. As it was, he recovered himself before I had perused the communication that had given rise to his emotion; and when we returned to his staff not a trace remained on his countenance either of grief or despondency."

With such antecedents Sydenham was a welcome guest, especially to the mistress of Acquabella—so the family seat in Devonshire was called.

The family of Imelda Gherardi had been devoted Liberals; and she, though now presiding over an English household, retained all her enthusiasm for the cause of her country's independence. "*Italia Unità*" was the idea of her life. An Italian republic, stretching from Switzerland to Sicily—of that she dreamed; for that, in her adopted country, she schemed and planned. Sydenham was charmed with her earnest zeal, entered into her patriotic projects with faith and sympathy, and became a great favorite with Mrs. Selbourne. Anna, sharing in a measure her mother's ardor, listened to their discussions with kindling eyes. In these discussions—under the influence of those eyes—Sydenham's sunny nature came out. His glowing fancy, his generous aspirations, his bursts of eloquence when encouraged by sympathy in his listeners, made a daily-deepening impression on the girl's heart. And Sydenham, on his part, unconsciously contracted a habit, as the conversation passed from topic to topic, of turning inquiringly to the dark eyes for approval or dissent. Could it all end except in one way?

With the intermission of a brief visit to Philadelphia, Mr. and Mrs. Sydenham had resided for several years in England, partly in London, partly at Acquabella. There they lingered, fearing the result of Mrs. Selbourne's drooping health. Shortly after her death they set out for Italy, taking with them their only child, the little Leoline, then seven years old.

After a brief sojourn in Switzerland, they passed, by Napoleon's wonderful road, the Simplon, into one of the most beautiful regions of Piedmont. How amazing the change! How lovely that first night at Baveno! The sweet Southern air—the moonlight on the placid lake, on the softly-rounded, olive-clad hills, on the trellised vines, so picturesque compared to the formal vineyards of France—all in such contrast to the scenes they had left behind—the giant mountain-peaks of granite, snow-covered, piercing the clouds, the vast glacier, bristling with ice-blocks, sliding down, an encroacher on the valley's verdure—in such marvelous contrast to all that region of rock and ice, and mountain-torrent and rugged path, and grand, rude majesty of aspect—it seemed like passing in a single day into another and a gentler world.

To Anna Sydenham a region of enchantment and romance! Her mother's native land, that she had never yet seen but in dreams! Once the Mistress of the World, and still the Queen of Art. But it was not of ancient renown or modern celebrity the daughter was thinking. It was of the fairy-land of her mother's adoration—the Italy which that mother, even in her pleasant English home, never named but with wistful eyes.

And Anna loved it now, at first sight,

for its own beautiful sake. Mere life was a pleasure to her in its balmy, dreamy atmosphere and under its pure, deep-blue sky. She drank in enjoyment as never in her life before. They made charming, quiet excursions on the lakes —Maggiore, Lugano, Como; rowed by young girls with pensive, oval faces, who sung barcaroles as they rowed. They returned always, however, to the spot where they had spent their first Italian night—Baveno; for they had come to like its humble, country *albergo*, clean and fresh, and had taken a fancy to their simple apartments, with gay furniture and polished, tesselated floor. Little Lela, too, as they usually called her, ever begged them to go back to the pretty, pretty room where, on the first evening of her arrival, sitting at the open window on her mother's knee, she had gathered clusters of grapes from the overhanging vine.

One fine evening they had crossed to that wonderful Isola Bella, once a bare and barren island of slate rock, now a gorgeous garden teeming with the vegetation of the tropics. They had explored its vast palace, lingered in its orange groves; and Lela, passionately fond of flowers, returned with her pinafore full of magnificent specimens. When they reached the inn, the child, tired of pleasure, curled herself up on a couch and went fast to sleep, with the flowers in her arms. Sydenham and his young wife sat down by a large recessed window, set entirely open after Italian fashion. Beneath lay the Lago Maggiore, motionless, serene. The full moon, a few hours high and directly opposite, shone down on the dark blue waters, through that strangely transparent atmosphere, with a splendor which Anna, during all her island-life, had never seen matched. So brilliant was the long streak of light on the mirror-surface of the lake, formed under the line of the moon by her reflected rays, that one realized the poetical fancy which dreams of such as a path of radiance leading to some far-off world of beauty and of rest.

At first that glorious night-scene awed these young hearts; then gradually the awe gave way to gentler emotions. The delicious breath of Italy came over them, softening, inspiring—in Anna's case saddening too. Is the fullness of joy so nearly allied to fear? Her hand in her husband's, she sat long, in silence, tranquil. Then he felt her hand tremble—then suddenly grasp his own. He started.

"Forgive me!" she cried. "It was too strong for me."

"What is it, Anna?"

"Nothing. A silly fancy. Are you quite well to-night, Frank dear?"

"Perfectly. Never in my life, I think, was I better—or happier."

"Thank God!"

"What is the matter? Why, my child, you are shivering. My poor, little darling!"

"I will be stronger and banish such nonsense."

"What nonsense?"

"It has all come from a fisherwoman's sad story, I think. You remember, that, in returning from the Isola Bella, we passed close by that poor little Isola dei Pescatori, and that there was a crowd of fishermen and their families assembled round one of their rude hovels."

"I noticed that."

"But you did not hear the answer one of the boat-girls gave me when I asked her if anything was the matter."

"I did not catch the meaning: you know how much my Italian needs brushing up."

"Only because you devote so much more time to German. This was what the girl said: 'A fisherman was drowned yesterday; they brought the body home to-day: she will be very, very lonely, the poor woman.' I think a stranger's death never so touched me before. I could not even talk to you about it."

"I am an excellent swimmer. You foolish child, I shall not be drowned."

"No," with a faint smile—"No; but there was more, dear Frank. You remember what you were reading to me, yesterday, in the boat as we returned from visiting that gigantic statue of St. Borromeo?"

"Oh, Frank, you mustn't go there before me."

"Some very indifferent scraps of translations, I believe—bits from Schiller's 'Death of Wallenstein.'"

"Yes, and among them that exquisite heart-wail of Tekla's. While I was sitting with my hand in yours, just now, looking across at that Fisherman's Island, three lines of your translation came upon me so vividly I could not help grasping your hand. It actually seemed to me as if some one repeated in my ears—

'Thou, Father, in mercy thy child recall !
Earth's holiest pleasures I've tasted them all ;
I have loved, I have lived—let me die !'"

She shuddered—eyes moist, face pale. Sydenham put his arms around her, gently drawing her head to his breast. He touched her hands; they were icy cold.

"We have been overdoing it, dear," he said. "You must rest for a day or two."

"I think it is this eerie, dreamy climate," she murmured languidly, "and that moonlit pathway over the dark lake. It all makes me think of Heaven." Then, with a sudden burst: "Oh, Frank, Frank, you mustn't go there before me. If you did, how *could* I help praying—like Tekla?"

At that moment little Lela murmured in her sleep, scarce audibly: Sydenham's ear did not detect the faint sound. Anna was by the couch in a moment, kneeling over her. The child did not stir, however, relapsing into dreamless sleep.

Then the mother rose and crept back to her husband's arms. He felt that she was sobbing—silently, with an effort to conceal it. During all their married life he had never seen her so agitated without external cause. He stroked back the black tresses again and again, passed his hand gently, repeatedly—scarce knowing why or being conscious of what he did—over her face and person. The magnetic touch had a strangely-soothing influence. Her sobs ceased. Her breathing came free and regular: the long eyelashes drooped over her cheeks. Then, in a low, contrite voice, "What has come over me?" she said. "I am tormenting you for nothing, Frank. You are not going to die; and if you were, is our little darling to be deserted? Tekla was childless. God forgive my selfish thought!"

What a transformation may be wrought by a single night's quiet rest! The next morning Anna was all her bright, racy self again, the light in her eye, the healthy color on her cheek. The morning was perfect, a gentle breeze from the lake coming in through the open casements. Lela's merry outcry as she arranged her flowers was contagious.

"What a good-for-nothing wife you had last night, Frank!" said Anna, laughing gayly. "Are you sure some fairy did not steal me away, and leave that querulous simpleton in my place?"

"Likely enough. You look, this morning, as if you had been among the fairies all night. You are radiant, wherever you have been."

"I ought to look my prettiest, to atone for past folly. But the bad child begs pardon, and says it will never, never do so any more. And the *never* is to be such a long word. We are going to live together till we are—oh, so old!—till we have ever so many grandchildren clambering over our knees. And I shall not scold them, even if they do pull my cap and frills. Ah how we shall laugh then—you and I—over that evening at Baveno, with its doleful presentiments!"

"But you suit me, even if you are a querulous simpleton."

"Fie! How can you expect the bad child to reform, if you persuade it it wasn't bad at all? You ought to shut it up and feed it, for a day at least, on bread and water."

"Too glorious a morning for that! I want to take it out among some of these vineyards back of the village, and give it grapes for luncheon. Will it go?"

"Of course it will. Rogues don't fancy hanging, nor bad children being shut up in dark closets."

Their child, who had been listening attentively, opened her large, brown eyes in wonder. "Poor, perplexed Lela!" said the mother, laughing. "She's not accustomed to hearing about bad children and dark closets. Your papa was only laughing at me, pet. You've eaten all the grapes from around that window, and we are going out to get some more. Come!"

A servant entered just then to say that the principal guide to the Monte Monterone had come to offer a *portantina*,* in case their Excellencies wished to ascend the mountain; but they decided to adhere to their original plan.

They found an old calèche, easy and roomy, took a country road, shaded by chestnuts, and bade the postboy drive slowly, that they might fully enjoy the gay scene. He found some little difficulty in obeying, for he had a pair of large, spirited stallions that he was training for sale to the owners of the Milan diligence.

It was the harvest-home of the *vignerons*—why won't the dictionary let us call them *vineyarders?*—the season of recompense and rejoicing, when the result of the year's labor was collected and secured. The handsome, embrowned peasants, in their picturesque blouses, drove their teams along the road with light hearts, yet with a certain dignity, as if proud of the load. Every face was gay. The sounds of distant music, half lively, half plaintive, came over to them from the vineyards and olive groves as the travelers passed.

When midday came, they sought shade near a wayside spring, sheltered by a magnificent old chestnut. Ah, how every incident of that noonday rest haunted Sydenham's memory in after years!

But now, with light jest and careless hearts, they set about preparing their frugal meal. The cushions from the calèche furnished seats. Bread and a bottle of light wine of the country, with napkins and a table-cloth, were the contents of a basket which Sydenham emptied on the bank.

"Now I must fetch the grapes. This vineyard behind us looks promising, and the men are but a little way off." Then to Lela: "Will you go with me, little pet? I want your mamma to rest."

But the child had spied some gay wild-flowers on the opposite side of the road, and they were a greater temptation than grapes.

"I'm going to gather you a pretty nosegay for the centre of the dinner-table, papa. We mustn't dine without flowers."

So Sydenham took the empty basket and departed—*alone!* If guardian spirits there be, commissioned to watch over the welfare of mortals, where was Sydenham's then? Withheld, it may be, from interference by a Wisdom that sees deeper than ours.

Lela strayed off across the road to fulfill her promise to papa. Her English nurse, Susan, who had come with them, as on such occasions she usually did, made the little preparations for the meal, Anna being occupied in looking over Murray's Handbook, seeking to discover whether it was worth while to carry out an expedition they had projected to the top of Monte Monterone, in full view from where she now sat. Pietro, the postboy, meanwhile unhitched the traces of his horses and led them a little distance up the road, there to rest and feed. While he was busy attaching a nosebag containing barley to the head of the horse he had ridden, several dragon-flies darted, with the wonderful power of flight which characterizes these insects, right across the road to where the animals stood. One buzzed between their legs; another fastened, with ferocious grip, on the neck of the off-horse. Both animals stamped and snorted in terror. Pietro succeeded, at considerable personal risk to himself, in mastering the one he held; but the other stallion, a powerful brute, maddened by the sharp sting, broke away and dashed down the road.

It was Lela who first noticed the terror of the horses. She set out to cross

* A *portantina* is a species of easy litter, provided in Italy for the use of ladies unaccustomed to exercise, or invalids, desirous to ascend high mountains—Vesuvius, for example. The *Monte Monterone*, situated just behind the village of Baveno, between the Lago Maggiore and the little lake of Orta, is three or four hundred feet higher than Vesuvius; and the view from its summit is scarcely excelled, for extent and magnificence, by that from the Righi itself.

the road, but seeing one of the frantic animals loose and plunging toward her, she hesitated—stopped. At the same instant her mother rushed impetuously to her assistance. The horse was galloping directly toward Lela; but, with the instinct which characterizes his kind, even in his headlong speed perceiving the child, he swerved to the right, avoiding her. It was in the very moment when Anna had bounded forward from the other side, and this sideward movement brought him directly in contact with her. He struck her with his broad breast, casting her violently to the ground; then bounded over her as she lay prostrate, not touching her with his hoofs.

Susan, almost beside herself with terror, hastened, trembling, to her mistress' aid. Anna was insensible; and it was not until Sydenham, alarmed by the nurse's shrieks, reached the spot, that she was removed to the green bank under the chestnut tree.

CHAPTER VI.

STRONGER THAN DEATH.

It avails nothing that I attempt to picture the husband's wild despair. To a brave man—if alone in this world and believing in another—a summons to die is a thing to be received with passionless equanimity: it is but as a requisition issued to some sojourner in an indifferent country to take up his residence in a better. A little pain or trouble in the transit—soon over—that is all.

It is when he strikes us through others that Death thrusts home his dart. He is victor, not when he takes us hence, but when he wrests from us the life of our life, and leaves us here exanimate save only in the faculty of suffering.

Then holds the King of Terrors his carnival of triumph. Perhaps a brief triumph only. For the good and the wise there is ever, after a time, an exit from this valley of the shadow of death. After a time, not in the freshness of grief: not a gleam, then, indicating the way out. When the fearful blow first falls, the victim is stricken down, helpless, hopeless, prostrate, seeing around him but the blackness of darkness, and believing, in his utter abandonment, that such will be his lot for evermore.

So felt Sydenham at the moment it burst upon him that he had lost his Anna. The sun of his life had gone out. He groped about in the gloom, stunned, as one suddenly stricken with blindness. He noticed not even the child of his love, clinging to the helpless form, moaning, "Mamma! mamma!"

The untutored servant-girl had more self-possession than he. He sat gazing on the inanimate face: she had brought water from the spring, and was bathing her mistress' temples. A shudder seemed to pass over the features. A sigh! That awoke him from his stupor. "She lives! she may be saved!" he cried, bounding to his feet. In another moment he was beside the postboy, who stood stupefied, the bridle of the remaining horse still over his arm. "A portantina, Pietro! But instantly, instantly! It is life or death! In an hour you must be in Baveno. Ask what pay you please. Do you hear?"

"Eccellenza, yes," said the man, releasing his horse from its harness and tightening the saddle-girths. "In an hour, if—"

"No ifs! In an hour! Mount!"

But as the man threw himself into the saddle, Sydenham laid his hand on the rein: "A moment! This morning a guide offered me a portantina in case we ascended the Monte. He lives nearly opposite the albergo. Do you know him?"

"Eccellenza, yes—Francesco Ribaldi."

"Get it from him, and some conveyance to bring it here—at speed, remember! Twelve bearers, so they can relieve each other. Get carriages for them also. Any price, any price, so they are only here as fast as horses can carry them! Away!"

The man started at full gallop, and Sydenham, the flush of excitement fading from his face, retuı ned to the fatal spot.

For the first hour there was little

change—feeble indications of life, but apparent insensibility. At last the eyes opened, eagerly seeking the loved face; and the hand which Sydenham had been holding in his feebly returned the pressure. He touched her wrist—the pulse unnaturally low, as he made it out. He knew scarcely anything of medicine, but something seemed needed to sustain her. A few spoonfuls from the wine-flask revived her a little.

Gradually she seemed to return to life, speaking but feebly and at intervals, however—broken words of encouragement and of love.

Interminable, to the excited watchers, seemed the delay; yet in less than three hours the long-expected carriages drove up—their horses white with foam—bringing the litter and its bearers.

It was evident that the sufferer endured acute pain as they placed her on the portantina; but the well-trained bearers kept step perfectly; the motion was easy, without jar; and she did not seem worse on her arrival.

Sydenham, unwilling to trust any village doctor, and having ascertained the name of the principal physician in Milan, Dr. Lo Piccolo, instantly despatched an express courier to that city, with a letter to the doctor, imploring him to start as soon as the courier arrived. The distance is forty miles: the man promised it should be made, by the aid of relay horses, in two hours and a half, and he started about eight. Before four o'clock next morning the physician arrived.

Anna had passed a restless night—quite sensible, however, gradually improving, and without fever. She yearned to speak to her husband, but, fearing the excitement, he entreated her to desist. At her own earnest request, Lela had been laid beside her for a while. But the poor little thing, after struggling bravely with her emotion till she could restrain it no longer, sobbed so piteously that they were obliged to remove her to the nurse's room.

After a critical examination, the doctor prescribed bleeding, expressing regret that it had not sooner been resorted to. "Her pulse is feeble at present," he said as he passed, with Sydenham, into the adjoining room, where he had left his instruments—"slow and feeble; but fever will supervene in a few hours—by midday certainly. What have you given her?"

"Only a little wine from time to time: it seemed to revive her."

The physician shook his head: "Depletion, not stimulant, is the remedy at this stage. I do not think any bones are broken, but there are internal injuries, it is impossible to say of what organs, or determine how serious the lesion is. Blood must be let to arrest congestion of the injured parts."

The terrible question rose to Sydenham's lips. He became so pale that the experienced eye of the medical man detected his secret at once. "The shock to the system," he said, replying as if the other had spoken, "has been very severe, nor is it possible, as yet, to predict the issue. With these," taking up the lancets, "we combat the febrile symptoms. The signora appears to have an excellent constitution. Let us hope that we may be able to save her."

I have often wondered whether—with case succeeding case to disperse and distract attention—the physician continues to realize the despotic power over the heart often exercised by his lightest words. "Let us hope" had been this man's expression, but uttered in a tone such that he might almost as well have said, "Let us despair."

The patient was bled, and the doctor departed, promising to return next day, and enjoining, meanwhile, absolute quiet. "All exciting conversation," he said, "must especially be avoided." He left an anodyne to be given in the evening.

The prediction in regard to fever was verified. It set in about eleven o'clock in the forenoon, yet it was not so violent as to be alarming, nor did it, at any time, seem to affect the mind. Anna was, indeed, very restless: she experienced a settled pain on the left side, where, probably, the horse's shoulder had struck her, and she suffered much because of the frequent change of position which her restlessness required. But she bore it all with wonderful equanimity, and the few words they would permit her to say were calm, considerate and like herself.

So passed that day and the next night. When the physician called on the ensuing morning, he bled her a second time, and ordered leeches to be applied to the chief seat of the pain—that dull, wearing pain, still unabated. It would be impossible for him, he said, to call next day, nor was it essential. "It might not be prudent further to deplete the system," he said to Sydenham: "the fever gives artificial strength for the time; but to-morrow, or at latest next day, there will be depression: then we must fortify with stimulants. Watch the pulse and do not omit this. Art can do no more. Rest assured that all her resources have been called forth, and not, I trust, in vain."

But a straw to grasp at; yet Sydenham, sanguine and hopeful by nature, clung to it. "Men are prone," he thought, "to exaggerate difficulties, even when confident that they can overcome them. He may speak guardedly, so as to enhance the merit that will be due to him for success. Ah, how little needed! If he could but imagine what he will be to me if he save her life!"

Another day, with little change. Toward evening she said to her husband, who had scarcely quitted her room since she lay there, "Frank darling, you never in all your life refused to gratify a wish of mine; and you will not do so now, I think. Will you?"

Utterly unable to answer her, except by pressing the hand he held.

"Two days and two nights you have been beside me, almost without stirring. See what a glorious sunset! You must go out for an hour—nay, only for a single hour."

He moved impatiently, as in dissent. An expression of suffering came over her face.

"You don't want to pain me, Frank?" Then, with a faint smile; "Besides, I shall have company. I want Lela this evening. She shall not see that I suffer: I shall forget that I do when I know you are out in the fresh air. The child—little darling!—has already learned to control herself. She will be quiet. Nurse shall take her away, else."

Sydenham was like one condemned to a dreary task. He took his hat, then returned to the bedside, gazed, through his tears, at the sweet face, but without a word.

"A full hour, Frank—for my sake!"

He imprinted a kiss on her pale brow and was gone.

Just one hour after, to the minute, he re-entered the room. His wife was more quiet than he had seen her since the accident. "I am proud of my little daughter," she said, drawing the child to her for a kiss. "She has been such a comfort to me!"

"I've been taking care of mamma all alone," said the child, triumphantly. Then a shade came over the little thoughtful face. "I can't make mamma not have pain, but she says it does her good when I talk to her. Doesn't it, mamma dear?"

"Ever so much good, my child."

Then Leoline relapsed into a very grave, sad mood—quite quiet, however; no sobs, no tears. What seemed to the father a sort of childish dignity now and then lit up her face. Were new thoughts, that had never been there before, busy in that little brain? Sydenham wondered what mother and child had been saying to each other.

During the night Anna slept a little: at least she lay, for an hour and a half, her eyes closed, her face placid, without a symptom of restlessness, quiet as an infant asleep. When she awoke the pain in her side had much diminished. Sydenham accepted all this as a good augury. Toward morning, however, the pulse had evidently become feebler. Lo Piccolo's instructions in such a case were strictly obeyed. Diffusible stimulants were freely given, and in the forenoon the patient rallied.

About midday she said:

"Frank, my husband, it did me good that you left me alone last evening, with Lela. Now you must let me have my own way once more."

"Well, dear one?"

"I don't want you to leave me, this

time, but to stay and to let us have a talk together. I have things on my mind—"

"But Dr. Lo Piccolo said—"

"Yes, dear, I know; but there are matters as to which he cannot judge. He wishes me to be free from excitement. I shall not be so until I have spoken frankly to you."

"To-morrow or next day, perhaps, Anna—when you are stronger."

She hesitated: "Part, at least, of what I have to tell you ought to be said to-day—now. You yourself will think so when you shall have heard it. I entreat you by our love."

"My own darling! Not another word! You were always wiser than I, especially when moved by impulse so strong as this. It shall be as you say."

"Thank you!" extending her arms to him. Sydenham kissed her fervently. She lay quiet for a little while. Then, in a low voice:

"I have been thinking of the life we have spent together. Eight years—yes, day after to-morrow: did that occur to you, Frank dear?—eight years since you gave me your name; nearly two years more since I first knew you! Do you know what you have been to me all these years? Do you know what the summer rain is to the parched soil?—what the sun is to the flowers? I wish you could feel, just as I do this day, how happy—how happy I have been! Ten years! and, except those few dark weeks when we watched by my dear mother's bedside and saw her pass away, not a cloud! I wonder if you know how happy you have made me—hour by hour, day by day. I had a glad thought always near me. It went to sleep on my breast at night; and in the morning, through my first waking consciousness, it whispered to me that you were there. Ever throughout the day, in the midst of other thoughts, there hovered about me a sense as of some good news—a feeling that I had something to rejoice at—vague—as it were veiled—while my mind was occupied with daily duties, but in the intervals of these coming over me like a bit of sunshine through an opening in fleecy clouds. At night again—the last thing—it was a sweet sense of protection and of peace. That golden thought, running through the whole tenor of my life—embellishing, enriching—ah, friend, lover, husband; you must always remember, come what will, that it was the consciousness of your presence, of your love, of your ceaseless, priceless care. Whatever happens, promise me—for my sake—for my sake, my own beloved—promise me that you will never forget this!"

Sydenham tried in vain to control his emotion. "Anna, Anna," he cried, "why do you say this to me—why *now?* You are better, quieter, the fever is abating—"

"If I could spare you this blow—if I could! But, whether I am here beside you, or whether I am waiting for you—" She hesitated; then, in a lower voice—"waiting for you where separations are not—it ought to gladden your life that you have procured such a life of gladness for me. A life, Frank!—a whole life! More than the happiness of a lifetime was crowded into these years. How often, as they passed, has my heart cried out, 'What am I, that my cup should have been filled to overflowing?'"

The husband was utterly unmanned. He felt what her premonitions were. They might bring about their own fulfillment! "I beseech you," he cried, "by the love that has been more to me than life—I beseech you, cast from you these terrible thoughts. You must not leave me, Anna—you *must* not!"

"Would I go if I might stay with you—and Lela?" The voice was calm, instinct with speechless affection, but calm, with scarcely a tremble in its tones: the bitterness of death was past. "I have been thinking over it, lying here: it is not terrible, but I must tell you just the truth. That wine you gave me when my senses returned, and through the first night, did me so much good, Frank. I thought then I might recover. I dare say Dr. Lo Piccolo is a skillful man, and I have always heard that in case of an accident like mine one ought to be bled. But when he bled me the first day my life seemed to go out with the red stream; there was—oh, such a sinking of heart and spirit! When the fever came I felt a little stronger; but after the second bleeding I knew—I felt—you must not weep, Frank darling; this is a world where Death must be—where all we love lives but by his forbearance. If you had gone first—you must remember this that I am going to tell you, Frank, and you must forget that evening of my weakness and my forebodings, and that prayer of Tekla's—yes, if you had gone first, I should have waited patiently: I should have lived for our little Lela—and so must you!"

The strong man shook like a child. "My burden is greater than I can bear." That was his one feeling for the moment. But he was awakened to a sense of its selfishness by the increasing helplessness of the sufferer. The effort seemed to have quite exhausted her. Even the hectic flush was fading. He administered a stimulant.

That revived her for the moment. Alas! for the moment only! Each time that the remedy was resorted to the effect was feebler and more brief. There was, indeed, much less pain, but the pulse indicated a sinking condition of the system. Was her instinct in regard to the blood-letting correct? Had it drained the vital energies? At all events, relief from pain and fever had come too late—had come when there was no longer force to rally. Even to Sydenham, hoping against conviction, this became apparent. Yet she continued to speak to him from time to time.

How often, in after years, did the husband call to mind the beautiful thoughtfulness for himself and for others evinced by his dying wife! She seemed, especially, to have considered every minute detail connected with the welfare of her child—its culture, physical, mental, spiritual. Never had her mind seemed more clear. "Do not fear to bring her up in the country," she said: "simple goodness is better than brilliant accomplishment. And you have duties in the country, Frank. I have been thinking of that large Chiskauga property of yours. You told me there is a village there. How much you might do for these people! I think you neglected them for me: that thought came to me last night. It came to me from—" She seemed in doubt whether to proceed, adding after a pause: "Do you remember a text about dreams, Frank?"

"When you are better, dearest, we will talk of it: do not trouble yourself about such things now."

"Trouble!" The old fire lighted up the beautiful eyes once more. "Trouble! Ah, the brightness, the unspeakable beauty!" Then in a lower voice: "I saw mother there. Nay!" as she noted her husband's startled, uneasy look—"touch my pulse: see if I am not calm, quiet. In my dream mother said: 'You are coming to me;' and her eyes seemed to say: 'We shall be so happy!' Then I got the impression, though I don't remember the words, that she told me not to be sorry for you, for you would do so much good after I was gone. I try to do as she bade me; but if you busy yourself about thinking and caring for others, who is to think and to care for you? If dear Lela were only older! She will be such a comfort to you, some day."

"Oh, Anna, I cannot bear to hear you talk thus, as if it were all irrevocably fixed; and it was but a dream."

"My poor Frank! If you could but have been with me in that glorious dream! Think! I shall have everything there *but* you. And after a little while—a little while, dear—when your task is ended—then you, too, will find out that as we approach the Eternal Stream flowing between us and the summer-land, soft airs are wafted over to us, and sweet voices come to us from the other shore. Oh, Frank, try to be happy till then. One of us *had* to go first, darling. Do you grudge it to me?"

Thus, with her loving words and her sweet faith, that brave soul sought, even to the end, to wean the mourner, about to be left on the hither shore, from the indulgence of his grief. And not in vain was this last labor of love. Even in those supreme moments he came to think of her not as lost, but as going home the first: he came to realize that though, for both, there was a terrible parting here, for her there was a joyful greeting beyond. And in long after years she, being dead, yet spake. The balm of her parting words brought comfort and calm to many a lonely hour.

Toward midnight she became very feeble, having scarcely strength to ask that she might be moved before the window that opened on the lake. The same brilliant moon, the same track of radiance over the dark-blue mirror, as on the night of Anna's presentiments. She gazed dreamily on the calm effulgence of the scene, and, pointing to the streak of light, "It is not brighter," she said faintly to Sydenham, "than the path before me." Then gradually she sank into a stupor. Half an hour after she seemed to awake for a moment, with just strength to draw her husband to her arms and to whisper, "Not for long, dear love—not for long!" Her last words of comfort to him who had made the happiness of her life.

The trance-like condition into which she immediately relapsed continued until that earliest hour of the morning when so many have passed away. Then she stirred a little, her lips moved, but she recognized no one. After a time a seraphic expression lit up her features. What she saw, what she felt, we can never know. Except on the brink of the Dark River eye hath not seen it nor ear heard. She threw up her arms as in welcome. "Mother! mother!" she cried, in tones of tender exultation. Then the arms sank slowly, crossing themselves on the breast. The look of ecstasy faded into one mingled of calm joy and holy affection, and of peace passing all understanding. And that ineffable expression—earnest of another world—lingered there long after the glad spirit, freed from earthly surroundings, had passed to better regions, there to take up its eternal abode.

A little way up the Monte Monterone, on a small, picturesque, secluded plateau overlooking the placid lake—vineyard and olive grove around—there stands, inscribed with the single word ANNA, a simple monument of purest white marble. Never was earthly minister of goodness and beauty laid to rest in a lovelier spot.

CHAPTER VII.

FROM BAVENO TO CHISKAUGA.

One of Anna's last requests to Sydenham was that he should spend some time in passing through Italy with Leoline. She foresaw the dreary void, to fill which, at first, change of scene and the healthy excitements of travel are among the best appliances; but all she had said to him was, "It is my mother's country, and I should like my child to see it."

For most children of Leoline's age the impressions thus received would have been evanescent, but in her case many of them were never effaced. She was not as far advanced as girls of seven often are in the usual branches of education. Her parents, noting her quickness and eagerness to learn, had deemed it wise to restrain rather than stimulate her ambition. But her mental faculties and her powers of observation were of no common order, and her exuberant spirits were shaded at times by a dash of thoughtfulness rare in one so young. This last had been increased by her mother's death and the incidents therewith connected.

It was touching, even if it sometimes called forth a smile, to witness the sort of charge the little thing now took of her father, anticipating his wants and seeking to allay the impatience of his first grief. The day before they left Baveno he had shut himself up in his room, abandoned to thoughts of the heart-solitude that lay before him. She stole quietly in, sat down beside him without a word, and slid her hand into his. At first he scarcely noticed her, but, as she looked up with mute sympathy in her face, he took her on his knee and kissed her in a passionate burst of grief. She wiped his eyes with her handkerchief, and then startled him by saying,

"Dono' you cry, papa dear. It will make mamma *so* sorry!"

"Your mamma, my child? She is gone—"

"Yes, I know she is not here. She is up among the angels. She told me she was going there, to see grandmamma; and she said I mustn't cry after she was gone, because that would make her sorry, up there, in heaven."

Sydenham called to mind that hour which the dying mother had spent alone with her child. Lela's simple words strangely affected him.

"I'm going to see her, some day, myself," she pursued, a sweet gravity on the young face. "Mamma promised if I was good and took care of you, and tried to make you not sorry, that when I was bigger I should come and be with her and grandmamma; and after that she would never go away and leave us any more."

And then she startled him again with the sudden question: "Papa, don't you think mamma sees us?"

While Sydenham hesitated for an answer, the child added:

"Because, if she can't see us from up there, how would she know whether I cried or not. Don't the angels see us and take care of us, papa?"

How these little creatures with their daring questions sometimes stir up problems that the wisest among us may fail to solve! And yet we talk to them so heedlessly, and often say in their hearing what we little think they are noting and treasuring up for future thought.

Sydenham's nature was essentially spiritual: Spurzheim would have ascribed to him a large organ of veneration; but his religion had so far been rather a feeling than a system, and he had given little attention to doctrinal points. Lela's questions took him entirely by surprise. He had a vague recollection of certain texts about ministering spirits sent forth to attend on the good, and about taking heed not to despise these little ones, seeing that their angels always behold God's face. But he merely said, "We shall know more about these things by and by, dear child. Of this we are sure, that your mamma is happy."

"Then don't let us be sorry, papa darling. Mamma wouldn't be sorry if she knew we were happy, would she?"

Anna's influence was reaching her husband already for good. The ideas which Lela, in her unconscious simplicity, had aroused within him tended to soothing and tranquillity.

At Milan, one day, as they returned from visiting that elaborate wonder, the cathedral, Sydenham received a letter, which, by calling up old associations and bringing before his mind the needs and the griefs of others, had an effect wholesomely distractive. It was dated from Chiskauga, and was from an old and very dear friend, Eliza Pembroke, saying that her husband had died suddenly, six months before; that, feeling her own death to be approaching, she had very anxious thoughts about her only remaining child, Celia, then ten years old; and that her sister Alice Hartland, wife of a gentleman who had settled at Chiskauga, had strongly advised her to write to him.

"You were always a favorite of hers," the letter continued. "She and I remember so well the happy years of childhood we spent with you. Do *you* still recall our going to school together—how you used to aid us in our tasks—how you used to join in the quiet sports which were all that the strict discipline of Friends approved or permitted?

"To you, the friend and companion of those peaceful days, I now come for counsel, and—in case my Celia, left an orphan, should ever find herself in trouble—for aid and kindness to her; and I am sure that my appeal will not be in vain.

"The report is—how true I know not—that after a few years you may settle in Chiskauga. At all events, some day or other your large possessions here will probably attract you to the place. But in case of my death, I expect to leave my daughter here. I have, as you know, no brother, nor any sister except Alice. Her husband, Thomas Hartland, seems Celia's natural guardian, and her aunt's house her natural home. I know you will like my girl: a better or warmer-hearted child cannot be found. She has never given me an hour's uneasiness in her life. Hartland is an estimable character, to whom I can confidently entrust my daughter's property; but he is cold and impassive, and there will be little sympathy, I fear, between the uncle and niece. On the other hand, Alice will be a mother to my child. And there is another reason why I select Hartland as a guardian, and why I invoke your aid in case Celia should need it.

"There is a certain lawyer, named Amos Cranstoun, living here—a man, I think, without principle, whom I fear and dislike. He wormed himself, I know not how, into my husband's confidence, and even on his death-bed Frederick conjured me to do nothing to irritate or offend him. He has been studiously attentive to us since my husband's death, offering to attend, without charge, to any business of mine; and I know no reason why I should imagine that he might injure us; yet I do. A woman's logic, you will say. But Mr. Hartland seems to share my distrust, and I believe it was that which finally decided me to leave Celia in his care."

To this letter Sydenham immediately replied, pledging himself in the strongest terms to carry out Mrs. Pembroke's wishes.

They spent the winter in Italy, chiefly in Rome (where Sydenham met many of his wife's relatives, enthusiastic Carbonari—radical in their ideas of reform) and in Naples, where, through letters given him by the Gherardi family, he made the acquaintance of several distinguished reformers of the same stamp.

A nearer acquaintance with these Italian radicals somewhat weakened Sydenham's faith in their anticipations of prompt success. They were of a generous spirit, impulsive, enthusiastic, and had much of what the French term *élan*—the dashing ardor of the South; but they seemed to him to lack practical qualities—prudence, steadiness of thought and of purpose, power of endurance, equanimity. His confidence was especially shaken by a confession from one of themselves, Don Liborio Libetta, a distinguished Neapolitan lawyer.

"Signor Sydenham," he said, "I can speak with entire confidence to you, for you are Anglo-Saxon, and that is a reliable race. We live here under one of the worst governments in the world. There is no security, for a single day, to person or property. As regards persons of any rank or influence among us, the estimable, the intelligent, the industrious are considered dangerous characters, and are placed under a system of strictest *espionage*, dogged even to the privacy of their houses, tracked by spies, day and night; while the worthless and indolent, the spendthrift, the debauchee, are regarded as safe and inoffensive persons, and are left at liberty, without annoyance from the police."

"So bad as that?"

"It is the settled rule of policy—a premium, you see, on vice. The influence of such a system is terribly corrupting—so corrupting, you think, perhaps, that it ought to fall, in this nineteenth century, by its own weight. It *has* aroused the indignation of every man friendly to human rights. But, alas! we have no trustworthy bond of union. Do you know why we do not succeed against abuses so monstrous? Because we have no confidence in one another. I never feel assured that my nearest friend may not betray me to death. The iron, as one of your English writers expresses it, has entered into our souls. It is terrible to say, but we have no TRUTH among us."

"Terrible indeed!"

"And the result will be, that if, one of these days, we do get the upper hand, we shall not have sufficient faith in each other to retain it."

Three years afterward—during the revolutionary uprisings of 1848—Don Liborio's words were verified.

Naples, in its physical aspect, had a

beneficent effect on Sydenham. What a drive was that he took with Leoline on the far-famed *Strada Nuova*, leading in and out along the rock-bound, vineyard-clad shore to Baia—city of wonderful relics! The atmosphere, marvelous in its transparency, through which distant objects showed preternaturally distinct; the matchless bay, dotted with fairy islands—Capri, Ischia, Procida, Nisida—its waters lying in dreamy, glittering quiet, sharing (Fancy suggested) the national languor, in that they were stirred not even by heave of tide: then, as noble background, a lofty Apennine range, with Monte Sant' Angelo, cloud-capped, for a summit; and, more than all and seen from every turn of the road, the purple, lava-encrusted cone of Vesuvius, awaking a thousand memories; the smoke sullenly rising from its summit, a reminder of the power to destroy that slumbers beneath. All this made up a combination of natural beauty so wondrous and so varied that it took captive the senses as by a spell. Sydenham, charmed and soothed, felt little inclined to treat as hyperbole an encomium which he called to mind by a native poet, whose remains they had passed during the morning's drive—Sannazzaro, who, in allusion to the city of Parthenope and its surroundings, spoke of that region of enchantment, as

"Un pezzo di cielo, caduto in terra." *

Nor was it inanimate beauty on which, during their stay here, the travelers looked. The country breathed of the past. History was written all over it—over its ruins (once filled with Roman luxury and stained with Roman vice) of palace and temple and bath—the bath rivaling the temple in magnificence; over its tombs and its statues and its buried cities, now uncovered to modern gaze; over picturesque Naples itself, with background of rock and precipitous hill, sprinkled with charming villas and surmounted by castle and monastery.

And that was history, of which some of the stone-leaves date back, not only to the heyday of Roman splendor, or even to the times when Xerxes led his many-nationed host, with Lybian war-chariots and Arabian camels, against astounded Greece, but to a period of which the records were ancient history to Nero and to Xerxes—to an epoch before Homer wrote or Achilles fought. Through a dark grotto, partially invaded by water, Sydenham and Lela were conveyed, on the backs of guides, to a stone platform, the resting-place, they were assured, of the Sybil who prophesied the destruction of Troy. The long record stretches back full three thousand years.

They returned, by way of Marseilles and Paris, to England. After a brief stay at Acquabella, Sydenham's thoughts reverted to Chiskauga; and there came to him, as a behest, Anna's dying words: "How much good you might do these people! I think you neglected them for me." In spite of the entreaties of Mr. Selbourne and his sons, with whom Lela was a petted favorite, Sydenham embarked for America, spent some months, detained by business, in Philadelphia, and then set out for the village, where he had determined to take up his permanent abode. He was accompanied by a widowed sister, Hannah Clymer, one of those charming persons, not particularly bright, but instinct with benevolence, who "think no evil," and see, in every character, only its brightest side.

In Chiskauga, Sydenham found many changes. Mrs. Pembroke had died, leaving her daughter under Mr. Hartland's guardianship. A French physician, Dr. Meyrac, exile from his native country because of political opinions, had settled in the place. Another new-comer was Mrs. Mowbray, an officer's widow in limited circumstances, with one child, a boy, whom she greatly indulged. The business of the neighborhood was slowly but steadily increasing. A flour-mill, recently erected three or four miles west of the village on a rapid stream called Chewauna Creek, was in successful operation.

He found also, much to his satisfaction, that an old and valued friend, Mr. Harper, a man equally benevolent, simple-hearted, learned and eccentric, was settled

* A bit of heaven, dropped down upon earth.

in the place as Presbyterian clergyman. One of Sydenham's earliest recollections of this guileless enthusiast was the receiving a visit from him when he (Sydenham) was but seventeen years of age.

"My young friend," said the good man, "I like you. You are earnest, industrious, persevering; and I have remarked in you a reverence for sacred things which, alas! is rare in this thoughtless age. Have you facility in learning languages?"

Sydenham replied that his teachers had usually thought so; that it was a branch of study he had always liked; that he had obtained some facility in speaking French, and was now studying German.

"Ah, young man, these are but profane studies, not to be despised in their place, yet as dust in the balance compared to graver matters. Are you a good Latin and Greek scholar?"

"Greek, no: I am but an indifferent Hellenist; but I believe my knowledge of Latin is fair."

"I offer to you, my dear young friend, an entrance into higher regions. Come and study Hebrew with me. Thus shall you have the key to golden treasures. The writings of man are full of error and uncertainty. Come to me and we will study together the words of God, not as fallible men have translated them, but pure as they came from the great original Source. I do not ask you to come as a pupil, for I do not take pupils, but as a son to his father. It shall be to me a labor of love."

Sydenham had difficulty in parrying this cordial offer. He urged his law-studies, on which he had to depend for a livelihood, and the propriety of first completing the branches of philology he had begun. It pained him to reject a proposal so evidently made in generous simplicity of heart. "In after years, perhaps," he said, more in expression of gratitude, however, than with serious intention of ever seeking to master the Hebrew tongue, "he might be in a better situation to accept such kindness."

Thirteen years had elapsed since then, whitening good Mr. Harper's hair—for he was now approaching threescore—but leaving unchanged his primitive peculiarities and his pure and simple heart.

On making acquaintance with Dr. Meyrac, Sydenham found that he, also, was an original in his way. The following anecdote transpired through Madame Meyrac, a quiet, methodical, painstaking, well-dressed, well-mannered person, who ruled her own household rigidly, except that, in matters of importance, she was fain to let her spouse have his own way.

The doctor's health was usually good, but in case of casual indisposition, to which he was liable, it was remarked that he never called in the aid of any of his brethren of the profession. About a year, however, before he left Paris he was taken seriously ill; and madame proposed to send for a doctor, an intimate friend of theirs. To this, as usual, he positively objected. The wife watched and nursed her husband with her utmost skill, but the symptoms, fever especially, remained unabated. One morning, when Meyrac was evidently worse, madame said to him:

"My friend, this will not do. Your case is getting beyond my experience and management, and you know you have often told me that a man who insists on doctoring himself in a serious case has a fool for a patient. I must send for our good Montfaucon."

"I thought," replied the sick man, very politely, "to have already advertised you, my dear, more than once, that I do not desire to have any doctor attending upon me?"

"In an ordinary case, dear friend, very well; and you will do me the justice to admit that I have hitherto always obeyed your wishes on this point. But the symptoms, this morning, are very serious: I cannot take the responsibility of waiting longer. I must absolutely send for Dr. Montfaucon, in whom I know you have confidence."

"Before doing so, dear Elise," said her husband in his quietest tone, "do me the favor to ring the bell." Madame obeyed and the servant appeared.

"Jean," said his master, "in my study, over the fireplace, you will find my pistols. Have the goodness to take them down carefully and bring them to me. And—a moment, Jean ; that is not all—in the left-hand drawer of my escritoire there is a powder-flask and a small package of balls. Bring them also."

"My God!" said the terrified wife in an undertone, "his brain is disturbed." Then to the sick man: "Dear husband, but this is madness. What can you possibly want with pistols, lying here on a sick-bed?"

"Montfaucon is a good fellow, and I should be very sorry to do him harm. But if you really insist upon sending for him, my dear wife, and if he enters that door to prescribe for me, I shall blow his brains out: that is all."

"Just Heavens!" cried Madame Meyrac, now thoroughly alarmed. "Rest tranquil, my husband: if you feel so strongly opposed to having medical advice, be assured I shall respect your wishes."

"As you will, Elise ; but," turning to the servant, "let me have my pistols, Jean, at any rate."

No doctor was sent for, and Meyrac slowly recovered. On the first day he was able to leave his bed, "You are an admirable sick-nurse," he said to his wife, kissing her on the forehead. "If all men were as fortunate as I, my dear Elise, we poor blunderheads would make but a sorry living."

The villagers generally were friendly and social; and without other division of class or caste among them save that which superior cultivation and information naturally bring about.

Sydenham resolved to make his future home among them. In selling out some of his lands adjacent to Chiskauga, he had made reservation of a small farm of fifty or sixty acres, west of the village; partly valley-land, but chiefly picturesque hills—an old clearing, on which the tree-stumps had already decayed, and which ran back to the original forest. During a former visit to the place he had picked out a piece of table land, half-way up the hills; and, intending some day to build there, had had it planted out with clumps of shade trees.

Here he erected a dwelling of moderate size. The material was a fine-grained freestone, from the New Red Sandstone formation, found in a quarry which Sydenham had discovered on a tract of his forest-land at no great distance. The style he selected was the Norman, but in its later and lighter phase, prevailing during the twelfth century—simple semi-circular openings without tracery, but with labels of the same form, and bold corbel-courses devoid of the grotesque ornamentation with which our ancestors were wont to disfigure them; several sharp-pointed gables; on one side a slender campanile tower, with pointed roof and an Italian air about it; beneath it a handsome entrance, enriched on the jambs with a succession of small, receding pillars.

The variety of freestone selected had this peculiarity, that, when first quarried, it was comparatively soft, working freely before the chisel, and thus was readily carved into ornaments; while by exposure it gradually indurated almost to the hardness of granite. But Sydenham was not betrayed by this facility of ornamentation into the elaborate. The outer finish was in rough-tooling. A few graceful leaves or flowers on the lower points of the corbels and as capitals for the dwarf pillars peculiar to this style, a circular window with radiating mullions in the principal gable; a few carved finials—that was nearly all the architectural luxury he indulged in.

The tint of the material accorded well with the manner, being a lilac-gray, the shade which ladies, in their dresses, call ashes of roses. All this gave to the dwelling, at a distance, a quaint and somewhat grave and old-fashioned aspect. Nearer, it had a look of substantial grace, its fine proportions and beauty of outline giving warrant of a pure and cultivated taste.

Nor did the interior belie the external promise. It had an air of welcome about it. No gilding, no glitter; no buhl nor ormolu; no unwieldy tables with cold marble tops, irksome to move, unfit to write upon; no huge mirrors; no long, heavy brocatelle curtains excluding the light of day; no gaudy silk damasks too fine to lounge on; but, in variety of form, easy-chairs and sofas inviting to rest; cozy seats in oriel windows, suggestive of tête-à-têtes; furniture to last a lifetime—solid oak and walnut and rosewood; in the heats of summer covered with gay chintzes that looked cool ere one sat down,—in keeping with the India matting beneath the feet: during the chills of winter with warm colors—maroons, scarlets, dark crimsons and the like—imparting, through the eye, a genial glow as one entered the rooms—an effect which was heightened by adoption of the European fancy of *portières*, or door drapery, corresponding in color to the curtains and carpets, these last bearing no huge, gorgeous, mimic nosegays, but being of a uniform tint, with small stars or single flowers spotting the surface.

For the rest, the works of art adorning the walls were choice, rather than of great cost. Of statuary there was but a single example: a terzino statue (scarcely half life-size), in faultless white marble, of Eve, by Angelini of Naples. It was a charming figure, admirable in form and proportion, eminently womanly, and with a certain youthful dignity about it—a fit embodiment of the Mother of Mankind. She is seated on a mossy bank, at her feet the roses of Paradise. By her side is the serpent, in her hand the apple; but she does not look at either. She is gazing into vacant space—an absent, thoughtful expression, as if she were inquiring of the future touching the godlike knowledge of good and evil. It seemed as if one could interpret the expression and anticipate the direful result.

This little statue was in the parlor, set in a niche built expressly to receive it, and lined with maroon velvet, against which the purity of the marble showed with excellent effect.

Then there were two or three landscapes by American artists of celebrity; also a small Turner, one sea-piece by Achenbach, another by Isabey; several carefully-executed copies in oil of celebrated pictures; and, scattered all over the house, choice engravings executed in the first style of art. Almost all of these last illustrated some sentiment. One of them, entitled "The Gentle Warning," represented a young girl, in ancient costume, standing, with self-convicted air, before a table at which sat an elderly lady—mother or aunt, one may suppose—with a charming face; an open letter on the table before her to which she was pointing, but raising her eyes, the while, to the face of the fair culprit with such a look of love and gentle sorrow that one could almost hear the mild words of tender remonstrance she was addressing to her. Another, hanging over the fireplace of Sydenham's study—setting forth the great truth that the poor assist the poor—was an engraving by Jouanin of Dubufe's well-known "Denier de la Veuve." All the rooms, by the way, had open fireplaces, the fuel being supplied from the neighboring forest. How cheerful and home-like that primitive wood-fire's blaze!

A special fancy of one of the inmates gave, in summer especially, an additional grace to this dwelling. Leoline's early passion for flowers, still unchanged, showed itself in the beauty and variety of the flower-beds, chiefly cultivated by her own hands, from the spoils of which it was her daily delight to decorate the principal rooms. Every morning (in winter from the green-house) there was a special bouquet of the rarest—the delicate colors daintily selected and harmonized—for the writing-table in her father's study. A favorite with her, because of its odor, was the mignonette; and this, planted in narrow boxes, she set on the sills outside of the parlor windows; the summer wind, as it stirred, bearing the faint perfume, from time to time, over the house. One came, at last, to associate flower and locality. "I was reminded of you and of your charming residence," wrote an English friend one day to Sydenham, "by passing, the other morning, in Covent Garden, a flower-stall fragrant with mignonette."

It was a pleasant retreat for a man of letters, and now and then a select friend. Two spare rooms only. In an Italian villa on the Hudson, built with California gold, there are a dozen. But when Sydenham visited its owner, an old friend, and congratulated him on his magnificent residence, the wife said, rather sadly, "How much I prefer yours! If we leave these rooms untenanted, it is like living in an empty barn. If we fill them, it is a bustling hotel, with guests that never pay their bills, and of which I am landlady."

But Sydenham was more than a man of letters. It was as if he heard a voice, silent on earth except to him, saying, "You neglected these people for me: when you come to join me, bring an account of your stewardship." Upon that unspoken injunction he had acted. And so ten years had passed since the sad events at Baveno.

Our readers are now acquainted with the gentleman whom Miss Celia Pembroke and her aunt, Mrs. Hartland, set out to visit. Are they content, before learning the result of that expedition, to go back with us, for a brief space, to Philadelphia, and ascertain how Terence O'Reilly fared during his prison-life?

PART III.

CHAPTER VIII.

THE PRISON-CELL.

TERENCE had clung to the one idea that haunted him from the first: he *could* not be convicted, because he had not taken the money. He had dwelt on this till it assumed almost the character of a monomania. It had sustained him through all the varied excitements of the trial. Even the announcement of the verdict failed fully to dispel the illusion. It stunned him. He scarcely took in its import. He was but partially roused even when asked if he had any reasons to give why judgment should not be pronounced against him. He gazed vacantly at the jury, then at the judge. And it was not until the latter added, in a compassionate tone, "Have you nothing to say, prisoner?" that he broke forth:

"But I didn't do it, judge. And is it to prison you're sending me? They don't send innocent men to prison. I don't care for the money. Let the lying scoundrel have it, since he swears it is his; but for the Lord's sake, judge, don't be after sendin' me to prison. What will Norah do? And the poor, helpless childher? Is it a thief you'd make me out before them and their mother?"

A shriek from a distant corner of the court-room, and some one cried out, "A woman has fainted." Terence made a fruitless attempt, arrested by the officer in attendance, to rush from the dock, then sunk his head on his hands, with a desperate effort at composure. But that shriek had stirred the depths of his warm and passionate nature. A stinging sense of shame and pride came over him—in vain. His loud sobs, heard all over the court-room, awoke hearty sympathy in the bystanders. One or two of the jurors repented their verdict.

Nine months' imprisonment was the sentence. The seventeen eagles were paid over to the witness, Cassiday, and the rest returned to Terence, who, after brief delay, was conveyed to Moyamensing prison.

The preliminaries which preceded his actual incarceration produced a terrible effect on the high-spirited young fellow. First, his hair was closely cut; then he was put in the scales and his weight carefully recorded in a book kept for the purpose; next he was measured, and his exact height set down in the same official record. Then he was stripped: all marks or scars found on his person were noted and minutely registered. To this was added his complexion, together with the color of his hair and eyes, his age, his birth-place (alas ! alas !), the date of his conviction, August 24, and full particulars of his offence. Finally his prison-dress was put on, and his prison-number assigned him—two hundred and thirty-seven.

It is difficult for us, in these comparatively enlightened times, to realize what the suffering of some poor wretch condemned to the "*peine forte et dure*" may have been, when conveyed from the torture-chamber to a mediæval dungeon. Yet I doubt if it much exceeded the mental agony endured by Terence when consigned to the solitary cell which bore his number.

He was past all complaint now, or outward demonstration of grief. It seemed to him as if he had been stripped of his very identity. His former life had gone out, and, in its stead, had come up a despised and to-be-avoided thing—a felon, weighing so much, measuring so much, marked or scarred so and so ; and all this set down as a man records the brand he has selected with which to stamp his cattle, so that each animal may be recognized for ever as his own. It was all done and settled. It could never, in this world, be undone, any more than one can unlive the day that is past.

If he could only go to sleep and wake no more ! Norah was far better without him. His children too. If he died now, people might forget to cast it up to them that they had had a thief for a father. Norah might marry a decent man and change her name, and that would help to bury the past. He hated his new self. It had no business here. It could be of no use to anybody. Why should he live ?

Two days after Terence's incarceration, Mr. Kullen, the prison-agent, called. "Anything new ?" he asked the under-keeper, a good-natured fellow, Walter Richards.

"Yes, a young man, nine months for theft, who has not tasted food or water since he came—two days and two nights now. I shouldn't wonder if he died."

"What's the matter with him ?"

"Well, I don't know. A stout fellow, too, but looks as if he had lost every friend he ever had in the world. I could get nothing out of him, say what I would, except that he didn't want to eat or drink, for it was no use. I wish you'd see him—two-thirty-seven."

"What's his name ? Has he a family ?"

"Terence O'Something : Irish, from Connaught, I think. Married and two children. He needs looking after."

"I'll see him at once."

He found the prisoner seated on his pallet, listless, with the look of a man abandoned to his fate, seeming to notice nothing, not even the arrival of his visitor. On a small table near by, his dinner, untouched. Kullen drew up a chair and sat eyeing him for some time in silence :

"You have not eaten anything for two days : that is very wrong."

The other just lifted his eyes to the agent's face, but without a word.

"You have no right to throw away your life. No man has—least of all one who has a wife and children."

He started—that touched him.

"You don't look like a coward ; but nobody except a coward gives up and forsakes those that have a right to his help."

"An' is it a thief can help wife or childher ?"

"You're a thief, then ?"

Terence started up, defiantly ; then sank feebly back again on his bed. "Didn't the jury say I was ? And why shouldn't he ?" as if speaking to himself.

"Maybe the jury mistook ?"

It was the first drop of balm to that bruised spirit. "Are there people that think juries mayhap mistake ?" he asked, hesitatingly.

"I do. I've known many such cases."

"Thin the Lord above be blessed that sint ye here. It's no good now, but it comes grateful to a man, anyway."

"Why is it no good now ?"

"I'm no good. There's only one thing I can do for Norah and the childher."

"What's that ?"

"To git out o' their way. I'm a disgrace to them."

Kullen moved the table, with the untasted meal, toward him. Wistfully, for a moment, the man eyed the food: then his face hardened. "Ye're losin' yer time," he said, feebly: "I don't want to talk about it."

"Are you innocent of this crime?"

"Where's the use in tellin' you? In a day or two I'll be afore the Great Judge. HE knows. It'll be all right then."

"And if He asks you, as He asked Cain about his brother Abel, what you've done with Norah and the children, will you tell Him that you were not their keeper?"

"He knows better nor to ax me that. He heerd the jury, and the judge on the bench too, set me down for a thief. He saw them men here, when they ticketed me in their blasted book for a jail-bird, and weighed me and measured me, and wrote down every mole and freckle on me body as if I'd been a dumb baste, only fit for the shambles. And He knows that, after all that, I'll niver be aught but a millstone around the necks o' Norah and them babes."

"If you're innocent, Terence — and you look to me like an innocent man—that can be proved; and then they'll take it all back: they'll write down, in the same big book, that it was all a mistake, and that you were found out to be no thief at all; and then nobody can say you ever were a thief. And why can't you help Norah and the children then?"

"I'm not strong to argufy with ye," the poor fellow sighed: "the spirit's all gone out of me. But it's not a bit of use, no more than the wind that blows. Ye didn't hear Mister Bagster?"

"No: I wasn't at the trial."

"Thin it's no use, I tell ye, at all, at all. If the angel Gabr'el, with his wings on, had come down and stood afore that jury, he never could have spoke better, or done more, nor Mister Bagster did. If *he* couldn't get me out of it, there isn't a livin' soul that can come near it."

"I have no doubt he said all that could be said: I know Bagster, and there is'nt a better man before a jury at our bar; but as for what he did—how many days had he to prepare the case?"

"Three days the judge allowed him."

"Three days! No wonder they convicted you. Come, Terence: I dare say it will all come out right yet. But you must eat that dinner."

"Mister—"

"Kullen's my name."

"Ye mean the fair thing by me, Mister Kullen; and ye're a good man to come and speak to a poor devil as ye've spoke to me. But ye can niver do but one thing for me. Maybe ye'll do that."

"Anything I can, I'll do."

"Thin look a bit to Norah and them childher when I'm gone. But you mustn't never let the lassie know I wouldn't ate: let her think it was the jail-sickness that did it. Tell her God knowed she'd be far better off without the likes of me. It would break the dear heart of her if she thought I wanted to lave her and the two childher. And God, He knows I never did. I'd stay here and work my fingers to stumps, though there wasn't a stick to the fire or a bite to the table, if I didn't know that the very scum o' the street can throw it up to her, any day, that she has a thief for a husband. D'ye think I could stand that—me, that loves her as dearly this blessed day as when the darlin' first tould me she'd never have nobody but myself in all the wide world, and that she didn't care no more for that scamp of a Rory that was always coortin' round her nor she did for the worm that crawls?"

Kullen could not restrain a smile, but the prisoner did not notice it. Anxiety and excitement, and, latterly, lack of food, had done their work. He sank on the bed, adding, in a half whisper: "I never could stand that, and I won't try."

The agent, deeply touched, propped the poor fellow's head on the pillow, arranged the bed comfortably, and then sat looking at him, lost in thought. "Terence," he said at last, "you're very lonely here: that's not good for you. I'm at leisure this afternoon. I want to tell you a story. It will help to pass the time."

"It's very kind o' ye, Mister Kullen. But it's no sort o' matter now about me."

"But if I like to tell it to you?"

"The Lord reward ye."

"It's about Africa. You've heard of the slave-trade?"

"Not much," said Terence, listlessly.

"It's worth hearing about. It lasted a very, very long time—three hundred and fifty years. If you should ever read about it, you'll find it's a history of men and women and children that were hunted down by soldiers and caught and sold. There were fifteen millions of them—nearly half as many as there are people in this country—twice as many as there are in all Ireland. They had committed no crime: nobody pretended they had. They were not tried or convicted by a judge or a jury, but they were all sent to prison — every one of that fifteen millions."

Terence looked up, his attention evidently arrested, but it was a look of incredulity. He was probably considering where prisons could be found for fifteen millions of people. Mr. Kullen resumed:

"Bear in mind that this happened all through three hundred and fifty years. The prisons they were sent to were slave-ships, and the prisoners were carried from Africa to America. They were stowed away between-decks, like so many herrings. A full-grown man had fifteen inches by six feet, and no more, to lie upon—less space than they allow a corpse in a coffin. The men were all put in irons, fastened two and two, and the chains locked to the deck. Even if they had been unchained, there wasn't room to stand up. On the average, one of them out of every five died on the passage and was flung overboard. If the voyage was a stormy one, sometimes one-half died. So you see three millions of people out of the fifteen millions were thrown into the sea before they arrived. Their sufferings, from sickness and hardship and from thirst, were often so dreadful that many did as you are doing, Terence — they refused to eat, and then they were flogged, sometimes to death."

"To death!" with a faint look of astonishment.

"Yes, Terence, to death: that's the way they treated *them* when they wouldn't eat."

Terence winced a little.

"When they arrived in America," Kullen resumed, "they were forced to work from sunrise to sunset, for other people, instead of for themselves; and if they refused, they were unmercifully beaten. Afterward their children and their children's children were compelled to do the same thing. Yet none of that multitude were sent to these horrible prison-ships, or driven by the lash to work for other people, because they were guilty. They were all as innocent as you are."

The prisoner's sympathy was now fairly enlisted.

"What I particularly wished to explain to you," pursued Kullen, "was the manner in which they put a stop to this stealing and imprisoning of people that had committed no offence. Most of these prison-ships were owned by Englishmen, and they took their prisoners chiefly to Jamaica and other West India islands, where rich English subjects had plantations worth millions and millions of dollars, all worked by these forced laborers. On that account many very rich people were in favor of continuing this mode of getting labor. But there were others, good and just men, members of Parliament, who were very fine orators; and they tried to get a law passed to prevent so great a wrong. In defence of these innocent people they made speeches that were every bit as good as the speech Mr. Bagster made when he was defending you. But these speeches had no more effect than Mr. Bagster's had: the people were sent into the prison-ships, all the same.

"At last a man whose name was Clarkson—Thomas Clarkson—bethought himself that if the truth could all be shown about the sufferings of these poor people, the wrong would be righted, and no more of them would be chained down, under hatches, in slave-ships. He had observed that the surest way to have justice done to an innocent man is to search out what really happened in his case. He spent a number of years in finding witnesses and in getting the facts from them. He ferreted out the whole history of some of these prison-ships, and of all the cruelties that were practiced in them. Sometimes he got such horrible stories during the day that at night his brain was hot, and he was obliged to lay bandages soaked in cold water over his forehead for hours before he could get quiet and go to sleep. Every day he wrote down all the bits of evidence he had collected. Afterward he classified these and copied them out in large books, as a merchant does his accounts. He had a journal, with a complete history of the different slave-voyages. Then, in a great ledger, he had a page for every prison-ship he had heard about, and short notes of all he had heard about it—a separate page, too, for each witness (whether sailor or captain or surgeon of one of these ships), where he set down all he testified and his address, so that each man could be found and personally examined. He got heaps of affidavits, too, from different persons. All this was so well arranged that he could lay his hand, in a moment, on any piece of evidence that might be called for. When every thing was prepared, William Pitt, who was Prime Minister at that time, agreed to see Thomas Clarkson and to examine the testimony he had collected. He cross-examined him (as you heard the lawyers do the witnesses on your trial) for three or four hours. Clarkson had his books beside him, and answered every question, even about the smallest details, without the least hesitation. When it was over, Mr. Pitt said to him: 'Mr. Clarkson, all that I can do to put an end to the slave-trade shall be done.' He kept his word. A law was passed to prevent any Englishman from buying men in Africa and sending them on board prison-slavers.

"Now, Terence, what I want you to observe is, that as long as men made fine speeches, like Mr. Bagster's, in favor of these innocent people, it did no good: they were still put in irons and sent to these horrible ships. But when Thomas Clarkson found out the proper witnesses, and collected their evidence, and laid it before a man who had power to make it all right, then the great wrong that had been done for so many years was stopped at once. Can you guess, now, why I told you all this, and what I intend to do in your case?"

It was a study to note the various changes that passed over the prisoner's face, like clouds over an inclement April sky, as Kullen gave him this brief familiar sketch of one of the greatest episodes in the history of the world. Like many of his class and nation, he had hitherto cared little for the black man, and given scant attention to what concerned his sufferings or his wrongs. But Kullen had placed the matter before him in a new light, and at the very time his mind was prepared to receive it. Adversity was enlightening him. He was learning her lessons, bitter but wholesome. And the young man was coming slowly back to life. To Kullen's question whether he guessed his intentions, he replied, after a pause, "Maybe I do."

"I'm not an orator," said the other. "I can't draw tears from the eyes of jurymen, as Bagster does. But I'm a worker, like Thomas Clarkson. I am prison-agent of this State. It's my duty to look into cases like yours. Now hearken to what I've got to say. I've already told you that I don't believe you ever took that money. If you didn't, I'll do what living man may to find out the truth, and clear you. If I send you back, cleared, not a rascal of them all will be able to say one word against your character, unless he lies; and as to liars, I've a notion you can attend to their case yourself, when you get strong again and get out."

Terence smiled grimly, and Kullen went on:

"I'll do all this for you, and it shall not cost you a cent—on one condition."

"What's that?"

"You see I don't like to work for dead men: it's as much as I can do to attend to the living. When they've brought the jail-coffin for you and put you under ground, I shall have lost all interest in your case. If a man is a coward, and won't stay here to see his case through, and live down slander and perjury, and knock down every vagabond that insults his wife and children, he can't expect anybody else to do it for him. If the scum of the street, as you call them, throw it up to—"

"Norah," suggested Terence, as Kullen hesitated.

"Yes, if they ever throw it up to Norah that she's a thief's wife, or to her children that they had a convict for a father, it will be nobody's fault but yours. Now I want to know, once for all, whether you're going to starve yourself to death, or to eat that dinner?"

Another grim smile. Terence slowly drew the table close and cut himself a large slice of bread. At the first mouthful the animal instinct that rules a famished man came back in all its force. He began to devour the food.

"Slowly, man, slowly!" said Kullen. "That won't do. I'm going to put you on half rations for to-day and to-morrow, or we'll have you in the hospital after that two days' fast of yours. You'll have time enough. You can't track an old fox to his hole and dig him out in a day: then I've got other cases to attend to besides yours. It will be three or four weeks, maybe twice as many, before I get evidence enough to satisfy Judge Thomas." (The prisoner drooped at this, and the hopeless look came over his face again.) "Fie, man! Is that all the patience and the courage you have? What are six or eight weeks? You'll need that time to get strong, before you undertake the ragamuffins that are to cast up lies to Norah and the children."

The victory was won. And although, afterward, Terence did, now and then, chafe against the bars, like some caged wild beast, yet he behaved, on the whole, as well as could be expected of an impetuous and untutored nature.

A trifling incident that occurred that very day greatly encouraged him.

Interrogated as to his antecedents by Kullen, he stated that he had worked three years and a half on the farm of a Mr. Richards.

"Richards? Living where?"

"In Cumberland county, near Carlisle."

"Had he a son grown?"

"Yes, but I never saw him. He lived in Philadelphia, I think."

Kullen left the cell abruptly, and re-entered it a quarter of an hour later.

"Are you a believer in Providence, Terence?"

"Sure an' I was, Mister Kullen, till they sint me to prison for nothin' at all."

"Well, you'll have to come back to your old belief. Only think! The under-keeper that brings you your meals is old Mr. Richards' son, Walter; and he says he remembers his father talking to him last spring, when he went to see him, about a young Irishman that had been three or four years with him—the best hand and the honestest man he had ever had on the farm. Now ain't you ashamed to have lost heart as you did?"

Terence clasped his hands: "The Lord be praised! Well, I'll never misdoubt Providence again."

"Not till the next time. Take care, Terence! Suppose I don't get you out, after all?"

"And isn't yer honor after tellin' me ye're goin' to get me off as sure as there's a God above? And would I be doubtin' ye, Mister Kullen, and makin' a liar of ye, Mister Kullen? I know better nor that."

"Oh, you'll do! There will be no trouble about making you eat now. Well, I stand to my bargain."

CHAPTER IX.

THE RECONSIDERATION.

FAITHFULLY did that good prison-agent carry out his promise. He went first to Carlisle and obtained Mr. Richards' affidavit. Nothing could be more satisfactory. During the last years of

Terence's service the old man had entrusted him with large sums of money; had made him manager of a spacious market-garden, the produce of which Terence sold in the adjoining town; and had also occasionally sent him to Harrisburg with a drove of cattle to sell. He gave him the highest character for honesty and fidelity. During the term of his service, Terence had married the daughter of a neighboring farmer, and when he resolved to seek his fortune in Philadelphia, his master had agreed to his departure with great regret.

Returning to that city, Kullen made still more important discoveries. He obtained from Terence the name of the grocer with whom he chiefly dealt, P. R. Hardy, to whom Terence thought he had paid some money a day or two before his arrest. When the case was explained, the grocer turned to his books: "Yes, on the seventh of May, O'Reilly paid me ten dollars and a quarter."

"Did he pay it out of a linen bag, with gold pieces in it."

"Now I come to think of it," said the man, after a pause, "he did; and, more than that, the careless fellow left that very bag lying on the counter. I picked it up soon after he left; and as I wasn't sure whether it was his or not, I thought I'd make a note on a bit of paper of what was in it. It was a considerable sum, I remember, and Terence called for it that same evening."

"What became of the bit of paper?"

"Can't say. I generally put such things in the till. I'll see." Then, after a brief search: "Sure enough, here it is. I'd swear to that any day." And he tossed over the counter to Mr. Kullen a precious document, reading thus:

"MEM. *Money in linen bag. May 7, 1855.*

$170 00 in eagles.
45 50 in smaller gold and silver change.
20 00 in notes.

$235 50

"*Likely belongs to T. O'R.*"

The authenticity of this memorandum, and the circumstances under which it was made, were duly sworn to by Hardy.

It was two months after this that the man who was present when Terence so incautiously exposed the contents of the bag before Cassiday, returned from the South; but he remembered, and swore to, all the circumstances. This brought the *scienter*, as lawyers say, home to the accusing witness, satisfactorily explaining how, by rapidly counting the gold, he came to name a hundred and seventy dollars, in eagles, as the sum he lost.

While waiting for this testimony, Kullen set about the most difficult part of his task—to trace Cassiday's antecedents. He obtained a certificate from the clerk of the court of Berks county to the effect that no such person as Gottlieb Bauerman lived, or had recently lived, in that county; but he was not satisfied with that. Yet he was long at fault while searching farther. He could hear of no such person as Byron Cassiday, and he began to suspect the name might be assumed.

One day he cross-questioned Terence closely:

"Try to remember every word Cassiday said, and everything he did, that first evening. It's important, Terence. Did he hesitate when you asked him his name?"

"Well, I do' know as he did. I remember I called him Bryan, and says he—quite warm like, as if I had misca'd him o' purpose—says he, 'What for d'ye call me Bryan? it's Byron's me name.' I might a' known he was a false thief, and no Irish heart aboot him, to like Byron better nor Bryan for a name to go by."

Kullen was something of a detective. His experience in tracing out evidence had rendered him very observant of trifles. After a minute or two's thought he went to a drawer in the prisoner's table, where he usually kept the papers in this case, and took thence the manuscript notes which Bagster had made in anticipation of the trial, running them over carefully. Two of them arrested his attention, and he copied them out. The first was this:

"*No name on the Register of the police station at Port Richmond (except of persons well known to the officers*) *but one only*—BRYAN DELORNY, *and he came from Pottsville.*"

The second was:

"*Description of prosecuting witness: middle-sized, appears to be from* 30 *to* 35 *years old. No beard. Brown whiskers and brown, curling hair. A purple scar across the left ear. Features well formed, but injured by a furtive expression.*"

"It's worth looking after, at any rate," said Kullen, as he placed these memoranda in his pocket.

He went first to Terence's tavern, now carried on, after a fashion, by the barkeeper, Patrick Murphy, with Bridget to attend to the boarders. It had been shut up for several days after the trial; but Kullen had called on Mrs. O'Reilly, encouraged her about her husband, and, by his advice, the house had been re-opened. Kullen carefully examined the name in the register under date May 9: "*Byron Cassiday, Port Richmond:*" then, taking the book with him, he proceeded to the Port Richmond police station, and asked to be allowed to look at their record for May last.

"I want you to examine two signatures," he said presently to one of the officers, an experienced detective, "and tell me what you think of them."

The officer compared them critically for several minutes.

"Well?" said Kullen.

"The same man wrote both."

"Are you sure of that?"

"Dead sure! Look for yourself. There's the capital *B* in Byron and in Bryan; then there's the *Po* in Port and the *Po* in Pottsville, as like as two pins: there can be no chance in all that. Look at the *y's*, too—four of them—two in Byron Cassiday and two in Bryan Delorny. A half-blind man could see they're by the same hand. How's this?" He examined the date on the tavern register, then that on the police record: "Why, the man went right from our station to that tavern, and changed his name on the way. On the track of some villainy, ain't you?"

"It looks like it."

"Here's a memorandum by one of our men: '*Came on a coal train from Pottsville.*' Let's see: that's Tom Sullivan's hand. Tom!"

An officer entered from an inner room, and the detective said to him: "Here's a note of yours, Tom, isn't it? Do you remember anything of the coal-train passenger?"

"Not much to his credit," said the officer, examining the memorandum. "I took special notice of the man, for I didn't like his looks. A scaly customer, I should say. Couldn't look a man straight in the face. A scar on one of his ears. Been in rows enough, I'll warrant."

"A scar, you say?" asked Kullen.

"Across the left ear—a blue line, from a cut, probably. That your man?"

"Any beard?"

"No. Brown whiskers. Hair curling. Rather handsome, if it hadn't been for that down look of his."

"It's all right," said Kullen, referring to Bagster's memorandum. "What account did the fellow give of himself?"

"That he hadn't a cent to pay for his supper and night's lodging. Some story, I think, about losing his wallet at Pottsville. Any way, we gave him something to eat, and let him stay the night. It was a regular storm, I remember, and he was soaking wet."

Kullen felt pretty sure that he held the clue in his hand, and his next visit was to Pottsville. He went at once to a friend of his, John Clews, a lawyer of the place. To Kullen's question whether they knew anything in Pottsville of a certain Bryan Delorny, Clews replied:

"I should think we did!—more, a good deal, than we ever care to know again."

"Tell me about him. I have good reason for asking."

"Pretended to do business among us, but turned out a common loafer and drunkard. Swindled us here, right and left. First he cheated the keeper of a public-house where he lodged and boarded; then, several of our storekeepers: worse than that, his washer-woman, a hard-working soul, a widow with three children; worst of all, a poor sick seamstress who sat up, when she ought to have been in bed, to make three shirts for the scamp, and hadn't a loaf of bread or a ten-cent piece in the house the day she delivered them to him. When she entreated him for the pitiful sum he owed her, he laughed in her face and bid her sue for it and be damned. Some of the boys heard him. That was the drop too much for us. We got hold of him, gave him five minutes to pack his bundle, took the three new shirts out of it, and let the poor sick creature have them. Then we gave him his choice—either to have a tin pan tied to his coat-tails and be ignominiously drummed out of town for a vagabond, with a fair supply of odoriferous eggs and similar delicacies, or else to save us the trouble by taking the first train for Philadelphia. He pleaded that he had no money to pay his fare. We searched him thoroughly, and found, sure enough, that he had but fifteen cents, in a greasy wallet. There was a coal train just starting. We gave the conductor a dollar, told him that Pottsville would regard him as a public benefactor if he would give the rascal an outside seat and set him adrift—the farther off, the better we should like it. He set him down, so he told us afterward, near Port Richmond."

Kullen interested Clews in Terence's story. Through his aid he obtained a deposition, duly authenticated, setting forth all the main facts above related.

It took even longer than Kullen had anticipated to collect and arrange the testimony necessary to establish, beyond possible cavil, Terence O'Reilly's innocence. September and October passed: November came, and the poor fellow was still in prison. The repeated delays incident to such work greatly annoyed the kind-hearted prison-agent, certain as he now was of Terence's innocence. The prisoner might have had a visit from Norah and the children; for, under the separate system in the prisons of Pennsylvania, such visits are permitted at regular intervals. But he had made a vow to himself that his family should never come near him till he could embrace them as a free man, with character cleared of all suspicion. He adhered doggedly to this self-imposed vow; but, as the weeks passed, and he recovered bodily health and strength, that hope deferred which maketh the heart sick preyed upon him, till his impatience rose, at times, almost to frenzy.

At last, quite late in the evening of the seventeenth of November, Kullen procured the last of eight important affidavits, containing legal proof—

First: That two days before the alleged theft the prosecuting witness had but fifteen cents in his possession, while the accused had upward of a hundred and seventy dollars, in gold eagles, loose in a linen bag.

Second: That the said witness had deposed under a false name, his real name being Bryan Delorny; that he was a common drunkard and swindler, disgracefully expelled as such from the town of Pottsville.

Third: That the witness before going up to bed, on the night of the alleged theft, had had an opportunity to see and count the gold-pieces found in the possession of the accused.

And, finally: That the said witness had given a false reference when asked where he obtained the money which he alleged to have been stolen from him.

It was nearly ten o'clock at night when Mr. Kullen, fortified with these overwhelming proofs that an innocent man had been sentenced to nine months' imprisonment, and accompanied by the under-keeper, Richards, reached the residence of Judge Thomas. The servant at first refused to take up their names, saying that the judge was occupied with business of the utmost importance, and had ordered that he should not be disturbed. Finally he consented to deliver a message from the prison-agent to the effect that his business brooked no delay; and, after some demur, they were admitted.

The judge received them somewhat abruptly.

"Well, Mr Kullen," he said, "what is it?"

"A criminal case which I am very anxious you should reconsider."*

"I have no time to consider any case to-night. Call to-morrow evening."

"It's a case where the greatest injustice has been done, judge; as I can prove to your satisfaction, if you'll listen to me for half an hour."

"I tell you I have no half hour to spare for any such business. What's this case that's so important it can't be put off foı a single day?"

"A man you sentenced for larceny last August—Terence O'Reilly."

"Oh, it's that young Irish fellow, is it?"

"Yes—as clear a case of perjury as ever I met with in my life."

"Let me tell you, Mr. Kullen, that I sha'n't reconsider that case, neither to-night nor any other night. It was a protracted trial—two whole days. If the man's life had depended on it, it couldn't have been managed with more skill and care. I haven't a doubt of the prisoner's guilt. That Bagster's eloquence is ringing in my ears now. You're losing your time to talk to me after the defence he made. Once for all, I won't reconsider it."

"You're a just man, judge—impartial and merciful, too, when mercy ought to be shown. But you are hasty, especially when you have a lot of work on hand. If you stick to that last resolution and refuse to hear this case, and if, by and by, the truth comes to your ears, you'll never forgive yourself. I know you."

"Do you? Well, I can return the compliment. I know *you* for one of the most incorrigibly obstinate fellows I ever had the bad luck to encounter. Some of your ancestors must surely have been Scotch: are you sure you're not descended from John Knox? I see what I shall have to do. You may talk about my justice, but you'll force me to imitate an *un*just judge that you've read about. There was a widow, you may remember, who was as great a plague to him as you are to me; and he concluded to hear her at last, lest by her continual coming she should weary him. That's the shortest way to get rid of you. To-night it's entirely out of the question," putting his hand on a bundle of documents: "it will take me half the night to get through with these, and they *must* be disposed of before I go into court in the morning. To-morrow evening, at eight. Till then, good-bye to you."

"I'm very sorry, judge: I know you are worked a great deal too hard. But I've labored at this case for two months. My heart's in it. This is the twelfth week that poor young fellow has been in prison. He's half crazy now. I gave him my word that the evidence in his case should be completed and should be laid before you to-night. I got up this morning at four, and I've been at it every minute since then. Now I've made up my mind not to stir from this place to-night till I get a hearing."

The judge had taken his pen, unfolded one of the documents before him and commenced a memorandum. He threw the pen down petulantly and addressed the under-keeper:

"Richards, is craziness infectious in that prison of yours? Have you seen any symptoms of it in Mr. Kullen before?"

"I'm afraid I'm not a good judge, your honor; for I take a'most as much interest in the young fellow as he does."

"Oh, if you're all crazy, then the matter's hopeless."

"I did think the man would have died on our hands, judge, he took it so hard. I don't believe I ever should have got him through, if it hadn't been for Mr. Kullen; and it would have been a great pity. He's as good and as honest a fellow as ever lived."

"How do you know?"

"He worked three or four years for my father in Cumberland county. The old man set the greatest store by him,

* At the date of this narrative (1855) the Court of Quarter Sessions of the county of Philadelphia claimed, and exercised, the prerogative to reconsider the verdict under which a criminal had been convicted, and to discharge him from custody. It was but during the year 1868 that the Supreme Court of the State of Pennsylvania overruled that interpretation of the court below.

would have trusted him with untold gold, and took it awfully hard when he heard Terence was in jail."

"I see it's a regular conspiracy against me. Well, a man may as well submit first as last. Come, Mr. Kullen, since it must be, be as brief and as quick about it as you can."

Before the prison-agent had read two of the exculpatory documents, the judge, quite forgetting his impatience, began to take as much interest in the case as Kullen himself. Then came the grocer's memorandum. "Upon my word, Kullen," he said, "this looks like the finger of Providence." When there were laid before him the authenticated proofs that the prosecuting witness had deposed under a false name, and that he was a penniless, notorious swindler who had been expelled from Pottsville, the good judge brought his fist down on the table with a vigor that upset the mass of forgotten documents he had still to wade through.

Kullen saw that the cause was gained: "Will you reconsider the case and cause the clerk of the court to make out an order for the man's discharge to-morrow morning?"

"No, I won't" said the judge, taking up his pen.

"You won't?"

"No. Do you think I'd leave an innocent man like that, who has suffered so shamefully already, one night more in prison than I can help? Richards here will take an informal order from me at once, and I'll make it all right with the clerk to-morrow. Won't you, Richards?"

"God bless your honor's kind heart!" said Richards: "of course I will."

The judge wrote out the order accordingly, and handed it to the prison-agent. "You're a good fellow, Kullen," he said, warmly; "and if you only knew what an infernal lot of papers I've got to go through to-night—bless me! who scattered them all over the floor?—you would excuse my hastiness."

Kullen wrung the honest judge's hand without a word, the moisture rising to his own eyes; and he and Richards hurried off to the prison.

A little before three o'clock that morning, Terence, his convict-dress cast off for ever, yet the man scarcely convinced that he was at last free and beyond reach of reproach, stood once more at the door of his dwelling, and startled its inmates by a loud demand for admission.

CHAPTER X.

AMOS CRANSTOUN.

LET us revert some ten weeks and to Chiskauga, for that morning visit of the aunt and niece to Mr. Sydenham yet remains to be described.

Our readers may remember that while Byron Cassiday, or Bryan Delorny (let each select the paternal or maternal patronymic* as to him seems best), was seated on that grassy knoll and wishing Terence O'Reilly out of prison, without doing anything to procure his enlargement, the said Byron or Bryan, looking northward over Sydenham's residence, discerned, beyond the vineyards, on the line of a brook, indications of a waterfall.

On the banks of Kinshon Creek, beside that waterfall, under a rustic arbor of trellis-work overrun with grapevines, sat two young ladies in earnest talk. They were worth seeing, and, what is better, worth knowing—very unlike each other in appearance, but each possessing no little share of beauty.

The stature of the one just reached middle size. Her well-developed form, with its rounded outlines, was finely proportioned, and its motions were easy and graceful; small, dimpled hands, and small feet. Her eyes were blue, soft, thoughtful; her hair, curling in ringlets, was light brown, with a golden tinge in it. Her face, not quite long enough for the classical model, had a child-like expression about it, very pretty (that word, rather than handsome, occurred to one in looking at her); a chin slightly receding; a very fair complexion, and a delicate color in the cheeks. There was

*As we do not say *matronymic*, I assume that patronymic, like the word man, may occasionally refer to either sex; the etymology to the contrary notwithstanding.

a touch of languor about her, and she looked a little out of health and spirits. This was Celia Pembroke.

The other, a full inch taller, though evidently several years younger, contrasted strongly with her companion. She seemed in brilliant health. Her figure was lithe, agile, vigorous, but somewhat slender, giving promise of remarkable beauty when a few years more should have filled up the outlines and expanded the form. The limbs were a little longer in proportion than Celia's, and her hands and feet larger, but perfectly well formed; the fingers long and tapering, and the foot with the "Arab arch." Her face showed the faultless oval, more frequent in Italy than among us; the nose was very slightly aquiline: otherwise the features were classical, but with nothing of the tameness sometimes marking this type; the expression denoting high spirit, full of life and hope and energy and intelligence. Thoroughbred, one might have been tempted to style her. A clear, bright brunette, with large, dark-brown eyes, that could flash as well as melt. Her hair, too, was brown—long, thick, dark, silky—"une chevelure magnifique," as the French say, choosing to designate, by a single word, what we somewhat strangely call a "head of hair." The chin was well set and delicately cut, its form indicating (Lavater would have said) resolution. That was Leoline Sydenham.

What these young girls were saying to each other I do not purpose to disclose. The elder people, Celia's aunt and Leoline's father, were talking indoors. Let us listen to them.

They were sitting in the recess of a bay window opening east on the lawn. Sydenham had made the usual inquiries after the health and welfare of her family, to which Mrs. Hartland had replied with that absent, preoccupied manner which indicates a purpose to enter on an important subject that the speaker has not exactly determined how to broach, or has not mustered courage to encounter.

When Sydenham paused, the color came slightly to her cheeks, and she said, hastily:

"Mr. Sydenham, I fear that I am about to take an unwarrantable liberty with you, but our old friendship, your uniform kindness—"

"Alice,' said Sydenham, smiling, "I was beginning to think you had quite forgotten that happy old time when your excellent sister and you and I were children together. You have never called me Frank, as you used to do then, except the very first time we met on my arrival here; and we see you so seldom here among us."

"It is not customary."

"Not customary for old friends, living in a country village, and who certainly have not quarreled, to visit each other?"

"I did not mean that—"

"Ah! I am glad to see you smile once more."

"Surely you cannot doubt that to visit you and my favorite Leoline, and dear, good Mrs. Clymer, whom everybody loves, must be a pleasure to me. But Mr. Hartland—you know his ways. He is more devoted to his favorite botany and entomology than ever; and he seems never satisfied unless I am at home. While he is in the field he expects me to make colored drawings, for the work he is getting out, of every undescribed flower and insect he finds. Then I have to label his specimens, arrange his cabinets; and so, what with these and my domestic duties—"

"You have not time or thought to spare for your neighbors. Well, I will not quarrel with my friend Hartland about the importance of his scientific pursuits; but, upon my word, I hold this same science to be a villainous engrosser, an arrant monopolizer as ever sold salt in Queen Elizabeth's days. I shall owe it a downright grudge, Alice, if it carry you off too. We can't spare you out of the world. These insects are very curious—I have spent hours in admiring them—but they are not worthy of having the interest one takes in humankind wholly squandered on them. These undescribed flowers that grow under your pencil—I don't doubt their grace and beauty—but when Hartland gets out his work, I am sure I shall never look at them with patience, if they are to steal your affections away from us."

A painful expression crossed Mrs. Hartland's gentle face for a moment, and then was gone. "I strive to take an interest in my husband's pursuits," she said: "it is my duty. And I do take interest in them—much more than I once thought I ever could. You don't know," she added, with a faint smile, "how learned I have become in genera and species—"

"Dear Alice," interrupted Sydenham, "forgive me. I was wrong, and you are right. You shall come to us just when you please and when you can. You know how welcome you are. But you have not told me yet what it is that is not customary."

"Oh, I meant that it is not the custom for married persons, unconnected by blood, to call each other by their first names."

"Is it not? Well, I never wore the straight coat, though my father did. But I have quite enough of the Quaker leaven within me to sanctify, among old friends at least, that beautiful patriarchal custom, a reminder of the common brotherhood of mankind. And you too, Alice: your good mother wore the plain cap and bonnet to the day of her death. It strikes me that might justify her daughter in calling an old schoolmate Frank."

"I think I am quite as much Quaker as you—"

"Frank. Mr. Sydenham won't fit in there at all."

"Well, I think I am quite as much Quaker as you, Frank; but Mr. Hartland is not. Sometimes he seems as if he wished me to forget my Quaker origin."

"Is he so much prejudiced?"

"He is a strict Congregationalist, as you know; and I have heard him speak, in general terms, of the dangerous latitude which the followers of William Penn allow themselves. I never heard him say a syllable on this particular subject of Christian names. But, as I have always called him Mr. Hartland, I think, Mr. Sydenham, that you cannot object to sharing the same fate, my dear mother's plain bonnet to the contrary notwithstanding."

"Oh," said Sydenham, laughing, "I have not a word more to say. If you have never called your husband Thomas, I am not surprised that you should have forgotten to call me Frank."

The painful expression shot again, for a moment, across Alice's face; but Sydenham, not observing it, added: "And am I to call you Mrs. Hartland in return?"

"No, indeed no," she replied, earnestly. "You have always called me Alice; and if you were to change now, I should think I had vexed or offended you. Besides, it is your common habit. Do you not call my niece Celia?"

"Do I?"

"Always: I have particularly remarked it. And that reminds me of the purpose of my visit to you. I come to trouble you about affairs not your own."

"My dear Alice, you shall call me just what you please. But I shall quarrel with you outright if you ever consider it necessary to employ preface or apology in asking my advice or aid in any matter that concerns or interests you."

"Then, as I don't feel able, just at present, to encounter a quarrel outright with you, I shall come to the point at once. It *is* a matter that interests me, for it concerns the happiness of dear Celia."

"Of late she has not been looking so well nor so happy as usual."

"She is not happy, poor child. It is the old, sad story," said Alice, with a sigh:

"'The course of true love never did run smooth.'"

"Ah!" said Sydenham, "she has made a choice?"

"Does that surprise you? You know nothing of it? But you are so seldom with us, now. Yes, she has made a choice, and one that does not at all suit Mr. Hartland."

"May I know the name?"

"Certainly, if you have not already guessed it—Mr. Mowbray."

"And what are Mr. Hartland's objections to Mowbray?"

"In the first place, his poverty. His mother has not enough, aside from what her school brings in, for a humble support."

"Celia must have thirty thousand dollars."

"Forty thousand. Mr. Hartland has invested for her prudently and profitably."

"Barring extravagant ideas, that is enough for both."

"Ah, I knew you would look at the matter as I do."

"But perhaps I don't."

"You are not going to support Mr. Hartland's view, surely!"

"What is his view?"

"That a girl with forty thousand dollars is entitled to look for a corresponding fortune in a husband."

"You transport me back to Paris. A hundred thousand livres must marry a hundred thousand livres; and, to do really well, ought to attract and subdue a hundred and fifty thousand. Purses are mated. No wonder poor hearts take their revenge afterward. No, if that be Hartland's view of the matter, I never can support it. Besides, where, in this humble village of ours, is he to find forty thousand dollars for her? I am altogether too old: Leoline is within a few years of Celia's age."

"Oh," said Alice, quickly, "I assure you Mr. Hartland has no designs upon you. He favors a very different man."

"He *has* some one in view then?"

"You have already guessed whom: I see it."

"Indeed I have not. I cannot even imagine whom, in this neighborhood, he would select. Why should you think I had hit upon it?"

"Because you seemed to feel alarmed, as I do when I hear Mr. Hartland urging the claims of Mr. Cranstoun."

"Cranstoun! Amos Cranstoun! Impossible!"

"It is only too true."

"This is serious," said Sydenham after a pause. "The wishes of the dead, no less than the welfare of the living, urge me to interfere. Strange that this should so long have escaped me!"

He went to a cabinet of carved oak, dark with age, and, after a search of some minutes, returned with a letter in his hand.

"Her fears foretold the truth," he said, as he offered it for Mrs. Hartland's perusal. It was the same he had received, ten years before, from Mrs. Pembroke, at Milan.

"Dear Eliza!" The tears rose to her eyes as she recognized the familiar characters. "And three months only before her death!"

Sydenham paced the room while she read the letter, and when she looked up he stopped before her.

"Alice," said he, "this must be looked to, and it shall be. How does Celia feel toward Cranstoun?"

"Strangely. She undoubtedly dislikes and seeks to avoid him. Yet I think he possesses a certain influence over her. It has seemed to me to resemble fascination. I believe the poor child hears in her dreams her father's death-bed words about that man. They seem to haunt her."

"There is something I do not quite understand in all this. It certainly is remarkable that Cranstoun should have been tolerated—even favored, conciliated, recommended to his wife and daughter—by Frederick Pembroke."

"Eliza often expressed to me her aversion to him."

"She was right. He has a smooth, plausible manner, is not without ability, nor, I believe, without kindly impulses—"

"Your sister Clymer says that in her visits to the poor of our village she has several times found herself forestalled by the charity of Cranstoun. His name is seldom withheld from any subscription for benevolent purposes, and he has the character of winning to himself the attachment of those whom he employs."

"His character," said Sydenham, musing, "has been to me a study. Hannah has told me of his charitable deeds. The man is neighborly, compassionate, I suppose—indulgent, they say, to his dependants. And yet he has no more idea of honesty than if such a thing were not to be found in the world. He is an arrant knave—not a violent one, not what would be called a cruel one—but a knave without a single grain of rectitude, without the first spark of honor, and, with all his plausibility, devoid of every principle that stamps the gentleman."

"Is it possible that benevolence and such utter lack of principle can coexist in the same character?"

"Benevolence is too strong a term. But undoubtedly a rascal may be kind to his neighbors and family, compassionate to suffering that comes under his immediate observation, and disposed to save to his fellow-creatures all pain that is not necessary in carrying out his own sinister purposes. Cranstoun would bring suit against a poor widow—wrongfully too—he would suffer the constable to sell out the last article not exempted by law, and then, next day perhaps, if he chanced to see his victim and found her in want, he would send her a bushel of meal or a barrel of potatoes."

"So bad as that?"

"I have had little to do with him, thank God! but the case I have supposed is not an imaginary one. You know the widow Carson?"

"Betty Carson? Certainly. She washes for Mrs. Mowbray—as hard-working and as honest a creature as lives."

"You may remember Matthew, her husband—a confirmed sot, who led her a dog's life. Matthew had dealings with Mr. Cranstoun, and, at one time, fell in his debt some twenty-five dollars, giving his note for the amount, with Betty's name, by Cranstoun's special request, as security. About a year before he died Carson fell sick, and Mr. Harper, for whom he sent, so wrought upon him that he became, for a time, quite a reformed man, went to work in good earnest, and promised fair to be a credit to his family. During this interval, at his wife's earnest solicitation, he contrived, partly with her assistance, to pay off the debt to Cranstoun; but either he forgot that he had given his note, or carelessly neglected to take it up. The payment of this debt poor Betty mentioned at the time, with tears of gratitude in her eyes, to Mr. Harper. He has not the slightest doubt it was paid. Soon after, Matthew relapsed into worse than his former courses, coming home late at night from the grogshop, breaking open his wife's chest, and taking thence, to supply the next morning's orgies, the pittance she had earned by unremitting toil over the wash-tub, and laid by to procure bread for her children."

"Poor Betty! That was worse than I imagined. I knew Matthew was a drunkard, but did not suppose him a thief."

"Neither was he, that I know of."

"Not when he stole his wife's money?"

"I did not say he stole it—he only took it."

"Now you are jesting."

"God forbid that I should jest on so serious a subject."

"You say he took from her chest, without her permission, the money she had worked for—"

"Yes, money made painfully, toilsomely by going out to wash at seventy-five cents a day."

"And that was not stealing?"

"Not in the case of a husband who took the money from his wife."

"*Is* that the law?"

"In our State, yes."

"Man's law, then, not God's.'

"I hope it will not long be man's law in any State of the Union. Our neighbors of Indiana have got rid of it; and others are doing likewise. The rage for strong drink seemed to return upon Matthew with redoubled force after his brief season of sobriety. One article of furniture went after another to eke out the means of slaking his ceaseless thirst. At last—the best thing he could do then—he died of delirium tremens."

"And Cranstoun brought suit against Betty for the debt?"

"Not at first. He did his best to obtain work for her, and even set on foot a small subscription for her benefit. After a few months the chairs and tables were replaced, a list carpet once more covered the cabin floor, the children were decently clad for winter, and the widow was just beginning to feel that she might yet work her way through the world, thanks to the timely aid of Mr. Cranstoun and other kind people, when one day a writ was served, at Cranstoun's instance, for the amount of Matthew's note to him, soon to be followed by an execution of sufficient amount to sweep nearly all she had saved since her husband's death."

"How surprised the poor soul must have been!"

"She was thunderstruck—could not imagine at first that it was anything else but a mistake; and went to Cranstoun, who asked her, very coolly, if she had any receipt to show of payment made."

"You had this from Betty herself?"

"Certainly. I never take such things at second hand. She came to me, in her distress, to ask if there was no remedy. I examined the case with care, saw Mr. Harper and others, satisfied myself, first, that the money, beyond a shadow of doubt, had been paid, and, secondly, that no legal proof could be obtained of the fact."

"Did you call upon Mr. Cranstoun?"

"Yes."

"And he denied the payment?"

"No. He merely requested to hear my proofs; and the array, as to moral conviction, was perfectly overwhelming: that, I saw, was evident even to him. He listened very quietly, and then asked me which among them I supposed to be sufficient, in a court of justice, to bar his claim. 'Do you deny payment?' said I—indignantly I am sure it must have been, for I felt my blood boil. 'Not at all,' he replied, without the slightest apparent emotion either of shame or resentment. 'I am not required to deny anything of the sort. It is Mrs. Carson's business to prove payment, and if she does not, I have a legal right to the debt, and shall certainly get it.'"

"Atrocious!" said Alice. "And such a man as that has Mr. Hartland's confidence!"

"He made himself very useful in the way of business. To your husband the available part of his character has probably shown itself, while its baser traits have been kept under in the background."

"I know he has spared no pains to win Mr. Hartland's good-will and good opinion. At one time—about the time this letter of my sister's was written—my husband seemed to dislike and mistrust him. I think that was the chief reason why Eliza, on her deathbed, required from Celia a promise that she would not marry, before the age of twenty-three, without her guardian's consent."

"Did Celia give such a promise?"

"In the most solemn manner."

"And this consent Mr. Hartland now refuses to her marriage with Mowbray?"

"Absolutely. The poor child is in despair. I could not see these crosses and vexations prey upon her health, as I know they are doing, without asking your counsel and aid."

"Have you seen much of Mowbray?"

"Of late not much. Hartland's manner almost forbids him the house. Celia has been taking German lessons of Mrs. Mowbray, and thus has seen him almost daily; but Mr. Hartland has told her that at the end of the present quarter—that is, next week—these lessons must cease."

"And your own opinion of this young man—"

"Is favorable. Mowbray is young, handsome, well-principled, I think; and he loves Celia devotedly. Cannot you do something for her, Mr. Sydenham? No one who has not lived with her for years, as I have done, can tell what a dear, good, warm-hearted girl she is. And she might be so happy! And she might make him so happy! My very heart sinks within me to think of their early years darkened, saddened thus; and youth that never returns!"

There was a tone in Alice's soft, low voice that went to Sydenham's heart. Her eyes were fixed, absently, on the lovely landscape which, under a slight haze, stretched out before them.

"Do you know, dear friend," she suddenly resumed, "it has often been a puzzle to me that God's gift to us of His most beautiful attribute should so often—oh, so very often!—have been given in vain, worse than in vain!"

"It is one of the world's great mysteries," said Sydenham, sadly—"one of many. Who shall explain to us why, just outside the garden of our happiness, stands Death to enter—who knows at what moment?—and lay desolate hopes, affections, enjoyments, that seemed the direct boon of Heaven itself?"

"Death!" said Alice, following her own train of thought—how often we do this, unheeding our neighbor's!—"death! Ah, that is the least of evils!"

Sydenham looked up surprised. But she did not notice the look, and he merely said: "Have you pleaded Celia's cause with Mr. Hartland?"

"I dare not: besides, it would be useless."

"And you wish me to do it? Small chance of success for me if you feel secure of failure."

"Do not fear that, Mr. Sydenham," said Alice, eagerly. "He does not heed me: he thinks I cannot understand such things. But you—oh I know you can do so much, if you will. You will speak to him as her mother's early friend—nay, this letter of Eliza's gives you authority to interpose."

"It makes it my duty, at all events, to leave nothing untried that may prove of service to her daughter, be it much or little."

"I knew I could depend on you," said Mrs. Hartland, giving Sydenham her hand. "When we were children together you never refused me anything. It was a happy time, then; and you did so much to make it happy! If I come but seldom to see you now, Mr. Sydenham, and if I don't call you Frank, you mustn't think I am ungrateful enough to forget. Indeed, indeed, I have much to do at home"—she rose—"and I have been gone, I fear, too long already. Mr. Hartland takes it so much amiss if I am absent when he returns from his walk. Where can those girls be?"

"They must be close by; for I saw them, but a minute or two since, returning by the vineyard gate. But cannot you leave Celia with me? I ought to speak to her, and perhaps it would be better alone. Ah! here they come."

"Lela dear," said Mrs. Hartland as they entered, "can you spare the time to drive me home? We did not bring Potter: Celia was my charioteer; and, as your father has something to say to her and I am in a hurry, she cannot return with me. I know what a skillful driver you are, and, to tell you the truth, I am a little nervous about that brown mare Potter bought us."

"Ah, you are driving Brunette. I shall be delighted. I *am* a good whip, I think: am I not, papa?"

"If you would drive a little more cautiously down this steep approach of ours, I could recommend you with more confidence. But I think I may trust Mrs. Hartland with you."

"Well, that's a good deal for papa. You must know, Mrs. Hartland, he's afraid of spoiling me by too much praise, and deals it out by thimblefuls. But I find him out, for all his stinginess. He would not let me drive you, Mrs. Hartland—you, who are such a favorite with him — nay, you needn't look incredulous: isn't she, papa?"

"Certainly, my child," said Sydenham, with a quiet smile—"with me and with all her friends; but you are detaining her."

"Well, would he entrust you to me if he didn't believe, in his heart, that I drive, as our old coachman says, splendidly?"

"Go along, chatterbox," said her father, patting her cheek fondly: "Mrs. Hartland's time is precious."

"In a moment. My driving-gloves: ah, here they are. Now, Mrs. Hartland, I'm ready."

Sydenham accompanied them to the door, Celia following.

"That is a beautiful animal," he said, patting its arched neck as Leoline took her place beside Mrs. Hartland and assumed the reins, "but she seems high-spirited."

"Yes, papa, spirited, but not vicious. There's not a bit of vice in those large, bold, projecting eyes. I had a good look at her the other day."

"Drive cautiously, my child."

"I will indeed, papa," said Leoline, earnestly. "Do not fear for us. By-by, Celia." And, at a light touch from the whip, the high-bred animal trotted off, stepping in a style that delighted her young driver and would not have disgraced Hyde Park.

CHAPTER XI.

THE USE OF A VILLAGE POND.

"MRS. HARTLAND," said Leoline as they drove along, "I wish Celia could feel just as I do."

Mrs. Hartland smiled: "She *would* be the better of a little of your flow of spirits. But Celia used to be gay and light-hearted as any one. It is only of late—"

"Yes, I know: that is just what I am thinking of. I did not mean that I wished her to be like me—dear Celia is far better than I am, already: I only meant that, at this particular time, I could wish that she felt as to some things—"

"Some things! Ah, Celia has been opening her heart to you, then?"

"No. I never ask people about their hearts: it's not much in my way. What a beauty that Brunette is, and how nicely she goes! It is a real pleasure to drive her."

"Yes, dear, but if you were to go a *little* slower—"

"So I will, if you are the least afraid."

"Thank you. It was not about Celia's heart, then, that you were talking to me."

"Yes, it was; and perhaps I have no business to say a word, for Celia and I have not been touching on that topic at all, to-day; but I can't help hearing what people, in a village like this, *will* talk about, when they ought to let it alone. And it provokes me to think—it provokes me still more for others to think— There, Mrs. Hartland, she shall go more slowly: I didn't intend to touch her with the whip. Don't look so apprehensive. Brunette shall walk down this hill quite quietly, so that papa shall say I am a good child."

"You *are* a good child to think of my silly fears. Now tell me what it provokes you to think and for others to think."

"That Mr. Mowbray should have the power to make dear Celia's cheeks pale and her eyes sad even for a day. I dare say it's all wrong for me to speak so plainly, but that is the honest truth: and I only wish—" She hesitated.

"That Celia felt toward Evelyn Mowbray just as you do."

"I believe that was just what I was going to say," said Leoline, laughing; "and a foolish enough speech it would have been. But no: it's not quite that. My anxiety, I believe, went no farther than this, that—in short, that she should take things quietly."

Mrs. Hartland looked at that fair young face, unclouded by a care, and sighed.

"I am only wishing, remember," said Leoline, apologetically, as she met Mrs. Hartland's pensive eyes. "I know," she resumed, a sudden shade saddening her own, "we cannot take some things quietly. Poor, dear papa! what years he grieved about mamma! But that was death!"

"The death of those we love is a terrible evil, but they may be for ever lost to us, though yet alive."

"But there is no question of Celia losing Mowbray for ever; and if she did—"

"Well?"

"I am afraid my ideas are not very clear this morning, dear Mrs. Hartland. I come back to my wish that Celia could but take things a little more as I do. I like people to be happy. Not that I should object to Mowbray's looking a little forlorn or so; but darling Celia, who is too good for any of them—worth them all put together—I can't bear to think that she should droop and grieve. I believe—yes, I fancy that must be it—that my idea is, men ought to care more for us than we do for them."

There flitted across Mrs. Hartland's face a singular expression—sad, regretful, it seemed—which Leoline was trying to interpret when it suddenly changed to one of great alarm.

They had descended more than two-thirds of the hill which led from Sydenham's house to the level on which the village stood, and the mare had behaved perfectly well. They had passed the neat paling which fenced the garden and orchard, and now, on their right, was a rivulet, swelled by late heavy rains, and which, running down some distance parallel to the road, crossed it a few hundred yards farther on: then, passing to the left, its banks fringed with willows, it bisected and irrigated the lower portion of Sydenham's pasture-ground, dropping thence into Kinshon Creek below the fall. On the left of the road they were descending was the post-and-rail fence which enclosed said pasture, a pretty, undulating piece of meadow-land, with an eastern slope to the plain below, and extending some distance beyond the foot of the hills.

In this pasture were cattle and several horses, among them a colt, three years old and still unbroken, which, as soon as it saw the dearborn descending the hill, raced across to a point a little behind where they then were, stood for a second or two, head and tail erect, snorting loudly; then, after trotting slowly a few bounding steps, dashed impetuously down the hill, close to the road fence.

Whether it was that Brunette had been purchased by Potter of some of his racing associates, who had been testing her speed on the turf, or that the high-spirited animal had been but imperfectly broken, the sudden start, as the colt shot past her, was too great a trial, and, in a moment, she too was galloping at full speed down the road.

Mrs. Hartland's first impulse was to snatch the reins, but Mr. Hartland had once checked her harshly for a similar imprudence; and she recollected herself just in time to refrain from an act that might have proved fatal to both.

Leoline had not boasted vainly of her skill in driving, and her self-possession was admirable. With one foot planted against the dashboard, she gathered up the reins, and, though she could not check the powerful animal, she guided it steadily and without difficulty.

In an instant they had reached the foot of the hill. Leoline glanced at Mrs. Hartland's agitated countenance. "It is nothing," she said: "I can take her up, never fear; only pray, pray, sit still."

They approached the spot where the rivulet already mentioned crossed their path. There was but a foot-bridge, composed of a squared log with a rude hand-railing, close to the pasture fence, for the stream scarcely ever deepened so as to prevent vehicles from passing easily; and now there might be some eighteen inches of water. Fortunately, the descent on each side was gradual.

Leoline drove the mare close on the left of the road, toward the foot-bridge; then, as they reached the descent, drew her briskly to the right, cutting at an angle across the little stream and up the opposite bank, thus avoiding any dangerous shock in crossing. The rush of the water and the acclivity beyond caused the animal somewhat to slacken her headlong speed, and Leoline managed to guide her safely round the turn which, sweeping to the left, brought her into the main avenue, leading directly into the village, which was nearly a mile distant.

On the left of this road, fronted by a neatly-kept grass-plat, dotted with evergreens, was Mr. Harper's dwelling, a pretty, white-painted frame house of a single story, with green blinds, and a rustic porch shaded with woodbine; and before his gate, at this moment, stood his gig, which the good man was in the act of entering.

No sooner, however, did he see the plight of the ladies than he rushed forward, totally forgetful of the risk to himself, and, in spite of Leoline's warning exclamation, attempted to seize the runaway by the reins. The effect was to cause the animal to swerve and start off afresh, thus depriving the girl of the mastery which she had almost succeeded in obtaining.

But even at such disadvantage she did not lose heart. It was market-day, and she saw crowds in the distant street. "It will never do," such was her rapid thought, "to enter the village at this pace."

Now, about half-way between Mr. Harper's house and town, on the right of this road, was the village pond, a pretty piece of water, fed by constant springs, partially shaded by willows and acacias, and presenting, on a summer evening, when the cattle, returning unherded from their forest-pasture, stopped to drink there, a pleasant scene of rural quiet that Cuyp or Gainsborough need not have disdained to paint.

It was a usual watering-place for wagoners, being open to the road, and was accessible, by a short sloping descent, as well on the village side as that on which Mr. Hartland's dearborn was now rapidly approaching.

As they came in sight of it a sudden thought flashed on Leoline's mind, and she acted on it with instant promptitude.

With a single word of encouragement to Mrs. Hartland, she headed the mare, to that lady's consternation, right for the centre of the pond. Down the slope they went, and into the water, with a rush that dashed it over the animal's back and sprinkled the ladies pretty heavily. But Leoline, in that moment of decision, had calculated well. She drew the mare sharply to the left. The bottom of the pond was soft sand, the wheels dragged through it heavily, and before they had completed a semi-circular sweep toward the opposite landing-place, the panting horse was fairly brought to a stand-still.

"I could not help it, dear Mrs. Hartland," said Leoline, shaking the large drops from her dress: "I was so much afraid of running over some of the children in that crowded street. I hope you are not very wet. Indeed I could not help it."

"Wet, dear Lela! How can you talk or think of such a trifle when nothing but your courage has saved us perhaps from death! Oh let us get out!"

"What! Into the water? That *would* be a craziness! And let Brunette get home her own way, break the dearborn to pieces and frighten your household into fits? Oh fie, Mrs. Hartland! I was going to return you the compliment about courage, but now you've spoilt it all."

"Leoline, if I could but feel and act like you! I owe to you my life."

"It was nothing, Mrs. Hartland. If the mare had been vicious and had kicked, ah, then it would have been serious. A gentleman we knew in England had his knee lamed for life in that way; and I've been rather nervous about it, myself, ever since. But Brunette ran beautifully. Ah, good mare! See, she drinks: she is conquered now. We shall get home with her quite safely."

"How skillfully you drove over that brook in the road! I scarcely felt a jolt."

"Yes: I flatter myself that was not badly done. If you are going fast, never drive at right angles, but always slantingly, across a drain. 'Il faut couper les ruisseaux,' as good Monsieur Meyrac once told me. Now, Brunette, you are too hot to drink much. Come!"

And the animal suffered itself to be driven, quietly enough, out into the main road.

"Ah, here is Mr. Harper in his gig, come to look after the runaway damsels. Dear old man! He nearly upset us, but his kindness and courage are not the less for that."

"Are you safe?" said Mr. Harper.

"Perfectly," said Mrs. Hartland, "thanks to this noble girl! But how could you think of risking your life for us, as you did?"

"The truth is, I didn't think of it, or I might have done better. Zeal without knowledge was mine. But isn't that your man Potter coming to us? And, though Miss Leoline drives admirably, had she not better resign the reins for to-day?"

"On one condition, Mr. Harper," said Leoline—"that you will do me a great favor. I am so much afraid of dear papa hearing of this runaway scrape of ours before he knows we are safe. If you are not too busy, and Mrs. Hartland will spare me, would you mind setting me down at our lower orchard gate?"

"Most willingly shall it be done, my dear young lady; and you shall go safely, if not swiftly. My good old Trooper won't bear comparison with that brown beauty of Mrs. Hartland's; but he is a faithful servant, that has not failed me in fifteen years."

"Yes, dear Lela," said Mrs. Hartland, "you do quite right to carry the first news to your father. God bless you, my child!"

And with looks of love and admiration, Alice's eyes, fixed on Leoline, long followed Mr. Harper's homely equipage ere she bade Potter drive carefully home.

PART IV.

CHAPTER XII.

THE ADVANTAGES OF THE NINETEENTH CENTURY.

SYDENHAM and Celia had returned to the parlor. As they entered, a look of consciousness and painful embarrassment stole over the girl's anxious face.

"You have a dear and excellent friend in your good aunt," said Sydenham.

"No mother could be kinder," she replied, warmly. "I call her mother, and well she deserves it from me. What should I do now, if it were not for her?"

"Are you so hard bestead?"

"Oh, Mr. Sydenham," said Celia, the tears glistening in her eyes, "I am very unhappy!"

"You are very cold, poor child!" said Sydenham, taking her hand—"absolutely chilled through. Come to the fire and let us talk it over."

Now this speech did not please Celia at all. If the tone and the look had not been so kind, it would have offended her seriously. As it was, it effectually arrested her tears.

Sydenham seated her comfortably in a huge arm-chair by the fire, and stood looking at her. "What is the matter?" he asked, after a pause.

Celia remained silent.

"Cannot you trust me with the cause of your troubles? Cannot you talk to me as you would to a father?"

"No, sir."

"No?"

"No; and I don't wish you to call me 'poor child.'"

"Nor to tell you you have not been behaving well?"

"Not in that tone.'

"How old are you, Celia?"

"I shall be twenty next week—in ten days; and that is altogether too old to be a daughter of yours."

Sydenham smiled, well pleased: "What! Three whole years older than Lela?"

"Don't let us talk of that. I am quite willing to trust you, Mr. Sydenham. I will do as my aunt advised me and tell you all my difficulties; only—"

"Well, only what?"

"You never seemed to me the least like a father, and I am sure you never will."

Sydenham, who had remained standing beside Celia's chair, put back from her forehead a few stray hairs that had been displaced by her bonnet, passed his hand gently over the soft, rich, wavy tresses and touched the fair brow with a light kiss. "I suppose, then, I must be satisfied with the authority of an elder brother," said he, as he drew a chair beside her.

"Talk to me as your sister," said Celia, looking up well pleased, "not as if you were soothing a spoilt child, and you may tell me I have been behaving badly, or anything else you please."

"You *have* been behaving badly."

"So you told me already."

"You have been doing what many older and wiser people than you do every day—borrowing sorrow, causelessly, of the future; vexing yourself—I will not say for nothing, but for nothing that ought to make my sister Celia's cheek look pale and her step grow languid."

"What did my aunt tell you?"

"That Mr. Hartland disapproved the choice you had made; and that, unless he changed his mind, or you broke a solemn promise made to your mother, you cannot marry Mr. Mowbray—let me see!—no, not for three whole years and ten days."

"Oh, Mr. Sydenham, surely you don't think—"

"No; I don't think it ever presented itself to you before exactly in that plain, matter-of-fact point of view, else I might not have had to scold you for these pale cheeks. You felt that Mr. Hartland could not understand you, did not sympathize with you—that he was unjustly prejudiced against Mowbray, and was cruelly outraging your affections. It brought to your mind the various piteous cases of thwarted love and jailer guardians which you have pored over in novels—you thought yourself very ill-used, and persuaded yourself that you were very unhappy."

"Is that the way in which brothers talk to sisters?"

"If they care more about doing them service than pleasing them for the moment, yes, it is."

"Is it not wrong in a guardian to flout the suit of a good, estimable young man merely because he is not rich, and to insist on his ward marrying another, whom she fears and dislikes?"

"Both are very wrong."

"My uncle will never forgive me if I marry Evelyn. It is not a question of now or three years hence. Thrice three years would not change—no, not a hair's breadth—his rigid prejudice. He has set his heart on my marrying Mr. Cranstoun, and he will never cease urging it upon me to receive the addresses of that man—never, never! Oh, Mr. Sydenham, how can I help being unhappy, when I see nothing before me but endless quarrels, a struggle between myself—dependent, inexperienced—and a guardian, estimable to be sure, to whom I owe much, who wishes me well, I dare say, but who is bent upon what would make me miserable, wretched for life? And even that is not all."

"What more?"

"My father, during his lifetime, seemed strangely bound to Mr. Cranstoun, and on his deathbed urged it upon me, in terms the most earnest, always to look upon him as a friend, and to abstain from whatever might offend him. And I myself can scarcely get rid of the idea that he has power over me. He seems, when he speaks to me and looks at me, to feel that he has."

"Is that all?

"Is it not enough?"

"Enough to demand thought and call for prudence, but not enough—except in some romantic love-tale, in which the heroine may resort to every means of escape from difficulties except common sense—very surely not enough to be just cause for serious unhappiness; far less to be sufficient reason why the harassed mind should prey, as yours has been preying, on the body."

"I am not ill, though my aunt *would* send for Dr. Meyrac yesterday."

"You are not ill, but, if you go on in this way, you very soon will be. I have more faith in Meyrac than, report says, he has in his brother Galens: you have heard the story?"

"Yesterday, from his own lips. I have not laughed as heartily for a month."

"He showed his sense by getting you to laugh, and Meyrac *is* shrewd and sensible; but I hope to do you more good than he and all his brethren, backed with every nostrum in their pharmacopœia."

"What if I have no faith? Will not the charm lose its virtue?"

"You shall not choose but believe. Now, my good, persecuted, affrighted little friend, I pray you to answer me a few plain questions."

"That is the empiric's privilege—well?"

"You are getting sharp. I have more and more hopes of you. But do you know what empiric means?"

"Ah! the word touches Dr. Sydenham's professional pride?"

"On the contrary, it suits Dr. Sydenham, and he adopts it. EMPIRIC—one who practices from personal experience only, not from theory; one who tries experiments."

"And you intend to experiment upon me?"

"Precisely, relying for success on my own experience."

"Pray proceed, then. I will answer truly, on my conscience, as to all the symptoms."

"Do you remember who was Bacchus' lieutenant-general in his expedition into India?"

"You begin sufficiently far off, so as not to alarm your patient," said Celia, laughing.

"Nay, I approach the principal symptom. Have patience."

"But my mythology is rather rusty. Bacchus' lieutenant-general? I have forgotten."

"It was Pan. Bacchus being surrounded in a valley by a vastly superior force, the shepherd-god recommended that the men, at night, should give a general shout, which so surprised and terrified the opposite force that they incontinently forsook their camp, took to flight and left to Bacchus a bloodless victory. Hence, as you may remember, any sudden terror, without a cause, is usually called a *panic* terror."

"Ah, one cannot accuse you of flattery, Mr. Sydenham, nor deny that you speak plainly, if it be in parable. But your diagnosis is faulty. I have not, that I know of, been seized with any *sudden* terror."

"No, in your case the disease assumes its chronic form. So much the worse."

"Let us speak seriously, Mr. Sydenham. I am hardly able, to-day, to keep up the light shuttlecock of jest."

"With all my heart. Let me ask you a serious question, then: Are you not afraid of your guardian?"

"He is so stern and severe."

"What are you afraid of? Not a scolding?"

"Mr. Hartland does not scold. But he talks just as if everybody *must* do exactly what he requires of them, and especially a young person like me. My aunt always obeys him, without question or delay. He makes everybody obey him who comes near him."

"And suppose you were not to obey him—what then?"

"Oh, it would be terrible! You have no idea of his look and tone."

"Stern looks and severe tones are disagreeable, no doubt: I am very sensitive to their influence, myself; but the most favored of us cannot pass through this world without encountering a few disagreeables. Beyond these formidable looks and tones, what else do you fear from your uncle? What other danger impends?"

"Indeed I scarcely know. If I were to defy his will, I cannot tell to what lengths he might go. Oh, it would be dreadful!"

"Let us see. In the first place, *defy* implies a challenge, provocation, a calling out to a contest. I recommend only gentle firmness. You cannot tell what he might do."

"It seems to me that, if he were thoroughly roused, he might do anything."

"Just so—anything. I dare say those Indian troops whom Pan so scared with a shout had ideas of danger about as definite as you seem to have. Let us analyze this 'anything' of yours. It does not include a whipping, I suppose?"

"Mr. Sydenham!" said Celia, rising. Her indignation became her well. Sydenham could not help admiring the glowing cheeks, but he proceeded without change of tone:

"Ah, this will never do. I undertake

no cure if my patient starts up and runs away from my questions. Sit down. Don't you see that we must proceed in the matter regularly if we are to reach any practical conclusion? And let me tell you, ladye fair, that the time has been when your 'anything' included consequences that might appall the boldest. The Romans had the power of life and death over their offspring. And did they spare sex or age? There was Boadicea. Do you remember?—

'When the British warrior-queen,
Bleeding from the Roman rods,
Sought, with an indignant mien,
Counsel of her country's gods.'

Those must have been serious times for disobedient wards. Don't you think so, Celia?"

"I was foolish. But you have such a strange way of putting things, Mr. Sydenham. I see that my 'anything' has a restricted meaning. And you shall have an answer to your question. I am not at all afraid of sharing the fate of poor Boadicea."

"Good! Now we shall get on. I don't think my friend Hartland would be likely to lock you up in some upper chamber and starve you into compliance, or feed you there on bread and water till you promised to be a good girl and to say yes when he bade you."

"Mr. Hartland is despotic enough, but he is a gentleman—"

"Of the nineteenth century: that is the best part of it: those picturesque gentlemen of the good olden-time were not much to be trusted in such matters. And Hartland does not live in a remote castle, in some wild forest, with moat and donjon keep, with subterranean dungeons for prisoners and lone turret-chambers for refractory *damoyseles.* His house, without a single loophole or even window-grating, is situated in a quiet, unfortified, civilized village, in a republican country: a great convenience, all this, in your case, depend upon it. Bricks and mortar have a good deal to do with civilization and morality. An iron will in a feudal fortress, and an iron will in that pretty, comfortable two-story dwelling-house of your uncle's, with nothing worse than its neatly-painted green shutters to aid in a scheme of incarceration, are two very different things."

"I admit that I run no risk of hopeless captivity."

"Here, you see, is another point settled. Your person and your liberty are in no danger. One thing more. Can your guardian disinherit you if you use your own eyes, instead of his, in selecting a husband?"

"Not that I know of."

"Of course he cannot. You are your mother's sole heir. Just at present you are a minor, and he might, perhaps, curtail your allowance. But in another year and a few days he will be obliged to account to you for all your property: he will do so faithfully—Hartland is thoroughly upright—and will place it unconditionally in your hands. You will, thenceforth, have the entire control of forty thousand dollars, and will be free to select your own residence, choose your own friends, follow out your own mode of life. There is a great deal of independence, especially here in a Western village, in forty thousand dollars."

"I confess all this did not occur to me."

"Of course not. You do not know half your own power and privileges. You have a dash of romance about you, Celia. I like you all the better for that: I was seriously touched with it, in younger days, myself, and am not thoroughly cured yet. But romantic people never do see what lies in the plain path straight before them. Their eyes wander up to the heavens and off to the right and left—to those regions of earth to which distance lends enchantment. No wonder they are sometimes grievously puzzled to thread their way."

"Unless they find some kind elder brother on the road, who has still romance enough to sympathize with them, and not so much as to disqualify him for a guide," said Celia, looking up with a grateful expression to Sydenham.

His ideas seemed disarranged just for a moment: then he said quietly: "I dare say it was well your aunt Alice thought of me. But we are wandering from the point. How far had we narrowed down your 'anything?' "

"I believe I had to admit that it did not touch life, limb, liberty, property."

"Very well. You are sure your heart has made a choice?"

A bright blush for answer.

"I see it has. To that choice Mr. Hartland says 'No,' for the present at least, and may very possibly persist in saying 'No' as long as he lives. You have resolved not to marry without his consent till you are twenty-three—"

"Most positively. A violation of a promise solemnly made to my mother on her deathbed would haunt me to my own dying day."

"You are quite right. Then, to return to the point from which we started, it appears, in the first place, that your guardian may postpone your marriage for three years and ten days."

"And meanwhile?"

"That is my secondly. Meanwhile, Mr. Hartland may look sternly, speak severely—"

"And that is so hard to bear!"

"It is disagreeable, very, to come into daily contact with ill-will or anger. I once gave a man up a most just debt that could be obtained by litigation, and in no other way, because I had to pass his door each morning, and became impatient of being reminded, once in every twenty-four hours, that I had a quarrel with him."

"And I should have done just so."

"And you might have afforded to purchase exemption from a daily-recurring annoyance at a cost of fifty dollars, as I did. But what is the price of your uncle's good-will? Is it worth while, do you think, to marry Cranstoun in order to get it?"

"God forbid! I would rather die."

"The price, you see, is too high. You have quite decided not to purchase. You cannot afford to buy off your uncle's harsh words and angry looks at the rate of a lifetime's misery. It is like any other luxury which one's purse is not heavy enough to compass. I should very much like, in addition to what works of art I have, to possess one or two of Canova's statues for my entrance-hall, and a few of my favorite Murillo's best paintings to adorn these walls. But, seeing that my fortune is inadequate to such expensive indulgences, I do not set my heart upon them, and I cease to repine that they are beyond my reach."

"And you think I ought not to set my heart on my uncle's good-will and kind looks?"

"Not if he sets upon these a price unreasonable, extravagant, and which it would bankrupt your happiness to pay. Offer him freely, generously, what you really can afford—the little attentions to his personal comforts which men at his age value; cheerful obedience in minor matters, though it involve sacrifice of your taste and inclinations; the respectful fulfillment of every duty which a guardian, standing for the time in a father's place, can reasonably exact or expect of his ward. Remind him that you are young, are in no haste to marry, and that all you ask is, not to have a match forced upon you against your will."

"That is it, exactly—that is all I ask. If it were not for this Cranstoun—"

"Cranstoun seems to be the *bête noire* of your dreams. And, to be right honest with you, Celia, I think him a dangerous man."

"Ah, there it is! You have left him out of view altogether. I do think there is nothing he might not do."

"Pan's midnight shout again, Celia. Don't desert the camp and leave its spoils to the enemy until you have ascertained his force. 'Nothing he might not do!' Do you think, for example, that he might hire three or four ruffian-looking men, their faces covered with crape; have a carriage-and-four close by; set upon you some day when you were out botanizing in these woods; cause you to be gagged after the most romance-approved fashion; spirit you off to some out-of-the-way, mysterious, unknown region; and there, aided by a ghastly monk or chaplain, compel you, at the dagger's point, to marry him?"

"You are really too bad, Mr. Sydenham," said Celia, laughing.

"These mysterious impending dangers, you observe, will not stand question. They vanish as you approach them. They are ghosts from a bygone age. It is nearly seven hundred years since Dermot Macmorrough carried off, from her bog-fenced castle, the Princess Dovergilda. His exploit, then deemed a proof of gallantry and spirit, would now be rewarded, if in our day it were practicable at all, with ignominy and the State prison. Forcible abduction is, among us, an almost impossible felony."

"Certainly: I am not afraid of being stolen away."

"Very well. Can they marry you here, to this Cranstoun, against your consent? Not very readily, I should think. When Mr. Harper, or some other clergyman, asks you, 'Do you take this man for your husband?' you must take care not to say 'Yes.' That is all."

Celia smiled: "It is a comfort to think one has the privilege of dying an old maid if one chooses."

"It *is* a privilege, though you may not think so—one which women have not always enjoyed. You possess lands and houses; and if you had lived in England in the early days of King John's reign, you might have been forced to marry, whether you chose it or not, so that your husband might render, in person, at the head of a suitable number of armed vassals, that military service to his suzerain which, by feudal usage, attached to the ownership of land."

"Have such things been?"

"Undoubtedly. War, in those days, was more important than happiness. The right to compel such marriages was an ancient prerogative, though afterward abolished by Magna Charta. See what you have escaped! Then, again, you have no father to go down upon his knees before you, as selfish scoundrels of fathers do in silly novels, informing you that he has been committing some murder or other infamous crime, before you were born perhaps—that his life, or honor, is at the mercy of some rascally accomplice, and that you, by way of mending matters, must, like a dutiful child, swear at the altar to honor and obey this same rascally accomplice; thus condemning to a penalty worse than death a young, innocent victim, to whom he, the while, is not ashamed to profess unbounded love."

Sydenham rose and paced the room, as was his habit when excited; and Celia sat gazing absently on the dying embers for several minutes.

"I see," she said at last, "how reasonable all you say is. Mr. Hartland's control over me is for a limited time only, and meanwhile I may conciliate where I cannot obey him. But, Mr. Sydenham—if I have not already tired you—"

"Celia," said Sydenham, coming to her side, "your mother was an early playmate and valued friend of mine; and, if she had not been, you are a dear, good girl, whom I like for your own sake. Are you in the habit of getting tired when those you love tell you of their troubles and ask your advice?"

"Nobody ever asked my advice," said Celia, smiling. "But I remember that Franklin, when some one whom he had relieved expressed a fear that he might never be able to return the obligation, told him to pass it round when he found a suffering brother. And I, when I am an old lady with gray hair and a plain cap, looking venerable, and when young girls think I am very wise and come to consult me about their troubles, shall not forget my debt. I will listen to them—oh, so patiently!—as you have been listening to me; tell them that sharp words, after all, are not a killing matter; that nobody is likely to lock them up and feed them on bread and water, or to run away with them against their will; and that, as long as they keep saying 'No,' they can't be married."

"Admirable! I only hope you will find pupils who will learn their lesson half as aptly as mine has done. But there was something else."

"Ah, yes," said Celia, the playful mood fading away, "there *is* one thing more. I have no father, as you have reminded me, exposed to suffering which a hateful marriage might avert. But is it not possible that Mr. Cranstoun may be in possession of some important secret, perhaps connected with my father's past life, which he could still use?"

"Did he ever say as much to you?"

"Not in so many words. But he has left that impression on my mind by certain vague expressions dropped from time to time, and which I could not help coupling with my father's dying request not to do anything to irritate this man."

"You do well to tell me all this."

"Ah, even you are alarmed now," said Celia, turning very pale.

"Indeed, no," said Sydenham, smiling. "It is a matter worth looking at and thinking over, but I feel no alarm about it. Cranstoun was acquainted (intimately, it would seem) with your father in early life. It is possible that he may possess, or think he possesses, the clue to some undivulged transactions, which it might have been unpleasant to your father—might be painful to you, perhaps — to have brought to light. But if he has any such knowledge, and hopes to turn it to profit, I don't very well see why he should not have sought, ere this, to do so."

"He may, at this very time, be meditating such an attempt."

"Possibly. Yet I cannot believe he has much in his power. I was not intimately acquainted with your father, but I believe him to have been a man of honorable, gentlemanly sentiments—impulsive at times, somewhat infirm of purpose, perhaps, but incapable of anything that would disgrace his memory, or which, if known, ought seriously to pain his child."

"Oh, I am sure of it!" said Celia, eagerly.

"But, Celia, remember this," said Sydenham—"that even if we are both mistaken—even if this fellow Cranstoun possesses, and should hereafter disclose, matters redounding to your father's discredit, disgrace even—nay, dear child, you mustn't look as if all this had already taken place: I don't believe a word of it: I am putting a mere possible case—and if that possible case ever prove a reality, I wish you ever to bear in mind— Are you attending to me, Celia?"

"Indeed, indeed I am," said Celia, raising her downcast eyes to Sydenham's face: "you wish me to bear in mind—"

"That no man—I will not say who loves you, but whose good opinion is worth striving after or caring for—that no man who has the slightest claim to be called good or wise will visit on the daughter the father's sins. If any man ever does, Celia, take my word for it, you are well rid of him."

Poor Celia's eyes sank beneath the flash of Sydenham's, and her lip trembled as she faltered out, "Are you speaking of any one?"

"Of no one whatever, dear Celia," said Sydenham, in his usual gentle tone. "Pardon my vehemence. I have an unlucky habit, when I think of any mean or wicked act, of personifying the creature of my imagination, and speaking as if it stood in bodily form before me."

"How good you are!" said Celia. "I wish that I could only confide in all the world as I do in you."

Sydenham looked toward the door. It opened, and, her cheeks glowing with health and exercise, her bright eyes radiant with spirit, Leoline entered.

"Ah, still here? I am so glad!" she said, tripping lightly up to Celia.

Something struck her in the expression of her friend's face, and she looked from her to her father.

"I believe I had better go up to my room and lay aside my hat," she said, demurely.

"Put your hat beside mine on the piano," said Celia, "and sit down with us, like a reasonable creature. Did you think your father and I had been plotting treason that was to be kept from you?"

"Oh, I didn't know. You both looked as if you had had a long, confidential chat."

"So we have. Your father has been doing me so *much* good, dear Lela."

"Has he?" said Leoline, depositing her hat and shawl. "Good father! He shall have a kiss, to pay him for it, before I sit down. There! Confess,

Celia, that was more than you gave him, with all your gratitude. Ah, you were afraid. You needn't have been. Papa is not a dangerous man to kiss."

"How do you know, rattlebrain?" said Sydenham, smiling. "Celia thinks, at all events, that I am too young for her father."

"Does she? Wise girl! Her father, indeed! I often think you're not nearly old enough for mine. Do you know," turning to Celia, "I feel so tempted sometimes to call him Frank! How do you think it would do? But what great good has my young father been doing you, dear?"

"I came here, seeing nothing in the future but strife and unhappiness. And now I am going away with a heart—no, not as light as yours, Lela: nothing but a bird singing in the morning sunshine can match that—but hopeful, reassured; feeling as if some tempest had suddenly passed away, and a bright, genial sky had come out, with a few clouds here and there—maybe a dark one now and then—but only such as all skies that shine on this world of ours must sometimes have."

"That's my own Celia!" said Leoline, kissing her. "A practical philosopher! Papa is great on philosophy. And now, to do honor to his lesson, these eyes must grow bright again; these cheeks—let me look at them!—they show a little better just now, but they have been of late most unphilosophically pale—"

"Why, philosophy is privileged to be pale. 'The pale cast of thought.'"

"Not in our house. Ask papa. We are republicans, and don't allow philosophy a bit more privilege than the humblest handmaiden virtue in her train: pale cheeks least of all."

"Lela reminds me," said Sydenham to Celia, "that I intended to prescribe for these cheeks and eyes. But as my crucibles and alembics are out of order just now, and as the chief ingredient required is not to be found in our village drug-store—"

"You must cull the necessary simples," interrupted Celia, "just at midnight in the moonlit forest."

"No: I am more likely to be successful at midday, and in the neighborhood of some thriving farm."

"I don't think your father has one spark of poetry in his composition, Lela. If anything is presented to him with the least spice of imagination about it, he analyzes and dissects it after such an inexorably matter-of-fact fashion! And now he won't even gather the materials for the specific he promises me,

'In that hour
That scatters spells on herb and flower.'"

"Out, Celia—completely out in that guess! Papa not poetical! You don't know anything about him. As to the moonlight, I can't say. If he makes up a prescription for you at all, it's more than he ever did for me. He was telling me, the other day, that the Greeks employed the same word for *medicine* and *poison*."

"Nevertheless Celia shall have her prescription within ten days—to be taken once a day, if the celestial influences are favorable."

"This is some joke of papa's. Don't puzzle your brain to understand it now, Celia: it will unriddle itself one of these days. But for papa having no poetry about him, I must come to his defence there. Gravely as he may talk to you, he sometimes reads to me his favorite poets, English and German, by the hour; and I caught him, this very morning, translating from Schiller, I believe, some ballad or ode. What was it, papa?"

"Schiller's 'Ideale;' a favorite of mine—a lament over the loss, in middle age, of the beautiful Ideal cherished in early youth. And, by the way, Celia, as there are some of the verses not inapplicable to your case— You read German, do you not?"

"Not with facility. Read me your translation."

"I am sorry; for I have not at all succeeded in rendering the melodious flow and graceful spirit of the original. The idea is all I can give you. Lela, my child, you will find the manuscript on the sofa-table."

Lela brought it, and Sydenham resumed: "The opening verses I have not yet arranged to my satisfaction. Here are a few, picked out toward the conclusion :

" How rich the buds of promise that put forth
Along my life's path as I wandered on !
How few of these have 'scaped the chilly North !
How soon the freshness of these few is gone !

" With bounding courage winged, through fairy-land,
Happy in dreams that cheat the fleeting hours,
Untouched, as yet, by Sorrow's fetter-hand,
How sprang the youth along that path of flowers !

" Aloft to ether's farthest, palest star
His checkless wishes bore him in their flight :
No thought so high, no enterprise so far,
But on their soaring wings he reached its height.

" How lightsome was he borne through ambient air !
What task seemed weary in that joyous day !
How graceful swept, before his triumph-car,
The airy heralds of life's summer-way !

" Love, with her sweet reward, I ween, was there,
And Happiness, with golden wreath bedight,
Glory, with crown of stars that blazed afar,
And Truth, resplendent in her garb of light.

" Alas ! midway th' inconstant troop divide ;
The fair companions of his path are gone :
Faithless, they turn their devious steps aside—
Faithless, forsake the wanderer, one by one.

" Lone and more lone the dreary path doth seem,
And more forsaken still, and darker aye ;
Hope's fading torch scarce sheds one flick'ring gleam
Athwart the rudeness of the murky way !

" Of all the clamorous attendant train,
Who yet remains where'er my footsteps roam?
Who lingers still to cherish and sustain,
And follows even to the last, dark Home?

" Healer of ills with which the world is rife,
Thou, FRIENDSHIP ! of the soft and gentle hand—
Thou who dividest all the cares of life,
Whose love, unchanged, all ordeals can withstand ;—

And Thou who by her side hast constant stood,
And who, like her, the soul from grief canst sever,—
Thou, INDUSTRY ! who weariest not in good,
Creating evermore, destroying never ;—

" Thou who, to rear the sempiternal pile,
But grain, indeed, on grain of sand doth cast,
Yet from the roll of ancient Time, the while,
Days, years, a lifetime, strikest off at last."

Sydenham read well—a rare accomplishment. Celia thought she had never seen him look so handsome.

"Beautiful !" she exclaimed, "and so just ! I shall ask Mrs. Mowbray to let me go over the original with her. I must go." She rose : "Why, Lela, how wet your dress is ! What have you been about ?"

"That mare of yours is hard-mouthed."

"She ran away ?"

"Something like it. Nay, Celia, nay, darling papa ; your anxious looks frighten me far more than Brunette did. Mrs. Hartland is quite safe."

"How was it, my child ?" said Sydenham, his voice calm, though all color had forsaken his cheeks.

"Perhaps I was off my guard for a moment, interested in the conversation —it was about you, Celia. A colt racing in the pasture startled the mare near the bottom of the hill, and she started off. I'm satisfied I could have taken her up, only good Mr. Harper tried to stop her, and made things worse. So, as I had no mind to drive into town at that John-Gilpin pace, I ran the mare into the pond, where I knew I could stop her easily—at expense of a sprinkling, as you see."

"Thank God !" said Sydenham.

"She's not vicious, papa : I told you so. She ran beautifully. If I had had a stiff bit, instead of a snaffle, I know I could have held her. But perhaps Mr. Hartland had better sell her. She's hardly safe for you to drive, Celia ; and what a pity it is ! There isn't such another beauty in the county. I wish men and horses were always as good as they look. Dear papa, that was so frightened about his runaway daughter"—she kissed him fondly—"I'm glad I got him to smile once more."

Celia had put on her hat and shawl. "No," to Leoline, who was about to do the same. "My talk with your father has made me feel more independent already, and I shall go home alone. This is the hour of your drawing-lesson, I know. How do you get on ?"

"Charmingly, if you will trust to Aunt Hannah, who, you know, has not the heart to find fault with anything. Papa is not so easily satisfied, and he is right."

"Good Mrs. Clymer ! I do believe God never made a kinder heart. Where is she this morning ?"

"In the village, I believe, visiting the saddler's wife, who was taken ill in church last Sunday. I dare say you will meet her on your way down."

"Good-bye, dear Lela. Mr. Sydenham, I shall never forget your kindness, nor, I hope, your advice."

CHAPTER XIII.

CHISKAUGA MATTERS.

"He mourns the dead who lives as they desire."
YOUNG.

WHEN Sydenham, in fulfillment of his promise to Alice Hartland, called on her husband to speak of Celia Pembroke and her suitors, it was with slender hope that any good would result; and the cold and distant manner with which Mr. Hartland received his first allusion to the subject convinced him that any direct interference on his part would injure rather than benefit the girl's cause. This arose not only from Hartland's impatience of contradiction, and because he and Sydenham were mutually antipathetical, but also because circumstances that had occurred eight or ten years before had produced, on the part of the former, a coolness toward the other which seemed but to increase with time—a coolness growing out of a benefit conferred. In some natures benefits unwillingly received rankle as deeply as injuries.

Inasmuch as the circumstances referred to connect themselves with the earlier fortunes of the neighborhood in which our scene is laid, and afford an opportunity to present to our readers a member of Mr. Hartland's family better worth their acquaintance than that gentleman himself, they will bear with us, perhaps, while we revert to them.

Sydenham, when he made his home close by a Western village, entered what to him was a new world—a world differing more widely from that which swarms in our Atlantic cities than the people of these cities differ from those of the towns and villages of England. Still greater, however, was the contrast between the farmers and farm-laborers around Chiskauga and the same classes on the continent of Europe.

The young Philadelphian, when he first crossed to the Old World, had spent months in a pedestrian tour—for a time in the agricultural portions of England, afterward among the peasantry of France and of Germany. He had often found among them simple goodness, patience under hopeless toil, resignation beneath grievous burdens. He had met a cheerful smile, a ready welcome. But the spirit of the man was not there—the spirit that can look up with an honest confidence, and feel that while it is no man's master, neither is it any man's slave. One felt—*they* felt—that between themselves and the favored of fortune there was fixed an almost impassable gulf.

How great the difference he found in the lowliest cabin of our rural West! Humble, often the means; homely the forms; blunt, nor usually grammatical, the manner of speech; but a certain rude independence, natural not assumed, shone through—a quiet sense of equality in political rights and in the pursuit of honors and office. The tone in which hospitality was tendered assured one of this. Seldom any apology for rough fare or poor lodging; or, if such was made, not in the tone of humility one meets with on the Rhine or in the French *chaumière.*

A trifling incident brought this home to Sydenham. One evening, at the close of a political meeting held in the open air and in a remote portion of the county, he had accepted an invitation, from a farmer carrying his homespun coat over his arm, to stay with him until next morning. He found a large family inhabiting a double log-cabin, with an open entry separating the two compartments. "We're poorly fixed to take in strangers like you, Mr. Sydenham," said the farmer as they entered; then added, with a smile, "but I thought, as we've made out with our accommodations for fifteen years, that maybe you'd be willing to put up with them for one night."

Supper, plentiful but badly cooked, was served in the kitchen. Two grown-up daughters remained in that apartment for the night, while the rest of the family adjourned to the other. Three or four younger children there clambered, by a short ladder, to the loft above, while the guest and his host, sitting down by a blazing log-heap, dropped into a long chat; the wife, on the other side of the fireplace, knitting and listening as silently as her ancestress, Eve, when Adam was talking with the Angel Raphael on the origin of the world and other celestial mysteries.

The conversation branched off into arguments on government, and Sydenham had occasion—not for the first nor the twentieth time since his arrival among these primitive people—to note the common sense which marked the man's judgment of men and things and his views of national policy, albeit these were couched in uncouth phrase and interlarded with homeliest illustrations.

At an early hour the husband, after covering up the fire with ashes, retired to rest with his wife in one end of the apartment, while to Sydenham was assigned a cot bedstead, with clean sheets and abundant bed-clothing, at the other. The latter lay long awake, watching the effect of the moonbeams shining through the gaping apertures between the logs of the cabin wall, and calling to mind Waller's lines:

> "The soul's dark cottage, battered and decayed,
> Lets in new light through chinks that Time has made."

If a certain abrupt rusticity of demeanor, common especially to the older settlers, jarred, at first, on Sydenham's fastidious taste, yet, as he penetrated the rough shell, he found beneath such genuine qualities, so much that was fresh and racy, mixed too with a quick sense of humor, that his prejudice melted away. These people, for example, were strictly law-abiding; yet with their respect for the law's behests was mingled but little reverence for its external forms. Witness an old anecdote, current among them: Nancy Leavitt, known to all the county as widow of a thriving farmer who had made his home there at an early day, had been summoned as witness in a suit pending between two of her neighbors. This ancient dame was hale and hearty, and she began giving testimony with great self-possession. But as she had lost several teeth, her enunciation was somewhat indistinct, and her voice no longer as powerful as in her younger days it had been. Add to this that she wore what was called usually a sun-bonnet, sometimes a "poke-bonnet," made up of a liberal allowance of pasteboard, covered with gay calico, projecting farther than even the Quaker fashion permits in front, and with a voluminous cape, protecting the neck from the sun, behind.

"Madam," said the judge, "we will thank you to speak a little louder."

A second attempt did not seem to be more successful, for the judge again interrupted her:

"Witness, the court cannot hear a word you say. Please to take off that large bonnet of yours."

"Sir," she replied, "the court has a perfect right to make a gentleman take off his hat, but it has no right at all to require of a lady to take off her bonnet."

"Upon my word," retorted the judge, "you seem to be so well versed in law, madam, that I think you had better come up here and take a seat on the bench beside us."

Whereupon the old lady rose, dropped a low curtsy, and, with the gravest face, and to the infinite amusement of lawyers and audience, added: "I thank your honor very kindly, but there are old women enough there already."

When Anna Sydenham, on her deathbed, commended to her husband's care the inhabitants of Chiskauga, she "builded better than she knew." Yet it is doubtful whether Sydenham, with his lofty aspirations and his vague theories of perfectibility, would have succeeded in doing much practical good among these people but for a fortunate incident. While casting about, soon after his arrival, for some intelligent foreman or manager accustomed to land operations and farming business, and familiar with the habits of the West, he became acquainted with Ethan Hartland, son of

Mr. Hartland by his first wife, a young man who had returned, six months before, from a four years' residence in Germany, where, in an excellent polytechnic institute, he had qualified himself as civil engineer. Yet his tastes, formed before he went to Germany, were for farming pursuits. Modest and deficient in self-assertion, he preferred the independence of rural life to the chances in a profession where success depends, in a measure, on patronage. Sydenham made his acquaintance, and liked him. He found him steady, industrious, persevering—a great favorite, too, with the country-people on account of his good-nature and ready sympathy. Young as Ethan was, Sydenham fell into a habit of consulting him on his plans for the sale and improvement of his property, and for meliorating the condition and reforming some of the habits of the population in the village and its neighborhood. He soon discovered that the youth, under his quiet demeanor, had opinions and a will of his own, and he gradually began to entertain doubts whether sundry of the somewhat ambitious schemes he had himself projected might not be advantageously modified by the practical, business objections which the other interposed.

"I have more land," he said one day to Ethan Hartland, "than any one person ought to possess while so many hard-working men around me have no homes of their own; and I have been thinking of a plan by which this injustice might be remedied."

"What do you propose?"

"A workingman's land association. I am willing to place at the disposal of the members three or four thousand acres at two-thirds of the present market price. Let a certain number of laboring men organize a joint-stock company, with shares, say, of ten dollars. When the number of shares acquired by any stockholder is sufficient to purchase a home for him, let him take it up. I will accept payment for the land as it is sold. Let him who is first ready to buy have the preference."

"If you put the land at two-thirds its market value, speculators would be likely to come in and engross the whole."

"But I should make it a condition that the company pass a regulation to the effect that no member be allowed to buy until he is ready to build and improve; and that if, within a given time, he did not make the improvements specified, the land should fall back to the company."

"Even the passage of such a provision might prove insufficient protection against the greed of speculators."

"You are suspicious, Ethan, for so young a man," said Sydenham, smiling.

"The facts are in my favor, Mr. Sydenham. On my return from Europe I spent a month with an uncle in Philadelphia, and met at his house a Mr. Disland, who had promoted just such an association as you propose, and taken stock therein. The company made a judicious purchase of five thousand acres of unimproved land, partly on credit, and, guided by Mr. Disland's advice, adopted the very regulation you have just suggested."

"Indeed! This interests me. What was the result?"

"At first all went well. Several of the members turned their shares into building lots or small farms, and improved these. Gradually all the stock was taken up. Other settlers following the example of the first, the land began to increase in value. Thereupon the shares rose to a premium. This attracted the attention of land operators, who bought in pretty heavily, hoping for a farther rise. Disappointed in this, they wished to turn their shares into land, but the rule in regard to improvement stood in the way."

"Did not that induce them to sell out again?"

"No. They combined together, intrigued with the laboring men who held shares, represented to them what an advantage they would reap if each was allowed to secure a site at once, instead of waiting till he had money enough to build, and so losing the best lots. Then, taking advantage of Mr. Disland's absence from Philadelphia, they procured a call for a public meeting of the stockholders, had the obnoxious resolution reconsidered and rescinded, and the next morning, within a quarter of an hour after the office opened, they entered, to the amount of their shares, the most valuable portions of the property."

"The rascals!"

"They considered it a fair business transaction."

"Do you know how the matter finally resulted?"

"Mr. Disland returned the same day, and sold out all his shares before evening. The stock gradually declined, poor men being unwilling to enter and improve a bit of property lying by the side of a larger tract held by some rich man, who avowedly declined to do his part, waiting for others to move, and thus seeking to reap where he had not sowed. In four or five months afterward the association went to pieces."

"I think precautions might be taken to prevent such a result. In conveying the land to the company I might make it an imperative and irrevocable condition that it should not be sold out except under stringent improvement stipulations."

"Our people are peculiar, Mr. Sydenham. Wherever, in larger or smaller deliberative bodies, they have the right to debate and decide, they want, to use a common phrase, to have their 'full swing;' not to be cramped by restrictions, however wholesome, that have been arbitrarily imposed. I think they would not submit to the Constitution itself if they did not know they had the right to amend it."

Sydenham, struck with the sagacity of these strictures, pondered the matter; and meeting Ethan next day, invited him to spend the evening at his house. There the conversation was renewed.

"I still think my plan of a land association practicable," said Sydenham, "if the first movers are prudent in selecting their associates, and if they have a wide range of choice. But it might be less advisable here, where the number of land purchasers is limited, and one has to take them as one finds them. Have you any substitute to propose?"

"The idea of selling land below the current rates, and under strict improvement stipulations, seems to me practica and very important. But why not go directly to your object? Retain in your own hands the powers you propose to delegate to an association. Say that you set apart five thousand acres. Have these laid out, in the vicinity of the village, in building lots of a few acres each, and farther off have the land divided into small farms. Reserve from sale each alternate lot and farm, and offer the rest (giving several years' credit for part of the purchase-money) at low and fixed rates. Instead of a deed, give the purchaser a bond of agreement containing a covenant on his part to erect, say within a year, a habitation for purposes of occupancy, and to make certain other specified improvements, with the right to demand a warranty deed as soon as these conditions are fulfilled and the land is paid for. Before the first two thousand five hundred acres are sold out, the remainder will have risen greatly in value."

"I should be willing to stipulate that I will sell the reserved lots and farms at the same rates as before. The increase of price will be due to the labor of others, not to my own."

"That would be generous: yet I advise not to encumber yourself with any promise in advance. If the difference between the selling price and the actual value of these lands be great, great also will be the temptation to circumvent you. You may hereafter see fit to set apart a portion of the surplus which you now think of relinquishing, and to expend it in works of public value—to aid the schools of the village, or in drainage, in opening roads and avenues, and planting these out with shade trees. Possibly that might, in the end, be best for all parties."

Sydenham sat silent for some time: then he asked, "How old are you, Ethan?"

"Just twenty-two."

"You seem to have given much attention to this subject."

"I owe my ideas on it chiefly to Mr. Disland, who has made it a study for years."

The young man's modesty attracted Sydenham: "Have you determined to follow out your profession as engineer?"

"My father wishes it, but, so far, no situation has offered. The former president of the Riverdale Railway, an intimate friend of my father, had promised to give me a post on his road as assistant engineer, but he died, as you may remember, a month before my return. I can hardly say I regret that I missed the chance, for I greatly prefer a farmer's life."

"You managed a farm of your father's, I think, for two years before you went to Germany?"

"Yes, and should be glad to return to it."

"Perhaps I can offer you something better. You know, probably, that I have between nine and ten thousand acres in and around Chiskauga. I am quite ignorant of the details of Western farming and land management, and I want an educated young man as superintendent, to supply my deficiencies. I know how thorough German training is: it is an excellent preparation for our faster life. I think we should suit each other, Ethan. What say you?"

"As my father has recently finished paying for my education, I ought to consult him. But I feel most deeply the confidence with which you honor me, Mr. Sydenham, and should be delighted to accept the situation."

"I can afford a salary of eight hundred or a thousand a year. I know you could save me as much as that."

"Give me sixty dollars a month, if you find my services worth the amount. I can pay my own board and live comfortably for less; and that is more than a young man of my age can reasonably expect."

"One can see that you come from a German college, Ethan. Young America will leave you behind. By the way, when we talk business, let it be in German. How I envy you your accent!"

With that they parted, mutually pleased. Not at all pleased, however, when he heard of it, was Mr. Hartland, Sr.

Parents, especially those who, like Ethan's father, are of an arbitrary turn, are apt to forget that when their children reach adult age the time has arrived when advice should succeed authority. Mr. Hartland was angered that his son, after four years spent in preparing for one profession, should select another. "I hate such change of purpose in a young man," he said.

"You may remember, sir,' the son replied in a respectful tone, "that when you were about sending me to Europe, I begged you, instead, to let me study improved agriculture on Professor Mapes' farm. You yourself selected for me the profession of engineer. I am grateful for the expense you incurred in qualifying me as such, and in giving me an opportunity to see foreign countries and to learn German. I have always been ready, at a day's notice, to go into the field if a situation presented itself. But six months have elapsed, and I do not wish to be a burden on you, now that a chance offers to make my own livelihood."

"Have I ever sent you in a board-bill, or refused to pay your store-accounts?"

"No, sir: I am grateful that you have not. But that is no reason why I should remain dependent upon you longer than is necessary."

"You prefer to be dependent on Mr. Sydenham."

Ethan did not reply. He saw it was a matter of feeling, not of reason. The next morning, after Mr. Hartland and his tin case had gone out botanizing, Mrs. Hartland spoke to the son.

"My dear Ethan," she said, "there is no one living from whom I would sooner see you accept employment than from Mr. Sydenham. But don't vex your father. You know he could never endure opposition."

"I know, mother; but then *I* can't endure dependence."

"Not on your own father?"

"No. I would accept the Axton farm from him, and trouble him for nothing more; but you know he has no intention to give it me."

"No, he doesn't like putting property out of his own hands. But he never refuses you money when you want it."

"I am no longer a child, to ask him for every dollar I need."

"I have to do so."

"I know you have, and that's all wrong."

"Oh fie, Ethan! to talk of your father so!"

"It's the truth, mother."

"Must not a husband support his wife?"

"Yes, but he needn't dole out every five-dollar note as if she were a pensioner on his bounty."

"The money is his, to give or not as he pleases. He made it all."

"I don't see that. If we hadn't you, mother, how much would he have to pay for an ordinary housekeeper, not to say some one that would hold his property as well together and make us all as comfortable as you do? I wouldn't undertake it for five hundred a year. I do believe I can manage Mr. Sydenham's land with less trouble. It's nearly eight years that you've been with us, mother; and if all had their dues, I think father would open a bank account for you, and place three or four thousand dollars to your credit."

"Did you get these ideas in Germany, Ethan? When you marry are you going to pay your wife five hundred a year as housekeeper?"

"I shall be too poor for that; and then the mistress of a domestic establishment is far more than house*keeper*—she's house*holder*."

"How do you propose to manage, then?"

"I do not intend to ask any girl who doesn't understand housekeeping, and who can't tell what it costs. I'll ascertain how much she wants a month to keep house and to cover her personal expenses, and I won't marry till I can spare her that. Then I'll put enough cash to last for a month or two in her bureau drawer, and ask her for the key now and then, so I can see to it that it doesn't run out."

Mrs. Hartland laughed: "Bachelor's dreams, Ethan! I expect nothing else than to see you marry a girl who don't know whether coffee needs roasting before it is ground. Young people always do make up beautiful theories beforehand."

"Well, mother, my only theory just at present is, that it won't do for me to sponge on my father any longer. It's wrong."

"How hard set you men are in your opinions! Ethan, you've never disobeyed your father yet; and when he is dead and gone it will be a comfort to you to think that you never did."

"It must come to an end some time, mother. As well now as later. I may have a household myself in a few years, and then maybe he'll object to that arrangement about the bureau drawer."

The wife felt the justice of all this. But she felt more strongly still how serious is often the first breach between father and son. Alice Hartland was one of those of whom it is written that they shall be called the children of God. Human strife—even war itself, no doubt—has its mission, yet the peacemakers are to be the ultimate rulers of a civilized world.

"Dear Ethan," she said, "you have always been such a comfort to me in the house, especially since you returned from Europe. God knows how much more willingly I should see you accept Mr. Sydenham's generous offer than to have you going off, to remain for months or years from home, and then settling down at last, perhaps, as resident engineer in some distant State. I hope it will never come to that, and I know you have a right to choose. But you remember Paul says: 'All things are lawful for me, but all things are not expedient.' Your father has paid much for your education. Cannot you give way to him a little? Cannot you agree to wait a few months? Then, if there seemed no chance of a situation as engineer, I think he would give way."

Alice's mediation was successful. The

compromise was made. For six months, during which Ethan kept up his mathematical studies and sought in vain for employment in the field, Sydenham reserved for him the place he had offered. Then, without further opposition on his father's part, the young man accepted it. Hartland overlooked the contumacy of his son, but he never forgave Sydenham.

Now that our readers know something of Ethan's connection with Sydenham, and of the cause that led to the antipathy which grew up in the mind of Mr. Hartland, Sr., toward his son's employer, it is time that we return to the current of events that followed Sydenham's unsuccessful intervention in the love affairs of Celia Pembroke.

CHAPTER XIV.

THE MILLER AND THE GENTLEMAN.

TEN days elapsed. Then, one evening, Cassiday came to report progress to Cranstoun.

"A devilish hard time of it I've had," he said. "That miller of yours expects a man to do two days' work in one."

"You've found out nothing?"

"He gave me little chance. But I like to keep a promise when I'm well paid for it."

"Let us have it, then."

"Widow Carson's boy Tom has been hired by Mowbray, at a dollar a week, to rub down that gray gelding of his once a day and clean out the stable on Saturdays. I thought it would be convenient to take the widow for my washerwoman, so I got acquainted with the boy."

"Not bad, that."

"It's a stylish gelding enough, but there's a splint coming on the near fore leg."

"What's that to me, you incorrigible horse-jockey?"

"And the shoe of that foot—"

"You used to be straightforward, Delorny—"

"Cassiday, if you please, while I'm here."

"Very well. You used to be straightforward in telling a story, Mr. Cassiday. What do I care for splints and horseshoes?"

"A horseshoe's an important thing. The rider has been lost for lack of one before now; and the rider of that same gray may have cause to curse that very shoe."

"Go on your own way, then."

"On one side the iron has a notch in it, and on the other there's a nail that's been badly driven in, and the head's turned over a little. A man can tell the print of the shoe among a hundred."

"You've tracked him?"

"He meets Ellen—damn him!—about a quarter of a mile north of the road, and half a mile below the mill, near the bluff bank of the creek, where the brush is thick. It's an unfrequented spot."

"You saw him?"

"And heard him, last Saturday afternoon, reading to her — from my namesake, too—Byron's poems."

"How did you know it was Byron?"

"We had an old copy in the Squire's stable at home, and I used to read it at night, by the lantern, when the horses were restless and wouldn't let me sleep: that was what made me think of Byron for a name to go by. He was dealing out to her some love-verses. I could have throttled the infernal scoundrel where he sat."

"You take up Ellen's case warmly."

"Did not you tell me the girl mustn't be ruined, and ar'n't you paying me thirty dollars a month to look after her?"

"She's very pretty, isn't she, Cassiday?"

"If there are any prettier girls, I haven't been lucky enough to light on them. And she's as good and as modest as she's pretty. I'll bet all I'm worth the poor thing wouldn't let that rascal say three words to her if she didn't believe he intended to make her his wife. She *ought* to be some honest man's wife."

"Your's, perhaps?"

"Why not?"

"Well, there *are* some small matters—"

"That you and I were engaged in together long ago. Yes, I remember. But then we don't take any more heavy risks now. We have both reformed, you know. We're repentant sinners. And you would like to marry—"

Cranstoun's eye warned Cassiday that he might go too far; so he added:

"To marry some rich, handsome girl; and no doubt you'll do it, too, one of these days."

"Are you serious, Cassiday?"

"Never was more serious in all my life. Didn't I tell you I had set up respectable, as you've done. I've been thinking it must feel very comfortable when a man has a house of his own over his head, like this of yours."

"But then—" said Cranstoun, putting his hand to his mouth and turning up his little finger.

"Yes, I know," rather dejectedly. "That cursed drinking has been the ruin of me. But I haven't touched a glass since I came here, nor I don't intend to. I felt mean about it when I was talking, last night, to—to the miller at supper."

"I wonder," Cranstoun thought, "whether a fancy for a young girl really could reclaim a sot like that?" But he only said: "Was the daughter at supper, too?"

"Of course. The handiest girl about a table, Mr. Cranstoun! I believe she knows what a man's thinking about before he asks for it."

"The miller's pretty well off himself, and he'll look for a son-in-law that's well to-do in the world."

"And why shouldn't I be well-to-do? I've made some money here already."

"How was that?"

"I heard that Mr. Sydenham wanted a handsome pony for a lady. Nelson Tyler, who has an eye for a horse, told me where to find the snuggest fourteen-hand mare in three counties, and lent me a nag to go after her. Small, thoroughbred head; eyes like a deer's; shoulder thin and high, running handsomely back; arched neck; short-coupled; legs flat and clean and slender as any racer's I ever backed; the least little bits of ears; coat like silk; mane as fine as a young girl's hair, and dropping half way to the ground; color just the thing—dark bay, with black legs. Where the old Dutchman who owned her got such a beauty I can't imagine. He thought her too spirited and too light for his work: I got her for a hundred and thirty-five."

"And sold her to Mr. Sydenham—"

"For a hundred and seventy-five, and cheap at that. Forty dollars clear, you see, for a few hours' work."

"But Miss Sydenham has a saddle-horse already."

"It was not for her he bought the mare."

"How do you know?"

"Would you like to hear something about Mr. Sydenham's motions for the last ten days?"

"Such things never come amiss."

"Well, the same day I hired to the miller, Miss Pembroke and her aunt started out, at nine o'clock in the morning, to visit Mr. Sydenham. Mrs. Hartland returned about eleven, but Miss Celia didn't get back till nearly one, though Miss Sydenham wasn't at home."

"How do you know she wasn't at home?"

"She drove Mrs. Hartland back; there was a runaway scrape, and if the girl hadn't been a trump, and rushed the mare into that pond close to town, they might both have had their necks broken."

"Anything more?"

"Mr. Sydenham returned the visit next day. Then he set about getting a lady's horse. Then he bought, at Jacob Hentzler's, the handsomest side-saddle and double bridle—bit and bridoon, all bang-up—that were to be had in the village. And this morning, being Miss Celia Pembroke's birth-day, he sent down the old coachman on one of the carriage horses, leading that beauty of a pony—saddle, bridle, white saddle-cloth, ear-nets and all complete—a birth-day present to the heiress."

"Confound his impudence!"

"She don't care for him, Mr. Cranstoun: she's looking another way."

"Upon my word, Mr. Del—Mr. Cassiday—considering that you've been doing two days' work in one at that mill, you seem to have been making good use of your extra time. Pray how did you happen to find out the state of the young lady's heart?"

"I was on hand when she and the aunt started for Mr. Sydenham's. Mowbray came along on his gray, and I saw her color up red as a peony, and cast a look at the windows of her uncle's house like a guilty thing. It wasn't hard to guess that the young scamp was the favorite, and that old Hartland—well, that he didn't take to Mowbray, and probably did favor somebody else. I'm glad you think I've been industrious. If you care about any more information in that line, and will make it an object, I'm your man. There's one thing I'd like."

"Well?"

"The mare that ran away, and might have killed Mrs. Hartland, was sold to her husband by the coachman, Potter. I've made the man's acquaintance: he says Hartland looks as black as night at him, and he's expecting every day to get notice to quit when the month's out. A word from you would settle it."

"You want to leave the house where Ellen Tyler lives?"

"Next month, yes. It's no use for a fellow to see a girl every day as long as she cares more for another. Besides, I like being among horses better than among meal-bags. And then Hartland gives forty-five a month, and a house just across the street from the stables. It's small, but it's neat, and it's large enough for two."

"Did you hear what Mowbray said to Ellen?"

"No. He read loud, but when he spoke to her it was so low I could not make it out."

"I must have another witness before you leave the mill. I want you to watch your time and take the miller himself to the spot, so he can see them there together with his own eyes. They'll have a nice time. Mowbray's not good for much, but he's fiery enough; and Nelson Tyler, though he's hard to rouse, isn't a man to stand any nonsense."

"An ugly job!" said Cassiday, hesitating; and Cranstoun added: "*You* needn't appear. Don't you see it's for the girl's good, Cassiday? These clandestine meetings must be stopped, and who can put a stop to them but her father? Do you want her to go on meeting that kid-gloved fop in secret till—"

"Enough said!" broke in Cassiday. "I'll see to it that the burly miller has a chance at him."

"And I'll look to that matter about the coachman's place."

Thereupon the two worthies parted.

The next Sunday afternoon the stout miller and Cassiday might have been seen not far from Tyler's mill, on the road leading thence to Chiskauga, walking away from the mill, as two men might for a wager. Silent too. In the case of one of them, however, not (if physiognomy may be trusted) for lack of thought. The usual bold, frank, good-natured look of the miller seemed clouded with anxiety or anger, the lips set, the veins of the forehead swollen. Cassiday stopped at a point where two large poplars stood by the roadside close to each other. After passing back and forth along the road several times, examining the ground carefully, he said: "We are in time: he has not returned."

Then the men struck off into the woods at right angles to the road, proceeding north, and, as they approached Chewauna Creek, slackening their pace. When, at some distance through the trees, there became visible a gray horse, saddled and bridled, fastened to a sapling, Cassiday turned to note the effect on his companion. A flush on the cheek and a twitch of the right hand, in which the miller carried a stout hickory. "Rather him than me," thought Cassiday; then to the miller: "I did it for the girl's good, Mr. Tyler, but I don't want to appear in it. I'm not used to act the informer, and you don't need me."

"I should think not," was all the

other said as he strode through the brushwood alone.

Ellen was seated on a low ledge of rock, over which a horseman's cloak had been thrown: Mowbray on the grass at her feet, a book in his hand.

"It is such a pleasure to read to those bright eyes of yours, dear Ellen. You ought to be a poet's wife."

The young girl blushed with pleasure.

"It was like sunshine to me," he pursued, "when you used to come three times a week to mother's French class. Wouldn't your father let you come for another quarter?"

"No: he says I have learned French enough already; and you know I am nineteen."

"Then I must bring a French book with me next time and let you read to me, so you may not forget what you have learned. When can I see you again, Ellen?"

Ere the girl could reply, the sound of a heavy footstep caused Mowbray to start to his feet. Ellen turned, recognized her father, and, acting on the impulse of the moment, ran off through the underwood in the direction of the mill. The two men remained confronting each other.

Mowbray was by no means deficient in animal courage, but, as the Dane expressed it, "Conscience does make cowards of us all." He avoided the miller's fixed gaze.

"I'm not surprised," the latter began, "that you can't look a man straight in the face."

Mowbray raised his eyes: "Why shouldn't I look you in the face? I happened to be riding through these woods hunting a board-tree to cover our wood-shed. I met your daughter and stopped to have a chat with her. We got acquainted when she was taking French lessons from my mother."

"Yes. I wish I had run my hand in the fire rather than ever suffer the girl to darken your doors."

"Have you a good board-tree any where on your land that you want to sell, Mr. Tyler?"

"A liar too! Do you go hunting board-trees all the time in the same place?—yesterday was a week, for instance, when you came here with Byron's poems in your pocket?"

Mowbray flushed scarlet, but he restrained himself, conscience-smitten; and Tyler added: "You young gentlemen think it fine, spirited amusement to cozen a poor young girl that knows no better than to believe you. You have respect neither for God nor man."

"Ask Miss Ellen if I ever treated her otherwise than with respect."

"If you had—"

"I'll abide by whatever she says. I'm willing to suffer any punishment if she declares I ever did. Ask her."

"I'll ask her whether *you* ever asked her to be your wife, and the poor child will say no, and will weep as if her heart would break. *I'm* not going to ask you that question: God knows I want no such upstart as you for a son-in-law; but I've another question I'd like to ask."

"Well, sir?"

"Suppose you had a sister and I a son. Suppose that my son met your sister secretly, without your mother's knowledge, without yours. Suppose you found this out, and that you had every reason to believe my son never meant to marry your sister—was actually courting, at the very time, a richer girl—and only flirted with the other, and tried to win her foolish heart, for his own amusement—nothing worse, observe; and suppose you found him, one day, making love to her in a lonely spot, and telling her it was like sunshine to him whenever he met her. Suppose you had happened, that day, to have a good stout hickory with you, what do you think would have been the probable result?"

"But the case is not the same."

"Yes, I know. I'm a clod: you're some of the porcelain of the earth; or at least you think you are, and that often answers just as well. What you do to me and mine I have no right to do to you and yours. That doctrine may answer in Russia, where they sell the working-people along with the land they live on.* It won't do here. What's the difference between us, Mr. Mowbray? Nobody ever asks me twice for a debt; and the story goes that's more than you can say. There's not a neighbor I have that won't bear witness I never willfully injured him or his. You know there's one neighbor, at least, who would lie if he said that of you. Are you more respectable than I am? Not in God's eyes: I'm not at all sure if you are in man's, either. Now I want to know about that son of mine, and what would happen if you caught him courting your sister, and you with a stout cane in your hand?"

"You won't listen to what I have to say to you, and I don't choose to answer a question when it implies a threat."

"Oh, you don't?"

"No gentleman would."

"John Mowbray, you shall have a piece of my mind. I suppose you would scorn to break into my house and get at my strong-box, and, if you found a couple of hundred dollars there, to go off with it under the cloud of night. If you did play me a trick like that, you wouldn't deny that you deserved the penitentiary; and if anybody saw you at such work, you'd be very sure to get there. Now I think a midnight thief a decent, respectable man compared with you. He risks his life to get my money: there's some spunk in that; and he may need it—who knows?—to feed a wife and children. Then in a month or two I can make it up again. But you steal from me my very life—my child's heart, my child's honor. You do this in mere wantonness of purpose, out of no need, only out of profligate selfishness. She trusts you, and you deceive her: she loves you, and you betray her. None but a villain would do that: none but a base, treacherous coward would do that. John Mowbray you are both!"

And the old man, in his hot indignation, unconsciously raised the cane he held in his hand.

Up to this point, Mowbray, exceedingly desirous to avoid a brawl with Ellen's father, had done his best to curb his temper, though his blood boiled when the miller first called him a liar. But the villain and the coward! And the menace of the cane! It was more than his father's son could bear. His rage, long pent up, burst all bounds. Scarcely knowing what he did, he drew from a pocket a large spring-knife, snapped it open and rushed on Tyler.

The miller, who had kept his eye on him, stood quite still and threw away his cane. With a sudden jerk of his left hand he clinched, with the grip of a vice, Mowbray's uplifted arm; then with his right he seized the blade of the knife, wrenching it from the other's grasp with a force that sprained the wrist; then, letting him go, he snapped the thick blade in two as if it had been a pipe-stem, pitched the pieces over the cliff into Chewauna Creek, and signed contemptuously to the young man, saying:

"Get ye gone for a fool! What business had you to meddle with edge-tools?"

If Mowbray's blood had not been in a ferment, he might have appreciated the generosity that let him off so easily. But he was maddened; and he grappled fiercely with his opponent, his passion lending him a force which took the miller by surprise. Mowbray struck him two or three violent blows. Then, for the first time, the animal in Tyler was fairly roused. For a minute or two he had to do his best; but he was a veteran wrestler, who in his youth had never been beaten; and age had but little diminished his extraordinary strength. Closing with Mowbray, in a few minutes he had tripped him up, caught him, as he was falling, in his arms, and borne him, despite his struggles, to the verge of the cliff. It was a sheer descent of full forty feet to the bank of the creek, and that was covered with sharp-angled rocks. Had Mowbray at that terrible moment pleaded humbly for his life, it is just possible he might have lost it through the contempt he would have inspired; but pride and passion overcame fear: he said not a word, and when he had ex-

* The Russian serfs were not emancipated until 1862.

TYLER AND MOWBRAY.

hausted himself by terrible but fruitless effort, and felt in that clutch of steel that he was overmastered, he submitted silently to his fate. Nelson Tyler stood, for a few moments, as if irresolute—it was no bad subject for a group of Hercules and Antæus—then, turning from the precipice, he flung the young man on the ground with stunning force. In falling, Mowbray's head struck against a stray root of a tree just visible above the ground, and he lay insensible.

The miller stood looking at him, "He's had enough," he said; then hastily descending to the creek, by a circuitous path well known to him, he brought back a hat-full of water just as Mowbray had recovered consciousness so as to sit up. The wound on his head was trifling, and the cold water soon revived him. Not a word passed between the men except the question: "Can you ride home?" and the answer: "Yes."

Tyler brought the horse, assisted Mowbray to mount; and, as he gave him the reins, he said, in his deep bass tones:

"Thank God, young man, that He preserved you from death and me from murder."

PART V.

CHAPTER XV.

ELLINOR ETHELRIDGE.

CELIA told Leoline the exact truth when she said, after the conversation with Sydenham, that she was returning home hopeful and encouraged. But a few words, how wise and encouraging soever, so long as they fail to remove daily-recurring annoyances, afford alleviation only. One cannot take a fire in one's hand by "thinking on the frosty Caucasus." Hartland's grim looks were real things—as real as frost or rainy weather—for they chilled her more than either. Sydenham's mediation, she saw, had only irritated her guardian; but when his mysterious prescription reached her, on the morning of her birth-day, in the shape of a beautiful pony, it proved an habitual comfort, in substantial form, that almost offset the grim looks. Bess—so she named the little mare—became a petted favorite at once; and the spirited creature returned her mistress' daily caresses, after a time, with almost human affection. She would follow Celia everywhere, though at large, even through a crowd.

Morbid thoughts usually spring either from feeble health or from idleness. It is a difficult matter to get rid of such by sitting down and seeking to reason one's self out of them. We do better to remove the cause; and this we can often effect by some simple arrangement of external circumstances. This young girl, while she reaped the advantages, suffered also the evils, which money brings. With a competence already assured, she was subjected to no wholesome demand for exertion of mind or body. She had finished her education, or what is called such by those who forget that the development and cultivation of our faculties go on not only through the life which now is, but doubtless through that which is to come. Had she been at the head of her own household, a sense of duty would have kept her busy; and the actively busy have no time to be sentimental. But she had no vocation—nothing imperatively calling her off from trifles and summoning to the realities of life.

Sydenham, even if he did not realize all this, had prescribed wisely. Bess became educator as well as physician. As Celia gradually contracted the habit of riding out for an hour or two every fine day, the effect on health and spirits was notably salutary. She dwelt less on petty annoyances than formerly. On horseback she seemed to get away from them. The custom of the country permitted her to ride unattended; and when out in the woods her thoughts took freer scope and a fresher tone.

After a time she found a companion with whom to ride—one who was at once a puzzle and a pleasure to her.

In most villages there is to be found some mysterious personage, whom the villagers cannot exactly make out; who dropped down among them, they scarcely know how; with whose antecedents they are very imperfectly acquainted: some one, perhaps, whose manners and bearing are at variance with his apparent circumstances, and who becomes, by turns, an object of curiosity, of admiration and of suspicion.

Nor was Chiskauga without her sphinx's riddle, welcomed by village gossip. It had made its appearance about five years before the present epoch of our story, in graceful guise—to wit, in the form of a young lady of very striking appearance: not pretty, certainly. Handsome? Well, one scarcely knew whether to call her so or not. Stylish-looking she certainly was in face and in person, though her manners were very quiet, even reserved. Her features, though expressing dignity and intelligence, were irregular, but no one would call her plain who looked in her beautiful soft eyes. They were a little dreamy. Those might have thought her proud who did not note how uniformly unobtrusive her deportment was. Did these expressive features indicate spirit? One would have said so but for a despondent look that was habitual to her.

She had brought a letter to Mr. Sydenham, introducing Miss Ellinor Ethelridge from England, an orphan. It was from a Mr. Williams, an elderly Quaker gentleman of Philadelphia, with whom Sydenham had accidentally made acquaintance at Pisa. They had traveled together to Florence and Rome, and Sydenham had been delighted with the benevolence and the inquiring spirit of his new acquaintance.

What the exact tenor of Mr. Williams' letter was did not transpire, except that it contained a warm recommendation of the bearer as a person in every way well qualified to fill the post of teacher—a situation, it appeared, which the young lady desired to obtain in some quiet country place.

Sydenham's influence and exertions soon procured her a school, to which the principal people in the place gradually sent their children. He was himself a frequent visitor, and he was pleased and surprised with the good judgment and ability which Miss Ethelridge displayed. No such teacher had ever before appeared in Chiskauga. Aside from music, in which she was not a proficient, her qualifications were admirable — among them a familiar acquaintance with French, which she spoke with the fluency of a native. This brought about an acquaintance with Dr. Meyrac's family, and after a time they received her as boarder. With Madame Meyrac, fastidious in her likings, she became a great favorite.

Celia, desiring to perfect herself in French, had taken private lessons from her; and, notwithstanding a five years' difference in their ages, was strongly attracted to her teacher. For a year or two her advances had been met, on the part of Miss Ethelridge, with a degree of coldness which would have repelled her in almost any one else; but the soft eyes, with their spiritual light, and the cultivated tones of a low, sweet voice, drew her on with a strange fascination, and her persistent love thawed the frost at last. Beneath, she found rare qualities—a noble spirit, generous and impulsive, covered, however, with a reticence so strict that Celia knew no more of this stranger's early history up to the time of which we are now writing than the rest of the Chiskauga world did. But if this woman, to others grave and undemonstrative, withheld even from Celia her confidence, she granted her at last, in unstinted measure, affection—unwillingly, it seemed, as if she were yielding to a reprehensible weakness, but with all the warmth of a genial nature breaking over the bounds of self-imposed restraint. And for the little kindnesses which Celia's position enabled her to bestow she returned a measure of gratitude out of proportion to the benefits conferred. One of these, which the girl had recently offered, seemed to touch her more than any other she had received.

It happened that Cranstoun, in fulfillment of his promise to Cassiday, had spoken of the latter to Hartland; and having exhibited the certificate which the groom had received from Rarey attesting his ability as horse-trainer, he persuaded Hartland to try the newcomer's skill in reclaiming Brunette, the runaway. So satisfactory had been the result that when a young city friend of Celia's, a timid rider but fond of the exercise, came for a day or two to visit them, the uncle permitted his niece to ride Brunette and to lend Bess to her visitor. The "brown beauty" behaved admirably, and both young ladies came home delighted with the trip.

This suggested to Celia a plan, to which, as Mr. Hartland had somewhat demurred to her solitary strolls on horseback, she hoped to obtain his assent. One evening, when her uncle, with infinite self-satisfaction, had been exhibiting to her a magnificent beetle yet undescribed, and one of the finest specimens he had ever added to his collection, her instinct bade her avail herself of the rare good-humor which her praises of the insect's brilliant colors had called out. She broached her proposal, which was, that she might be allowed, occasionally, on days when her aunt did not require the dearborn, to have the use of Brunette for Miss Ethelridge, so that that lady might join in her rides.

Hartland, after reflecting a little, gave a hearty assent; for which Celia would have been more grateful had she been quite sure that his ready compliance with her wish was due to kindness alone. She *was* thankful, however, especially to her aunt, who joined warmly in the plan and placed Brunette at her disposal during three days a week.

At the German saddler, Hentzler's, Celia early next morning picked out a saddle, bridle and accoutrements, the exact counterparts of her own, and herself accompanied the man who carried them to Dr. Meyrac's. Ellinor was absent, but came up to her room, where Celia awaited her, a few minutes later. Her first look of surprise at sight of her friend's gift, which had been deposited on the floor, changed to one of sadness—it seemed almost of pain—so suddenly that Celia, disconcerted, presented her offering with hesitation.

"For me!" was all Ellinor said, in an incredulous tone—"for me!" And when Celia disclosed her project, telling what a pleasure it would be to have such companionship in her rides, she was startled by the effect her words produced. She had never seen her friend give way to deep emotion in all the five years of their acquaintance; and it was evident that Ellinor tried hard now for self-control. In vain! The tears *would* come—the sobs could not be restrained.

"Celia," she said, at last—"darling Celia, I used to have friends who called me Ellie: I have none now. They used to plan for my happiness as you do—as no one else has done since—since a dear friend died. If you treat me as you are doing to-day, I must be Ellie to you—Ellie, dear one, Ellie! What years since I heard my name!"

Celia, startled by this unexpected burst of feeling, threw her arms about Ellinor's neck, called her "Ellie," and "darling," and other pet names besides, and then cried heartily, as if she had just lost a friend instead of finding one.

Her tears arrested Ellinor's. She took the excited girl in her arms and soothed her as a mother might.

"Dear child!" she said: "how selfish I am, giving pain to you when you were recalling to me dreams of pleasure! I wish so much to give *you* pleasure; and then your gift was such a temptation!"

Celia looked up and met the sad, longing eyes:

"You are not going to let me call you Ellie, and then refuse the only little bit of comfort I have the chance to offer you? And the kindness is to me, not to you. Please, please believe me! there's nobody—not even Leoline—that I feel drawn to as to you."

"Yes, that's it. That is all wrong."

"All wrong that I should love you, Ellie?"

"Wrong that I should have asked you to call me Ellie, as things stand. What do you know of me, Celia? Who am I? Why did I come here alone? I was but twenty when I reached Chiskauga, and I have had dear friends. Yet I am sought for by no one, cared for by no one. I scarcely receive a letter—never but from one person, and upon him I have no claim. You have given me your love, from pity maybe, or because your heart is warm and trusting, and you knew I needed love. But have I a right to accept it and explain nothing? You are so young and guileless! You do not know the world and its false pretences and its crooked ways. Ought I to take advantage of that?"

"I know you are an orphan as I am; and I dare say there was no uncle and no kind aunt, like mine, to take the orphan in and care for her. Is not that enough? Have I ever asked to know more?"

"Never: that is the worst of it. If you had been inquisitive, I should have had an excuse for reticence."

"It needs none. I have known you five years, Ellie, and have loved you nearly as long. If you are not good, nobody is."

The tears glistened again in Ellinor's eyes.

"If I live," she said, "you shall know, some day, whether I am worthy of your love or not. Keep that beautiful faith of yours till then. We grow old when we lose it. God, in his mercy, send that your trust in his creatures may never be betrayed!"

"Mr. Sydenham said, the other day, that you had done *so* much good here—that your pupils, as they grew up, would be an honor to the place."

"Thank God!" Then, after a pause: "When they are mothers of families and I an old woman, I shall have friends in them."

"But as you are a young woman still, and working hard for them, you ought to have a ride now and then to do you good. Macbeth asked that 'doctor of physic,' with the long black gown, if he could not 'minister to a mind diseased?' I think Bess can. That's my experience."

"What do you know about 'a mind diseased,' little pet?"

Celia blushed: she would have been ashamed to talk of her sorrows to one like Ellinor — forsaken, alone. The quick eye of the latter saw and interpreted the emotion at once. "Forgive me," she said; then picking up the bridle Celia had brought for her, with its white web-reins and blue silk frontlet: "Where did you find anything so pretty as this?"

"Mr. Sydenham had a set of horse equipments made, or sent for, expressly for me, by Mr. Hentzler, and this is a duplicate set which the saddler got up, or procured, at the same time, thinking, I suppose, that Bess would set off mine to advantage, and that somebody might fancy the pattern."

"One recognizes Mr. Sydenham's taste: it is faultless. Every article is perfect, even to this beautiful riding-whip with its knobs wound with silver wire. Ah! from Swayne & Adeney! I thought I detected London work. The covered buckles of that bridle were never made in Chiskauga."

"I am so glad it all suits you."

"I could not help admiring it, but it does not suit me, dear Celia." She stopped, seeing how much pain she gave: "You ought to have a companion in your rides, but there is Leoline, nearly your own age, in your own rank—a far more fitting associate than I."

"Leoline is a dear, good girl, merry as she can be, and I like her ever so much. Now and then she rides with me—more usually with her father. But I want *you:* I need you, Ellie."

"Me, dear child?"

"Yes, you do me good. I feel better and quieter when I've had a real chat with you. And we can have such long, long talks on horseback in the woods. Don't you like riding?"

"I used to like it very much."

"Did you ever take riding-lessons?"

"For nearly two years, before I left London. It was my chief amusement then."

"Ah!"—Celia took her friend's hand and patted it coaxingly—"now do be a good girl, Ellie. I've been wanting so much, for two years past, to take riding-lessons. I know I need them. Mr. Sydenham gave me some hints about my seat in the saddle: I'm certain he thinks I ride badly. You have praised me for my progress in French. Who knows but what I may do as well in riding?"

Strange! Still that despondent look. Celia read refusal in her friend's face.

"Ellie," she continued, "I'm not too proud to accept a gift from you. Won't you make me a present of a quarter's riding-lessons?"

"Little plotter!" It was said with a sad, sweet smile, but something in the tone or look convinced Celia that she had not reached the depth of her friend's objections, whencesoever arising. She made one last effort:

"There's another reason why I want you;" and with that she blushed a little, and Ellinor's expression changed. "My guardian is a good man, but he is not a cordial one. Yet he agreed cordially to this proposal of mine when I spoke to him about it. I think I know the reason. There is a young man against whom Mr. Hartland has very strong prejudices; and he imagines that I shall not be able to meet him so often if you and I ride together sometimes."

"It is Evelyn Mowbray."

"Yes."

"Do you wish to meet him alone?"

"Not often. We can be friends only, for two or three years at least; and I am so anxious to do nothing that shall offend my guardian."

Ellinor sat silent for a minute or two. "God forgive me if I do wrong!" was the thought which occupied her. "You are right," she said at last: "it is best not to meet Mr. Mowbray too often."

"Then help me do right—there's a darling! See!" taking up the riding-whip: "here's a tiny silver shield: mine has exactly such a one, and Mr. Sydenham had my initials engraved on it. There's just room for 'Ellie:' it won't hold 'Ellinor.' I'm going to take it to the watch-maker's—you know he engraves nicely."

"I don't need a memento of this day, Celia."

"Well, I shall carry off your whip with me, at all events; and—let me see, to-morrow is Saturday: you do not keep school, and we can take the morning for it—to-morrow at half-past eight I'll be here. Potter shall call for your saddle and bridle at once: I only had them brought here to show to you. It's your hour for school, Ellie: you haven't time to argue with me any longer. Good-bye!"

The little strategist had carried the citadel by assault. Ellinor let her go, saying only, "It's such a comfort to be able to teach somebody without asking payment in return! You shall have your riding-lessons, Celia."

Ellinor mounted Brunette next day. Even Celia's unpracticed eye detected the finished grace with which she rode. Whether she felt the inspiration which Bulwer may have realized when he declared that, "give him but a light rein and a free bound, he was Cato, Cicero, Cæsar," I know not. But, as they cantered swiftly through the woodland glades, her eye appeared to kindle with a spirit, and her stately figure to dilate with a commanding power, which Celia had never seen in her before. Some old character, hidden till now under the veil of grief or despondency, seemed emerging. The village teacher was transformed. For a time her thoughts had strayed off, far off, beyond her control.

Then, awaking to the present, she drew rein. She was in the Chiskauga woods once more.

"The elbows a little closer to the body, Celia," she said. "That is well: if it seem stiff at first, the feeling will wear off by habit. I think I had better knit up that bridoon rein for you till you obtain more complete management of the bit."

"I thought that was the snaffle rein."

"A snaffle, as my riding-master took pains to tell me, has a bar outside of the ring, on each side, and it is used alone: the bridoon, you see, has none—it is used along with the bit, but independently of it. The bridle hand lower, dear. That is important, especially in rapid riding."

That new creature whom Celia had admired, curbing her horse in queenly fashion beside her, a few moments before, was gone. It was again Miss Ethelridge, the village teacher, painstaking, with an eye on her pupil and giving her advice from time to time. As they were approaching home on their return, she said, with a smile: "My riding-pupil will do me as much credit as my pupil in French did." Then, with changed tone and manner, she added: "You have given me such a day as I have not had for years, dear child—for years! Dante was only half right when he spoke of the grief we suffer by recalling happy times in the past."

Two days a week was all Celia could persuade Ellinor to agree to. "I took only two riding-lessons each week myself," she said. The second day, when they were about to mount, she asked Celia, "Would you mind letting me ride Bess a little?"

"You shall have her most willingly."

"She doesn't rein back readily, and she should be taught to passage."

"To passage?"

"To move off sideways, her head turned just a little, so as to let one foot cross in front of the other. It is very convenient sometimes, when one is riding in company."

They were not to have their talk to themselves this time. After a ride of some miles in the woods, they heard galloping behind them, and turning saw Ethan Hartland and John Evelyn Mowbray approaching. Celia was a little surprised, for the young men were seldom seen together. Mowbray rode up at once beside Celia, and Hartland, with apparent hesitation, slowly moved his horse to the other side.

"Cousin Celia," he said, "we had no intention of intruding on you and Miss Ethelridge. Mr. Mowbray asked me to show him a piece of land belonging to Mr. Sydenham which he thinks of purchasing."

Ellinor, after a single glance at the speaker, turned quickly to Mowbray, who spoke, almost as if her look needed a reply: "Yes, mother finds cord-wood getting to be so expensive that she proposes to buy a bit of woodland, from which we can supply ourselves."

They rode on, a little way, four abreast, then came to a spot where the road, cut into a hill and flanked with ditches, narrowed considerably.

"We crowd you, Miss Ethelridge," said Hartland, reining back.

"Perhaps we had better ride on," said Mowbray, and, without waiting for Celia's answer, he put his horse to a canter, Brunette keeping up. Ellinor checked Bess, prompted by the evident incivility of leaving Hartland behind; but the animal—much to her surprise, for it had hitherto seemed perfectly docile—reared, made one or two dashes to the front, then, when checked, stamped impatiently, neighing the while; and, when put in motion again, curveted so violently that a rider with less practiced hand and less assured seat might well have been in danger. But Ellinor, thoroughly trained, sat with skill and self-possession, such as is said to have deceived the poor Peruvians into the belief that Pizarro and his followers formed a portion of the animals they rode. Hartland forgot his apprehensions for her safety in admiration of her horsemanship; but when, after the mare was reduced to submission, she still fretted against the bit as impatiently as ever, he said:

"Celia has stopped, alarmed, I think, for your safety, Miss Ethelridge. Had we not better ride up? The road is wider now."

"It is spoiling Bess to let her have her own way," replied Ellinor; yet she acted on the suggestion and touched the mare with the whip. No dog ever showed joy more plainly at his master's return than did the high-spirited animal when once more by her mistress' side. She rubbed her head against her as if seeking the accustomed caress. Celia could not withhold it, but she said: "I am ashamed of you, Bess: how *could* you behave so?"

It seemed almost as if the creature understood the tone of reproach. She drooped her head and submissively obeyed the slightest touch of the rein.

"Have you had any difficulty in detaching her from Brunette when you were riding her, Celia?" said Ellinor, thoughtfully.

"Not the least: I have separated them again and again, and Bess has always obeyed at once. I cannot understand her behavior to-day."

"I can. It is not her comrade, it is her mistress, she is unwilling to leave. I knew just such an instance once," in a low voice. "Poor Bess!" she added, patting the mare's neck, "if that is your only fault—" What memory was it that gave so touching a tone to the broken words? Whatever it was, it was harshly dispelled the next moment.

"Celia," said Mowbray, "it will never do to let that pony get so willful. You'll have no peace with her. She ought to be broken of such tricks at once. I wish you'd let me take her in hand for a day or two."

Ellinor's eyes had been fixed on Mowbray during this speech, and she turned to Celia as if anxious for her reply.

"Thank you, Evelyn, but I prefer to manage her myself. Miss Ethelridge will help me: I am taking riding-lessons from her."

Mowbray's brow clouded. He seemed on the point of making some additional remark, but checked himself. They rode on for some distance, silently at first—afterward exchanging a few commonplaces, until they reached a cross-road, little more than a bridle-path, leading deeper into the woods. Then Hartland said:

"Our road leads off here to the right, Mr. Mowbray."

"Are you very busy this afternoon, Mr. Hartland? We might accompany the ladies as far as their ride extends, and then have time, in returning, to look at this land before sundown."

"Another day I shall be glad to show it to you, but I have several things which I have promised Mr. Sydenham that I would attend to this afternoon."

The tone was barely civil. Celia, who knew her cousin well and liked him, had a dim feeling that there was something wrong, especially when she saw a frown darkening the face of Mowbray, who, having no longer excuse for delay, coldly doffed his hat to the ladies and rode off with Hartland.

If either of the riders who remained regretted this departure, one of their horses evidently did not. Bess resumed all her spirit and gentleness, arching her neck, as with pride or pleasure, and glancing with her bold, bright eyes at her mistress—a mute protest, one might almost have supposed it, against another separation. Ellinor ran her fingers through the long silky mane admiringly.

"I shall not have the heart to correct this pretty creature for her one sin," she said. "I have the same weakness for her mistress that she has. She means only love, not harm. Should one be blamed for that?"

"We are told that to him who loveth much shall much be forgiven."

Ellinor looked up quickly: she saw that Celia was not thinking of her. "That is God's own truth," she said, reverently: then after a pause—"yet we have no right to indulge even love at expense of others."

This time it was Celia who looked up. Ellinor turned it off: "Bess won't annoy you with her fondness: she'll be good at your bidding, if she is perverse with others."

A fit of musing fell on the girls as they rode home. Something had jarred on Celia's consciousness, but she had forgotten it next day. Not so Ellinor: she laid up what seemed trifles in her heart.

CHAPTER XVI.
THE CANDIDATES.

"Audi alteram partem."

"PAPA dear," said Leoline, as they rode one morning toward Tyler's Mill, "who is this Mr. Creighton that we are going to hear?"

"Candidate to fill a vacancy in Congress, against Mr. Emberly."

"Yes, I know; but *who* is he?"

"Have you any recollection of Mr. Williams? But no—you were too young then."

"The Quaker gentleman who traveled with us in Italy? Why, I remember the very day we made acquaintance with him."

"Are you sure of that, my child?"

"It was in the cathedral at Pisa. He asked the guide about Galileo's lamp. No, not Galileo's, but the lamp that was accidentally set swinging while mass was going on, and Galileo noticed it, and it helped him to invent the pendulum."

"It suggested to him the principle of the pendulum, you mean: yes, that is the very Mr. Williams. Eliot Creighton is his nephew—a young lawyer living about fifty miles from here."

"A good speaker, is he?"

"They say so. I take an interest in him. He is, I believe, a Unitarian; and I saw, this morning, an anonymous handbill attacking him on account of his religious opinions, and abusing him as an infidel."

"I'm glad of that: I mean I'm glad he will have to defend himself."

"Why, my child?"

"It will be nice: we shall see what he's made of. We shall see whether he'll let them catechise him. A man that's a coward won't do for me."

"I like pluck myself. Moral courage is the rarest of qualities among our public men. But, in a political contest, where the party vote is so nearly balanced as in our district, there is great temptation to temporize, and smooth things over."

"Surely you wouldn't vote to send a man to Congress who could not stand temptation, papa?" said Leoline, indignantly.

"Not if another offered who could," smiling at her warmth.

"I hope Mr. Creighton can."

"We shall see."

The trysting-place was Grangula's Mount—so called after an Indian chief who had formerly held sway in these parts. It was in the woods, about two miles west of Sydenham's residence. The topmost summit of this eminence was bald, but a little way down, on its eastern slope, were loosely clustered a few broad-branching trees—old oaks and elms and dark hemlocks. Under the spacious shelter of this detached grove the eye commanded a magnificent view over the village, the pretty lake beyond and the expanse of forest and champaign that surrounded both. The spot was a favorite resort of the villagers on their pic-nic excursions; and Sydenham, desiring to encourage these easy, healthful social gatherings, had caused rustic seats to be placed where the shade was deepest for comfort and accommodation. This had caused it to be selected, also, as a convenient spot for public meetings, political and sometimes religious.

A crowd was gathering fast. It was a magnificent day—calm, cloudless, but the landscape veiled with the light, transparent, illuminated haze which marks that beautiful episode in the autumn season of the West, known as "Indian Summer." As Sydenham and his daughter advanced to their seats, Leoline exclaimed in delight; and her father, albeit familiar with whatever is most striking in European scenery, stood still in admiration.

It was at the epoch when the first light finger-touch of frost sprinkles magical coloring over dark-green oceans of foliage. The woods, far more brilliant in their decay than in the tropic of their perfection, showed like groves in fairyland, pranked with all that is gayest in the rainbow—golden and primrose yellows; tawny orange of every shade; deep, blood-red crimsons; scarlets with color of flame; gorgeous purples, with here and there a lilac tinge; bright, rich browns, shaded off into russet and olive; yet all harmonizing with a felicity which human pencil seeks in vain to emulate. A lover of Nature might well have traveled a thousand miles to witness the scene, if nearer home such exhibition of sylvan splendor was not to be found. Yet most of the spectators who now sat down in full view of the wondrous prospect scarcely vouchsafed a second look or a single comment.

Their thoughts were on something less familiar—the two candidates, both personal strangers in the county, who had just made their appearance on the ground. They had agreed to travel together and to speak alternately. On this day, Mr. Emberly had the opening speech. He ascended an elevated platform, occupied, on festal occasions, by the village band.

A thin, middle-aged man, clad in black, with a slow step and somewhat solemn aspect; known by reputation to many of the spectators as having filled, a few years before, the post of president-judge in an adjoining circuit—a fluent rather than forcible speaker. He began by a compliment to the audience, eulogizing the appearance of the village and surrounding country, then ran glibly over the political topics of the day in partisan fashion, hitting his opponent from time to time with a touch of asperity, but without allusion to his religious sentiments, unless his concluding remark might be so construed.

"Fellow-citizens," he said, "I here rest my cause, assured of helping hands. I am happy to have found among you many who agree with me, not only in politics, but on topics transcending in importance all matters of secular debate—men with whom I have a bond of fellowship closer than any party ties; dear friends who sympathize with me in those opinions which will determine our Future when earthly scenes shall have passed away. That I have the hearty good-will of all such men I know, and with that I rest satisfied: it is not for me to inquire whether I shall obtain their votes also."

At this all eyes turned toward Creighton; and Leoline, glancing round, noticed that one or two men, who had been reading a handbill before the speaking began, nudged their neighbors. She felt a little nervous as Creighton rose. The young man himself did not seem quite at ease.

Instead of ascending to the platform which Emberly had occupied, and which stood a little on one side, he took his stand at the foot of a noble elm, directly in front of the audience, who were chiefly seated, row above row, on the sloping hillside, so that he looked up as he addressed them.

During the first ten minutes most of his auditors had come to the conclusion that the fluent Emberly was the better speaker. No easy preface; no conciliatory commendation of themselves or of their neighborhood: no sueing; no allusion, in deprecatory tone or otherwise, to his own claims or to his inexperience. A plain review of the facts at issue, curtly but carefully stated, rather as if it had been committed to memory. This called forth no token, expressed aloud, either of dissent or of approbation; a Chiskauga audience never indulged in any such—it was contrary to the habit of the country; but the faces were cold, and there was a smile, not of friendly import, on the lips of several prominent men—on those of Amos Cranstoun among the rest. Such a moment is a turning-point in the career of a young speaker. Creighton noticed the mute irony: it stung him, shaking him free from embarrassment at once. He took up the subjects he had laid out, one by one, just a little bit defiantly at first; but, as the spirit began to work, with such earnestness and candor that, before half an hour more had passed, the audience had forgotten to criticise or to admire; had forgotten that it was Eliot Creighton who was speaking to them; thought only of the facts submitted and of the arguments made; so completely, by the magnetic tones, had they become wrapped up in the subject itself. Several had stretched themselves on the grass near him, their rifles beside them, and now, the chin propped on a hand, sat with eyes as eagerly fixed on the speaker as if they had been tracking a deer.

Animated by the attention he had won, Creighton indulged, once or twice, in a vein of humor that was natural to him; his allusions to Emberly and to his arguments, sharp as the wit was, still untinctured by ill-nature. That won simple hearts, always open to a pleasant jest. Several old farmers slapped their thighs, in a manner which said as plainly as a slap could say it, "He'll do!" And when at last, in illustration of some point he had made, the speaker introduced, with graphic gestures, a sportive anecdote, the hillside rang with laughter.

Then he paused, a sudden change passing over his features, sternness succeeding the light pleasantry. The whispered comments which his amusing story had called forth instantly ceased, and there was a hush of expectation. Picking up from the grass beside him, where he had laid it ere he began to speak, a printed handbill, he unfolded it as if to read its contents: then, seeming to think better of it, he cast it from him again; and, selecting from among several documents a small, time-stained-looking pamphlet, and alluding now, for the first time throughout his speech, to the fact that he was a candidate, he said, quietly, but with that emphasis which subdued emotion imparts:

"If you send me to Washington City, it will not be as a propagandist to take action for you in matters of religion: it will be as agent or attorney to transact your worldly business. But it is not usual to ask a lawyer, before he is entrusted with a cause, whether he be Presbyterian or Universalist. Nor do you catechise the tailor who sews your coat, or the shoemaker who fits you with a pair of boots. You want your business well done—that is your affair: you leave the man's creed alone—that is his. Now the same common-sense principle which prevails in every-day life would govern in politics also if voters, in this matter, were left to themselves. Yet ever since the commencement of our government there have been found, from time to time, those who have taken pains to lead astray, on this point, the good sense of the people.

"Would you hear what was put forth, in the year 1800, when the author of the Declaration of Independence was candidate for the Presidency? Then let me read to you from a pamphlet of that day. The writer says: 'Consider the effect which the election of any man avowing the principles of Mr. Jefferson would have upon our citizens. The effect would be to destroy religion, introduce immorality and loosen all the bonds of society.'

"Such was the prophecy. Shall we ask whether, four years afterward, when he whom his enemies persisted in calling 'the infidel President' took his seat, the predictions of evil were fulfilled?—whether religion was destroyed—whether immorality was introduced—whether the bonds of society were loosened? The questions are an insult to the illustrious dead!

"Now, as then, we find men who engage in politics as they would gamble at cards. But it is not the religion of the heart that busies itself in this profligate game. True piety is quiet, unobtrusive, a keeper at home, a peacemaker. She enters into her closet and prays there, after she has closed the door. She does not thrust herself into the turmoil of party politics, catechising candidates and sowing broadcast the seeds of intolerance and of all uncharitableness. True piety, let it differ from me in the articles of its creed as it will, I honor and respect. From my youth up I have been trained to honor and respect it. But, for its base counterfeit—say, freemen of Ohio! answer and say, whether I should better deserve the suffrages of brave and upright men if I lacked the spirit to scorn its slanders—if I consented to bow down my soul before its pharisaical sway?"

Creighton's voice was a low tenor, musical and of great power; and its tones, as he warmed with indignant emotion, swelled out over the hillside and reached the edge of the forest, where some little children were nutting. They crept back on tiptoe, "to hear what the preacher was saying." When Creighton recommenced it was in a quieter key:

"When a friend asks me about my creed — when any good man, anxious for my spiritual welfare, makes inquiry touching my religious opinions—I have an answer for him, full and frank. But when political intriguers, conspiring for sinister ends, go out of their way to charge upon me sentiments which as little resemble those I ever held as their whole conduct in this affair resembles uprightness and fair-dealing — to such men, impertinently obtruding such a subject, I have no answer whatever.

"It may be that some of you, if I told you my creed, might deem a few of its articles heterodox. So be it! They are my own. I am answerable for them at a higher tribunal than man's. I claim for myself, as the good and noble Roger Williams did of yore, that right of private judgment and free speech which it is our country's proudest boast that every American citizen may demand at the hands of his fellow-citizens. To the greatest it has not been refused—to the humblest it may not justly be denied. Jefferson claimed it when he asked your fathers' votes for the office of chief magistrate of the republic: I am equally entitled to its sacred shield, though I stand before you but one among the undistinguished hundreds who now aspire to a seat in the councils of the nation."

Not a sound nor a movement in the audience. No one stirred from his place. They sat with eyes intent on the speaker, as if waiting for more. It was not till Creighton, noticing this, stepped forward with a smile and a blush of pleasure at this mute compliment to his eloquence, and thanked them gracefully for the marked attention they had given him, that the spell was dissolved and the crowd arose. Then, indeed, all tongues were loosed.

Some of the comments, even when laudatory, were more forcible than elegant. As Sydenham stopped to speak to Celia and her aunt, Leoline overheard, from a knot of four or five gray-headed men near them:

"If that young fellow didn't give it to them good! Now ain't he a horse?"

"Well, he's slick on the tongue—very," said another; "but he's mighty high and independent. He didn't seem to care a chaw of tobacco whether we gin him our votes or not. If a man goes for him, he won't get a thankee for it. Emberly's something like: he has a civil tongue in his head."

"They're both blooded nags," broke in a younger man who had come up during the last remark; "but I'll tell you what it is: fair play's fair play. That handbill sort o' sticks in my craw. A fellow ought to have a chance. Here's just three days to the election, and it's only yesterday these dirty sheets showed their faces here. I hear'n they were kep' back in the other counties till the candidates had spoke and gone. That's stabbin' a man behind his back. A scamp that'd be guilty of such a trick'd steal cold corn-bread from a nigger's saddle-bags."

"Ye can't say Emberly had anything to do with the handbills."

"No; but, to my thinkin' there was a touch of the sneak in the way he wound up his speech about 'bonds of fellowship.' A man could see with half an eye that it was a tub thrown out to the Methodists."

"And you're a Hard-shell Baptist."

"Not soft enough, any way, to be caught with such back-handed tricks."

Leoline's party passed on toward the stand, so she heard no more. Sydenham gave his hand to Creighton. "We must become good friends," he said, cordially. "Come and have a quiet cup of tea at my house this evening. Or cannot you ride home with us now?"

"Thank you, much. But a candidate is public property for two hours after his speech, and I must call on my friend, Miss Ethelridge. By six I can be with you."

"That will suit us perfectly."

Celia, having come on horseback, joined the Sydenham party as they rode home. "So he knows Ellie?" she thought to herself; "'my friend Miss Ethelridge,' he said. And she has only one friend who writes to her. I wonder if it is Mr. Creighton?" But all this she kept to herself.

"Isn't he splendid?" said Leoline to Celia: her father was riding in advance with Ethan Hartland.

"Mr. Creighton? I liked his speech; but you surely don't think him handsome, Lela?" Celia was comparing him, in her own mind, with Evelyn Mowbray.

"I really can't tell what ladies call handsome. Dr. Meyrac has a fine portrait of Kosciusko, and Lucille Meyrac and I were looking at it the other day. She said it was an ugly face. Well, I don't know. I think if its owner had courted me right hard, I might have had him."

"And you think Creighton resembles him?"

"Wicked creature! You would entrap me into giving as broad a hint as Desdemona gave to Othello—

> 'And bade me, if I had a friend that loved her,
> I should but teach him how to tell my story,
> And that would woo her.' "

"Well, Lela, why shouldn't you admire him?"

"I like him. I like all brave and frank men, who speak their minds nobly—who won't temporize and truckle—who won't be taken to task and trodden on. But it's against my principles to care for any one—that is, *really* care, you know—who will never care for me."

Celia laughed: "So you've made up your mind already that Creighton never will."

"Quite," Leoline replied with the most sober and thoughtful air. "He never would, even if he were to settle here among us. I'm not the least the sort of person to take his fancy. I'm too like him. If I were fairly brought to bay and hard put to it, I'm not at all sure but I could make some such speech, myself. I felt like it when he talked about bowing down his soul—how was it?—beneath Slander's pharisaical sway. Such sort of men like sweet, quiet, domestic women. Ah! if you were not disposed of, Celia! The very person to suit him!"

"But then I should never take a fancy to him."

"No. It's a pity, though." And Leoline looked as serious as if she had the whole matter on her own shoulders: she was thinking of Mowbray, and comparing the two men. Then she branched off to the speech again: "What a gesture that was!"—she threw up her own arm as the thought crossed her—"and what a look, as he talked of Roger Williams and claimed the right of free speech! How came it, I wonder, with that slender figure and just medium height, that he could throw so much dignity into his bearing?"

Sydenham overheard her and turned: "In a measure, no doubt, because noble sentiments impart noble expression; but it was partly due, I think, to an accident or an intuition."

"How so, papa?"

"Instead of getting on the platform, as Emberly did, he took his stand on the grass below his audience. Thus, in addressing them, his head was naturally thrown back a little, his eyes raised, and when his emotions sought expression in action, the gestures were all upward, corresponding to sentiments elevated and aspiring. I think clergymen do wrong to ascend high pulpits whence to deliver their sermons. There was a simple dignity about Creighton to-day such as young men seldom attain. But if he had been boxed up and looking down upon us, much of the expression would have been lost."

Creighton came to tea. So, at an invitation from Sydenham, did Ellinor Ethelridge. Celia kept a promise given to Leoline to come over in the course of the evening, her cousin Ethan Hartland accompanying her.

Ethan informed Sydenham that the chairman of a certain committee that was about to convene sent a pressing request for his attendance.

"You will excuse Mr. Hartland and myself, I know, Mr. Creighton: it is in your interest we meet. I leave you in charge of the ladies."

They had a pleasant, lively party—after a while, music. Leoline played a portion of the overture to the *Trovatore*, then a fresh importation and just coming into Cisatlantic favor. Afterward Creighton sang "Ah che la morte ognora" to Celia's accompaniment, and persuaded Leoline to join him in "Ai nostri monti," though she could but just reach the lower notes.

After one or two of Schubert's songs, Creighton spied a volume labeled "Mozart." "Ah!" he said, as he opened at some selections from *Don Giovanni*, "it is refreshing to see anything so old-fashioned." At his request Celia sang "Vedrai, carino;" and together they executed the duett, "La-ci darem." Their voices harmonized admirably.

"You had music-lessons in Germany?" said Ellinor to Creighton.

"Yes; and I was about to ask the same question of Miss Pembroke," turning to her. "Have you been abroad?"

"In Europe? Never. But I had a German teacher in Philadelphia."

"Ah! I thought so." Then he conversed with Miss Ethelridge. His manner toward her was cordial and unembarrassed. Celia blamed herself afterward for having observed them so narrowly. She could not make out Ellinor's demeanor toward him. They were old acquaintances, certainly; but it was not the manner usual between intimate friends of the same age, even if of opposite sex. There was deep respect in it, as if Creighton had been twenty years older than she—her guardian, perhaps, who had cared for her from her infancy. Yet he seemed to be rather the younger of the two. Evidently she took the warmest interest in his welfare.

"Is your election doubtful?" she said.

"Very doubtful. I shall probably lose it."

Celia, who had taken one of her friend's hands between hers, felt it tremble as Ellinor asked, "Because of that vile handbill?" her eyes flashing.

"It will cost me a good many votes."

"Surely not!" exclaimed Leoline; and she proceeded, in her animated way, to repeat the conversation she had overheard as they were leaving the ground.

Creighton laughed heartily: "It's very amusing, this electioneering, though it is tedious enough sometimes. I feel flattered by the old man's comparison. The horse *is* a noble animal, and the farmer's best friend, too."

"But you have no idea how well your defender's hit about the cold corn-bread came off," said Leoline. "I know your speech made a good impression."

"There is in our people a strong sense of justice and love of fair play, to which one seldom appeals in vain. The handbill would probably have aided rather than injured me, had they left me a chance of reply. But they chose their time well."

"Ill, you mean," said Leoline, indignantly.

Creighton smiled.

"How *can* you take it so easily?" she went on. "I do believe you forgot, while we were singing just now, that Monday next is election-day."

"One likes to shake off the dust in the evening. Do not grudge it to me, dear Miss Sydenham. That last duett took me back to Göttingen. Miss Pembroke's voice and style reminded me so much of a charming family of musicians I used to visit there."

"And you actually forgot that handbill?" persisted Leoline.

"The evil which others seek to do us is worth forgetting only." Creighton turned toward Miss Ethelridge as he said it.

Again that tell-tale hand! But this time Ellinor gently withdrew it from Celia's clasp.

At this juncture Sydenham and Ethan Hartland returned.

"Mr. Creighton," said the latter, "your concluding remarks were taken down in shorthand, and are now in type for our *Chiskauga Gleaner*, of which we have hastened the publication one day, so that it will appear to-morrow. An extra thousand will be printed and sent over the county. Do not fear the result at our precinct. There is reaction already. Here you will outrun the party vote."

Creighton expressed his thanks in strong terms.

"It is we who are your debtors," said Sydenham, warmly. "We have temptations enough to hypocrisy already among us, without suffering an honest man's creed to be made a political test. I am sorry you live so far from us."

"I liked the expression of those faces

on the hillside to-day. I like the social atmosphere of your little place; and I have serious thoughts, when the election is over, of returning this way and asking you if you have not a small dwelling-house to rent or sell."

"You shall be heartily welcome. Come and make your home with me for a day or two."

"But if Mr. Creighton has to go to Congress, papa?"

"Then his time will be short; but we shall be thankful even for a flying visit."

"One doesn't like to be beaten, Miss Sydenham," said Creighton, "and I have had dreams of being useful if elected; but if Emberly is to be Congressman, it may be all for the best. A man's traducers often do him good. I am very sure I shall spend a pleasanter winter here, if I succeed in finding a home in this pretty village of yours, than I should in Washington City."

"At all events," said Leoline, "we'll do our best to make it up to you if these rascals, with their handbills, hoodwink the people. Won't we, Miss Ethelridge?" she added with sudden impulse, noticing that lady's anxious looks.

Ellinor colored just a little, was embarrassed for a moment, then replied, in a quiet tone: "Mr. Creighton deserves all we may be able to do for him."

Creighton seemed about to reply to her, but he merely bowed and expressed, in warm terms, his sense of the kindness with which he had been received at Chiskauga.

They parted, with sentiments of mutual esteem.

That evening Celia spent twice the usual time in doing up her hair. The comb dropped on her knee, and she dropped into a musing fit: "He liked the faces on that hillside! Did he, indeed! I think I could pick out one in the village that has more attractions for him than that whole audience, and can do more to make a winter pleasant to him than all of us put together: I saw him glance across at her when he talked of settling here. Then I should like to know what chance a man has of judging the 'social atmosphere' of a place which he has inhabited for just two-thirds of a day; especially when half of that protracted period was spent in two rooms —Dr. Meyrac's parlor and Mr. Sydenham's drawing-room. How transparent men are when they fall in love!"

Then the labor of the comb was resumed, but by and by there was another intermission: "I wonder whether a woman ought to reverence a man before she marries him—he about her own age, or even if he were two or three years older. I don't the least believe that I could. Isn't there a text about 'perfect love casting out fear?'" Another pause: "It's best not to let even a dear friend hold one's hand when it's not convenient to have it known what one is thinking about. But never mind, poor, dear Ellie! If that's your secret, it's safe with me."

Before Celia went to sleep she had come very decidedly to the conclusion that Ellinor Ethelridge either was, or very soon would be, engaged to Eliot Creighton.

The vote was close, but Creighton lost his election; and six weeks afterward Chiskauga gained an addition to her population in the shape of an honest lawyer and estimable young man.

CHAPTER XVII.

LABOR LOST.

ONE day, about a week after the election, Celia received, through the post-office, the following anonymous letter:

"MISS CELIA PEMBROKE:

"You are basely deceived, and you ought to be informed of it. J. E. M. has private assignations with Ellen Tyler in a lonely part of the woods on the bank of Kinshon Creek, about half a mile below her father's mill, where he reads poetry and makes love to her. Not long since the father caught them at it, and they had a tussle which M won't forget in a hurry: he carried the marks home. The girl is simple and innocent, and no doubt believes that he intends marriage. You know best whether he does or not. The miller might give her a couple of thousand dollars, but there is a good deal of difference between two and forty.

"The writer has seen you often, but is unknown to you. If you wish to know whether he is telling you a lie or not, ask Nelson Tyler. The new groom that Mr. Hartland lately engaged, and who worked several weeks at the mill, could, if he would, tell you something about it. ONE WHO KNOWS."

"Cranstoun!" was Celia's first thought when she read this startling epistle. She went over it a second time. The spelling throughout was correct, but not a stroke of the writing seemed his. She was familiar with his hand, having copied several law-papers made out by him for her uncle. And this almost resembled a school-boy's handwriting.

It annoyed her very seriously, especially the innuendo about her forty thousand dollars; but it did not unsettle her faith in Mowbray. She knew that her lover was acquainted with Ellen, for she had seen her frequently at Mrs. Mowbray's, when the girl came thither for her French lessons; and she thought it likely enough that Evelyn, in the course of his rides—perhaps in search of woodland to purchase — might accidentally have met Ellen, and even, for once, have read to her. But what of that? She called to mind that only two or three months since, one day that Ethan Hartland met her in the woods, they had sat down together on a log and he had read to her, from a pocket edition of Thomson's *Seasons*, some passage appropriate to the sylvan scene around them. To be sure, Ethan was her cousin; but then cousins do marry sometimes, though she had heard Sydenham express the opinion that they never should.* Celia was not the girl to discard one to whom she had given her confidence because he laughed and chatted with some one else: those who do ought to delay marriage until they learn better. She had read that wonderful thirteenth chapter of First Corinthians, and she acted up to its declaration, that Love thinketh no evil.

She thought: "Shall I trust an anonymous scribbler rather than one I have known since childhood? And then the creature thought me dishonorable enough to act the spy on Evelyn's actions—to go asking a comparative stranger whether the man I am engaged to is a rascal or not, or putting the same question to a servant who came not six weeks ago to the village, from nobody knows where? What a mean wretch he must be himself!" And, with that, after glancing once more over the letter, she threw it contemptuously into the fire.

Thus, as generous natures are enlisted in favor of the persecuted, this covert attack on Mowbray reacted in his favor. His mistress held but the more faithfully to her troth because others sought to malign and to injure.

Ten days later, Cranstoun and Cassiday sat together, in the evening, conversing. The latter spoke, in reply to some inquiry addressed to him:

"It's hard to come round them, Mr. Cranstoun—these highflyers especially, like Miss Celia. You never can tell how they'll take things."

"You're sure she got it?"

"You posted it yourself. How could it miscarry?"

"What makes you think it did harm rather than good?"

"First, the black looks she cast at me for three or four days after we sent it. She's over that now, I take such capital care of Bess; and then I told her what a splendid seat she had, and how much better she handled her reins since she took riding-lessons from the school-teacher. She's a stunner, is Miss Ethelridge. I've been out fox-hunting with the old Squire that fathered me, and I've seen those Irish girls take their

* Celia, like many others, had probably failed to distinguish between *affinity* and *consanguinity*. Ethan was not Celia's cousin-german, being a son by Thomas Hartland's first wife, not by Celia's aunt. He was, therefore, related to her by marriage only, not by blood. But it could only have been to marriages of cousins by blood that Sydenham, a man of discrimination, had objected.

fences—it's a sight to see, Mr. Cranstoun!—but if she's not up to any of them, may I never back horse again! I praised her to Miss Celia, too. She liked all that. She knows I'm a good judge. So I've got into favor again; but if she'd had her way the first day or two, good-bye to that snug little shealin' where I hope to see Ellen one of these days."

"Is that all your evidence? Black looks don't amount to much."

"No, it isn't all. Yesterday we had the sorrels out—Mr. and Mrs. Hartland, Miss Celia, and who else, do you think, in the carriage?"

"Not Mowbray?"

"Mowbray! Why he dar'n't come within our doors. The beaten candidate, Mr. Creighton."

"What! Currying favor with Hartland already?"

"Looks like it. He told the old man he'd make him a present of some specimens, I think he called them — stones or something—that he had collected in Europe."

"So he *is* going to settle here?'

"Did not you hear he was bargaining with Mr. Hugo for his house, just this side of Mrs. Mowbray's, on the lake shore? As pretty a cottage as there is in the village, with a handsome lawn clear down to the lake."

"What does he want with a house?"

"His mother's a widow, and she's to keep house for him."

"Mr. Cassiday, you were explaining to me how you knew that our letter had missed its mark. What has all this to do with it?"

"I'm coming to that. Hartland and this Creighton hitch horses together in politics. When we were out driving they had a heap of talk about that handbill, you know."

"Well?"

"Miss Celia, she joined in. And the way she abused every man that would not sign what he wrote! I did not quite hear it all. She was telling some story, I think, to her uncle: in course she didn't say a word about our little affair. But she was as bitter as gall; and somehow she brought it round that any scamp that would abuse another, and not set his name to it, wasn't too good to steal cold corn-bread from a nigger's saddle-bags."

"You are surely mistaken. She could never have said anything so coarse as that."

"Her dander was up, I tell you. I heard her as plain as I hear you. Pretty hard on us, wasn't it?"

"She may repent that one of these days."

Something in the tone caused Cassiday to look up surprised; but Cranstoun was not thinking of him, and didn't notice it. The groom feigned indifference, and said, in an easy tone: "Anyhow, that's a lost ball. I thought it was well shot, too. I've known a good deal less than that play hell in a family before now. I wonder what on earth the girls see in that stuck-up coxcomb of a Mowbray to cajole them so? If I were as mean as that fellow is, I'd want to creep into a nutshell."

Cassiday understood the meaning of the smile with which Cranstoun received this, and replied to it:

"Well, Mr. Cranstoun, you've a right to think just what you like about me: we've done some hard things, in our day, to raise the cash—you and I. But if I loved a girl as well as I—as well as maybe that rascal himself loves Ellen, for I'd like to see the man as could stand that smile of hers—may the foul fiend catch me if I'd turn away from her for money-bags! You don't believe what I'm telling you, and a fellow that's as bad as me has no right to complain. But I'm a gentleman's son, if it is on the wrong side of the blanket. And if gentlemen *are* wild, there's some things some of them won't do. That father of mine never paid his tailor's bill that I know of, but he'd have shot himself sooner than let a racing-debt run over the day it was due."

"Maybe somebody else would have shot him if he had tried that game on them."

"He had his faults, the old Squire had—rest his soul!—as mother knows and me, to our cost; but he'd stand the click of cocked pistol just as you would a knock at your door; and he'd put a ball through a good-sized wedding-ring at fifteen steps, every other pop."

"So you think Mowbray's meaner than you?"

"We say just what we like to one another, Mr. Cranstoun; so it's all right for you to ask me that. But if John Mowbray should take it in his head to follow suit, he might have a chance of finding out which was the best shot—him or my father's son."

"I have no objection to your trying, and I hope you'll hit him, Cassiday. But all I meant to ask was, whether you didn't think Mowbray was after the dollars, and not after Mr. Hartland's niece."

"I'll give you a plain answer to a civil question. If Ellen and Miss Celia had a fair start, with two thousand a piece, the niece would be nowhere, distanced, beaten out of sight. I'll bet two to one on that, and put up fifty any day."

"Stranger things have happened than that you should have a chance to find out, before another twelvemonth's gone, whether that would have been a safe bet or not."

It was more than Cranstoun would have said had he not been thoroughly out of humor, as baffled plotters are wont to be.

Cassiday took his hat and departed without a word, except the remark that it was time his horses had their supper. As he was measuring out the oats, the import of Cranstoun's last speech seemed to dawn upon him. "I must look out for my wages," was his reflection: "these guardians are the very devil. Who would have thought it, with that sanctimonious look of his? Cranstoun ought to know; he's constantly here, closeted with him; but the old fellow must be hard up if he has laid hands on Miss Celia's cash. Any way, he has promised he'd pay me the last day of every month, and I'll hold him to it. He can't get anybody that'll keep things as tight and bright as I do. I hope he won't run high and dry and have to sell his horses. I'd be hard put to it to find such another place."

It *was* a snug berth. Cassiday had thriven on perjury so far. Some rogues do thrive to the end of the chapter—the *earthly* chapter, which is but a small portion of the great Book of Life. Some accounts seem to be squared here. Others, unsettled, are carried over. The Roman who said that no man should be accounted happy till Death sealed his good-fortune looked but a little way. There are heavy debits of which he took no account.

What has been happening to Cassiday's victim? Did the world smile or frown upon him after his release from prison? We left him knocking at his own door for admission.

CHAPTER XVIII.

GOOD OUT OF EVIL.

How wonderfully does the principle of Compensation intervene in human affairs! How bright—as a grand old Reformer, poet and philosopher has suggested—how bright is often the silver lining of the darkest cloud!

It was a terrible injustice that had befallen our friend Terence; and yet, had the lines always fallen to him in pleasant places, it is doubtful whether, throughout a prosperous lifetime, he would ever have known such supreme and unalloyed happiness as when—just emerged from the gloom of prison-life—he took in his arms his weeping wife—weeping because no language other than tears could express the fullness of her joy. If all had gone well with him, it is doubtful if he would ever, with so stirring a conviction of mercies vouchsafed, have kissed his sleeping babes, lying there unconscious alike of the storm that had passed and of the sunshine that was succeeding it.

He was better as well as happier. There had been, till now, little or no evidence of the spiritual to be detected in that thoughtless, careless nature. Yet it was there. It always is where warm affections exist. It came forth now, at the moment when these affections were stirred to their depths. Not with much outward demonstration: the man did not go down on his knees, but his heart knelt to the Giver of all good. No set form of thanksgiving came to his lips, beyond the single exclamation that burst from him as Norah, between sobs, returned his passionate kisses:

"The Lord be praised for this blessed hour!"

Only an exclamation, yet almost as long as that of the publican who implored for mercy to him a sinner. All that sleepless night, as the young Irishman gradually came to realize his great deliverance, his soul prayed in more than words. The effectual fervent prayer—the availing one—often ascends ungarmented by human phrase, in robeless purity.

I do not assert for Terence anything like a change of heart. Nature, as Linnæus has expressed it, makes no great leaps. She does not deal in sudden transformations. The seed, the plant, the blossom, the fruit,—these are the types of her gradual workings. If there be examples of men regenerated by a single experience, these are so rare as only to prove the general rule of patient progression. In the present case the young man's better nature had been stirred: that was all. After influences must decide whether the first impression was to grow and strengthen, or to fade out, leaving him to sink back again to the level of his former life.

One of these influences followed close on his release. During the evening of the next day, Kullen, the prison-agent, came to see his emancipated client. No need to say how he was received! Norah gave him both her hands, unable at first, in her agitation, to utter a word; but, in default of speech, she offered to the preserver of her husband her matron cheek to kiss. Terence spoke with all the warmth of his country:

"Mister Kullen, it's owin' to you that I'm alive, and, more nor that, that I can stand up and face the world like an honest man. It's all owin' to you, wid yer cheering ways and yer lovely stories, that Norah's got a husband and the childher's got their father back agin. It's no earthly use to speak about payin' such a debt as that; but sure ye know, Mister Kullen"—here the tears rose to the poor fellow's eyes—"sure an' ye know, without iver my tellin' ye, that, as long as Norah and me's got a roof over our heads, come rain, come shine, let it be mornin' or noon or black midnight, ye'll be as welcome to our fireside as the flowers in May."

Then he hesitated, as if he didn't know exactly how to proceed. At last he brought out: "An, Mister Kullen, you wouldn't be refusin' a poor fellow the little he can do for you. I heard down yonder—it was Walter Richards tould me—that yer salary's but a small one, Mister Kullen, for all the good ye do. Now, ye see, I've got two hundred and fifty dollars in the bank, and sorra a bit o' use I have for it now, becase I can't buy the house, and that was all I laid it up for—"

Here the prison-agent interrupted him: "You need not say a word about that, Terence: the State pays me for what I do, and it wouldn't be honest to take pay twice, you know. But, since you are willing to do me a pleasure, what if I were to ask you for something that might cost you more than two hundred and fifty dollars?"

Terence's face brightened: "Sure an' I can borrow the rest," he said.

"No, I don't approve of a man getting into debt. You can do it without borrowing. How long have you the lease of this house?"

"Till the first of May comin': that's near five months and a half."

"Have you done well with it?"

"Very fair. Last year it cleared me seventeen hundred and fifty dollars. And this year, if it hadn't been for that damned—"

Norah laid her hand on his arm: "Not to-day, Teddy darlint—not to-day, just when the Lord sint ye back to me."

"Well, thin, I won't swear, Norah, ef ye don't like it. But ef it hadn't been for that scoundrel Bryan—bad luck to him!—sure there's no harm in callin him what he is, and wishin' him his desarts — I'd have made two thousand dollars clear this very year; and I can live on half o' that and lay by the other half."

"How much of the profit you make is from the bar and how much by lodgers?"

"It's close on half and half."

"So you expect to clear from the bar, between this and the first of May, some seven or eight hundred dollars?"

"Full that."

"Unless some rascal like that Delorny should play you just such another trick as he did."

"Yes, Mister Kullen; but I've hearn old sailors, as has been to the war, say that a cannon-ball niver comes through the same hole twice."

"Well, Terence, to confess the truth, I don't think it likely that anybody, in the next six months, will accuse you of going into a bed-room at night and stealing a hundred and seventy dollars. But something as bad might happen. Norah, did Terence use to swear when you lived in Cumberland county?"

"No, Mister Kullen, niver a bit: he's larnt it—"

"Behind the bar-counter?"

The young wife flushed scarlet, and looked at her husband.

"You're a good girl, Norah," said Mr. Kullen. "I see I shall have your help. Terence, what would you say if that eldest boy of yours were to come out with an oath?"

"Derry knows better nor that, Mr. Kullen: his mother's larned him better."

"I'm glad to hear it. I once knew an excellent man who had served as lieutenant, and then as captain, for fifteen years under the First Napoleon. He came to this country poor and learned English perfectly. He had received a college education before he entered the army, and he set up school and became an excellent teacher. One habit of the soldier, however, clung to him. When his pupils proved unruly he *would* swear. One day he was much shocked to hear a youngster of twelve, who had been with him a year or two, utter a round oath. 'Dick, don't you know you mustn't swear?' said his teacher: 'it's wrong and it's vulgar.' 'But if it's wrong, Mr. Tinel,' said the boy, half afraid to finish his question — 'if it's wrong, why do *you* swear?' 'Because I'm a damned fool,' was the rejoinder: 'don't you be one too!' Now, Terence, if little Dermot, imitating his father, should venture on an oath, would you like to give him such a reply as that?"

Norah interposed: "Where's the loss to be droppin' a word or two out o' yer talk, Teddy asthore—and a bad word at that—that ye should be refusin' the likes o' Mr. Kullen?"

"Well, it's little enough to promise for them as has done so much for me: I won't swear no more."

"But for your children's sake, and for your own, I want you to do something else, Terence. It's a good deal to ask you. I want you to give up that seven or eight hundred dollars — in a word, to close your bar."

Norah clasped her hands with a look of entreaty. Her husband sat silent, looking first at her, then at Mr. Kullen. The proposal evidently took him by surprise.

"Listen to me before you answer," pursued the agent, "and then I'll leave you to talk it over with Norah there. It would be a terrible thing, Terence, if a man like you, that God has given so good a wife to, were to go to the bad. And, let me tell you, that might happen. Men are not depraved sots because they frequent a bar-room, but they're on the way to be good for nothing, or worse. Then, a tippling-house attracts riff-raff. Yours attracted Delorny, a common drunkard. See what came of it. You're not safe among such men."

Norah turned pale, changed her seat to one close to her husband and took his hand in hers.

"It's true, Terence," added Kullen. "You're easy and good-natured—just the sort of man that might take the color of his life from the ways of his associates. Just the man, too, to be imposed on by swindlers. But no man is safe with thieves and perjurers around him. An innocent man's always more or less at their mercy; and next time I mightn't be there to help you out."

The tears were in Norah's eyes. Terence wiped them away with a gentleness one would hardly have expected of him, and kissed her.

"That's not all," said Kullen. "Do you think a man *deserves* to be helped out, if, after he has once been warned, he still keeps on with a business that makes men worse instead of better? I lived many years in the West, where crimes then were rare and could be easily traced to their source; and I know that two-thirds of them began in tippling-houses, and in the habits that grew out of them. Two crimes out of every three that were committed, Terence! and growing out of just such places as that room of yours below, where Patrick Murphy is tending bar."

At this juncture little Dermot came into the room. Kullen and he had made close acquaintance during the visits of the former to Mrs. O'Reilly, when he brought her news how her husband fared during his imprisonment; and the child ran, delighted, to his friend. Kullen took him on his knee and resumed:

"The very day you were arrested, Terence, you would probably, but for the arrest, have bought this house. The chances are you would have kept it, selling brandy and whisky to all comers, till this boy of yours was a young man; perhaps till he got into the habit of coming, two or three times a day, for a dram; perhaps till he learned to make companions of such men as Bryan Delorny. Are you quite sure Providence did not send you to prison that day, so that this chubby little fellow might grow up under more wholesome surroundings and with better associates? You love that wife of yours, Terence, and well she deserves it. Have you ever thought that it might break her heart if Derry turned out a drunkard?"

Norah had listened with ever-increasing excitement; and now she threw her arms round her husband's neck, gave him one bright, hopeful look, then laid her head on his bosom and sobbed as if her heart would break.

Love has its triumphs in the humblest breast. The good fellow, more than half persuaded by Kullen's earnestness, was wholly won over by his wife's silent emotion.

"Whisht, lassie," he said, passing his brawny hand soothingly over her long soft hair — "whisht, then, me darlint. D'ye think I'd bring up that babe to be a drunkard? I know what ye'd be axin' me, acushla, and d'ye think I'd refuse ye, this very day that the Lord brought me back to yer arms?" Then to the prison-agent: "Maybe the arrest was His doin', Mr. Kullen. It looks like He sint you to that cell to save me life and me character; and who knows but what He's sint ye here to-day to talk to me about Derry and that bar? It'll be all I can do"—he winced a little at this —"to make the two ends meet without the bar. But, ony way, I'll not be after standin' out agin the Lord and you and the lassie. I'll sell off the liquors and quit the trade bright and early to-morra."

Norah looked up, smiling through her tears. "Thin my heart's continted," was all she said.

Before Kullen went he said to Terence: "I heard when I was in Cumberland county that Norah's a famous dairy-woman. You understand market-gardening and keeping stock and managing horses. If you choose to go into the country when you leave this house, I'll recommend you to a friend of mine in the West, who wants a man and his wife to take care of his farm. Would you like to ride a real horse, Master Dermot?

"Wouldn't I, Mr. Kullen?" said young America.

Terence kept his promise. His former companions were not a little surprised; and one of them, a strapping young fellow, said that same evening, when Terence announced to them his intentions:

"So, Teddy, you've turned milksop since they had you under lock and key."

Terence's eyes flashed and he had an

oath on the tip of his tongue, but he remembered his promise to Norah :

"I've changed some of my opinions, Mister Malone, bein' I don't intend to sell no more drinks to the likes o' you. But there's one opinion I haven't changed at all, at all, Mister Malone."

"What's that?"

"That whatever a man's sintiments is, he ought to stand up to them *like a man!*" the last three words very distinctly accented.

Thereupon Terence deliberately laid off his coat on a chair, and took his place in the centre of the room ; adding, in a civil tone : "Any time ye're ready, Mister Malone."

But Malone didn't seem quite ready, and the others interfered :

"Not the last evening, O'Reilly : let's part good friends, any way."

"Ye're no coward, Terence," said Malone : "nobody ever said you was. And sure a man has a right to his opinions, and a right to sell liquor or not as he pleases."

Terence resumed his coat, and they all parted in amity. Whether Malone's conciliatory speech — just though the aphorisms were which it contained—tended to raise him in the estimation of the man he had offended, we need not too curiously inquire.

PART VI.

CHAPTER XIX.

THE SIX-ACRE LOT.

THROUGHOUT the winter that followed Terence's liberation from prison and Creighton's defeat for Congress, events of great importance to some of our Chiskauga acquaintances were ripening; yet on the surface matters seemed to proceed smoothly enough. The place made progress, socially and intellectually.

Under Ethan Hartland's supervision, Sydenham's land operations had turned out (as all bargains worthy to be called good, do) profitable alike to seller and buyer. There had, indeed, been attempts to evade the prescribed stipulations for building and improvements: men pleaded illness or bad luck—pleas sometimes feigned, sometimes real—and Sydenham's easy temper induced him to grant indulgence. This, as Hartland showed his employer, usually resulted in a sale to third parties, who bought on speculation and refused to improve, setting up the plea that the seller had waived his right to enforce the provision on that subject.

The young man said, one day: "Mr. Sydenham, may I speak to you very frankly?"

"If you think well of me, Ethan, you will speak to me frankly at all times."

"Thank you. If a purchaser, through ill health or bad management, is unable to pay his land-notes at maturity, and if you give him an extension of time in which to pay them, it is entirely your affair. If you can afford it, and if the man has done his best, I think it kind and wise in you to do so. But if he fails to comply with the stipulation for improvement, have you the right to indulge him? You gave public notice, through me, to all who desired to purchase, that your land would be sold only to those who would build and occupy it. You permitted me, also, to head the bonds of agreement with the words '*No purchase without improvement.*' It was a virtual promise on your part, upon which men depended; and, because of it, your land has been sold much more rapidly, for purchasers know well that the tendency of occupancy and improvement is to give additional value to all adjacent property. Thus it is no longer your affair only. Others are injured if you give way."

"That is a just view of the case."

"May I bring suit against these non-complying speculators?"

"Yes."

It made quite a flurry among them.

One man, who had bought up three or four farms, was overheard threatening personal violence against Mr. Sydenham. This coming to his ears, he sent for Ethan.

"Hereafter," he said to him, "I will take no excuse or apology whatever for violation of our improvement covenants. If you find any case where a deserving man, from continued sickness or other unavoidable misfortune, cannot comply with these, report it to me, and I will lend him the money that may be necessary to fulfill his engagement. In all other cases press the suits to a verdict."

Ethan smiled: "Have you heard of the threats Tom Bellinger has been making?"

"Yes."

"I thought so."

"I hold it a duty to see to it, so far as I can, that those who defy the law shall make nothing by it."

"Tom is from Western Missouri: they're a wild set there. Shall you arm yourself?"

"With a good, stout cane—yes; but I have no idea I shall need it. There is an old proverb that 'threatened folks live long.'"

Tom Bellinger subsided; and several other well-dressed men, who, for a month or two past, had been seen sauntering, with gilt-headed canes, through the streets of the village, gradually disappeared. Chiskauga survived their absence.

One, however, more obstinate than the rest, remained and resorted to law; his plea being that covenants for building and other improvements to be completed within a given time were of no binding force, and that a purchaser, even after such covenant in writing, was entitled to a deed as soon as the purchase-money was paid. The court, however, decided that covenants of that character constituted a lawful consideration, in which time was an essential element, and that non-compliance with them was legal cause of forfeiture.

From this time on, Sydenham added to the covenants of his land-agreements a provision that no assignment of such agreements should be made before the improvements were completed; and that on pain of forfeiture. This and the other covenants somewhat retarded the sales for a time; yet within five years from the day Ethan became manager the first two thousand five hundred acres were all sold and occupied. The alternate farms and lots that had been reserved from sale had, meanwhile, risen in value about seventy-five per cent.

Then Sydenham instructed his agent to offer these remaining two thousand five hundred acres at seventy-five per cent. advance on the prices to which, so far, he had adhered; but as this left the land still at two-thirds only of the current market rates, and as, by this time, it had become evident that Sydenham's stipulations of sale resulted quite as much to the benefit of the purchaser as to his own, this last-offered land went off even more rapidly than the first. At the end of three years more—which brought it up to the preceding spring—Ethan, one afternoon, reported the whole sold out.

"What net gain have I made," Sydenham asked Ethan, "by the advance of price, on this second installment of farms and building lots?"

"So far, about fourteen thousand dollars; but when your land-notes are paid up, there will be some eight or ten thousand more."

"You have managed well. The sales, I think, do not include a six-acre building site on the lake, just north of the Elm Walk—a site you admired, one day, Ethan, as the prettiest we had."

"I remember. It is unsold; I followed your instructions to reserve it, and to have it neatly fenced in and nicely graded, and laid out and planted. I could have sold it fifty times over. I refused two thousand for it last week: it is worth much more than that."

"Make out a deed of it to yourself, and bring it to me for signature to-morrow morning. Nay," he added, as he noticed the young man's look, "it is my turn now: you had your way last time. You made me do violence to my conscience by accepting your services for three years at seven hundred and twenty dollars."

"Which you increased, first to a thousand, and then to twelve hundred."

"It ought to have been fifteen hundred long ago. Please credit yourself at that rate from the close of this half year. As to the two thousand, I owe you twice that sum, fairly reckoned; only I thought the lot was as much as I could get that obstinate nature of yours to accept. And then, listen! I have additional work for you to do. You need not look so incredulous—I have."

The tears glistened in Ethan's eyes, but Sydenham proceeded as if he had not noticed them:

"You have been studying practical architecture of evenings, I know, and I've had proof enough what a neat draughtsman you are. I want a plan of a house. Now, don't be frightened, man: I'm not going to offer to build you one: you'll have to lay by money, and attend to that, one of these days, yourself."

Ethan could not help smiling.

"Ah!" said Sydenham, "now we can attend to business. I wish to have a 'Land-Trust Account' opened on the books of the estate. Let it be credited with that fourteen thousand dollars, or whatever the gain by advance on land has been. Then add to the credit whatever more may come in from the same source. You must help me expend this fund for the benefit of the village and of the neighborhood."

"It is a pleasure to work for you, Mr. Sydenham."

"Then pray set about the plan of my building."

"When I know what you want."

"Tea, in the first place," said Sydenham, as the bell rang. "Stay with us, Ethan, and let us talk this over."

Mrs. Clymer had gone out for the evening, and Leoline presided at the tea-table.

To an understanding of Sydenham's views, it should be premised that there were in the village two small public libraries—one belonging to a "Working Man's Institute," established ten years before, and the other the township library. The first had been aided by a gift from Sydenham and by a legacy of one thousand dollars left by an eccentric old gentleman named Lechaux: it contained about twelve hundred volumes. In the township library, to which Sydenham and others had contributed, there were six hundred; but both were in small, inconvenient premises, and were kept open one evening only in the week, when books were lent out; there being no fund to pay a librarian. The one public hall in the village would seat five hundred people, but was owned by a company of young men, some belonging to the brass band and others members of a Thespian society, and could only be had on rent from them. It was used for balls, concerts, theatrical representations, township meetings, political gatherings and the like.

"What I want," said Sydenham to Ethan, "is a plain, substantial, two-story brick building—the lower story laid out, at one end, as a library and reading-room, and at the other as a small lecture-room, to hold two hundred persons; the library to contain all the books belonging to the Institute and to the township, with room for two or three thousand more; and the lecture-room to be free for public readings, for literary or scientific lectures, and for the meetings of the Agricultural and Floral societies. The upper story I intend for school-rooms."

"For Miss Ethelridge?"

"Yes. I learn that she is likely soon to be crowded out of the two rooms she is now occupying in the public school; and they have long been too small for her."

"Altogether too small. She engaged a second assistant teacher last week. But there is one objection to the plan."

"And that is?"

"The noise of the school-rooms above might disturb the frequenters of the reading-room. Ah! I have it! Eight or nine inches of deafening below the upper floor. Then Miss Ethelridge's classes are always so orderly and quiet. It can all be arranged, Mr. Sydenham."

"We have a half-acre lot just opposite Mr. Hartland's: take that. Will six or seven thousand dollars put up the building."

"The latter, at all events."

"Then set apart, for the object, seven thousand from our land-trust fund."

Leoline startled them by breaking in here: "Papa, I do believe you are the very best man that ever did live. I'm so glad for dear Miss Ethelridge."

Ethan's face brightened with pleasure, and, as he looked at Leoline's kindling eyes, with admiration.

"I'm delighted that you think I've been behaving well, dear child," said Sydenham, smiling: "perhaps I shall stand some chance now of a second cup of tea. I've been wondering when you would make up your mind to pour it out."

"The common lot, papa! Good deeds shine like farthing candles in a naughty world. But, since virtue is not its own sufficient reward, there! not a grain too much sugar, not a drop too little cream."

"Lela dear, I want you to take a good look at that engraving, in the library, from Dubufe's picture."

"Of the poor widow who put two mites into the treasury?"

"Do you remember what was said of her?"

"That while others had lavished their charities, she had given more than they all."

"Yes. 'They, of their abundance, cast in offerings, but she, of her penury, cast in all she had.'"

"I think you'd have handed out the two mites, papa dear."

"Who knows? I have never been tried. In giving these people this building I do not abate one comfort, either yours or my own."

"But I think they ought to do their part."

"So do I, Miss Leoline," said Ethan; "I wish you would try to persuade your father to let me head a subscription with his name for seven thousand dollars, to be paid only on condition that half as much more is subscribed by others. The fitting up and furnishing of such a building will cost some fifteen hundred dollars, and we ought to have two thousand, in addition, to purchase standard works that are much needed. That would make the thing complete. It isn't the best plan, Mr. Sydenham, to let people, in a village like this, get into the habit of depending on one man for all public improvements. They value more that to which they have partly contributed."

To this Sydenham finally assented. "They shall have the management of the library and lecture-room," he said, "provided no charge beyond lighting and heating is made for the latter."

"And you retain in your own hands the disposition of the upper rooms?"

"That would be fair, and perhaps I had better do so."

"Decidedly." Then, after a pause: "You wish to give Miss Ethelridge what aid you can?"

"Certainly. She is an honor to the place."

"Then perhaps, as I shall have leisure on my hands now that we have sold that land, you would not object to my offering to give German lessons in her school twice a week. Some of her pupils are desirous of learning that language, and I am anxious to keep up my familiarity with it. But I shall have to say that it is your time I am giving her: she would not accept my volunteer aid."

"It is an excellent idea, Ethan. Carry it out."

"May I join Mr. Hartland's class, papa?" said Leoline.

"By all means, my child. Thanks to Miss Ethelridge, you read and write French fluently enough. I shall be very glad that you give some time now to a language that has always been a favorite with me. Ethan's accent is perfect."

When Ethan Hartland left Rosebank that evening he could not make up his mind to return directly home. A full moon shone down brilliantly from a cloudless sky. His heart needed the quieting influence. It was full of gratitude, and not without hope, but it was restless: the hope was dashed with uncertainty.

The figure that Ethan saw on the Lake shore.

[Beyond the Breakers.]

He took a path leading up the hill which surmounted Sydenham's residence, and, when he reached the edge of the forest at a point which overlooked the valley for miles, he sat down to commune with that restless heart of his.

It was a warmer heart than Ethan's common acquaintances at all imagined it to be; coming to him, not from his hard father, but from the quiet, anxious, affectionate mother he still remembered so well; as gentle, though not with as much character, as his stepmother. Strange, that these austere social dictators so often seek and win their opposites!—perhaps from an instinctive feeling of the need that, in the next generation, their own asperities should be corrected.

"If he knew, if he could but imagine"—that was the first thought—"what a kindness he has done me! How much more of a father than my own! In another year I shall have saved enough to build—in a very humble way, to be sure—but perhaps—" Then the heart began to sink a little. "So far above me—so beyond my sphere!—in education, in manners, in accomplishments! She ought to be a queen! Not that she assumes; ah no: who has less pretension than she? But there is no station she would not grace. And what have I to offer?"

He looked dreamily out into the soft moonlight: "It is not so brilliant as the blaze of day, but how peaceful! Who knows but that she might be satisfied with my lot? Peace is so much in this world—peace and affection. And how many, how many, miss them both!"

With that his thoughts reverted to a large, formal dwelling down in the village, where the heart of one parent was closed to him, and the pensive eyes of another awoke sympathy and sorrow—reverted to that half home, then wandered down toward the lake, past a stately avenue of elms, to a charming spot, untenanted yet, but where Nature and Art had combined to prepare a site for a simple, happy home. Nothing, indeed, to tempt worldly grandeur: a few acres only, decked out with no ambitious embellishment; fresh greensward sloping gently down to the pebbly shore of the lake; back of that a little tastefully-selected shrubbery intersected with a gravel-path; then a few clumps of trees so disposed as to leave vacant a building spot on the highest point of the site; back of that again, two or three acres of blue-grass pasture. Commonplace a worldling would have thought it—dull and commonplace: Ethan's thoughts invested it with a halo of light. The young man dreamed dreams—dreams of a picturesque cottage among those clumps of trees; and from its porch, shaded with woodbine and eglantine, he looked out eastward on the lake; then across, on the left, to its pine-crowned barrier of cliff, and saw the summer sun rise from behind the pines. And in his dream he thought: "Ah! if she were but here to rejoice with me in that glorious sunrise!" And, with that, there was a light step coming from within, and there was a gentle touch on his shoulder; and he turned to look into eyes that he had never yet ventured, except in dreams, fairly to encounter. Such eyes! He had found out their color at last!

Then it all faded away, and he was out in the dim world again, talking to men, attending to business. How tedious they were! He thought it would never end. But at last there came tender moonlight, and he was walking, all alone, down a familiar avenue, and thinking that while he had been gone, exiled from happiness, she had been sheltered from the fervor of the noonday sun by those old elms, and that she would come forth, by and by, fresh and bright, to meet him—brighter than the sun, more tender than the moonlight. Suddenly he saw, within that paradise of his, standing on the edge of the shingly beach, looking out on the silver-tinted lake, a figure in white: there was but one form in all the world as graceful as that; and was it waiting for him? He approached it slowly, with hesitation, as only half assured that he might, until it turned upon him those eyes—the same, only darker in the moonlight; and then he felt his welcome. He struggled to speak—as in dreams we often do—in vain. He awoke, on the hillside by the edge of the forest, alone.

Was this Ethan Hartland, the plodding, the practical? — the hard worker who had gone his round of humble duty year after year?—the prudent manager who had made so much money for his employer? What business had he with such dreams? Would any of his friends —even Sydenham who knew him best— believe it of him? Not one of them. Yet this was the man himself: they were acquainted only with the outer, work-a-day semblance.

Nor—though under the glamour of Hope phantasms had been evoked—was this dream of Sydenham's man-of-business all a dream. The moonlight was there; and there, in the distance, lay the lake, with a streak of silvery light dividing its blue waters. The Elm Walk, too—a dark line of foliage from the village to those blue waters; and near to it, out in the moonlight—

Ethan started up, strode down the hill, through the silent streets of the village, and then, urged by a strange impulse, along that dark avenue, turning to the left near its termination. No white figure on the lake shore—he almost expected to see it—but there, under his eyes, and in a few hours to be his, lay the fairy-land of his dream— the dotted groups of trees, the dainty shrubbery, the sloping lawn. These, at all events, were real. And something else which he had heard at Sydenham's, that evening, was real too. "Twice a week at least," he said, as he turned toward home—"twice a week! Thank God for that!"

The summer had passed, and the autumn, bringing with it events which we have already related. The subscription, as suggested by Ethan, had been filled out. The proposed building had been erected and fitted up: the libraries consolidated, additional volumes purchased; and the lecture-room had been opened, with all due ceremony, by an address from Sydenham. Three weeks after the election, Ellinor Ethelridge removed to her new rooms. Ethan's German class had increased in numbers; Celia and Lucille Meyrac had joined it, and Leoline, the brightest scholar among them, was a constant attendant. She thought her new teacher "was very nice."

This brings us again to the time when Celia Pembroke received that anonymous letter. It was not followed up by any others, but reports injurious to Ellen Tyler's reputation were bruited about, and became, after a while, a staple article of village gossip. No one was able to trace these tales to their source, except Cassiday, and in his heart there sprang up a cordial hatred of Amos Cranstoun. "The infernal hypocrite!" he said to himself. "To pretend friendship for the girl, and tell me she mustn't be ruined, and then set to work in the dark and blast her name!" But Cranstoun was still paying him thirty dollars a month to watch Celia; so he avoided an open breach with him, and contented himself with bitterly denying all scandalous stories about Ellen, and knocking down Mrs. Wolfgang's stable-boy, Sam, who was speaking ill of her.

Mrs. Wolfgang was a widow lady, past middle age, who had been many years in Chiskauga. She was a sister of Mr. Hartland the elder—an unfortunate woman, sour and vicious, who seldom said a good word of any one, and never missed a chance to pass round a piece of scandal. Through her, in the course of the winter, Cranstoun contrived that the evil rumors touching Ellen Tyler should reach Celia's ears; but when Mrs. Wolfgang broached the subject, the girl received it so frigidly that the narrator was fain somewhat to abridge her story. Her comments upon it, however, were sufficiently pointed and envenomed —so pointed, at last, that the resolution Celia had made not to reply gave way.

"Perhaps you can tell me," she said, "who is the author of these slanders."

"I only repeat what is the common talk of the town," said Mrs. Wolfgang, taken a little aback.

"You spoke so confidently that I supposed you must know who set the common talk of the town afloat. I dare say it was the same tale-bearer who sent me a letter two or three months since on this very subject, and was ashamed, as he well might be, to sign his name to the falsehoods it contained."

"Oh, if you take it in that way, Miss Pembroke, I have nothing more to say."

"I am glad of it, Mrs. Wolfgang."

The lady flounced out of the room. "The pert hussy!" she said, as she issued into the street. "Cranstoun shall hear of this. He's a fool if he'll stand that, even for forty thousand dollars."

Cranstoun did stand it for some time. He was playing for a large stake, which he was unwilling to lose by rashness, or to forfeit so long as a chance remained. But during a casual interview with Celia, one day, at her uncle's house, that young lady's manner was so unmistakably discouraging that he began to lose hope and patience. A letter from England which he received in April brought him to a decision. "I may as well try my fortune first as last," he said to himself: "she drives me to it; and, at the worst, half a loaf is better than no bread."

Thus, progress and plotting kept pace in our little village. A village is often an epitome of the great world.

CHAPTER XX.

PREPARING FOR AN IMPORTANT MOVE IN THE GAME.

CRANSTOUN was a man of quiet nerves and well-controlled temper. He was rarely excited beyond equanimity, and not easily startled out of his self-possession.

But any one who could have looked now through the Venitian blinds of his office — they were carefully dropped— would have doubted his right to the character.

Whatever the cause, he exhibited a degree of nervous agitation very unusual with him. Now he paced the small room in moody thought, head sunk and arms crossed behind his back. Now he seated himself before a large, baize-covered table, backed by numerous pigeon-holes for papers; absently took up his pen and drew a blank sheet before him; then threw the pen down, pushed the paper impatiently away, and fell into a long and apparently unsatisfactory fit of musing.

"I wish to God it were over!" he said at last, half aloud. Then he took from one of the pigeon-holes, and began to read, a half sheet headed: "COPY: *Letter to C. Pembroke.*" The letter, dated the day before, might have puzzled any one else to decipher, for it was covered and blotted with erasures and interlineations; and the final document seemed very short, compared to the original draft. It contained only these words:

"DEAR MISS PEMBROKE:

"When I inform you that I have a communication of the utmost importance to make to you—one which will disclose to you much connected with your mother's early history, and much involving your future welfare; and one which, if you do not hear it from me, may reach you unexpectedly through some less friendly source" (he had it, at first, "less *agreeable* source," but *agreeable* was erased and *friendly* substituted), "and under less advantageous circumstances—I trust you will favor me with an interview to-morrow at ten o'clock, or at any other day and hour more convenient to yourself. I name to-morrow at ten, because I learn that your uncle and aunt will both be absent at that hour, and I am *quite sure*" (these two words underscored) "that, when you learn the nature of the communication, you will wish it made without witnesses. I entreat you to believe this, and also that I am, most respectfully,

"Your friend and well-wisher,

"AMOS CRANSTOUN."

How that brow cleared as the keen eyes ran over the paper! The brief and unwonted signs of agitation had passed away, and there sat the man in his normal condition—the passionless player considering his next move in the world's great game, calculating its chances, settling down into conviction of its success. A complacent smile flitted over his features—a smile born of such thoughts as these:

"Nature cut you out for a diplomatist, Amos Cranstoun. A fool would barely have asked her for a private interview on matters of importance to her happiness, and would have had a plump refusal for his pains. But '*her mother's* early history,' and then 'a communication which might reach her unexpectedly through some less friendly source'—that brought her down. Curiosity, anxiety, apprehension—I stirred them all. And they, being stirred, dictated the message: 'Miss Pembroke will be at home at the hour named.' The gypsy would not risk a committal on paper! She thinks herself cunning. Well, I must play the game warily. But the devil is in it if I don't win with such cards as I hold in my hands."

We are told that the children of this world are, in their generation, wiser than the children of light. And so, in one sense, they assuredly are. Cranstoun, a true world-child, spurred on by lust of wealth, of station, of power, had studied his fellow-creatures—not profoundly, for the most astute rascality is not profound—but with sharp and careful eyes and shrewd judgment. In regard to a large portion of his species it might be said that he knew them well. Especially had his study been their weaknesses, failings, besetting sins, selfish ambitions, vulnerable points of temptation. To these he had the clue within himself, and he detected them with keen scent, and employed them with efficient certainty in a thousand cases in which a better man would have overlooked or neglected them.

Thus, in the race after riches and honors, the world's children, wise after their kind, often distance men who in all true knowledge are as far above them as the heavens above the earth.

But there is a point beyond which this worldly wisdom reaches not. Cranstoun had heard, and had often read in books, of generosity, self-devotion; uprightness that was proof against earthly temptation; love that was stronger than death. He had a vague belief that such things might be—a belief about as strong and definite as our grandmothers' faith in ghosts. These romantic fancies were not "dreamed of in his philosophy;" but somewhere, in heaven or earth, they might, for aught he could tell, have existence. He had never detected them, however; and he never seriously calculated upon them as disturbing elements having power to defeat any plan upon which he had set his heart.

Had Cranstoun, then, in his walk through life, never encountered any man without the taint of mercenary motive about him?—never met the generous, the devoted, the unselfishly loving? Beyond doubt he had met them, had come face to face with them, time after time.

But seeing, he perceived them not. There was nothing in his character to respond to or call out the noblest parts of theirs. The key was wanting. The highest virtues do not stalk forth ostentatiously in the sunshine. They do not, like the almsgiving hypocrites in Jesus' day, sound a trumpet before them in the synagogues and in the streets. They enter into the closet of the heart; and he who would thence win them forth to speech and sympathy, must possess the signs and passwords of the soul's freemasonry.

There were men, then, beyond his reach, because beyond his apprehension. Virtue is a generously careless leader, falling into many an ambush, paying many a time the penalty of over-confidence; but then, to fall back upon, she has an inner citadel, its pure recesses impregnable, because unknown, to her enemies—accessible to those only whom she vouchsafes to guide.

The clock in Cranstoun's room struck the half hour after nine. He started, replaced the copy of his letter to Celia, took from another pigeon-hole a package of papers, the separate titles of which he carefully examined before placing them in his pocket; closed and locked the many-celled depository of his secrets; and, after adjusting his dress in an adjoining room, issued into the street.

CHAPTER XXI.

THE DISCLOSURE.

WHEN Cranstoun was ushered into the parlor, he found Celia sitting at the centre-table, an open letter before her—the letter he had sent her the day before, as his quick eye instantly detected.

She rose, indicating a chair. Cranstoun had made the ordinary inquiries after her health, and then, somewhat unexpectedly to him, she took the initiative.

"You have written to me," she said, taking up the letter, "that you have some important matter connected with my mother's history which you wish to communicate. Have the goodness to inform me what it is."

There was a subtle something in the tone and the grave manner, rather than in the words, which fell unpleasantly on Cranstoun's ear. This young lady had hitherto seemed somewhat embarrassed in his presence, especially when he met her alone. She had avoided his look, and evinced trepidation sometimes when he spoke to her. Now, though she trembled a little, she looked him steadily in the eye, and awaited his reply in a quiet way for which he had not been prepared. He felt that his power over her was lessened—Sydenham's influence probably. No matter. He, Cranstoun, was master of the situation now. All this glanced through his mind during the second or two which elapsed ere he replied:

"It *is* of the utmost importance, Miss Pembroke; and I deeply regret to say it is of an unpleasant character: I most deeply regret the pain I shall have to give you. Let me hope that you will disassociate, in your feelings, the evil tidings and unwilling bearer of them."

Her sudden pallor and look of alarm reassured Cranstoun, and he went on with more confidence:

"The property which you have always considered yours does not legally belong to you."

"Am I not papa's heir? Is that what you mean?"

"You were so young at the time of your father's death, Miss Celia, that you may not have noticed in his manner indications of a secret burden."

"I remember," Celia forced herself to say, "that papa was often sad and thoughtful."

"He had good reason to be so. At the time he married your mother, and for many years afterward, he had a wife living in England. You will require proof of this. It is contained in your father's own letters."

He took a small package from an inner pocket, untied the red tape which bound it, and handed her the contents.

Poor Celia! The stern realities of life were upon her now. The actual shadow had fallen across her path at last. Mechanically she took from Cranstoun the offered letters, opened one of them, gazed on its contents. Her father's hand was remarkably fair and legible, but the characters gave back, for a time, no idea — no more than to an unlettered Indian they would. Her mind, after the first stunning blow, wandered far away, back to her years of childhood—to her earliest memories of her father—of her injured mother.

"Did she know it?" were her first eager words.

"Your mother? No. She died believing herself your father's legal wife."

"Thank God! oh thank God for that!" and the fast-flowing tears, for the first time, would come.

Cranstoun looked on, in curious astonishment. He had just been communicating to an orphan girl, who till now had borne a reputable name and enjoyed a handsome fortune, the fact that she was entitled to neither. He had thought to overwhelm her with the idea of dependence, of poverty, of the world's contempt. And her first expression was one of gratitude—almost of joyful gratitude, it seemed—that another had been spared the misery which seemed closing around her!

"No matter," was his next thought: "this can't last long." And in the expressive countenance before him, marking every change within, he already read that she was gathering up the severed links of thought, arranging and combining, out of sudden confusion, what were at first only vague shadows—beginning, in short, to realize her actual position.

"Miss Pembroke—" he began.

"Pembroke is not my name. It was not my mother's—poor mother!—but she thought it was! She always thought it was." And then the tears, in spite of her best efforts, would force their way afresh.

"Miss Celia—"

"Yes, that is mine still. They can't take it from me. Mamma gave it me."

"A name is of little consequence. The chief point is, that the property which you have always supposed you inherited belongs to another. You are not—" He hesitated.

Celia turned very pale, but she said, in a low tone, "I know—I understand—I am not a legitimate child. I have no right to my father's property."

"No, only to your mother's. Your father's estate goes, by law, to the nearest legitimate heir."

He had awakened a new train of thought: "Is she—I mean, is my father's wife alive?"

"No, she died nearly three years before your father."

"And he had an opportunity to remedy the evil he had done, and did not do it! I don't believe it. I am sure—oh sure!—that he loved my mother. You are not telling me the truth."

"I am, indeed I am. You need not trust to my word for it. One of these letters will prove what I say. But your father had every disposition to legalize his marriage with your mother."

"Every disposition, and not do it?"

"Yes. He was extremely sensitive to the opinion of the world, and he feared that a second marriage with your mother, no matter how secretly solemnized, might become generally known. Still more, he feared to disclose the truth to her. The very strength of his affection for her held him back from confessing that he had deceived her, and that she had been living with him for years as—"

Cranstoun stopped involuntarily. Was this Celia? How the world's lesson was telling upon her! Every trace of tears was gone. The glance was steady, almost stern, and her tone was cold and firm as she broke in upon his unclosed sentence:

"You have no right, sir—*he* had no right—to couple my mother's name, even in thought, with any term except such as may be applied to the best and the most virtuous. She deserved—and well you know she commanded, even to the last moment—my father's unbounded confidence and respect."

"It was that very respect, Miss Pembroke, which caused him to delay, day after day, what he earnestly longed, but had not courage, to do. Had he not, he would, at least, have made a will."

"Could he have left his property, by will, to mamma?"

"To her, or to you or to any one. His wife being dead, the dower in the real estate was extinguished. He had the entire control, free from incumbrance, of all his property."

"And even that he failed to do! But perhaps—" How new ideas were crowding on Celia as the several phases of her position, one after another, presented themselves!—this time, however, the new emotion had joy mingled with its sorrow. "Perhaps he meant—" She stopped again, and with flushed cheek and lighted eye she asked Cranstoun, abruptly, "Have I a sister?"

"Your father had, by his wife, one child, a daughter. But I know he never intended she should have any of his property in this country. When he left her mother, they separated by mutual consent, and he made over to her half his property, real and personal. At her death it would go to her child."

"A sister—a sister!" Celia repeated. But the light gradually faded from her eye, and she added: "Perhaps she would despise me. She might feel as if I had wronged her, and hate me. *Am* I her sister, or does the law say I am not?"

"You are undoubtedly her sister of the half blood, but I am not sure she is alive."

"Has she been ill?"

"Not that I know of. I am sorry that I have to tell you a melancholy story, that leaves everything in uncertainty. At her mother's death, as your father had not been heard of for years, and had caused a report of his death to be circulated, she was received into the family of her nearest relative, a Mr.—a Mr. Dunmore, her father's first cousin, a gay man of the world, addicted to horse-racing, and who was afterward appointed her guardian. There she remained several years. Among the fashionable frequenters of this gentleman's house, a captain of the Guards paid especial attention to Miss Mary—"

"And she married this captain?"

"She eloped with him, under promise of marriage, it seems, but has not been seen or heard of by her mother's relations since."

Celia sighed deeply. She felt as if the only gleam of sunshine in a stormy sky had been suddenly shut out. She would have given up all her property willingly, she thought—joyfully—if thereby she could but have won a sister, a sister's love!

"But some explanation must have been given," she said at last. "This captain—"

"He prevaricated—told first one story, then another. There was a duel, I believe. Finally, he protested, in the most solemn terms, that he knew not where she was; that she had disappeared in the most unaccountable manner; and that he had made every effort to trace her, but in vain. The cousin believed, or affected to believe, the story. Indeed there seems pretty strong ground for the conclusion that she came to an unfortunate end."

"Poor, poor sister!" And though Celia's chaste ignorance failed to suggest to her the horrors of which such a narrative opened up the possibility—for a great city has darker depths than those of the swollen river, last refuge of the suicide—still, she could not but feel that her own fate was mild and endurable compared to what had possibly been the portion of one who was born to name and to fortune.

Cranstoun was obliged to recall her thoughts to her own situation. "Miss Mary, if she be alive," he said, "is undoubtedly heir to all the property which you imagined that you had inherited from your father, she being his only legitimate child. If she is dead, Mr. Dunmore is heir-at-law. But ten years have elapsed since your father's death. He had evidently not been traced by his English relations. They know nothing, in all probability, of your existence, nor have any clue to the property that is in your guardian's hands. As you have enjoyed it unmolested until now, I do not see why you may not continue to do so as long as you live, if—if you will only act prudently at this juncture."

"What has prudence to do with it? I know, now, that the property is not mine—you have taken pains to tell me that—and you know it also."

"Very true. I know it; and if I were to sit down and write to your father's cousin, whose address I have, he, as heir-at-law, would sue and undoubtedly recover. But I have known the same thing for twenty years, and have never written to him a word about it."

Celia was silent for some time, and Cranstoun sat anxiously watching the effect of the hint he had given. At last she said:

"Mr. Cranstoun, you must have had some motive for concealing all this so long and for disclosing it to me now. What was it?"

Most persons would have been taken aback by so downright a question, and might have replied, in the commonplace style, that if the young lady would but consent to marriage, she would save fortune and name; otherwise, she would surely forfeit both. But Cranstoun, though a man incapable of appreciating nobility of motive, had been partially enlightened as to Celia's character by the preceding conversation, and was too shrewd not to perceive that such a move would be false and unprofitable. In a quiet tone he replied:

"As a member, however unworthy, of the legal profession, it was, in one sense, my duty to have made these disclosures long ago to those concerned, so that the persons to whom the property lawfully belongs might obtain possession of it. Cannot Miss Pembroke imagine why I have not done so?"

"I prefer to learn the reason from you, sir."

"It is very simple. I have ever been unwilling—at this moment I am more than ever unwilling—to take any step that should give you pain and do you an injury."

"But this does not explain why you have broken silence to me at last."

"If I could have believed that I stand as high in your esteem as I most earnestly wish and hope to stand, you should never have known a syllable of all I have told you to-day. As it is, can you blame me for seeking to inspire you with some sentiments of—of gratitude, of good-will, through the knowledge that, by my forbearance, you have lived in ease and affluence, your name has been saved from dishonor and your father's memory from reproach. Miss Celia, I desire, above all things in this world, your good opinion."

How smooth the villainy! How fair the words in which it was clothed!

Celia *felt* her way through it, as the blind sometimes safely thread field and forest, by an inscrutable instinct.

"Allow me to ask another question," she said, after a pause. "Supposing the forbearance of which you have spoken to continue in the future as in the past, do you expect me to live, as heretofore, but with the consciousness ever present that not a dollar I spend, nor an article I possess, is, of right, my own?"

"Most assuredly I do, Miss Pembroke. It was your father's intention to make your mother and yourself his heirs. I have personal knowledge of that. I am willing to make oath to it."

"No oath can make that mine which belongs to another."

"I beseech you, Miss Celia, to make no rash move, as you seem to purpose. It would be the very extravagance of Quixotic humiliation."

"You *do* expect, then—or did expect, at least—that, if no one disclosed to the heir-at-law—to Mr.—"

"Mr. Dunmore."

"—That if no one disclosed the truth to Mr. Dunmore, I would leave him in ignorance, and go on using his property as if it were mine. You are mistaken."

A man of the world might, on mature reflection — after taking into view the miserable anxiety which attends the holding of property by uncertain tenure, the chances of black-mail and like contingencies—have come to the same conclusion as Celia. She, at the moment, had no such thoughts. Her womanly instinct, cutting across them all, went direct to the precept, "Render to every man his due." Be such instincts ever kept unspotted from the world!

Cranstoun's version of it was, that, instead of being actuated by common-sense considerations of practical consequences—as of the risks she ran, the imprudence of placing herself at others' mercy, to all which it might have been hard to reply—the girl was moved by a mere romantic fancy, a figment set up under the name of honor, which he might succeed in combating.

"This is madness," he said, earnestly —"sheer madness, Miss Pembroke. It may be law, but it is not justice, that a far-off relative of your father—a gambler and spendthrift whom he despised—should inherit his property to the exclusion of his own daughter. The *spirit* of the law is, that the intentions of a dying man, if they can be ascertained, should determine the disposition of his property. You propose, as to your father's property, by your own act to bring about a disposition of it which you are quite sure he never wished, never intended, and which, if he were now alive, would be abhorrent to his feelings. Most deeply do I regret that I said a word to you on the subject. But how could I for a moment imagine that it would bring about such a result?"

"Is common honesty so rare a thing?" was Celia's thought, but she did not ask Cranstoun that question. She said to him: "You desire to take back with you my father's letters?"

He bowed in assent.

"Then allow me a few minutes to look over them."

They confirmed everything that Cranstoun had said. A portion of one of them, in which the main facts were the most distinctly stated, she read with amazement. Her father therein accepted an offer which, it appeared, Cranstoun had made to him, to maintain silence on the subject of the previous marriage so long as Mr. and Mrs. Pembroke should live, on payment of ten thousand dollars hush-money. She was so startled when she came to this passage that she interrupted her reading to ask, "Did you intend me to see all these letters?"

"Certainly," he replied.

He had asked her in marriage, he had just expressed eager desire for her good opinion, and yet he was willing she should see this memorial of his shame! Even in the midst of her own bitter griefs she could not help saying to herself, "What manner of man is this?"

As she handed him back the letters, she said: "Some time since you did me the honor to make to me, through my guardian, a proposition which I declined. I think you must be glad now that I declined it. We have neither thought nor principle in common. You think me, no doubt, a young woman lacking common sense; and I think you" — she paused, and then added—"the last person who would wish to connect himself in marriage with one who will henceforth bear a stain on her name and have to work for her living. I feel confident I may now assure my guardian that your proposal will not be renewed."

He rose, as much exasperated by her coolness as it was in the nature of his impassive character to be. He had made his great move and been checkmated by a simple girl.

"You will do me a favor," Celia added, "if you will send me Mr. Dunmore's address."

He bowed, and left her without another word.

Two hours afterward Celia received the following note:

"Mr. Cranstoun trusts that Miss Pembroke will excuse him for delaying to comply with her request for the address of the gentleman to whom the request referred.

"Mr. Cranstoun will not write to England for a week to come. If in that time he receives no letter or message from Miss Pembroke, he will conclude that the resolution she has expressed to-day is irrevocable, and will act upon that resolution.

"Mr. Cranstoun reminds Miss Pembroke that a knowledge of the facts he communicated to her this morning is as much a piece of property as any other. He placed it at Miss P.'s disposal without condition attached; and Miss P. did not see fit to avail herself of it.

"At the end of a week from this day (under the contingency above referred to), Mr. C. will proceed to dispose of it elsewhere. Whether the information be given in the proper quarter by Miss Pembroke herself or by Mr. Cranstoun, the result to Miss P. will be the same, but the result to others will be very different. In the latter case (*i. e.*, if given by Mr. C.), a reckless spendthrift will probably secure for himself half the amount involved, while the other half may become the rightful property of a man who will not spend it in dissipation and horse-racing.

"CHISKAUGA, *April* 9, 1856."

CHAPTER XXII.

THE FIRST DARK DAY.

"If there be an evil in this world, 'tis sorrow and heaviness of heart. The loss of fame, of wealth, of coronets and mitres, are only evils as they occasion sorrow. Take that out, the rest is fancy, and dwelleth only in the head of man."—STERNE.

THE shield of our fate has ever two sides, but, like King Alfred's headlong knights meeting at the cross-roads, we too often look but on one of them.

There is no stroke of earthly happiness so unquestionable that it entails not mischiefs unforeseen, and no human misfortune so heavy that it brings not its attendant mitigations. Barring the worm that dieth not, our short sight scarcely suffices to distinguish what *is* calamity. Evil changes to good, good to evil, even before our eyes. But this is a lesson taught only by experience. It is especially in the days of impulsive youth, fresh to enjoy, quick also to suffer, that we fail to discern the reverse of the shield. When the sun shines out, we rejoice as if it would never be obscured; and when the clouds arise and cover it, we droop as if its light were gone for ever.

If there be, aside from the stings of conscience, one unmitigated evil, it is that which a common phrase aptly expresses: we "lose heart"—a loss, as Sterne has well reminded us, worse than of wealth, of station, of all this world affords. For the world's goods and the world's high places may be lost and won again if, in the storm which swept these away, we did not lose heart along with them.

We speak of the night of adversity, but the darkness is often within us, rather than without; and if we but preserve the spirit to retrieve, the courage to undertake, the perseverance to prosecute, Ajax's noble prayer will be answered in our case. The struggle we may not escape—to contend is man's destiny—but we shall have light to struggle by.

It was dark enough now around Celia, poor child! And when Cranstoun was gone, and she was left alone with her thoughts, she remained in the gloom, for a time, with but a dim sense of some vague and terrible misfortune—of disgrace, of desolation.

Gradually, as she recovered the power to recall and arrange the thoughts that had wandered off, like worldlings deserting the unfortunate, the realities of her situation rose up, one by one, in array before her.

Not at first the ruin of her fortune, for the young and the generous, bred in easy affluence, and to whom life's comforts have come as comes the air to refresh and the sunlight to cheer us, do not feel, at the time, even at its true cost, the loss of money, though it be all they possess.

But it was the position in which her mother had stood—she so good, so loving: it was, even more, the conduct of her father—so fondly remembered, and who had always treated herself and her mother with indulgent affection.

Could it be? That father to whom she had ever looked up so dutifully, whom all men had seemed so highly to respect—had his life with her mother and herself been but one long, acted falsehood? Was this the world in which she had to live? Who was true? Whom was she to trust? Could any one have seemed more worthy of trust than her father?

It is youth's sorest trial when on its warm, trusting faith comes the first icy breath of suspicion. Well may the wounded spirit pray to be saved from the infidelity of the heart, from skepticism in human virtue, from unbelief in Truth and Righteousness upon earth!

Who was to be trusted? Was he to whom she proposed to commit the happiness of her life? What would Mowbray say? What would Mowbray do?

It was with a start almost of terror that Celia met the question as it arose in her mind. Could it be that she was *not* sure how her lover would feel—how he would act? Was she, indeed, losing faith in humankind?

Not quite that. But now, for the first time, she became conscious of an instinctive impression that both Mowbray and his mother prized station, set store by wealth.

And what was she? What had her mother been? Not her father's wife. The terms which a world, heartless and undiscriminating, applies alike to the vicious and the unfortunate—terms that grate so cruelly on the ears of the pure and the young—thrust themselves upon her. She seemed to hear them spoken, and she shrank, as from the public gaze, under a feeling of degradation.

Her mind dwelt on this until the thought stung like a venomous reptile. She rose and moved about, as if thus she might shake it off. She closed her eyes, as though to shut it out. But it seemed only to stamp itself the more vividly on her imagination. Then she began to reflect that it would never leave her as long as she lived—that she would bear it with her day by day, year by year—at night when she lay down, at morning when she arose. The thought became intolerable.

Ah! if she could only go back twenty-four hours!—could only feel as she had felt yesterday, the day before, throughout her life up to this very hour! What would she not give to be again as she was then!—to awake and find that all she had just been suffering was but in a frightful dream!

It is often as true of happiness as of time, that we take note of it only by its loss. Celia suddenly bethought herself (it seemed to her hardly credible now) how miserable she had sometimes fancied herself!—for what slight cause she had bewailed her hard fate to her aunt, to Sydenham!

Sydenham! A new train of ideas arose with the name, the first faint glimpse of light through the storm.

The words he had once spoken to her—the very words—came back to her now, in her sore affliction, as with a new sense. She remembered the flashing eye, she seemed to hear again the indignant tones in which he had said, "No man whose good opinion is worth caring for will visit on the daughter the father's sins. If any man ever does, take my word for it you are well rid of him."

She felt that she could yet count upon one sure friend. If the rest of the world forsook her as the child of shame, he, at least, would pronounce her innocent—her and the unmarried mother, well deserving the love and reverence she inspired, who had lived and died unconscious of her fate, unconscious of the stigma that was one day to attach, through her, to her daughter.

But even this gleam of comfort was obscured a moment after. It flashed upon her, as she recalled Sydenham's words, that at the moment she first heard them she had experienced a vague apprehension, dispelled afterward by Sydenham's disclaimer, that they might apply to Mowbray.

How was this? She trusted Sydenham, a mere friend; her faith in him was even stronger now, in the hour of trial, than before; but the man she had loved and had chosen from all the world as her future husband—twice, while these gloomy thoughts had been sweeping over her, there had mingled with them almost a doubt of his loyalty. What had Mowbray ever done to deserve this at her hands?

And then again she thought, if her present position *did* change his views, ought she to blame him? It was not that she was poor now: he was not much richer himself. It was not as if she had discovered that she was born of parents in the humblest condition of life: she did not, she believed, think so meanly of him as to imagine he would despise her because of a lowly origin, so that her birth was only honest; but now, disgraced as well as disinherited, could it reasonably be expected—

She was going on with this reasoning when there suddenly crossed her train of thought the idea—What if the case had been reversed? What if Mrs. Mowbray had been the deceived one, and the stain had been cast on Evelyn's birth?

Oh how warmly the conviction gushed to her heart that she would have met him with open arms—with a love far stronger, in his day of sorrow, than when all went well; that she would have rejoiced unspeakably to be able to soothe when the world frowned; to prepare a home, sheltered by changeless affection from the blasts without—a home where, if her constant devotion could make it bright to him, there should ever be genial warmth and pleasant sunshine! But it was not—and she sighed—it was not, she supposed, with men as with women!

She forgot, when she made this excuse for her lover at expense of his sex, that she had not, even for a moment, lost confidence in Sydenham. But it is little to be wondered at if the poor girl's ideas, all startled into disorder by the news that had burst upon her like a clap of thunder from a summer sky, strayed hither and thither, without much order or consistency.

A carriage at the door! It was her aunt and uncle returning. She retired hastily to her room, there to reflect whether she should communicate to them what had passed. Her first impulse was to speak of it openly. Then she reflected that without fortune she became, as it were, a pensioner on their bounty, until she could arrange some self-supporting mode of life. Her aunt, she was quite sure—shocked and pained as she must be—would never regard, in that light, her sister's child; but how her uncle would look upon it she did not quite know. So she concluded that she would think over her plans for the future before saying anything. This, at least, was the reason she gave to herself. There was another, unacknowledged, that probably had greater weight — the natural reluctance to make the first trial as to the effect which her disclosures would produce on those around her.

She made a strong and not unsuccessful attempt to master her agitation. And when, after half an hour, she descended to the parlor, no suspicion was excited. It is true that she went through the petty duties of the day with a sort of mechanical unconsciousness, and that her aunt once rallied her, in a tone of pleasantry, about her evidently absent thoughts. But the day passed, as the weariest days will; and she retired early to her chamber to sink into a long reverie, crowded with the thoughts she had so resolutely shut out while the eyes of others were upon her.

When she sought rest, her mother's image rose before her so distinctly, so vividly, it seemed but yesterday she had received her parting kiss. If she could but have laid her head once more on that faithful breast, and poured forth all she felt, and told how her love for that dear parent, that had grown with her growth, seemed increased and renewed within her, now that they were companions in misfortune! (It was thus Celia put it: her mother was alive to her still.) And oh, if she could but have heard, in reply, a mother's answering words of sympathy!—those words of the dear old time—what was ever like to them in after years?—that fell on the young heart like fresh spring flowers on the surface of a brook bright with glad sunshine. The earnest longing so grew upon her that she stretched forth her arms as if to embrace a tangible form. And then, as a sense of lonely grief came back, she wept long and silently. But at length youth and health triumphed over sorrow, and she dropped into a heavy sleep; not, indeed, unbroken by wildering dreams, but which lasted till the slanting rays of the sun, just risen, came cheerfully through an eastern window athwart her bed-chamber.

CHAPTER XXIII.

TAKING HEART.

" Quale i fioretti, dal notturno gelo
Chinati e chiusi, poi ch'il Sol gl' imbianca,
Si drizzan tutti aperti in loro stelo;
Tal mi fec 'io di mia virtute stanca."*
DANTE, *Inferno*, *Canto* II.

WHEN any powerful emotion, whether of joy or grief, has possession of us, it can hardly be said to depart, even during the forgetfulness of sleep. It rests, almost with a palpable weight, on our slumbering senses, as if importunate for recognition on the first instant of returning sensation. And thus the moment of awaking on the morrow after some heavy stroke of affliction is like a renewal of that on which the blow originally fell. Our earliest consciousness is a sense of some misfortune waiting to assail us the very instant our eyes open on the world.

But, after the first shock, Celia found herself more capable, than under the weary depression of the preceding evening, of reviewing, with some degree of calm, the new phases of her destiny. Sleep, that gives fresh power and zest to enjoy, renews also, in youth especially, our courage to suffer. A cold bath, her

* "As flowerets, by the frosty breath of night
Shut up and drooping, soon as daylight glows
Spring on their stems all open and upright,
Even so my wearied courage freshly rose."
PARSON'S *Translation.*

constant daily practice, while it braced her limbs, seemed to extend its invigorating influence to her mind likewise. Her toilet completed, she threw open a window that looked out southward on the valley, and sat down beside it.

To the healthy mind there is something strangely hopeful in the fresh morning air and the calm beauty of the early landscape. It comes to the sorrowful a reminder of happiness yet remaining. Celia felt the encouraging impulse it imparted.

All, except it be impassive or defiant spirits—and our heroine was not one of these—bend before the first blast of adversity, the brave heart and the cowardly alike. But there is this difference: some are of an inherent feebleness that is beaten down, like the slightly-rooted maize-stalk, hopelessly prostrate, to rise and flourish no more. Others, who at first seem equally overwhelmed, have within them a recuperative principle—an elastic spirit not to be subdued—that rallies when the immediate pressure is removed, and rises, like the lithe willow, erect, when the storm has passed. Happy he who is numbered among these children of hope!

It is often difficult, until the day of trial comes, to decide to which of these classes one belongs. This was now to be determined in Celia's case, and the first indications seemed favorable.

Hartland's house was situated, as we have said, on the southern extremity of the village. Beyond the shrubbery that immediately surrounded it lay a pasture dotted with small clumps of trees: the green herbage, with Spring's freshness on it, glistening in the morning dew. Beyond that again were grain-fields, their boundaries marked with a fringe of dwarf copsewood; and to the right, some three-quarters of a mile distant, rose that semicircular range of hills to which we have already alluded, with orchards which the rich pink blossom of the peach, now in its early bloom, decked out in gayest beauty.

Celia gazed on this placid, rural scene, pensively, sadly it is true, but without bitterness. The terrible impatience of suffering which, the day before, had caused her to pace the room as if to escape from a burden too heavy to bear, was gone. She sorrowed, but no longer as those who have no hope. The charms of the external world brought soothing, not flouting, to her sorrow. The small birds that made their home in the branches of the neighboring acacias, their blithe notes ringing out cheerily in the morning air, were welcome. Burns' poor, lost songstress complained to Nature of the earth's freshness and bloom—to the very birds that their songs broke her heart; and never did hopeless desolation find truer interpreter of its despair. He is steeped in misery to the lips who is beyond the reach of consolation from our great Mother, smiling on him in her daily beauty, speaking to him in her thousand voices of love.

But though the sense of an intolerable burden had passed away, poor Celia's heart was very, very heavy. And she began to think, more than the evening before she had, of the loss of property, and of the plan of life which it behooved her, in consequence, to adopt.

A chance thought first brought home to her a consciousness of the practical workings of poverty. She felt an especial longing, this morning, for her daily ride—for the free air, the quiet of the shady forest, the bracing excitement of quick and easy motion. But these were luxuries which she would now have to deny herself. She recollected that, in her guardian's accounts, he had charged her two dollars and a half a week for the keep and care of Bess. She had never bestowed a second thought on the item; but now it occurred to her that, if she was to seek her own living, a hundred and thirty dollars annually added to her expenses, for an object not at all of necessity, was an imprudence which she must avoid. It cost her a pang to come to this conclusion. To part with her beautiful pony, so gentle, so spirited, that she had learned to love so well—Sydenham's gift, too!

The breakfast-bell broke in on these unwelcome cogitations. Hartland kept early hours, according to the primitive habits of the country: it was half-past six.

The breakfast passed over without comment. The uncle's thoughts were engrossed with a butterfly—a new species he had found the day before—and he dilated to Celia on its beauty. Mrs. Hartland looked anxiously at her niece several times. As they rose, and after Mr. Hartland had gone, she said,

"Celia, my love, are you not well?"

"Quite well, dear mother, except a slight headache, and, I believe"—she tried to say it lightly—"a touch of low spirits. An hour or two in the saddle will do me good."

"Is anything wrong, my child? Has Mowbray—"

"Do not alarm yourself about Mowbray and me. Nothing has occurred between us except what you know. I dare say it is all best just as it is."

"There *is* something wrong, Celia, or you would not—"

"Between Mowbray and me, nothing, I do assure you, mother. I have not seen him, or heard of him, for several days."

"It is so unnatural for you to say, while your uncle seems to become daily more averse to your marriage, that it is all for the best."

"Did I say so?"

"Did you not?"

"I was thinking, I believe, how necessary it is to be very, very sure of a man's character before one marries him. And you know, mother, that in two or three years I shall be absolutely free to choose, if, in the mean time, neither Evelyn nor I change our minds."

"*If* neither of you change!"

"Why should we not? This is a changeful world. Circumstances change, and they say we are the creatures of circumstances. And how much better that a lover should change before marriage than a husband afterward!"

"This from you, Celia!"

"Is it not true, dear mother? And in a world of such uncertainty, is it not well to be prepared for the worst? Have I been so thoughtless hitherto," she added, with a faint smile as she noted Mrs. Hartland's increasing anxiety, "that if I utter a sage reflection or two on the instability of human affairs, you must needs conjure up mystery and misfortune?"

"I do not know you, this morning, my child. Your dear mother felt, when she confided her orphan to my hands, that she would never want a parent's care or sympathy while I lived. And you used to confide in me, Celia.'

Poor Celia's tears, with difficulty restrained till now, filled her eyes. She threw her arms round Mrs. Hartland's neck and kissed her again and again. "I do, oh indeed I do!" she said. "My own mamma could not have been kinder. Pray, pray, don't cry. You shall know all that has been vexing me. But not now. I know Mr. Hartland expects you in the library to color the sketch of that wonderful butterfly he has been describing to us; and there is Bess at the door. When I return you shall know all."

"It has nothing to do with Mowbray?"

"Dear mother that cares so much about my happiness! I have already told you that nothing whatever has passed between Mowbray and me that need distress you."

"Then I dare say all will be well yet."

"Perhaps."

"You are a riddle to me this morning, Celia. But there is Mr. Hartland's voice. A pleasant ride, dear child."

Through bypaths that skirted the village, Celia reached the main road leading west toward the railroad station: then she put the little mare to a canter, caught a glimpse of Mr. Harper at work in his flower-garden as she passed, arrested the animal's inclination to take the side road which turned off to Sydenham's residence, and galloped on, without drawing rein, until she was fairly in the shelter of the woods. There she checked Bess's speed, and, a little farther on, diverging from the main road into a path on the right hand—an ancient Indian *trace* that led to Tyler's mill—she found herself traversing the same solitude that had been broken, a hundred years before, only by tread of wild beast, or of the red man, scarcely less wild, who was pursuing him.

There is something wonderfully tranquilizing in the deep stillness of these primeval forests. Alone with Nature in one of her most impressive garbs, that which is natural and genuine in our feelings expands, and asserts the mastery over the meretricious and the conventional. Under that stately shelter we seem, in a measure, protected from the capricious influences of an artificial world. In the haunts of men the eternal principles of right and justice appeal to the reason: here they speak to the heart. We distinguish truth in society, but we feel it in the solemnity of the forest.

This was telling now upon Celia. Her rapid ride, too, had had its usual inspiriting effect. The fresh bloom came in her cheeks; the languor was gone from her eye; her courage rose. The spirit of the place was upon her: the very color of her destiny seemed to change under the influence of the scene.

As, in such mood and with slackened rein, she passed slowly on, an incident occurred, of which the results materially influenced her fortunes.

PART VII.

CHAPTER XXIV.

A TALK IN THE FOREST.

"L'alternative des succès et des revers a son utilité. Nous nous plaignons de l'inconstance de la fortune. C'est de sa constance que nous devrions nous plaindre; alors, en effet, elle a plus de moyens de nous corrompre."*

DEGERANDO, "*Du Perfectionnement Moral.*"

ONE of the long vistas characteristic of the rude country-paths by which the early settlers threaded their way from cabin to cabin opened before Celia; and the animal she rode, raising its head and pointing its small, taper ears, caused the rider to look round, in expectation of some one's approach.

The road before her was vacant, but off to the right, through the open woods, gay with blossoms of the dogwood and the redbud, she thought she distinguished in the distance a horseman, riding in the same direction as herself.

"It must be Sydenham," she thought, for she knew that the bridle-path from his residence to Tyler's mill led through these woods, and connected, a few hundred yards farther on, with the road she was pursuing. Yes, it was he. But how was she to meet him?—what to say to him? Should she reveal all, and ask his advice?

An hour before she would have shrunk from such a disclosure. But now a quickened pulse gave bolder impulses. She took heart. She felt that the world must soon know her real position; and who so worthy of her confidence, or so capable to counsel her in her present strait, as her mother's trusted friend, to whom she was already beholden for so much encouragement in her former troubles—ah, such petty troubles they seemed now! But if she was to say anything to him at all, it must be at once, ere courage cooled: she felt that.

If she had any remaining hesitation, it was dispelled by Sydenham's manner—the evident pleasure with which he met her, the cordial earnestness with which he extended his hand and inquired after her welfare.

"And Bess still continues to behave well?" he asked as they rode on together.

"No creature could behave better. So full of spirit and so docile, too, as she is! She knows me, and I do believe loves me, for she will come at my call, from the farthest corner of our pasture. It is hard to part with a favorite," she added, sadly, stooping over the pony's neck and patting it fondly.

The tone, more than the words, arrested Sydenham's attention.

"I know, Mr. Sydenham," she rejoined, looking up, "that you must have thought me foolish and unreasonable."

"When?"

"Do you remember the day Brunette ran away with Mrs. Hartland and Lela—the day we had that long conversation together?"

"As if it were yesterday."

"You thought me weak and childish then: do not deny it."

"I thought you inexperienced — depressed without sufficient cause. I did miss in you a certain force of mind — a spirit that often lies dormant within us till circumstances call it forth."

"I am ashamed of myself when I look back upon it. I know now exactly what you must have thought of me. I hope you are right when you say that there is often within us more than appears during prosperity. I had everything to make me happy in those days—everything: kind friends, a respected name, an easy competency. I had nothing, absolutely nothing, as an excuse for low spirits. The delay of my marriage with Mowbray, how little, in reality, did that signify! I once heard you say that girls marry too young in this country.

* "The alternation of success and reverse is useful. We complain of the inconstancy of fortune, but its constancy would corrupt us more."

PEABODY'S *Translation.*

So they do: they marry in haste, to repent at leisure."

Sydenham was thoroughly alarmed. "What is the matter?" he said. "Tell me at once."

"Why do you imagine that something terrible has happened?"

"What is it, Celia? It is useless to attempt to deceive me. Some influence is changing your character. It is not the old Celia I used to know."

"Do I look as downcast now as when I came to complain to you that day of my hard fate?"

"No: you are a different creature. You are agitated, and I am sure something is amiss. But there is a light in your eye and a determination in your tone that seem anything but downcast."

"I am glad of it. At least you will not feel contempt for me."

"Celia, do I deserve this? Did I not promise your mother that I would watch over her daughter's happiness? Why will you keep me in suspense? What is it?"

"My father deceived that mother you knew so well. He was already married. I am an illegitimate child. Not a dollar of my father's property belongs to me. I am a penniless orphan, who must work for her bread and mâke her own way in the world."

"Good God!"

And Sydenham involuntarily checked his horse so sharply that the spirited animal started and reared against the bit.

For a moment the girl and her auditor seemed suddenly to have exchanged characters. She sat erect and quiet, her graceful form drawn up to its full height: her young face, shaded by the wide-rimmed riding-hat, very sad indeed, but quite calm; and though her voice trembled somewhat, she spoke so deliberately, and met Sydenham's first agitated glance of alarm, astonishment, incredulity with a look so steady and collected, that it took him almost as much by surprise as the astounding tidings she had just imparted.

But this was for the first moment of excitement only, and then nature and habit reasserted their power. Sydenham's evident dismay was communicating itself to Celia. He saw it, and it recalled his self-possession at once. Putting his horse again in motion, he came close to her side and spoke in his usual tone:

"So! You *have* surprised me. Ah, this comes from Cranstoun."

"Yes."

"The man is capable of any duplicity. Did he give you proof?"

"Papa's own letters, written about seventeen years ago, admitting the fact of his previous marriage, and adjuring Cranstoun to silence."

"You are sure of the handwriting?"

"Perfectly sure. Mamma preserved many of papa's letters: I have read them often, and I cannot be deceived in this."

"It may be," said Sydenham, after a pause, for the strange influence Cranstoun had maintained for years over one so dissimilar to him in character and station occurred forcibly to his mind. "It may be — probably it is. At all events, the facts can be positively ascertained, and they shall be."

"Oh they are true: do not doubt it, Mr. Sydenham. They explain so much in papa's conduct that was unaccountable till now."

"I have admitted that they are probable. Well, Celia?"

"It is very terrible, is it not?"

"No. I fear I have forfeited all claim to be believed when I say so. You did startle me, Celia — that is the truth— coming out with that sudden, solemn announcement, but there is nothing terrible in what you told me."

"Have I not just cause for unhappiness?"

"For unhappiness, no: for regret, certainly. It is a very painful thing to hear of a parent's misconduct."

"Oh so very painful!"

"And it would not be one's duty, as it is, to watch over the preservation of one's property if its loss were not an evil."

"I remember well your once explaining to me how much independence there is in forty thousand dollars."

"You have a good memory, and I

will not gainsay that opinion. Independence is the power to act, within lawful limits, as we please; and money adds greatly to that power. I am very sorry for your loss; yet, after all, it may prove a gain to you."

"I have often read," said Celia with a sigh, "of the chastening and purifying effects of adversity."

"That sentiment is to be taken with some grains of allowance. Many, doubtless, have been able to say from the heart, 'It is good for me that I have been afflicted.' But there *is* a grinding adversity that crushes oftener than it reforms. I have seen terrible things in the course of my life, Celia—not here, but in the Old World—terrible things that make one shudder to recall them: entire masses of human beings dying for lack of food; selling their youth and their health, and at last their very lives, for a pittance too small to keep body and soul together. I was in Ireland during that dreadful famine of 1847. It haunted my dreams for years! Ah, Celia, if you could but imagine the utter destitution that is the lot of millions, how small would seem your present loss! — how numberless the comforts that are still within your reach!"

Sydenham's kindling eyes and stirring words touched Celia to the soul. How faithfully the heart feels for others when it begins to learn sorrow by experience of its own!

"It is true," she said, submissively. "I should be most unthankful if I forgot that I have far more to rejoice at than to deplore. If I may but retain the affection and esteem of my friends! But some of them of course I shall lose—"

"Is that your idea of friends? I esteem you much more than I did before. To me there was always something pleasant and attractive about you, Celia. But I confess you have sometimes seemed to me, like many other girls one meets with in the world, very good and amiable doubtless—"

"Love-sick damsels, in short."

"I never thought you that. But one felt the lack of something vigorous, racy, self-relying. You are gaining that. You bear this trial admirably well. I see that it will be of real service to your character. Why, it has strengthened it already. You are coming out grandly, Celia."

How grateful sometimes—more genial than sunshine, more welcome than the first fresh air of spring — comes the breath of praise from those we love! It brings on its wings healing to the wounds of sorrow, healthy invigoration to the spirit sick and depressed. Wholly unwonted as it was from Sydenham, it proved to Celia, at this juncture, inexpressibly soothing. Her heart felt braver at each word.

"Ah, Mr. Sydenham," she said, "if others did but feel as you do, how easily I could bear the loss of fortune, and even of name! But you, who never deceive any one, even in kindness, will not tell me that of those who flattered the heiress none will desert the penniless girl with a stain on her birth."

"You are right. I shall certainly not try to persuade you that you will lose no flatterers. I do not even say that you will have the same chance which the heiress might have had of enlarging your circle of acquaintances."

"I know it well. Ah! that true line of the ballad — 'The poor make no new friends.'"

"Now you are running away with the idea. That line *is* touchingly true, and it came from the experience of the heart, whoever wrote it. But there is little chance that it should ever apply to you. You do not know — I hope you never will—what poverty means."

"I must work for a living now."

"But that is not poverty in this country, especially in a village like Chiskauga. It is not even hardship, if one has an education to fit for useful and profitable employment, with good friends to interest themselves in procuring it; and you have both, Celia. No new friends! Look round you, and see how many maintain themselves happily, reputably, increasing both in money and in friends, with far less resources. Your education has been no common one. You have a good knowledge of two foreign languages:

Ethan speaks highly of your progress in German. Your talent for music, rare by nature and carefully cultivated, is, in itself, a competence. I admit that you no longer possess the independence which a surplus of money bestows; but you have a surer one, of which no man can deprive you—the independence which lies in labor—less honored than the other, but more honorable. And if, in seeking it, you find those whom you call friends dropping away, let them go! You are better without them."

"You think, then, that this reverse of fortune is a gain instead of a loss to me."

"The future must determine that. Many pleasant things, of course, you will lose by it—the opportunity of traveling, for instance. I know you have had dreams of Switzerland and Italy, and I'm afraid I had something to do in nursing them. The very butterfly acquaintances that come round us when the sun shines, though they may not be friends, are often agreeable, well-informed people, whom we may like to meet and be sorry to lose. But then you gain one of the essentials to happiness."

"What is that?"

"A regular, settled object in life — a steady pursuit (I see you have determined on that), requiring daily exertion of body and mind. I'd like to give you —for it touches your case—a recollection of my childhood?"

"If it is not encroaching on your time, Mr. Sydenham, I should be delighted. But you came out on business, did you not?"

"Chiefly for exercise this fine spring weather, with a message from Leoline to Nelson Tyler about flour." They were then within a few rods of the mill. "Let me deliver it, and my time is entirely at your service for the rest of the morning."

They rode up, and the miller, his gray clothes well sprinkled with dust, came out to greet them, and to ask Mr. Sydenham what he could do for him. After he had taken an order for two barrels of flour, Celia, whose thoughts had reverted to the anonymous letter, inquired after Ellen's welfare. A slight shade came over the miller's hearty manner and open face, but after a moment's hesitation he called to his daughter, his deep, base tones reaching their dwelling, which stood a little way off. Thence Ellen came forward, fresh and neat indeed, but with a look of depression over her pretty features. When she recognized Celia, a sudden blush overspread face and bosom.

"Ellen," said her father, himself somewhat embarrassed, "Miss Celia has been asking after you."

Celia extended her hand and shook Ellen's cordially.

"We seldom see you in town now, Ellen," she said: "are you no longer taking French lessons from Mrs. Mowbray?"

The blush, which had been passing away, deepened again. But the girl struggled for composure: "No, Miss Celia. Mrs. Mowbray's French class is broken up, and—and it's expensive to take private lessons."

"Do you wish to join another class?"

Ellen looked at her father.

"The reason I ask," added Celia, "is, because I may have a French class myself one of these days."

"You!" said the girl, her blue eyes dilating with astonishment. "I thought rich folks—"

"I am not rich; and, besides, it is a good thing for young people to do something for a living."

"I should be very glad, Miss Celia—that is—if father—" She stopped, reading dissent in his face.

"It's very kind of you," he said—"*very* kind, Miss Celia: I shall not forget it. If Ellen takes any more French lessons, I'll send her to nobody but you. But I think she's had as many as will do her any good for the present. That was a true word you said, miss, that young folks should do something for a living; and this lass of mine" — he patted her head—"she's a good girl, if she does dress out now and then, and even herself to them that cares little for her—she does what she can to take her dead mother's place. I want to do the best for her, if I only knew what *is* best. If anything were to happen to me—"

"Oh don't, father, don't!" said the girl, her eyes full of tears; and then, ashamed of her emotion, she made a sudden retreat to the house.

"You must excuse her, miss," said Tyler to Celia: "she don't mean to be uncivil, and it's done her good that you spoke so kind to her; but she can't stand it to think the old man must go one of these days. Mr. Sydenham, you may count on having that flour this evening."

They bade the miller good-morning, and turning homeward rode on for some time in silence. Then Sydenham said:

"I am glad that we called there this morning, and very glad that you spoke to Ellen as you did. As the father said, it did the poor child good."

"I like Ellen. But I was afraid you might think me premature in beginning to electioneer, as politicians say, for pupils already."

"Far from it. Promptitude is one of the elements of success."

"But that anecdote, Mr. Sydenham—or was it an anecdote you were about to tell me?"

"Yes. My good father—a man who, even to extreme old age, maintained habits of active employment—was speaking, one day, of an English friend of his, Mr. Walsingham — one of those whom the world considers eminently fortunate. A man of letters, educated to every classical attainment and the inheritor of a princely fortune, he had been able to gratify, at a wish, his cultivated tastes. He had married, in early life, an amiable wife, and had seen his children (though he never personally concerned himself with their education) grow up around him with the fairest promise. He had a handsome town-house in a fashionable square in London, and a country-seat ten or twelve miles off, in the midst of one of those magnificent English parks—the ideal of stately rural elegance, with its trimly-kept lawn and its widespreading chase, dotted over with clumps of noble old trees, where the deer sought refuge from the noonday heat and a lair at nightfall."

"I have so often heard of these beautiful English parks, and dreamed that some day I might see one."

"The dream may come true, for all that is past, Celia. Mr. Walsingham had traveled over Europe, and brought back, as mementoes of his journey, paintings and statuary by some of the best masters, ancient and modern, with which to adorn his favorite retreat. The house itself (I have seen it since), with its rich marble columns and balustrades, was a fine specimen of the purest Palladian manner, where all that luxurious refinement could devise had been unsparingly lavished. There my father found his friend with no occupation more pressing than to pore over the treasures of his library, and no graver care than to superintend the riches of a conservatory where wealth had brought together, from half the world, its choicest plants and flowers."

"What a charming life!" exclaimed Celia. "How happy he must have been!"

"That was my father's thought. They spent some days in undisturbed quiet: not an incident, beyond the conversation of a sedate and intellectual family circle and the arrival and departure of a friend or two, to break the complete repose. Delightful it was to my father, no doubt, in contrast with the city bustle and the constant occupation he had left. One morning he said to his host: 'I have been thinking that if I ever met with a man who has nothing left to desire, you are he. Health of body, cultivation of mind, a charming family, wealth and all it procures — whatever Nature and Art present of most beautiful — you have them all. Are you not completely happy?' Never, my father said to me, should he forget the dreary sadness of the unexpected reply: 'Happy! Ah, Mr. Sydenham, I committed one fatal error in my youth, and dearly have I abied it! I started in life without an object, even without an ambition. My temperament disposed me to ease, and to the full I indulged the disposition. I said to myself, "I have all that I see others contending for: why should I struggle?" I knew not the curse that lights on those who have never to struggle for anything. Had I created for myself a definite pursuit—literary, scientific, artistic, social, political, no matter what, so there was something to labor for and to overcome—I might have been happy. I feel this now—too late! The power is gone. Habits have become chains. Through all the profitless years gone by, I seek vainly for something to remember with pride, or even to dwell on with satisfaction. I have thrown away a life. I feel, sometimes, as if there were nothing remaining to me worth living for. I am an unhappy man.' That was my father's story. I never forgot it, and I trust I have profited by its lessons."

"And so will I, Mr. Sydenham. Indeed, indeed, you shall not have to forego your good opinion of me. I know how much you have been doing to benefit our village and its inhabitants. Perhaps—oh, in a very humble way I know it must be—but yet perhaps I may be able to aid you, just a little, while I provide for my own support."

"You are thinking of a school. That is right. You really possess a gift for teaching, as grateful Ellinor Ethelridge can testify."

"Dear Ellie! I have been able to assist her so far; but then—ah, what a pity! If now I begin a school in oppoition to hers—"

"It might be an injury to her, you think? So it might. But yet, if that is really necessary, there is nothing wrong in it. Every merchant who begins a business may take from the profits of those already engaged in the same. We ought to be generous to others, as you have been to Ellinor, while we can afford it; but it may become equally a duty, if circumstances change, to be just to ourselves."

Celia sighed: "I am beginning to find out the pleasant things I have lost."

"The exercise of generosity *is* one of the most pleasant things that money permits."

"But I am resolved never to take any of Ellie's scholars away from her, even if they apply to me."

"Very good. One can be generous, you see, without being rich; and such generosity is worth more, for it costs more, than what we carelessly give from superfluity. But perhaps there need be no competition between you. I know that Miss Ethelridge has almost daily offers of pupils whom she refuses, fearing to take a greater number than she can do justice to. These applications would be more numerous still if she could teach music, as you can. What if you were to join her and carry on the school in partnership? I am sure there will be found enough for both to do."

When they came to talk over the details of the plan, Sydenham asked, "Have you not some money which came to you through your mother?"

"About sixteen or seventeen hundred dollars, I think my uncle once told me. That is legally mine, is it not?"

"Undoubtedly, even if all the rest is gone. Now let me give you one or two business hints that occur to me. Shall you propose to Miss Ethelridge to be equal partner with her in her school?"

"That would not be just. She has worked hard to establish it and build up its reputation."

"You are right. For this you ought to give some equivalent. I happen to know that Miss Ethelridge thinks it an admirable plan to teach children as much as possible through the eye, and that she wishes much to obtain a set of handsome illustrations; some representing objects of natural history, including geology; others, charts exhibiting what has been called the stream of Time, bringing tangibly before children the leading events and revolutions of ancient and modern history. Then she would like to have a large magic lantern, with slides affording other useful illustrations; also to have photographs of the most interesting scenes in our own and in foreign countries. It would be of great advantage to the school. But all that is expensive."

"Would the money I have purchase it?"

"A thousand dollars, she said, would be enough. I offered to advance that sum, but she is sensitive about obligations, and declined. I think she would receive it from you as an equivalent for the privilege of equal partnership; and then the illustrations, when they are bought, should be considered the joint property of both. There would still remain to you six or seven hundred dollars, which you ought to keep, in case of accidents."

The discussion of this and other matters connected with the proposed partnership brought them to the point where the road to Rosebank diverged, and there they parted.

How things were smoothing themselves in Celia's path! How "way," to use the Quaker phrase, "was opening before her!" Sydenham's proposal saved her from even the appearance of doing a hard thing—that severest trial of straitened circumstances.

CHAPTER XXV.

BREAKING THE ICE.

A FRIEND once said to me: "Do you know I think those old martyrs must have been very uncomfortable people to live with?" At first the idea struck me as very odd—afterward as very true. I should not have relished a life among the Puritans in the days when Hester Prynne walked about with that scarlet letter on her breast. Yet they were a grand old race, those Plymouth-rock pilgrims — the stuff that heroes and founders of empires are made of. What they thought right they did, and seldom asked whether it was pleasant to do it. They were hard on themselves: it is not surprising that they were hard also on others. If they were not amiable, they were estimable. If they were not pleasant people to deal with in daily life, they were men and women to trust to in the day of need or in the hour of trial.

Thomas Hartland, born in Connecticut, had a considerable touch of Puritan severity about him. He was, indeed, an improvement on his father, a stern old Englishman who took credit to himself for admitting that a man must not chastise the wife of his bosom with a rod any thicker than his thumb. He meant to be kind to the gentle Alice, and he thought he was because he abstained from all physical coercion. But he inherited so much of his father's spirit as devoutly to believe that domestic discipline was wholesome just in proportion as it was strict and exacting. If he acted the tyrant to his wife and son, it was on principle, not from wickedness: it was because his ideas of marital and paternal authority were none of the clearest, and because the heart was not warm enough to correct the errors of the head.

Sydenham and he frequently came into conflict. One day, for example, on a school committee of which they were both members, the question of corporal punishment coming up, Sydenham had taken ground against it, and Mr. Harper had added a few words on the same side. This aroused Hartland.

"These new-fangled, sentimental notions," he said, "may suit squeamish people, but the old-fashioned scriptural morality is good enough for me. A rod is for the back of him who is void of understanding! If that text is not plain enough, there are others plainer yet—direct injunctions: 'Thou shalt beat the child with the rod, and shalt deliver his soul from hell.' Gentlemen will not, I think, deny the authority."

"The texts are correctly quoted," said Sydenham, quietly: "we know that this has been said by them of old time, but we know also that the word *rod* does not occur even once in all the recorded teachings of Christ."

A bitter reply rose to Hartland's lips, but he restrained himself. "What is the use?" he thought. "A man who will encourage a son to rebel against his father's will!"

In this spirit it was that Hartland had hitherto treated his niece—with judicious firmness he called it; acting a father's part, he thought, when he thwarted her inclinations and pressed Cranstoun's suit. She was now afraid to encounter him. She found Mr. and Mrs. Hartland both out when she returned from her ride, and it was with fear and trembling she resolved, that same evening, to disclose all to her formidable uncle, not having had an opportunity previously to converse with her aunt alone. She expected her Cousin Ethan to go out, as he often did, after tea, but he remained. "He is good and kind," she thought: "they may as well all hear it at once: then it will be over." Yet she shivered, like some faint-hearted swimmer about to take the first plunge. Even in her distress she had a droll sense that she was going to break the ice about as willingly as a poor wretch might who had risen before sunrise in a fireless bed-room, some morning when the thermometer was below zero, and found the water in his pitcher frozen hard.

Hartland's first surprise almost equaled Sydenham's, but the two men took the disclosure differently. The uncle felt keenly the social disgrace that had overtaken his niece, and thought bitterly and resentfully of his dead brother-in-law's offence. Yet toward the poor girl herself the better part of his nature came out now.

Celia began her relation with hesitation and in an unsteady voice, but she gathered confidence as she proceeded. We often lament that the first keen relish of a new pleasure fades in proportion as it is repeated: we forget that, by the same law of our nature, the sting of a fresh misfortune abates as, by recurrence, the idea of it becomes familiar. Even the lapse of a single day had dulled the edge of Celia's sorrow; and the fortitude with which she met her fate, and the composure with which she declared to Mr. Hartland her resolve to earn her own living in the future by teaching, won his esteem. He had been far from giving her credit for so much spirit and independence, and he did not guess the share Sydenham had had in sustaining and encouraging her.

Celia's newly-acquired equanimity gave way for a time, however, before the burst of grief and the tender endearments of her aunt. Alice, who had drilled herself to repress all manifestations of deep emotion or outbursts of affection in the presence of her husband, sat at first with fixed eyes and clasped hands and in breathless silence, scarcely taking in the full import of Celia's appalling communication, but when the latter came to the expression of her resolution to be a burden to no one, it seemed all to burst upon her at once. Unable longer to restrain herself, she fell on her niece's neck, her tears and sobs attesting her grief and sympathy; called her her dear child and her darling daughter; and then, forgetting the presence of the master of the house, protested against the idea of her working for a livelihood, asking her if she did not know that she would always have a home with them, whatever might betide.

This unwonted encroachment on his domestic authority, which nothing but his wife's ungovernable excitement would have tempted her to commit, almost upset Hartland's favorable disposition to his niece, but he tried to restrain himself.

"Alice," he said, "Celia shows more sense than you do. You spoil the child when you ought to encourage her." Then to Celia, who had released herself from her aunt's embraces, and was drying her own eyes: "I never had much sympathy with your father, but he is gone to his account, and it is wrong to speak ill of the dead. At all events, your mother was not to blame, and neither are you. I have thought you obstinate sometimes, disposed to take your own way more than a young person should; but you deserve credit for the manner in which you have stood this blow: it is more than I expected of you. If you see fit to teach so as to procure pocket-money for your little expenses, I see no objection; I suppose it would be pleasanter for you than to take the money from me. But I hope you knew, before your aunt thought it necessary to tell you, that the orphan of my sister-in-law will always find a home and a welcome in her uncle's house."

Celia's acknowledgments would have been more cordial but for the tone Hartland had assumed toward her aunt. Yet she was grateful, and did thank him, adding:

"If my health should fail, or if by teaching I cannot earn enough to pay all my expenses, then, dear uncle, I shall accept your kindness without scruple. But while I am well and able to work, it is my duty to pay my own way, if I can. And you have always told me that I ought to act up to my highest ideas of duty."

"Well, Celia, you are a good girl, and I shall stand by you through this matter. The first thing to be done is to ascertain its exact legal bearings. Did Cranstoun give you Mr. Dunmore's address?"

"I asked for it, and this is his answer," handing him the letter she had received the day before.

Hartland read it twice, his face darkening the while. "The impertinent scoundrel!" was all the comment he made; then to his son: "Ethan, step down to Mr. Creighton's and tell him I wish to see him, on important business, as early after breakfast to-morrow as he can spare me an hour or two. Lucky that he settled here!"

There was a school-committee meeting that evening, which Hartland had to attend. Thus, as Ethan had gone on his father's errand to Creighton, the aunt and niece were left alone.

Both had restrained themselves, by a strong effort, in Hartland's presence; and the first thing after he went was to have a hearty cry together, which did them good. Then Alice said: "It was very wrong in your father, no doubt, Celia dear; but then his first wife may have been a high, haughty dame, who made no true home for him; and it's *so* hard to live with a famished heart! Then your mother was a woman that any man might risk his soul for; and they did love one another so dearly! Don't think I excuse him, my darling: it was a great sin, and see what it has brought upon his child! But you know that I stayed at your house for five years before I was married—five years!—and there was not a day in all that time but he made me feel that it was a pleasure, as well to him as to your mother, to have me there. He was a sinner, but he was very, very kind to me!" Then she looked at her niece, and with a passionate burst of tears she added: "And oh, Celia, Celia, you mustn't be hard on us now!"

"Hard upon you, mother?"

"Hard upon me. After others had made me feel that I was a burden to them, I sat for years an honored guest at your father's table, and half an hour ago his daughter told us—you never thought how cruel that was, Celia!—you told us that you must pay us if you sat any longer at mine."

"But you know, auntie, what a comfort, and what a help too, you always were to mamma. You know what care you took of me: you were always doing something for me. And what have I been? A useless idler that has never done anything for anybody. But that's over, now."

"Never done anything for anybody! God forgive me the thought, but I've felt — I'm glad you don't know how often, Celia — that life would not be worth having if it were not for you—and for Ethan, maybe. You've been the best joy in my life—the greatest comfort I've had—always, always, cruel child, until now!"

When the fountains of the great Deep of feeling are broken up and the windows of the soul are opened, hidden things come to light upon which the heart has set jealous guard through half a lifetime. Celia was so amazed at the glimpse which her aunt unwittingly gave her beneath the placid flow of a quiet, regulated life that, for a moment, she had not a word in reply: then her aunt added:

"But there's one comfort still: your uncle will never take money from you—never! He's hard, Celia—I won't deny it—but he's just."

The girl, quite overcome, was about to throw her arms around her aunt's neck, and tell her she would do anything in the world she wished if she would not cry so, when Ethan entered.

He saw that both the women were deeply moved, and stopped as if, uncertain whether he was an intruder or not, he was about to leave the room. Celia broke the pause that ensued.

"Sit down, Cousin Ethan," she said. "Let us refer the matter to him, mother: he is kind and wise."

Ethan smiled: "Pray don't make a Nestor of me, Celia. Tell me if I can help you: that's better."

"Yes, you can help us to decide—can't he, mother?—what is right to be done." And, taking her aunt's silence for consent, she stated the case.

Ethan reflected for a little; then he asked:

"You are anxious not to be a burden on your uncle?"

"Yes."

"Celia, Celia!" said her aunt, imploringly.

"It is best so, dear mother," said Ethan—"best for her."

"Best that my own sister's child should go on paying us board and lodging as if she were a stranger?"

"No, that is not my opinion."

Both Celia and Mrs. Hartland looked up surprised.

"Do you happen to know," Ethan asked Celia, "how much your uncle has been charging you for board and lodging? You need not blush if you have been looking: it was right you should."

"I *have* been looking—a hundred and ninety-five dollars a year."

What Ethan said next must, in maintenance of historical truth, be set down just as he said it, even though he lose caste in consequence. Deal not too hardly with a villager's ignorance, O fair young aristocrat, reading these pages, perhaps, in the boudoir of a Fifth Avenue palace! You know better than to mistake a poor forty thousand dollars for riches; but plain people, with country ways, who find that one can obtain all one needs or desires in this world for that paltry pittance, should be forgiven if they rise not to the level of your enlightened views, and forget to add on the right hand of the sorry sum that additional cipher which would make it worth talking about. When Celia stated the rate at which her uncle had charged her for maintenance, Ethan, simple fellow! not at all in jest, said:

"By a guardian who has a rich heiress for ward the charge is moderate enough. Good board and lodging can scarcely be had in Chiskauga under four dollars a week."

"But the dear child," interrupted Alice, "does not cost Mr. Hartland half that sum. Her chamber would stand empty if she did not occupy it. We should not have one servant the less. We have our own washing done in the house: what matters it whether her's is thrown in or not? Does the butcher, even, send us one pound of meat the more on her account?"

"Perhaps not," said Ethan. "Yet an additional person in a family must, necessarily, add to the expense, were it but in the consumption of tea, coffee, sugar, flour and the like; lamplight also, and many trifling incidentals."

"While you're about it, Ethan," said Alice, half amused, half indignant, "I think you'd better take out your pencil and make a nice calculation how much ought to be charged against the poor child for wear and tear of our carpets and door-mat."

"I have the fear of Walter Scott before my eyes," replied Ethan, laughing. "Who has a right to say that Celia is heavier-footed than Ellen Douglas? But you know

> 'E'en the slight hare-bell raised its head,
> Elastic from her airy tread.'

I'm a poor hand at calculating infinitesimals."

"I'm glad you've so much conscience."

"But, seriously, I don't think father pays out a hundred additional dollars because of Celia being one of the family."

"Surely you don't want Mr. Hartland to make money out of the poor child, now that all her fortune is gone."

"No, nor would he consent to that; but if Celia gets a good situation as teacher, and finds that she can afford it, I think a hundred dollars a year for her maintenance would be a fair compromise between uncle and niece. You are not so savagely independent, I hope, Celia, as to refuse from father and mother such kindness as they can offer you without actual cost to themselves."

Celia smiled: "Since I endorsed your character for wisdom, Cousin Ethan, I suppose I must accept your decision."

"You are as bad as she is, Ethan," said Alice: "you encourage one another in foolish notions."

But they coaxed her, at last, to use her influence with her husband to allow Celia, besides furnishing her own pocket-money, to pay him a hundred dollars a year as her contribution to the expenses of the household. And so, at last, it was settled, with some grumbling from the uncle about the niece's stiff-necked unwillingness to accept his hospitality, and a condition attached that the hundred dollars was to be received only if Celia found that, after clothing herself and paying other incidentals, she could spare the amount without any inconvenience whatever.

This was a great satisfaction to Celia, both because it relieved her, on the one hand, from a painful consciousness of dependence, and—truth to say—because, on the other hand, it unexpectedly lightened the burden which her new and untried task of self-maintenance imposed.

Next morning Mr. Hartland, Sr., was closeted for two hours with Eliot Creighton.

Lawyers learn to look with a quiet eye on the calamities of life. Surprised, deeply concerned at the unexpected tidings Creighton undoubtedly was, but he did not take them to heart, as the uncle and guardian expected.

"My first impression is," he said, "that it will not be proper or even safe to give up your ward's property until compelled by law."

"You doubt the previous marriage? Celia says her father's letters which she inspected were conclusive on that point."

"That may be: Cranstoun can readily prove it to us if it is so. But there are questions back of that. There may have been a will."

"Mrs. Pembroke knew of none. None, of course, was offered for probate, either in this county or in Philadelphia, where part of Celia's property lies."

"Still, there may have been a will: possibly left in Cranstoun's hands, and—I beg his pardon if I suspect him unjustly—suppressed."

"But why not shown by Pembroke to his wife during his lifetime?"

"He may have been living under an assumed name. Those who risk the punishment of bigamy generally take that precaution against detection. He would, of course, be unwilling to show Mrs. Pembroke a will executed under his real name; and Cranstoun, for his own purposes, may have persuaded him that a will signed by him as Frederick Pembroke would be valueless."

"If your conjecture is right, such a document would be worthless, would it not?"

"No. One not versed in law, like Mr. Pembroke, would be likely to suppose so. But a will is valid if the identity of the signer with the person entitled to dispose of the property be established."

"Yet if such a will has been suppressed or destroyed, of what avail that it was executed?"

"It must have been witnessed, and we may discover by whom?"

"By Cranstoun himself, perhaps?"

"Likely enough; but in this State two witnesses are required."

"If there was a prior marriage, and if no will can be found, then, I suppose, the English heir-at-law takes the property."

"The statute law of Ohio, unfortunately for Miss Pembroke, permits an alien to inherit real estate as well as personal property; but there are law-points involved in your question which I must study before I can reply to it. The cruel rule of the Common Law is that one born out of wedlock is *filius nullius* — nobody's child — and as such can inherit neither the property of his father nor—strange to say!—of his mother. Our statute law remedies the latter injustice. Under what circumstances — indeed whether at all — it affords relief under the former I cannot yet say, never having had occasion to examine that point. Indeed, I am not as familiar with the Ohio statutes as I ought to be. I studied law chiefly in Pennsylvania. Did Cranstoun speak positively on the subject?"

"He told Celia that, being illegitimate, she could not inherit a farthing of her father's property."

Creighton looked grave. "Cranstoun is too shrewd," he said after a pause, "to make such an assertion except on plausible authority; and he is doubtless far better acquainted with the law of this State, and the decisions under it, than I am. With so much depending on it under his rascally calculation of profit to himself as informer, he has, in all probability, sifted the matter to the bottom. To be frank with you, I don't like the look of it; yet I am not entirely convinced even of Miss Pembroke's illegitimacy."

"It surely must be, if her father was a bigamist."

"Not necessarily. Under the old Spanish law, once prevalent in Florida and Texas, as I happen to know, she would have been legitimate."

"But our laws are not so lax. With a former wife alive, the marriage of Mrs. Pembroke must have been null and void."

"Yes; at all events at the time it was solemnized, and probably as long as it lasted. The rest seems a natural deduction. The case is probably against us; and I beg of you not to mention to Miss Celia the doubts I have expressed, which may be entirely without foundation. It would be cruel to raise hopes only to be disappointed. How does she stand this?"

"The disgrace of her birth affects her seriously. Otherwise, I must say, she bears it well. She is gone this morning to talk to Miss Ethelridge about a partnership in her school. And the gypsy is too proud to stay in her uncle's house without paying for it."

Creighton's face brightened. "I was not deceived in thinking there was character beneath that soft exterior."

"She is obstinate enough, certainly."

"She will come out all right, even if we are beaten, Mr. Hartland: you will see. But if you think fit to entrust the case to me—"

"That is what I have been thinking about."

"You do me honor. It is a great responsibility for one so young in the profession as myself. Yet it will go hard but I shall deserve your confidence. If industry and painstaking may avail, we shall not be defeated. And this at least I may promise you—that I will work up the case as faithfully as if the young lady were my own sister, as faithfully as if life and death were on the issue."

Self-confidence breeds confidence in others, as young and small and slender General Bonaparte, taking command of the army of Italy, shiningly proved. Hartland agreed with Creighton on politics, and found in him a patient and interested listener when speaking on natural history and expatiating on his (Hartland's) favorite pursuits. On the other hand, the young man often startled him, and sometimes shocked his conservative proclivities, by coming out with some daring radicalism; so that he had hesitated a little about putting his ward's interests in his hands. But Creighton's bold assurance awoke faith in his powers as an advocate, and Hartland hesitated no longer.

"You shall have the management of the case, at all events," he said; "and if you desire to have other counsel associated with you, let me know."

CHAPTER XXVI.

JEAN'S SERVICES NOT NEEDED.

> "And one, in whom all evil fancies clung
> Like serpent-eggs together, laughingly
> Would hint at worse in either."
>
> TENNYSON'S *Enoch Arden.*

"No, Miss Celia—not jist exactly at home. Miss Ellinor went out to Betty Carson's on some business for the madame. A half hour she said she'd be gone, and it's mor'n that already. Won't ye step into the parlor?"

"Yes, Nelly, I'll wait for her; but don't tell Madame Meyrac I'm here, I know she's always busy at this hour."

Beyond the parlor was a small extension-room, used by the doctor as office and library. The door that communicated with it standing open, so that Celia saw it was vacant, she sauntered thither in an absent mood and sat down by an eastern window, looking out on the lake; for Dr. Meyrac's dwelling was on the eastern edge of the village, not far from the Elm Walk. At another time Celia would have rejoiced in that sunny spring morning and admired the graceful little sail-boat that was just leaving the wharf. But her mind was preoccupied, and the bright scene was lost upon her. Business was in her thoughts. She was congratulating herself that this was Saturday, and that she would probaby find her friend at leisure for a long talk. Mechanically she picked up and opened a book from a small table that stood near. It was that wonderful story of *Jane Eyre,* instinct with pathos drawn from the very depths of sorrow; and she had opened it at the incident of the wedding in the dim village church, so nearly solemnized, by such startling disclosure interrupted. "And she married him, after all," the girl thought. "And I remember I was *so* much afraid she would marry that handsome, pious St. John; and so glad when she found Rochester, blind and lame, in that gloomy parlor. Ought she to have kept away from him? Ought she to have married the missionary?" Her thoughts were in a maze, and she dipped into the absorbing volume, reading page after page, till she was interrupted by voices in the adjoining room. It was Madame Meyrac and some one who had entered with her, unnoticed by Celia in her abstraction. A voice said:

"It would be a great accommodation, madame, if you could give me up Betty for Monday. I have friends coming from Mount Sharon on Wednesday, and I must absolutely get through house-cleaning before they come."

How that harsh, sharp voice grated on Celia's ear! Well she knew who was the speaker! She could not make up her mind to encounter her just then; and so, unwilling to become privy to a conversation not intended for her ear, she stepped lightly across the library, intending to go up to Ellinor's room. But the door that opened on the passage was locked outside; so that she was fain to remain a prisoner. "It can only be for a few moments," she thought as she reseated herself; "and it is a mere matter of every-day business."

"I much grieve, Madame Volfgang," was what she heard next. "Ah, if the voman Carson might aid me Tuesday, or, vell, Vendesday, very good. But no, she has said me she is retained for these days there by Madame Hartland."

"I don't think sister Hartland cares about having her house cleaned this week. I could speak to her about it. She has something else to think of—something not very pleasant."

"Is monsieur ill? He has not sent to seek my husband."

"My brother is not ill, but in great trouble."

"I am much afflicted to hear it."

"Mrs. Hartland's sister made a pretty mess of it when she married Frederick Pembroke."

"A praty mase! Vat is happen? He is dead, there are ten, eleven years—is he not?"

"When Eliza married him he had another wife living in England."

"My God! vat you tell me?"

"It was no marriage at all. She was no more his wife than you or I."

"Ah, vat unhappy ting! And that charmante Célie! Poor litel mignonne! She is not—she is one—"

"A bastard, of course, and not entitled to a cent of her father's property.'

"Is it that the first vife lives still?"

"No: she died three years before her husband; but that's of no consequence."

"Your law says it so? Ve have much better in our Code Civile. If de second vife know noting and marry all of good faith, then if de first vife come to die, de children of de oder can have de goods—vat you call propertay."

"It's just as likely as not that Mrs. Pembroke knew it all the time. Of course she kept the secret. She was dying to have him before he married her. Everybody could see that."

"But if de poor soul did truly not know anyting?"

"Whose fault was that? It was her business to find out whether he was married or not before she took him; but she didn't care if she was his kept mistress. It served her just right."

Celia choked down her sobs, pride coming to her aid. She was terribly afraid now of being detected. The next words she heard were:

"You are one very hard voman."

"Hard! I see no hardship in it. That mawkish fop of a Pembroke was a felon, yet he wasn't sent to hard labor in the penitentiary—the more's the pity: you won't deny that the bigamist deserved it. Well, the daughter will suffer for it, that's one comfort."

"Madame Volfgang—"

"Mr. Cranstoun told me that just such a case as hers had lately been decided—I forget in what county of this State—and not a penny were the bastards allowed to inherit. The saucy minx is a beggar."

"I vill not hear—"

"There's no need for my brother to trouble himself about John Mowbray now. The Mowbrays stand on their dignity, and don't marry beggars. Ellen Tyler always was a prettier girl than that whey-face, and now she's a far better match. Her mother was an honest married woman, and the old miller can spare a son-in-law three or four thousand hard dollars if he likes him. The Pembroke girl hasn't a ghost of a chance."

"Madame Volfgang!"

Such a menace was there in the tone that Celia, beaten down as her very soul had been by that malignant outburst of abuse, started to her feet, expecting a blow to follow the words. She need not have feared.

"Madame Volfgang! I have de honor to remind you dat Mademoiselle Célie is my vary excellent friend. I did tell you I vould not hear, but you speak, speak, ever more. Jean is digging in my garden at dis moment—it is a moch strong young man, is Jean—and what I say to him, he do it. It vill make talk de world to turn some lady out of my house. But what to do? If you say only one litel vord more, I vill make seek' Jean, and he shall have you in his arms, and I vill make him descend the front steps and set you down outside de litel door of de garden, in de street: den I shall say you, 'Good-morning, madame!'"

What a world is this! — tragedy one moment, comedy the next. The hot tears were already dry on Celia's cheeks: she saw, in imagination, the stout young Frenchman picking up, at his mistress' bidding, Mrs. Wolfgang's solid weight of a hundred and sixty or seventy pounds. But his prowess was not called into requisition. The lady shook with rage, but she moved quickly to the door without a word. Celia saw Madame Meyrac sweep out after her with an air that would have graced the stage, and heard her say, as Mrs. Wolfgang stepped out on the gravel walk: "Ah, madame shows herself sage at de last. Dat is much better, for vy should one make talk the world?" Then Celia heard her muttering to herself, as she passed up stairs to her domestic duties: "Dieu mercie, elle s'est en allé à la fin, cette diablesse-là!" *

CHAPTER XXVII.

A GLIMPSE INTO A LIFE.

> "Work—work—work,
> Till the brain begins to swim;
> Work—work—work,
> Till the eyes are heavy and dim!"
>
> HOOD.

CELIA ascended to her friend's chamber, and ten minutes afterward Ellinor entered. She went up to Celia without a word, kissed her tenderly, and then, the tears rising to her eyes, passed her hand caressingly over the auburn tresses.

"Ah! you know all?" said Celia.

"My darling, yes—from Betty Carson this morning."

"All the world knows my disgrace already!" was the poor girl's bitter thought.

* "Thank God, she's gone at last, that she-devil!"

Ellinor added:

"That odious Mrs. Wolfgang had been trying to poison the poor creature's mind against you: but Betty — brave soul! — is a champion of yours. She washed for your family, it seems, when you were a mere child, and your father and mother seem to have been objects of her veneration."

"Dear, good Betty!" — her eyes filling with tears.

"She told me what an angel of goodness your father had been to her when her children were sick and her husband raving with delirium tremens."

"Ah, if others could feel so about him!"

"Your father's misconduct is the worst blow. Is it not, little pet?"

"I can't bear to think of it, Ellie!" shuddering as she said it.

"Do you doubt that he repented of his misdeed!"

"No, indeed, no," eagerly. "As I remember dear papa, sad, depressed, like one bearing a secret grief, his life with mamma must have been one long repentance."

"Yet you mourn as without hope. Do you remember the words of One who needed no forgiveness himself, touching the joy in heaven over one sinner that repenteth? Joy, Celia—joy because of the repentance, not sorrow because of the sin. How often I have thought of that!"

"Papa *was* a good man, Ellie: I wish you had known him."

Ellinor took down a small volume from a book-shelf. "I like 'Vivien,'" she said, as she turned the leaves over, "less than any other of the *Idyls*, yet it has some of the finest lines Tennyson ever wrote. Here, for example:

'The sin that practice burns into the blood,
And not the one dark hour which brings remorse,
Will brand us, after, of whose fold we be.'"

"Dear Ellie! No one like you to come to, when one is miserable and needs to be comforted! You are merciful."

"Am I?" — a sudden, solemn look shadowing her face—"am I? Thank God! The merciful, we are told, shall obtain mercy."

The two girls sat silent for a minute or two: then Celia took one of Ellinor's hands in both hers, and the expressive features, as she looked up to them, brightened again. "I came to talk to you about business, Ellie dear, but I have almost lost heart. That Mrs. Wolfgang was here this morning, and I heard—I could not help hearing — oh such terrible things! The full sense of my position never came home to me before. Name, fortune, good repute, all lost! Everything, everything gone!"

"Everything? There are these little dimpled hands left—" kissing one of them — "and they have not forgotten their cunning. The eyes are somewhat dimmed, I admit, but they can still read Liszt's music at a glance, and win hearts besides, provided they are worth the winning. I hear the very voice that charmed us all—and Mr. Creighton especially — in Schubert's 'Ave Maria,' the other night. These golden curls are the same I used to admire, and this little brain beneath them has just as much French and German and history and logic and literature, and just as many kind thoughts and generous sentiments, stowed away in its delicate cells, as there were there a week ago." The look from those brilliant eyes spoke deep affection more strongly even than the words as Ellinor proceeded: "Everything gone! Why every bit of my own precious Celia, who stole my heart in spite of all I could do to keep it, is here still. That money, if *it* be gone, was no part of her. As little any name the law may assign her. Like Juliet's rose, she is just as sweet under one as another. Young girls *will* change their names, you know, and do their dearest friends think the less of them for that?"

"I am so glad you don't despise me."

"Naughty child! What sort of love is it you give me credit for? A weed, that has root among dollars and titles, and withers when these are plucked up? Do you take me for one of those who mistake money or a name for the chief part of that 'noblest work of God' that Pope talks about? *You* are unmerciful. Come, Celia, I'm not so bad as that: tell me what business it was you had almost lost heart to talk to me about."

Celia disclosed her plans. At first Ellinor listened eagerly, well pleased it seemed. Then, as if some painful thought had swept over her, her face saddened and her manner betrayed nervous excitement.

"It does not suit you, dear: never mind," said Celia, struggling bravely to conceal sad disappointment.

Ellinor's quick apprehension detected the feeling instantly. "Dear, good Celia!" she said after a moment's pause, "it is cruel to say a word to you of my misfortunes when you are overtasked by your own. But between the closest friends there should be the most scrupulous good faith in matters of business." Then she hesitated, adding, at last: "Did you ever notice anything peculiar about my eyes?"

"Never—" bewildered by the sudden question—"never, except that I think they are love-eyes, that I should have lost my heart to if I had been a man."

"They told *you* the truth, at all events," faintly smiling, "yet they are not trustworthy eyes, for all that."

"Good Heavens! It can't be, Ellinor—" and Celia turned deadly pale.

"You have guessed it. If I were to accept your offer, you might have a blind partner on your hands one of these days."

When Cranstoun came out with that terrible announcement: "Your father had a wife living in England," it was scarcely a greater blow to Celia than this. She gazed at her friend, unable at first to utter a single word. Then she fell on her neck, sobbing, "Ellie, Ellie!"

Miss Ethelridge had spoken quite calmly, but under this uncontrollable burst of sympathy her equanimity also gave way.

Celia was the first who broke silence: "Don't cry, darling. I'll try to be as brave as you. But your eyes—you see me, Ellie?"

"Yes, little pet, quite well."

"Your eyes are weak, that is all?"

"Come on this sofa, beside me;" and she put one arm round her and took a hand in hers. "I said you *may* have a blind partner. Till darkness comes there is hope. God may spare me this, but I do not think it is His will."

"Is it only a presentiment, Ellie?"

"No. I must tell you a little bit out of a sad, sad story. I hope I was not bad—though I sometimes think I was—but I never intended to be, or I would not have let you love me, Celia. I was in cruel hands — cruel and powerful hands" — Celia felt her shudder convulsively — "and at times I scarcely knew what I did or what I ought to do. I promised to tell you all about it some day, and I will, but not now. I left my friends — what the world called so, I mean. I dare say they considered me dishonored; and they would probably disown me if I showed my face among them again, which I never will—God be my witness!—never will. I'm afraid I thought of doing a very wrong thing, for when one is forsaken by all the world, there's such a temptation to slip out of it. But when all the world forsook me, God sent—" she hesitated. "I think there are those on this earth who will be angels in the next world; and some of them act an angel's part here. Such an one — God bless him! as He surely will—saved me from myself, and found for me such home as was within his power. I accepted life from him: I could not accept money. To preserve the life he rescued, I had to win my daily bread. I am usually considered a skillful needlewoman, but others had to make profit of my labor. The miserable pittance they left me—well, it is the fate of thousands: I was not worse off than they. You know that fearful 'Song of the Shirt,' Celia: I hardly dare read it now: it terrifies me. I don't think the English language was ever wrought into another such picture: it conjures phantoms that haunt me still, yet it scarcely exaggerates what was my lot. The summer's earliest light often found me bending over my work. Perhaps even such labor as that would not have seriously injured my eyes, for they were strong, had it not been—you mustn't cry, Celia dear: nothing so weakens the eyes as tears."

"But at last?" was all Celia could say.

"At last, when sight had almost failed, an old gentleman—he was a Quaker and from your country—found me out. He spoke to me of America, of green fields and summer skies in a land where labor was honored and brought fair reward. Even then, though his words were like tidings from Paradise, my pride revolted against pecuniary obligation. Then he spoke to me as one of Christ's apostles might have spoken: 'Pride is sinful and goes before destruction: suicide is a crime. In another month thee will probably be quite blind: then thee will die a miserable death. Thee has no right thus to cast life away, for thee may employ it still to benefit, maybe to bless, our fellow-creatures. Thee may be able to repay them a hundredfold the trifle I offer thee.'"

"Ah, Ellie, how true that was!"

"I dared not reply to it. I accepted money enough to pay for a second-class passage across the Atlantic. In Philadelphia I remained six months in the house of a charming old lady, sister of my benefactor, as governess to her niece. An eminent oculist restored comparative strength to my eyes, but warned me against ever again taxing them severely, especially by artificial light, and strongly recommended country air and exercise. Mr. Williams—that was the good man's name—gave me a letter of introduction to Mr. Sydenham; and here too, I think, as in that London garret, I have been ministered to by angels unawares."

"But your eyes, Ellie—they are beautiful as they can be. Surely the danger is past. Do they pain you?"

"Don't grieve, dear, but I have no right to conceal the truth from you. They have been gradually failing—more, I think, this year than ever before. I *must* use them a good deal, sometimes by lamplight. But they do not pain me much."

"What does Dr. Meyrac say?"

"He is a faithful friend and speaks the truth. What a sigh was that! Don't trouble yourself about me, poor child. You have burden enough. You have your own affairs—your own way to make. You may find some one else as a partner; or perhaps — who knows, Celia, whether it may not be all for the best that I should become blind and give up school? Somebody must take my place."

"Hush, Ellie! I want to talk to you about something else."

"Well, dear?"

"Had you ever a sister?"

"Never."

"Nor a brother?"

"Nor a brother. I was an only child."

"So was I. Would you like to have a sister, Ellie?"

Such a look of love! but not a word in reply; and Celia went on: "I need a sister; and then—you and Dr. Meyrac may both be wrong; God may not intend that you should suffer this. But if He does, Ellie—if He does—you will need a sister, too." And with that she threw her arms round her friend's neck, and after a time all that she felt and all that she meant came home to Ellinor—warm kisses say so much more than words.

After they had become a little more calm, Celia spoke again: "I have complained for such small cause: I have so little fortitude in suffering. I am a poor, weak creature compared with you, Ellie —little worth your love except because I love you so; but then you have no other sister; and besides — there is a secret I must tell you, Ellie."

"Well, darling child?"

"Do you believe in magnetism—human magnetism, I mean?"

Ellinor started with an expression almost of terror, but she controlled herself, answering calmly, "Yes, I do believe in it."

"Because—you will scarcely credit me, Ellie—but when you first came this morning I had been trembling all over: that woman's venomous words had got hold of me, so that I was scarcely myself. I think my nerves were shattered: I could not keep my hands still, and when you opened the door I could hardly restrain a scream. But when you came up to me and kissed me, and passed a hand over my hair, I felt quieter and able to sit still. Then, afterward, when you bid me come and sit beside you on the sofa, and put your arm round me and took my hand in yours, it all gradually passed away — the fear, the nervousness, the restlessness: even that odious vituperation seemed to drop off from me like some soiled garment, and I began to feel stronger, braver, more hopeful, and then, after a time, almost like a soothed child that could go to sleep in your arms. I have often felt something of the kind before when I was near you, but never anything like that dreamy luxury of to-day. I know this must all seem fanciful to you, ridiculous perhaps—"

"Far from it, dear child. It is real."

"Then see, Ellie! For my sake we ought to be sisters and partners, so that I can be often with you. I am weak, and through you I gain strength; I am nervous and irritable, and near you I find solace and peace. Then after a time, maybe, I may get to be better worth living with, more like you—brave, energetic, self-possessed. You'll never find a sister you can do so much good to, Ellie, nor one that will honor and love you more. Will you have me, darling, just as I am?"

"Just as you are? — God forgive me, if I am selfish in this—yes, Celia, just as you are."

There are many more estimable and more meritorious people in this world than Celia Pembroke; but toward those she loved there was a witchery about her that few hearts, save very cold ones, could resist. It almost silenced Ellinor's misgivings, and before evening partnership articles between the two orphans were agreed upon.

Before leaving Madame Meyrac's, Celia took an opportunity of apologizing to that lady for having been an unwilling listener to Mrs. Wolfgang's tirade, speaking in French, as she always did to her.

"Ah, poor little one!" replied madame, sympathetically, "you heard it, then? It afflicts me that you should have been so cruelly wounded. But what would you have? That sort of creature has neither sense nor common decency. Without these, one becomes brutal. Dogs will bite and cats scratch. One can guarantee one's self only by selecting for associates bipeds and quadrupeds that are too well bred to do either. For the rest, I owe to you much, my dear: through you I shall obtain relief from ennui and disgust, for I do not think that madame will trouble me again very soon."

PART VIII.

CHAPTER XXVIII.

JOHN EVELYN MOWBRAY.

> "Then she took up her burden of life again,
> Saying only, 'It might have been.'"
>
> WHITTIER.

EARLY in the afternoon of the next day, Ethan and Celia were standing at Mr. Hartland's front gate.

"Are you going toward Mr. Sydenham's, cousin?" Celia asked.

"No. I—I thought of calling on Dr. Meyrac."

'Give him my kindest regards, and—shall you see Ellinor Ethelridge?"

"Probably."

"Tell her I hope to be with her this evening."

The cousins separated, Celia taking the road to Rosebank. She passed the house, however, and a little way beyond turned into a path to the right, which ran outside the west fence of the vineyard, and was bordered by a light fringe of shrubbery. It led her to that rustic bridge over Kinshon Creek already mentioned, and she crossed it, entering the village cemetery beyond.

Nature had done much for this little secluded spot. Its surface, some eight or ten acres in extent, was gently undulating, with a slope to the east. It was bounded on the north and west by the forest, on the south by Kinshon Creek, and was open eastward toward the village. A few of the handsomest forest trees had been left: there had been planted cedars, willows and graceful weeping birches, and around the whole was a hedge of laurel, thick set, the lower line of this hedge reaching Kinshon Creek just above the fall. Over a simple arched entrance on the east, built of the same warm gray freestone that Sydenham had selected for his residence, was the inscription:

> "Why should not He whose touch dissolves our chain,
> Put on His robes of beauty when He comes
> As a Deliverer?"

The memorials to the dead were, with few exceptions, quite simple and unpretending: some were of the same gray stone as the entrance, others of white marble: here and there a touching inscription, usually from some well-known author. Celia paused before one of these, over the grave of her aunt Alice's only child, which had died when but five years old. Selected by Alice herself, but only faintly depicting the desolation that fell on the mother as she laid her little one to rest on that hillside, it read:

> "Above thee wails thy parents' voice of grief;
> Thou art gone hence. Alas, that aught so brief
> So loved should be!
> Thou tak'st our summer hence: the light, the tone,
> The music of our being, all in one,
> Depart with thee."

A little farther on she passed a marble slab which she had not seen before, for it had been but recently placed. It recalled to her a melancholy incident. A few weeks before a German professor and his wife, friends of the Meyracs, had spent a few days at the doctor's house, on their way to Iowa. Their infant died there suddenly, of croup, and this was the grave. The inscription was in German; and Celia, struck with its grace, translated it:

"Ephemera all die at sunset, and no insect of this class ever sported in the rays of the rising sun. Happier are ye, little human ephemera! Ye play in the ascending beam and in the early dawn and in the eastern light; drink only the first sweet draughts of life; hover, for a little while, over a world of freshness and blossoms, and then fall asleep in innocence, ere ever the morning dews are exhaled."

Celia glanced around the cemetery: she was its only visitor. Slowly she passed on to where, under the shade of an old oak of the forest, lay the remains of her father and mother. The sight of the spot awoke a new train of thought: "She knows it all now, and she has forgiven him." Celia was as sure of that as if her mother had suddenly appeared before her, there by her grave, in robes of white, and told her so. "On earth as it is in heaven," were the next words that occurred to her. But *was* it on earth as in heaven? What is forgiven there must be punished here. Her father had saved himself from the penalty of penitentiary labor only by years of deception. And if his crime had come to light during his life, what a frightful blow for her mother! How *could* he risk the happiness of one he loved so much! Herself, too, his child: she had escaped being a convict's daughter by mere accident—through the lie that her father had lived.

And not a man or woman, or child even, in Chiskauga but knew it now, or would know it all before another week had passed. Was she justified in proposing that partnership to Ellinor? What if the mothers of Ellinor's pupils should object to send their daughters to the child of a malefactor—a girl, too, who was—oh the vile epithet from that horrid Mrs. Wolfgang's lips! It had seared like burning steel. Could mothers be blamed if they sought to preserve their daughters from contamination?

Evelyn Mowbray!—his name swept over her next. A man must protect his children — from reproach as much as from any other injury. Children living in fear that others should know who their mother was! Had she a right to marry at all? One thing was clear as noonday. It was her duty to absolve Evelyn from his promise to make her his wife. If he did not come to see her, she must seek him, to tell him that.

The murmur of the waterfall, wafted up by a soft southern breeze, had soothed her when she first reached the spot, but her ear was deaf to it now: bitter thoughts overpowered Nature's soothings. Impatient of inaction, she retraced her steps.

As she passed along the vineyard, she had one of those dim premonitions which sometimes intimate the approach of a person to whom the thoughts have been directed. Looking down the road by which Sydenham's house was approached, she saw some one ascending it. The villagers often passed that way, it being the most direct route for foot-passengers from the village to Tyler's mill. Celia *felt* who this was, but it did not occur to her that he might be on his way to visit a rival. Stern feelings engrossed her, excluding all inklings of jealousy: she forgot Ellen's existence. Her thought was: "Shall I accost him or avoid a meeting?" She saw him now distinctly, but the high paling and the shrubbery which fringed the path on the side next the forest afforded protection sufficient if she resolved to escape observation. She was too restless, however, to delay the issue. With a sort of desperate feeling she quickened her steps, confronting Mowbray as she turned the corner of the vineyard fence.

When a man occupied by secret thoughts of a friend or a foe — thoughts which he would fain hide from all the world—comes suddenly and unexpectedly on the object of his cogitations, he must be an adept in dissimulation if he can wholly conceal what he has been thinking. Celia read in her lover's face a conflict of feelings—embarrassment, hesitation. He rallied quickly, however, greeted her cordially and asked after her health.

"Which way were you going?" Celia asked, after replying to his inquiries.

"I sauntered out for exercise, and my good angel must have guided me here. Where have you been?"

"In the cemetery."

A pause; then Mowbray said: "Shall we walk a little way into the woods, they are so fresh and beautiful?"

Celia turned in assent. Mowbray walked by her side a few steps; then added: "I see you so seldom now, Celia. I feel as if it would be an intrusion to enter Mr. Hartland's house, he is such a crabbed old fellow. What a pity you have such a guardian! We might have been married before this if he had behaved like a decent man."

"Probably."

"Do you think, dear, he will ever get over that grudge he has against me?"

"I cannot tell: it is not likely. But he will not press Cranstoun upon me any more: he considers him a scoundrel."

"That is one point gained."

"My uncle is a strict, austere man, subject to prejudices, but he is a man to trust in time of trial; and that is a good deal in this world. He is upright, and means to be kind."

"Let us hope, then, that he will change his opinion of me, as much as he has of Amos Cranstoun."

"Would that be important?"

Something in the steady tone, more than the words, startled Mowbray. The look of embarrassment came over his face again. Celia turned very pale, but she asked him quietly: "Have you ever thought about choosing a profession, Evelyn?"

"Yes, often, but I've never been able to make up my mind what it is best for me to do. I'm not as clever as you, Celia dear."

"I don't see that. You're as far advanced in German as I am; and if you would only cultivate Dr. Meyrac's acquaintance, you would soon speak French fluently."

"But how would French and German help me to a profession?"

Another pause. Celia broke it, saying: "I hear your mother is not as well as usual."

"No; mother's health is certainly failing. I tell her she works too hard, and that she ought to give up some of her pupils, but she thinks she can't afford it. She has been in the habit of doing our ironing, so as not to make it too hard on Susan—you know we have only one girl—but I persuaded her to get Betty Carson for half a day each week. Betty's so busy she had only Saturday afternoons to spare, but we made that suit."

"You had Betty yesterday afternoon, then?"

"Yes."

They had reached the forest by this time. Here a footpath, diverging to the left from the direct road to the mill, led, in a circuit through the woods, back to the village. "Let us return home by this path," said Celia: "I am a little tired."

As they walked on, she looked up in the face of the man she had loved so dearly and trusted so utterly, and had always thought so generous and kind. It was as much as she could do to restrain her tears, but she did restrain them, and commanded her voice so as to say, in a steady tone: "You know what has happened to me, Evelyn. I'm sure Betty Carson must have told it to your mother yesterday."

Mowbray blushed scarlet, like a girl. "I believe"—he stammered—"I think I heard mother say—Betty told her—"

"What did Betty tell her?"

"It was some difficulty about your father's marriage, as I understood."

"That he had a wife living in England—was that it?"

"I think that was the story, as far as I made it out."

"Did you believe it?"

"I hope it is not true, dear Celia. I should be so glad to hear from you that it is all a fabrication."

"You didn't say a word to me about it when we met?"

"Why should I repeat to you such a scandalous report?"

"You expected, then, that we should meet day after day, and pass it all over, without any explanation, without any consultation?"

"Your denial is sufficient."

"My denial? Every word of it is true, Evelyn—every word. My father was a bigamist. A bigamist is a felon. If he had been found out, he would have worked in the penitentiary, a convict. I am a felon's daughter. I am—" She caught her breath, but hesitated only for a moment: "I am a bastard—a bastard! I heard myself called so yesterday. I heard my mother called my father's kept mistress. Do you hear that? Do you think we can live on and say nothing about such things to one another—you and I, lovers, two people who are engaged to be married—engaged to stand up and take each other for better, for worse, till death part us?"

Mowbray was weak, of facile nature,

inconstant, but he had a certain generosity withal, and Celia had roused it. He turned to address her, but stopped, fearing she was about to faint. By the side of the path, close by, there lay a large poplar that had been blown over a few days before. He begged her to sit down, supporting her toward it, but she recovered herself, saying, "Never mind, Evelyn—I'm better: let us walk on slowly."

"Surely, my darling Celia," Evelyn said, offering her his arm—"Surely you know how much I love you. What difference can it make to me whether your father behaved ill or not?"

"What difference? You don't care whether your children might live to be ashamed of one of their parents or not? You wouldn't care if, some day, it should be thrown up to a girl of yours that her grandfather was a felon, who cruelly wronged the one he loved dearest on earth, and that her mother was an illegitimate child? You *would* care, Evelyn: you could not help it. You once told me the Moubrays were in Domesday Book. You stand on the honor of the name."

He was about to protest, but she stopped him: "One word more. I must think for you, dear friend, as well as for myself. You have no profession. You have never seriously thought—you don't think now—of studying one. Your mother is barely able, faithfully as she works, to support herself. If her health gives way, she cannot continue to do that; and then to whom can she look but to her son? I saw all this before, when we were first engaged; but I knew then that I had enough for both, and that your mother could always have a home with us—"

"Dear Celia, how unjust is fortune to disinherit one so generous as you!"

"I thought then that, in any event, neither you nor your mother would suffer; but now—I'm not a beggar, Evelyn, though a woman (my uncle's sister) said I was: it was in Dr. Meyrac's parlor; I heard her; her words haunt me—but I'm not a beggar: those who have health and friends and good-will to work need never beg; but I *am* a poor orphan, without power to help any one, only too happy if I can earn my own support."

"And you think I am dishonorable enough to desert you in your adversity?"

"Your father left your mother and you little but an honorable name and an unblemished reputation. You must guard these—you must take care of your mother, and—" the color left her cheeks as she added firmly, but in a low voice—"you must find some other wife than me."

"Celia, Celia!" said Mowbray earnestly, "I would marry you, in spite of everything that has passed—I'd marry you to-morrow and brave it all, if your uncle would only consent."

Now, for the first time, the tears filled Celia's eyes, and she could scarcely reply. They had come to a turn in the path whence a vista opened down on the village and distant lake. Sydenham had caused a rustic seat to be placed there, whence to enjoy the view. This time she was persuaded to rest: the agitation she had passed through had unnerved her.

"It's very kind of you, Evelyn," she answered, after they were seated, "to say that you would marry me still, but it cannot be. Your mother would not wish it. We have not the means of supporting a household: that will confirm my uncle in his opposition. He is certain, now, to adhere to his refusal so long as my promise to mamma gives him the right to do so; and I'm glad of it."

"You, Celia!—glad of it?"

"Yes, glad."

"Then the hints Cranstoun threw out to me about Creighton's frequent visits to your uncle's house were true, after all? *He* has a profession—he can support a wife. He is an orator, and the ladies always admire orators. Mr. Sydenham speaks highly of him, too. You and Leoline Sydenham called on his mother last week. I see it all. I have nothing to say to it: it's all right. Only you might have told me honestly, Celia, how the land lay, instead of fooling me with these long stories about your father and mother. You had only to give me a hint that another was preferred, and I would have released you at any time. I might have known—"

Mowbray stopped, amazed at the effect of his words. Celia had dried her eyes and had spoken to him quietly, kindly, in reply to that offer of marriage. But now hot tears burst forth without restraint—convulsive sobs shook her frame from head to foot. Long and bitterly she wept, covering her face with her hands. Mowbray, repentant, began in humble tone to apologize for his suspicions. She did not intimate, by reply or gesture, that she heard him. Then he spoke to her tenderly, using terms of endearment: still, not a word, not a sign, but the passion of grief seemed gradually to wear itself out. As she became quieter he gently took one of her hands: she left it passively in his grasp. Then he put an arm around her waist. The touch seemed to awake her at once. She rose to her feet, confronting him. He rose too. They stood there for a minute or two, neither speaking — Mowbray actually afraid; poor Celia struggling desperately for composure. At last she spoke, faintly at first, but gathering courage as she went on:

"I used to think we had so much in common. It seemed to me we suited each other. I thought you understood me, Evelyn. Eight months ago you asked me to marry you. Did you take me for a girl who would say yes, as I did, and then leave you bound by the promise you made to me in return, after I had changed my mind and preferred another? I loved you, Evelyn: I thought so much of you."

"Forgive me — oh forgive me!" he broke in.

"Slanderers tried to poison my mind against you. They sent me an anonymous letter telling me that you met Ellen Tyler and made love to her, secretly, at a lonely spot in the woods near her father's mill, and that her father had surprised one of your interviews."

"Did you believe all that of me, Celia?"

"Not a word of it. If I had, I should have spoken to you about it that very day. I burned the letter, and have scarcely thought of it since—till now. I trusted you."

"How nobly you have acted!"

"Have *you* trusted *me?* Do you know what you have just been telling me?—that, after I had solemnly promised to be your wife, and without ever asking to be released from that promise, I played you false, secretly encouraging another because he was better able to support a wife than you. You accuse me of this—on whose authority? On the authority of a villain who traduced yourself (I'm certain that anonymous letter was from him)—on the say-so of a scoundrel who took ten thousand dollars from poor papa — hush-money to conceal the English marriage — and who has just written to the heir-at-law in England, offering to bring suit against me and recover the property for him, on half shares. You set his lies against your faith in me, and they outweigh it?"

"Spare me, Celia, spare me."

"I am sorry—*very* sorry, Evelyn—" in a softened tone—"but you force me to defend myself. And the truth *must* be told: the happiness of both our lives depends upon it."

"I absolve you from all blame, Celia."

"As to Mr. Creighton, he is a brave, generous man: any woman might be proud of him as a husband. I do honor him—you touched the truth there—because he selected a profession and works hard at it, as every young man should. He has a right to ask any woman in marriage, and I hope he will find one worthy to be his wife. But he is nothing to me. I do not love him, and I never shall. He does not love me. I don't even think he likes me. He thinks me purse-proud, I believe: at least his manner has seemed to say so. When I told you that I was glad my uncle persisted in refusing assent to our marriage, I had forgotten there was such a man as Mr. Creighton in the world. I was thinking of you — not of him. I was thinking that if I had been free to marry, and you had proposed to make me your wife to-morrow, it would have been wrong in me to accept the offer. I was glad that, if you did persist in seeking me, two years and a half would intervene, so that you could make no sacrifice on the impulse of the moment. If you had understood anything about me, you would have felt that at once."

"Celia, Celia, leave me hope yet."

"It is too late. We have not the power of trusting whom we will. If I had my property back, I would give it all—freely, joyfully—to regain the faith in you that I have lost. Oh, Evelyn, you have uttered suspicions—you have spoken words to-day—that will stand up for ever a barrier between us. You said"—she trembled, reseating herself and pausing, as if to gain courage—"you said that I had dealt falsely by you, and that, to conceal my encouragement of Mr. Creighton's addresses, I was fooling you with tales about my father and mother. It was an insult—an insult to their memory and to me. I know it was caused by a petulant burst of anger. But the words were said, and can never, in this world, be recalled."

"Is this your final decision?"

"Yes, final and irrevocable. I shall never marry. I don't want any man to brave reproach for me. I can bear my own burden. I release you from all promise, and you shall have a witness in proof. I shall see your mother to-night, and tell her that her son is free."

"And you throw me over, without more ado, like that, as if I were a worthless scapegrace. What am I to think of your love, Celia?"

"Do not let us part in anger, Evelyn. I don't think you worthless. I think we are unsuited to each other, and that we should be unhappy together if we married. And it is not you who have to fear insinuations about being thrown over, as you call it. It is not a rich girl jilting a poor man. I accepted you when I was able to offer a competency. A penniless girl, I reject you—a penniless and nameless girl, whom nobody would care to own. You ask what you are to think of my love"—again that tremble in the tones: "it may be a comfort to you some day, Evelyn, to remember that a young girl once loved you dearly, trusted you implicitly, would have given her life for yours. I am not ashamed to own it, even now that you and I—" If she could have arrested her tears, how gladly she would have done it! but tears are tyrants and will have their way. "We must part friends, dear Evelyn: that may be, and ought to be, and shall be, unless you reject my friendship. You will not do that?"

Mowbray gave her both his hands; and long afterward, when he was far away and at the head of a household in which Celia was a stranger, the girl remembered, with feelings of tender regard, that when they rose to walk home—nevermore to enter these woods as lovers again—hers were not the only eyes that were wet. The man had been touched to the soul at last; and all he could say was, "Can you ever forgive me, noble girl?"

"I have forgiven everything, dear friend. Do not let us say a word more about it."

And they walked home—these two—talking quietly and amicably of commonplace things, attracting the inquiring looks of many villagers whom they met, until, near to Hartland's dwelling, they reached the cross street that led to Mrs. Mowbray's cottage on the lake. There Mowbray wrung Celia's hand in silence, parted from her—and it was all over!

CHAPTER XXIX.

ON THE LAKE SHORE.

"I do believe it,
Against an oracle."
SHAKESPEARE—*The Tempest.*

WHEN Celia parted from her cousin at her uncle's front gate that afternoon, some tone or look of his suggested to her that his projected visit was to Ellinor only, not to Dr. Meyrac. Yet it seems she was mistaken. When Ethan called at the house he asked for the doctor, and was closeted with him for some time. Afterward, it is true, he inquired for Miss Ethelridge, and she came to the parlor.

"It is a charming afternoon," he said, "soft and balmy, like a day of early summer. I thought, perhaps, you would not object to a stroll on the banks of the lake."

She hesitated for a moment, and Ethan added: "You are so much confined during the week, Miss Ellinor—"

"I'll put on my hat and shawl and go with pleasure," rising to prepare for the walk.

April is proverbially inconstant, yet in temperate latitudes, when the sun shines out and a southern breeze stirs the air, what more delightful days, fresh and inspiring! — all the fresher and brighter that they shine upon us, like joy succeeding sorrow, after a season of murky clouds and drifting rains. No days in all the year when hearts, if they be true and warm, so gratefully yield to tender and trustful influences. The anniversaries are they of Faith and Hope and Love.

These two, Ellinor and Ethan, were faithful and cordial; and as they passed down the shady avenue, and thence to the left along the pleasant lake shore, there came over them, with genial glamour, the spirit of the hour and the place.

Ethan had been a frequent visitor of the Meyracs, whom he liked: he had often joined their walking-parties when Ellinor was of the number; occasionally he had accompanied his cousin and her friend when they rode out together; but this was the first time he had ever invited Miss Ethelridge to walk with him alone. Ellinor felt that it was, and the consciousness of it embarrassed Ethan. After a little commonplace talk, they walked on for some time in silence. Then Ellinor was the first to speak.

"What a beautiful spot for building!" she said, as they passed a certain six-acre lot that our readers wot of. "Has it been bought?"

"No. Mr. Sydenham had instructed me not to sell it."

"How prettily it is laid out! Is it for sale now?"

"No."

"Somebody has shown much taste there. Mr. Sydenham entrusted the laying of it out to you, did he not, Mr. Hartland?"

"Yes. I'm glad it pleases you. I like to lay out pretty spots, and this always took my fancy. It's embellishment was a labor of love."

"I have not seen a more charming site for a picturesque cottage for many a day."

Then they relapsed into silence again. After a time Ethan said: "Cousin Celia tells me you and she are to be partners in carrying on the 'Chiskauga Institute.' I am very glad of it—glad for her sake, for, though she is a dear, good, willing girl, she is inexperienced, while your management and method are excellent; and glad for yours, Miss Ethelridge, because the labor and the responsibility are too much for you alone: your brain and your eyes have been overtasked."

Ellinor looked up quickly: "Did Celia speak to you about my being overtasked?"

"No: she only spoke to me of her great love for you, and of her joy that you were willing to receive her."

"Dear child! It was your own idea, then?"

"Forgive me, dear Miss Ethelridge. I have no right to interfere—" he paused in search of an expression—"to interfere in what regards your welfare. But I have remarked—it has seemed to me sometimes—that when you have used your eyes long in school, you felt pain or uneasiness."

"I do occasionally. But is that your only reason for supposing my eyes weak?"

"No. I fear that I shall appear presumptuous, but—I wanted so much to know the truth, and I spoke to Dr. Meyrac about it."

"And he said—?"

"That it was important you should not overwork your eyes, especially at night."

"Nothing more?"

"No. You are not offended by my intermeddling?"

"Offended! I have met with much kindness—more than I expected—far more than I had any right to expect—since I came here; but no one has treated me more thoughtfully and generously than you. I am too dependent on my friends to quarrel with kindness; and if I have said little about yours, Mr. Hartland, don't think I am ungrateful."

"I am ashamed to hear you speak of it. What little I have been able to do for you by taking that German class was done during time that belonged to Mr. Sydenham and at his desire."

"You suggested it to him?"

Ethan did not reply to this.

Ellinor saw through it all now. She understood why he had sought to relieve her from the senior class, two hours a week, by the German lessons; why he had offered to read to her of evenings; why he so often proposed, to Madame Meyrac and herself, to translate to them passages he had selected from his German favorites. She understood why he had volunteered a thousand little services that saved her eyes from strain. "You are a good man, Mr. Hartland," she said, warmly. "God requite you! for I never can."

Ethan's face—not a handsome one, if one looked to regularity of feature, but a face in which one read firmness, benevolence, honesty—Ethan's face lit up with joy. But he changed the subject, speaking of details connected with the projected partnership. Thus conversing, they passed the fair-ground, where, the day before, there had been a baseball match between rival clubs, and reached a spot where a footpath ascending in zigzag the face of the hillside, through thick underbrush of laurel bushes, led up to the summit of the cliff, which, as our readers know, rose precipitously from the shore of the lake a little way beyond its north-western extremity.

Here, in a grove of cedars near the verge of the cliff, the villagers had erected a summer-house, sheltered from the north, but open on the side next the lake. The view thence was quite equal to that which had struck even Cassiday with admiration on his arrival.

The sweep of low hills, from one of which that worthy had first caught sight of the village, could be traced, trending off to the south for several miles, till the outline was lost in the forest. The lake, seen from this spot throughout its full extent, lay, like some huge creature in lazy beauty, at their feet; its banks, on the village side beyond the Elm Walk, dotted with pretty cottages, spacious gardens behind them. The valley-land beyond, chequered throughout with a carpeting of fresh green, spoke of teeming harvests and a bounteous summer to come. Over all—valley and village and placid lake—shone the slanting rays of the sun, now declining to the west. One might light on a thousand more striking aspects of nature, but on few more suggestive of peace and cheerfulness and rural comfort.

They found the summer-house vacant, and seated themselves in full view of the quiet scene. Ellinor's glance wandered over it, a tender melancholy gradually shading her face. She was seeking to stamp each feature of the landscape on waning sense; laying up, in store for possible years of darkness to come, bright memories of a glorious world.

"You regret, sometimes," said Ethan in a low voice, "that you have settled, here out of the world, among us? You look back, with sadness, do you not, on far different life in Europe?"

"With sadness, yes, but never with regret. Do you regret, after spending some years in the Old World, that you have returned to Chiskauga?"

"I? Oh no! But that is quite different. I was born in New England, but I came here so young that Chiskauga seems to me almost my native place. I like it more and more day by day. If—if the good fortune that has followed me so far endures, I should be willing to live and die here."

"Your engagement with Mr. Sydenham is a permanent one, is it not?"

Ethan hesitated—coloring and showing unwonted agitation. When he spoke something in the tone of his voice caused Ellinor to breathe more quickly—in the low, pleading tone it was, not in the simple words: "Will you let me tell you something of my life and my prospects, Miss Ethelridge, and not think me egotistical?"

Ellinor smiled: "We were speaking, a little while ago, of my plans and prospects. Did that strike you as egotism in me?"

"How kind you are! It shall not be a long story. I wish you had known my mother—my own mother. She was as gentle and warm-hearted as my step-mother is; and I think there never was any one who so forgot herself in her child as she in all she did for me. It is very sad to think of it, but I know now that she must have accepted my father from motives of respect and esteem—her love was all lavished on me."

"I have heard those who knew her well speak of her in terms of high praise."

"I never realized till I lost her what she had been to me. I was very lonely then, but after a few years I went to Germany; and then new scenes and hard work filled my thoughts. On my return I couldn't find employment as civil engineer; so I accepted from Mr. Sydenham the post of land-agent. Of his own accord he has gradually increased my salary from seven hundred and twenty dollars to fifteen hundred dollars a year. Last year—but you know how generous he is — he gave me what you were admiring to-day—that building site with the Elm Walk on one side and the lake in front. You were right, Miss Ellinor: there is not a more choice spot for a modest residence on the whole property. Last week he told me that just as long as I could find no more eligible situation he wished me to retain the position I hold as manager of his Chiskauga estate, were it for life: he even offered me a further increase of salary, in case"—he hesitated—"in certain contingencies. I have saved, while in his service, enough to build—perhaps not to furnish—as handsome a house as I desire." Ethan paused.

"I am not surprised," said Ellinor, "that you like Chiskauga and are satisfied with your lot."

"I am not satisfied with my lot, though I may lose your good opinion by saying so. I am ambitious."

"I should never have thought it: you seemed content to live and die here. Are you sorry to have lost the chance of distinction as engineer? or have you political aspirations, as my friend Mr. Creighton has had?"

At the name a shade as of disappointment crossed Ethan's face. He replied gravely: "My ambition rises higher than a seat in Congress or an engineer's post with a ten-thousand dollar salary."

"I didn't guess that," said Ellinor, smiling.

"No wonder. I doubt if there be a man or woman or child in Chiskauga that would guess it, or that would not laugh at me if they did," a little bitterly.

Had Ellinor an inkling of what was coming? It seemed probable that some shadow of the truth was stealing over her, for that color in her cheeks came somewhat too suddenly and brightly to be due merely to air and exercise. Yet it could have been a very vague intuition only, or she would not have said: "You are reticent, Mr. Hartland: you don't share your plans with your friends."

Some undefined suasion in the tone or in the words, or perhaps it was the heightened color, gave him courage. "You think me reticent," he said. "If I had ever believed that I could confess to you how far my ambition reaches, without incurring — no, not your contempt, you are too noble for that—but your displeasure, the confession should have been made long ago."

Then he told her what had lain hidden for years in that shy heart of his—how he had taken himself to task for aspiring to one so far above him—one who had always seemed to him to have come down from some upper sphere: how the feeling of that disparity between them had grown and strengthened the more he had seen of her, the better he had learned to know her. "God is my witness," he said, "it's not of rank nor of social position I'm talking: these have no oppression for me. If I were to be presented to a queen to-morrow, it would be without anything akin to abasement:

we learn independence of feeling here in the West. But there is a subtile something that enshrines you; an atmosphere of delicate culture and refinement, that is partly due no doubt to lifelong seclusion from all rude agencies."

"Seclusion from all rude agencies? If you only knew, Mr. Hartland, what has befallen me!"

"I do not know. I do not ask. The past is nothing to me. It's of the future I wanted to speak. I think I should not have had courage for it to-day, if you hadn't said those kind words—far, far beyond my desert. I feel that I am country-bred, rudely nurtured, and with a mere humble competence to offer. I have no claims—but none of us have any claims on God for mercy and love."

"You say this to a poor, penniless country teacher?"

"I say it to Ellinor Ethelridge. I knew I should have to say it some day or other. It's too strong for me. I thought perhaps I might escape it by throwing every energy into my work: I used to like that for its own sake; but I've come to feel that work without care for something beyond oneself has no life in it—is nothing but a task. It was a little thing, that bit of land to build on: how the magnates of this world would laugh if they knew what joy I felt when Sydenham's generosity threw it into my hands! But for me its charm was in hope, not in possession. The solitary feeling I had when I lost my mother had come again; and one night I dreamed that the pretty cottage I had been thinking of stood there in the early sunshine, and—that I was no longer solitary. Dreaming still, I went out to work, not for myself alone and impatient till evening came: then, when I returned, in the moonlight—there on the lake shore, all in white—I knew it was not a spirit, yet I approached it with misgiving. But I *was* welcomed, as some poor wanderer, when earth-life has passed, may be received in heaven. Now you know all the extravagance of my ambition. You know on what conditions I'm willing to live and to die in this little village of ours. My life is dark, my work is irksome, that pretty home-spot is a mockery, without you, Ellinor. You may not care for my love—perhaps you love another: then you shall never be pained by one troublesome word from me. I cannot live in sight of Paradise and feel that its gates are closed against me for ever. But the world is wide, and every man must do what God allots to him till the day of release comes."

These undemonstrative creatures who walk through life with heart in check and feelings "like greyhounds in the slips," have sometimes, under the frigid surface, a humble well-spring of enthusiasm that will overflow on occasion. To-day Ethan's time had come; the hidden fount was stirred. It was a new revelation to Ellinor.

Though her cheeks were flushed and the tears had stolen to her eyes, she sat quiet and silent, gazing dreamily on the placid landscape before her. Ethan said not a word more—half-hoping when he saw her hesitate—content, for the moment, that his temerity had not called forth sudden rejection. At last the answer came in a subdued tone: "Mr. Hartland, I think the highest honor one human being can confer on another is the homage of a faithful heart. But I owe you more than this. You trust me implicitly, knowing nothing, asking nothing, of my past life. Yet my position might well create doubts, even in those least inclined to suspicion, whether misconduct might not have had something to do with this exile from my native land."

The lover thought he felt his way clear now. His tongue was loosed: his heart spoke from his eyes. Ellinor did not recognize the Ethan she had known for years as he replied: "Whatever concerns you must interest me. But you know little how I love you if you think it necessary to say one word in exculpation—in explanation, I mean—of your coming here among us to do us good. Can love be faithful and have no faith?—a pitiful imposture without it! It is not in the power of human being—not even in yours—to convince me that you have ever knowingly, willfully, done anything that God or good men will remember against you for judgment; but I don't care—I mean, that except for the pain which sad memories may give you, I don't care—what you have been. I know, as I know my existence, what you are. I think—God forgive me!—that I couldn't believe in Divine Goodness itself if I lost belief in you. My faith in you is like my faith in the beauty of God's world—in His stainless sunshine—in the pure stream He sends for blessing—in His very promises of immortality. See!" he added in a low, reverent tone: "if every particle of historical truth set up in support of the Christian scheme of morals and eternal life were swept away to-morrow, it would still be to me the revealment of love and light it is—itself its own witness. And you are my revelation of human excellence and gracious refinement: if I have you, Ellinor, I have holier evidence than all human testimony can give about you. But it's no use," he broke out after a moment's pause—"it's not a bit of use to go on. I can feel it all—how it comes over me!—but to tell it—"

She was touched to the heart-core. "I did not know," she said, "that there was such nobility of faith in the world." Then she relapsed into what seemed sad thoughts, sighing. At last: "There is an obstacle. Do not fear," she said, earnestly. "I am not going to conceal anything from you: trust like yours must not be all on one side. Do you think I would let you speak to me as you have spoken to-day, and then keep back one sin I may have committed? Do you think I would hide from you now what reduced me to poverty and dependence? I meant to pass my life here in this quiet place, God and my own heart the only judges of the past. But you shall know all."

Then, after a pause, she told him of her early life while her mother, a widow, yet lived; of what befell her, in a cold home, at cruel hands, after her mother's death; of a terrible crisis in her life that led her to the brink of despair; then—what she had already told Celia—of her bitter sufferings and her final rescue.

Ethan listened as one might listen to tidings from the next world, his very soul in the fascinating story, now moved to pity, now stirred to hot indignation. And when Ellinor closed her narrative by saying, with a deep sigh of relief, "I have kept nothing from you, and now—thank God!—I am here, never, never to return," Ethan broke forth:

"And is that the obstacle? The world is faithless and heartless: Love's name is profaned by the base, the treacherous, the inhuman; and that's to be a reason why you can't marry me! I knew it beforehand—what it must all amount to—though that infamous plot passes imagination. What of it? Can you never be my wife because worthless creatures close their doors against you?"

"No, that's not it. God, who sees secret causes and influences, may justify where men condemn. At all events, now that I've told you the whole truth, I am willing to abide by your judgment."

"Thank God!"

"But if you don't think it cause enough to desist from seeking me, that my relatives regard me as outcast—"

"I entreat you—"

"Well, I shall not say another word about it; but that is not the obstacle I spoke of."

"It's some one else?"

She shook her head.

Such a sigh of relief! Then, eagerly: "What is it, Ellinor?"

"If ever man deserved a good wife, you do—one who would make you a bright, cheerful home — one who would see to all your wants and comforts — one who should be care-taker, it may be, of your children, looking to their habits, watching their shortcomings; in short, overseeing and providing for your household."

"And you, with your business tact and admirable judgment—you can't do this?"

"Had God so willed, it might have been. Possibly, possibly—but I mustn't shrink from looking in the face what may be the inevitable."

"The inevitable?"

"Dr. Meyrac was less honest to you than he has been to me."

Ethan hung on her words, scarcely breathing. Could it be? Ellinor went on: "The good man knew that the truth is always best, and he told me that any day there might be paralysis of the optic nerve. A blind wife—"

"Hush, Ellinor. It is in God's hands. Shall we rebel against Him?"

"I do not. Once, in the extremity of misery, I might have done so: then there came to me, as if some angel had stooped down and spoken, the words: 'Adversity never crushes except those who rebel against it.' I do not rebel. But God intends this affliction for me alone. It must never fall upon you."

"It's hazardous to say what God's intentions are. We see His doings—that's all. He brought you here. It was His will that I should be near you year after year. It was His will that out of all this glorious world of His I should crave one blessing, weighed against which all else is dust in the balance. I know that hearts have hungered until Death stilled the yearning, but if—" He paused, adding at last: "You are the soul of truth, Ellinor. If what seems to you an obstacle did not exist—"

"You shall have more than an answer to your question. If in one year from this time Dr. Meyrac thinks the danger has passed—" she gave him her hand.

* * * * *

The sunset was one of those gorgeous manifestations of coloring that seem, as we gaze into their magic depths, revelations from another world—an effulgence of which no human skill has ever transferred to canvas even the shadow. A consciousness of its unearthly beauty gushed over Ethan's heart as never in all his life before—as if some new sense had that moment been born within him. He turned to Ellinor: "Have you charity for extravagance?"

She looked up inquiringly, and he added: "I have had, of late: there is often wisdom underneath it." He took from an inner pocket and handed to her a scrap of paper. It contained but a single stanza:*

* From a fugitive poem by Mrs. SARAH T. BOLTON, of Indiana.

"There was no music in the rippling stream,
No fragrance in the rose or violet,
No warmth, no glory in the noontide beam,
No star in heaven, dear love, until we met."

"Is it absurd?" pursued Ethan, when he saw she had read it. "Is it ridiculous? Yet I never knew what the glory of sunset was till now."

As they walked slowly home they gradually came back to earth. They had passed the age of thoughtlessness. Ellinor was twenty-five and Ethan six years older, and they were business people, if they were lovers.

They agreed that, except to Celia, nothing should be said of their engagement and its proviso. Ethan could not help touching on that proviso: "Whom would you cherish the more dearly, Ellinor—one of your pupils who enjoyed all her senses, or one who, by loss of sight, doubly needed your protection?"

"A year, a year!" she persisted: "let us await the decree of God." Then, as they passed on, nearing the Elm Walk, her eyes following his wistful gaze to a small clump of shrubbery, the soft voice added in a lighter tone: "Dream-cottages are pretty things in the moonlight, but there are rainy days, you know, Ethan."

"Ethan!" He started.

"Besides," she went on, "even if all else result—result as we hope—there's the furniture: I've a small purse at home that perhaps in another year might be heavy enough—"

"In another year, then. Since you've found out my scriptural name, darling Ellinor, I am content to work and to wait, for I know now—if we both live—what the will of God is."

It was a cheerful party that evening at Dr. Meyrac's tea-table.

CHAPTER XXX.

AN ARRIVAL.

"Vengeance is mine, I will repay, saith the Lord."
—ROMANS.

"AN' is it you, Terence dear, at last? What's the matter? Ye look as if ye'd seen a spook."

"Worse nor that, Norah. Did ye ever hear of a spook stealin' a man's money and sendin' him to jail?"

Norah turned pale: "Sure and it isn't—?"

"Yes it is—that very black-souled, infernal— Ye needn't grip the babe, mavourneen: don't scare the childher. It's me that has the whip-hand o' the scoundrel now."

The time of this dialogue was three days after that on which the two cousins parted at Mr. Hartland's gate—one to return with crushed heart and saddened life; the other with exultation, in a tumult of wildering joy. The place was a room in the Chiskauga "Hotel."

No Inns now. No unpretending, homely nooks of shelter where, when one has been exposed without to cold and hunger and a long day's fatigues, man and horse may be taken *in* to warmth and quiet, and the rider may stretch his limbs and say, "Shall I not take mine ease?" We don't care about ease in these days of rush and railroading, except such as is to be had in a sleeping-car, and we hate simple names. Glasgow, the most populous town in Scotland, has her Green, and Boston, the modern Athens, her Common; but these are examples of extinct rusticity. Modern cities rejoice only in Hotels, noisy and glittering, where "distinguished guests" are entertained; and in Parks, gotten up at a cost of millions. And why should not Chiskauga—village if it was—be allowed, in this land of liberty, to pick a French term (once designating the stately mansions of the great) from the fashionable vocabulary, and appropriate the same to her humble house of entertainment?

It was at the Chiskauga Hotel, then, that our old friends, Terence and Norah, with their two children, Dermot and Kathleen, now found themselves. Kullen had kept his promise as to the letter of recommendation. It was to Mr. Sydenham, whose acquaintance he had made while traveling, three years before, as temperance lecturer in Ohio. Terence had given up his tavern, spent a week with his father-in-law in Cumberland county, and as soon as he reached Chiskauga had presented his credentials. It was on his return from Rosebank, and just before reaching the hotel, that he met a plain but nicely-kept carriage drawn by two sorrels.

"But are ye sure it was him?" Norah asked, under her breath.

"Am I sure that's you, acushla? Am I sure this is little Kathy?" taking her on his knee. "D'ye think them poor craturs that's burnin' in hell don't know the Divil when they catch a sight of him?"

"Ye scare the babe, Teddy, with sich talk."

"Well, thin, I won't." To the child: "There isn't no ugly black man comin' to take daddy or my Kathy: they don't have ugly black men here. We're goin' to a garden a'most as nice as grand pap's, where ye kin play to yer heart's contint, my little darlint. And, Derry, there's a stream o' water right convanient—Kinshon Creek's the name it goes by—where ye kin sail that boat o' yours."

Dermot clapped his hands.

"So ye've settled it all, Terence. Ye saw Mr. Sydenham?"

"Didn't I? A gintleman, every inch of him. He 'minds me o' the Ould Country, barrin' he's as civil-spoken as though he was nobody at all—"

"Did ye tell him about the trial and the jail and all?"

"An' what for shouldn't I tell him the whole, out o' the face? It's no more nor right for him to know where I've been; and then maybe Mr. Kullen wrote to him a'ready. So I tould everything, both about me and you. Says I: 'Mr. Sydenham, if she don't make the beautifulest butter that's ever been set on your table, we don't want a cint, nayther she nor me.' That settled it."

"So ye'r to manage the farm and me the dairy, and we're to have the place?"

"The house and the garden and a potato patch and a cow's milk, wood to keep the pot boilin' and the childher warm, and sixty dollars a month. It don't pay like the bar, Norah, but then, ye know, I promised Mr. Kullen—"

"Oh, Teddy, to talk of the bar! an' me and the childher goin' to live wi' the flowers and the green fields round us, and the blessed cows to milk and the lovely butter to make, and everything just like it used to be when you came over from ould Mr. Richards' in the gloamin'! But ye've forgot that."

Not quite, it seemed. And it was very well there was nobody there just then but the children—nobody to laugh at the foolish fellow when he dropped Kathleen in a hurry and stopped short his wife's panegyric on farm-life by a kiss very much of the old Cumberland county savor.

"Thin it's all jist right, mavourneen," he said. "I was sort o' tired o' them stone pavements and brick walls and white shutters, any way. It's a snug shealin' enough, Norah — four good rooms, forby the kitchen. The ould coachman had it, but his wife died last month, and he's sort o' lonely, and we'll have to give him a room. Mr. Sydenham's to pay us four dollars a week for his board; that'll help some, and maybe the poor man won't eat no great dale. I think he takes it hard, the ould woman's death. I'm not misdoubtin' but what we've done the right thing, if that divil *is* here."

The farm faded from Norah's imagination, the bright look from her face, and anxious misgivings about Cassiday, the perjured witness, clouded countenance and thought.

"Ye came here to please me, Teddy asthore, and ye haven't forgot them times when ye used to set by the kitchen fire and tell father stories about ould Ireland to please him for my sake. Maybe ye'll do somethin' more for me."

"Ye're a darlint, Norah, and so was yer ould father to let me have ye. Sorra thing can ye ask me—in rason, that is—but what I'll do."

"It's for your sake, Teddy, and the childher's. I dreamed last night about them days when ye was in jail, and me like a bird wi' a broken wing that wanted to go off somewhere and die: it's awful to think of; but then — ye can niver tell—it might be God that sint ye there: Mr. Kullen thought He did, to keep ye from helpin' on drinkin', and from keepin' company wi' bad men like that Cassidy, and to bring ye out here where ye can hear the birds sing, and where ye can let them childher run out and not find them, the next minit, wi' the riff-raff of the street, playin' in the gutter. Who knows but what it was the Lord put it in that bad man's heart to harm ye—all for yer good?"

"Sure, an' it wouldn't be God that would put sich a thought in a man: that's the Divil's work."

"I do' know," said Norah, thoughtfully: "He tould Moses he was goin' to harden King Pharaoh's heart and them Egyptians, afore they got drownded; and he did harden it awful; and that was the way the childher o' Israel got to the promised land. I was readin' it last week, and there's nothin' about the Divil there."

Norah was getting out of her depth in the Red Sea of theology, and Terence was afraid to follow her. He tried to bring her back to the dry land of practical business: "An' what was it ye wanted me to do for ye?"

But Norah was not quite ready to answer that question yet. "Cassiday was a desperate wicked man," she said, "but I don't think he was wickeder nor Pharaoh: he niver wanted to kill Derry nor nobody else, that I hearn of; but Pharaoh, he tried to murder all the boys them Israel women had jist as soon as the poor babes was born, and niver to leave them nothin' but the girls. Ef it had been Derry, what would ye have done, Terence?"

"Sure an' wouldn't I have shot the bloody blackguard, ef I could?"

"I expect ye would. But ye see God niver tould the childher o' Israel to shoot Pharaoh. He took it in hand himself, and drownded him. So you jist let that vagabone alone, Terence. Ef God wants him drownded, it's easy done. There's plenty o' them steamboats blows up every day; or maybe he'll go sailin' on that bit water we saw as we came in, and the boat 'll tip over. Any way, it's good the rascal's done ye, though he was minded to do ye harm: ef he hadn't sworn agin ye, ye'd niver have got to no promised land like this. I'm sure it's far better here nor it was in the wilderness, with nothin' but manna, or maybe some birds, to eat all day. We're to have a cow's milk, and they say there's bee trees in them woods out here in the West, that a man can cut down ef he wants a bucket o' nice honeycomb;—and thin, ye know, there's the garden besides, and the potato-patch. And sure the Israelites niver had no potatoes, and niver came to nothin' better, after they got done with the wilderness, nor milk and honey. Now, Teddy—there's a darlint!—let bygones be bygones: let the ugly spalpeen go, and let God have his own way, and don't ye be getting yerself into another scrape for nothin' at all, at all: that's what I wanted to ax ye."

Terence reflected: "It's nothin' better nor to be kilt over the head with a good shillalah the rascal deserves; but thin ef we all got our desarts, maybe there's some of us might come out sort o' badly. I don't niver like to think much about keepin' them men drinkin' half the night, instead o' comin' decently to bed to you, Norah, an' you lying there wakin' and waitin' for me. I don't jist think God liked that. So maybe, as ye say, I'd best leave Him to manage Cassiday, or Delorny, or whatever name the Divil's cub has picked up by this time. But it's mighty aggravatin'-like to see the mansworn rowdy set up there wi' a bran-new coat and hat, drivin' the prettiest pair o' sorrels ye ever set eyes on, Norah; and me that knows all the time where the money came from that made him a dacent man to look at."

"But ye niver can get back that money without you go into them law-courts again; and I think that would kill me," said Norah, with a shudder.

"Sure an' didn't I tell ye, acushla, I'd let the scoundrel run, for your sake and the babes? Thin I've got no time to go after him wi' the shillalah; for that house of ourn's is all ready, and I made a fire in the kitchen, and the ould coachman said he'd see to it till we came on. I'll go seek a dray to take the trunks and the plenishin'."

"There ain't no drays here, daddy," said that observant young urchin, Dermot, who had been exploring Chiskauga while his father was gone.

"Well, thin, a cart or a wagon, or whatever they carry things with in these parts."

Before evening they were installed in their new habitation. And Derry was sailing his boat on the creek, and Kathleen, with gaze of infant delight, was watching Norah milk "them blessed cows," warm recollections of a homestead in Pennsylvania flushing the mother's cheek and tears of pleasure dimming her eyes the while.

PART IX.

CHAPTER XXXI.

GRANGULA'S MOUNT.

"Charity for his fellow-creatures arrested half his words."—MADAME DE SÉVIGNÉ, *speaking of the good Monsieur de Gourville.*

ON the lower portion of the lawn in front of Sydenham's house stood a stately elm, which, when the axe leveled the surrounding forest, the woodcutter had spared. Under its broad shelter, in full view of the village, sat two ladies—Mrs. Clymer on a rustic chair, calmly knitting, and our friend Leoline on a camp-stool, a small table with drawing materials before her.

The latter seemed greatly discomposed. "It's no use, Aunt Hannah," throwing down her pencil: "I can't draw a steady line this morning. I wish some old man would marry that horrid creature and carry her off to California."

"Thee shouldn't talk so, Lela dear. We should make much allowance for Catherine Wolfgang. Thee is too young to remember much of her husband, but she must have been sorely tried with that man."

"If his tongue was half as abusive as hers, I think she must, auntie. 'Seems to me if we have suffering ourselves, that ought to make us feel compassion for the sufferings of others."

"Yes. But she didn't know Celia was within hearing, and had no intention of hurting her feelings."

"She's too cowardly to say it to her face: these creatures always are. They haven't a bit of real courage. She only abused the darling child, and insulted the memory of her parents, behind her back."

"Maybe it wasn't so bad as thee thinks. People sometimes exaggerate without intending it."

"I wonder if there ever was anybody you could not find some excuse for, aunt."

"We all need forgiveness, Lela."

"More or less. But I think if I had ten thousand Aunt Hannahs, just like you, they wouldn't need as much forgiveness for the sins they committed all their lives through, as Mrs. Wolfgang needs for the backbiting she does with that bitter tongue of hers in a single year. I'm wicked myself, I know: if that woman had waited for Jean to carry her out to the garden gate, I'd have liked, of all things in the world, to be passing, just then, on the other side of the way: it would have been a sight to see. But I'm not vicious: I don't wish anybody any harm: if Mrs. Wolfgang were on her deathbed, and had nobody else, I'd be willing to sit up with her all night, provided they didn't insist on my crying if she died next morning. Then, you know, auntie, I've heard you repeat the texts about breaking the bruised reed and crushing the soul already nigh to perishing. I think anybody who would do that is too mean and cruel to live in this world."

"God does not think so."

Hannah Clymer was almost startled out of her equanimity when the warm-hearted girl sprang from her seat, threw her arms round her neck and kissed her: "You're an angel, auntie, that's the truth—an angel with a good-for-nothing niece. I wonder I don't contrive to be better, with you in the house all the time."

"Do I ever complain of thee, dear child?"

"Never, nor of Mrs. Wolfgang either. Ah, here comes papa. Who is that he has just parted from?"

"Some one who brought him a letter of introduction this morning."

"Who is it, papa?" as he came across to them.

"An Irishman. He and his wife are coming to live in the coachman's house and manage the farm and dairy. You remember Mr. Kullen, Hannah?"

"The temperance lecturer? I remember him well."

"He recommends this man highly.

The poor fellow, it seems, suffered three months' imprisonment on a false charge. Kullen proved his innocence, and he was released on the spot. A hard case."

"This foolish child," said Mrs. Clymer, with her kind smile, "has been grieving so sorely over another hard case, this morning, that she has scarcely touched her drawing."

"Celia Pembroke's? Mrs. Wolfgang—"

"Ah, you've heard of it, papa? And you said nothing to me about it?"

"Why should I vex you, my child, by repeating the coarse slanders of a cruel woman?"

"Poor, dear Celia! And no father, no mother, nobody to stand up for her!"

"Except you, my child, and sister Hannah; and myself, if you think me worth counting; and the Meyracs, and the Hartlands—the uncle has come out most creditably—and Mr. Harper, and the Creightons, and ever so many more of those whose good opinion is worth having. Mrs. Wolfgang has a party who hold with her—I'm very sorry it numbers as many as it does — people who like gossip seasoned with scandal, and take comfort in the misfortunes of others. They will run Celia down, of course; talk of pride having a fall, and justify Mowbray in casting her off—that will be their version of it—because her father deserved the penitentiary and left a stain on her birth."

"Mowbray!" said Leoline, her eyes flashing—"is that broken off?"

"So Ethan tells me—by Celia herself."

"Brave girl! I want to kiss her."

"Mowbray behaved badly — some jealous quarrel, I believe—"

"Just like him; all a pretence to shirk out. I'm so glad! I'm scarcely sorry Celia lost her money, since that selfish Adonis is gone along with it."

"You are harsh in your judgments, my child."

"So Aunt Hannah says; and as both of you agree about it, no doubt it's true. But consider, papa. How would you like me to marry a young man who had made up his mind it was better to do nothing in this world except to live on the money you might be able to give me? How would you like a son-in-law without either trade or business or profession—the laziest young fellow about town, who spent half his time riding a horse he couldn't afford to keep, while his mother was slaving at home, teaching school and keeping house too? I won't say a word of the scandal about Ellen Tyler: I despise such things, and wouldn't hear them if I could possibly help it. But what is he good for, papa? What has he ever done in this world? What is he ever likely to do, except to wear kid gloves and a stylish necktie? Compare him to Ethan or to Mr. Creighton— By the way, I wonder if it wasn't Creighton he was jealous of?"

"Possibly. But, Lela, let me advise you not to meddle with your friend's love-affairs. I believe that Celia will not marry Mowbray now, and I am not sorry for it: there is too much truth in what you say about him; but she loves him still, depend upon it, and could not bear a disparaging word said to his discredit. And pray don't go recommending anybody else that you might think—"

"Papa, what *do* you take me for?"

"For a dear, kind, impulsive child, that is so indignant against wrong, and so eager to help her friends and make them happy, that I never do know what strange thing she will do next."

"Well, I'll try to behave well this time, papa," said Leoline, recommencing her drawing. "Please tell me how you like Mr. Harper's church."

"I think you've done the church correctly enough, but I can't say so much for the steeple. You must have been thinking of Celia when you drew these lines?"

"No, papa; it was not that."

"Your steeple leans all to the left. Look at it."

"It's not my steeple. If I had built it, I'd have made a better job of it. Here, papa," handing him a large opera-glass, "judge for yourself."

"Upon my word, you have a quick eye, Lela."

"You see it *does* lean on one side— to the north. The builder ought to have been ashamed of himself. It's a crooked steeple, and nothing else." Then, with mock gravity: "'The truth of history must be vindicated,' as somebody said in the newspaper the other day. As a crooked steeple it shall go down to posterity in my drawing."

"Now, Lela dear," said Mrs. Clymer, in her gentle, coaxing tone of remonstrance, "why cannot thee let the poor steeple alone?"

This was too much for the young girl, and even Sydenham joined in her merriment. But the old lady took it so good-naturedly that Lela, repentant, exclaimed, "Well, I'll forgive the steeple for your sake, Aunt Hannah: I'll rub out the builder's transgression and set his work upright, as all men and all steeples should be."

"After that good deed is done, my child," said Sydenham, "I want you to walk down to the village and invite Celia to join our riding party this afternoon, as soon as school is dismissed."

"Yes, papa: I'm so glad."

"What with the communication from Cranstoun, then that scene at the Meyracs, and finally this rupture with Mowbray, no wonder if the poor child feels miserable and forlorn. The ride, at all events, will do her good."

When Celia rode over, she found that Lucille Meyrac had come to practice duets with Leoline; so the latter was unable to join the riding party.

"You prefer the forest road?" said Sydenham to Celia.

"Very much." She was quiet, but with a look of much suffering and depression.

Sydenham tried to win her from sad thoughts, relating to her Aunt Hannah's compassionate plea for the steeple, then branching off to talk of the school and of Ellinor Ethelridge. "She is like a sister to me," said Celia.

"It is good for both that you are associated," said Sydenham. "I am not acquainted with the details of her early history, but I know it is a melancholy one. Adversity has given her strength of mind and courage."

"I'm so weak and worthless! I have no fortitude."

"The best of us have days when the heart asks if there be any sorrow like unto ours."

"Ellinor has suffered far more than I, yet she—"

"Did not win the battle in a day. Darkness and tempest must be. The soul must cry out sometimes in the gloom—as poor Burns did when the burden was more than he could bear—

"O life! thou art a galling load,
Along a rough, a weary road,
To wretches such as I!'"

Celia started. The very words that had been haunting her ever since that terrible scene with Mowbray! And the tears rose, do what she would.

"To all of us the road is barred sometimes," Sydenham added, after a pause; "but how can we tell whether it may not be in mercy?"

Celia thought of Sydenham's widowed life, and of all the good he had done. Gradually she became calmer: but little more was said till they reached Grangula's Mount, the scene of Creighton and Emberly's political discussion. A little way down its eastern slope, as our readers may remember, was a sparse clump of umbrageous forest trees. Patriarchs were they, that had survived the fate of their companions—isolated patriarchs; not, as their fellows still in the crowd of the dense forest, shooting up tall and slender and restricted in their spread, like the constant indwellers of a populous city, cramped, by the crush and press around them, in scope of action and circle of habit; but spreading erratically out, like the lone-dwelling pioneer, who has taken root apart from his fellows, and whose uncribbed notions and doings dilate to the ample proportions of the wild and exuberant nature in which they grow.

It was one of those afternoons, typical of human life, when detached clouds flit across the sky and the landscape lies in chequered patches of light and shade. The riders drew rein and turned to the charming scene. "Shall we rest a while?" said Sydenham. "I seldom pass this spot, especially on so beautiful an evening as this, without stopping to enjoy a prospect that never tires."

Celia assenting, they dismounted: Sydenham made fast each horse's bridle-rein to a depending branch, then led the way to the shelter of the grove.

Sydenham had too much wisdom and delicacy to advert to Mowbray. Though he well knew that the girl's disappointment in her lover weighed far heavier than loss of property or even of name, yet he knew also that time is the only styptic for a bleeding heart. He sought to divert her thoughts from what, for the nonce, admitted of no cure. When they were seated, "Celia," he added, "have you ever felt what a good thing it is to get away from one's fellow-creatures now and then, and renew acquaintance with inanimate Nature?"

"Of late more then formerly. I used to prefer—who is it that so expresses it? —having some one to whom to say how sweet solitude is."

"Yes; it is with years the conviction comes that to be alone, sometimes, with Nature in her beauty not only refreshes the feelings, but also invigorates thought. I don't know what world it is that Young bids us shut out before we can wake to reason and let her reign alone. If he spoke of the noisy world as it swarms in the thoroughfares of men, good and well; but if he meant such a glorious world as spreads out before us here, he is quite wrong. It is precisely before so grand a tribunal as this that the mind can grapple with the sublimest questions. If I had to argue against a man's prejudices, I'd like to undertake the task, not within the four walls of a room, but where we are now sitting. I'm glad we came here this evening, Celia."

"Have you some prejudice of mine to combat?"

"Perhaps."

The color rose in her cheeks.

"You have guessed aright," Sydenham continued. "It is of your mother and your own birth and position that I wish to speak to you."

Celia struggled for composure. "Speak to me freely," she said at last. "I know it is right that it should be talked over."

"Tell me how you feel about this matter. It grieves you more than your loss of property?"

"Much more. I confess I have felt dreadfully about it. I can scarcely tell you how: as if I had been debased, degraded — as if every one had obtained the right to look down upon me, to despise me. The Pariahs of India came into my mind."

"Now I can answer your question. I *have* a prejudice of yours to combat."

"Is it a prejudice? Yet we must often suffer for the evil-doing of a parent. Are we not told that God visits the sins of the fathers on the children?"

"The sentiment is Jewish, not Christian: you would look for such an one in vain among Christ's teachings. But I will answer you more directly. In one sense—often in a terrible one—it is most true that the sins of the fathers are visited on the children."

"Just so."

"It is patent to all of us that a child neglected by ignorant or vicious parents often suffers through life the penalty of a crime or a neglect not his own. And the curse may descend more surely still. A parent persisting in a career of reckless dissipation may transmit to his offspring terrible disease. Nay, phrenologists assert, and I partly believe it, that violent passions or vicious inclinations, which years of indulgence have stamped on the nature, may go down—a frightful inheritance! — from parent to innocent child. If there be one motive, outweighing all personal considerations, that ought to warn off from excess of body or intemperance of mind, it is to be found in the reflection that we are becoming the deadly enemies of our posterity—that we are consigning to misery or vice the beings to whom we have imparted existence. In this sense well may we be reminded that God visits on the children the fathers' sins."

"I see that. Then, since so many thousands must suffer for the misconduct of their parents, why not I for the sin of mine?"

"How are you to suffer? By God's fiat? Has He doomed you to misery? Did your parents neglect or mislead you? No: from the wise training of one or both—"

"Oh, of both, Mr. Sydenham — of both. Let my father's misconduct in other respects have been what it may, to me he was always the kindest, the best—" She stopped. Warm recollections of past days melted her heart and filled her eyes, but she mastered her emotion and resumed: "Mr. Sydenham, I cannot tell you what consolation I feel in the favorable opinion of me you expressed the other day; but I should be most unworthy of it if I could forget that I owe whatever good may be in me not to my mother only, but also to the care and instructions of my dear, dear father."

"Your parents, then, both trained you in the way you should go. You have inherited, chiefly perhaps from a mother's gifted organization, health, beauty, talent, good dispositions. If you are to suffer for a father's sin, it will be man's doing, not God's."

"But if God does visit on children parents' sins, can it be wicked in man to do so?"

"Yes, Celia, wicked. You shall judge. Suppose that in the school you are now teaching you find some scholar ill-nurtured, untrained, sickly too perhaps, suffering sorely for a parent's faults. Have you a right to add, by your act, to the heavy burden? Have you a right, because the sins of others may have been visited on that poor creature, to neglect or vilify him?"

"Oh, none, none! I see it would be wickedness. I feel that such a castaway should have more kindness than those who have been favored by Nature and Fortune."

"Your sense of justice informs you what is your duty to others. Be not less just to yourself. Because of your father's misconduct you will probably lose a comfortable fortune; but whatever you suffer, on the same score, beyond that, you will suffer through the base prejudice, or the baser malevolence, of worthless people, just as any other innocent person might."

"But there is so much prejudice in the world, especially on this very point."

"It is daily diminishing. But you are right, Celia: there is much of it still. Try to listen to it as you do to the growling of a thunderstorm or the pattering of sleet against your windows. Try to encounter it as you would any other evil thing—envy, malice, hatred and all uncharitableness. That which is unmerited may, by a brave heart, always be borne. Lift up your brow with a noble confidence, and if offence come, bear in mind that the woe and the shame attach not to you, but to the offender. Be independent—how well you can afford it!—of the self-installed arbiter. Even in the slanderer's evil pride there may be real benefit to you. If any one, puffed up with self-righteousness or blinded by false conceptions of right and wrong, seek to disparage you because of your birth, and assume that you ought to stand aside—he or she, spotless-born, being holier than you—remember that any such Pharisee is utterly unfit to be an associate of yours. If by any such you are avoided, how great the gain to you! The good-for-nothing are often winnowed from our acquaintance by what the world calls adversity."

The conversation continued for some time longer in this strain. Then they began to talk over the business points in the case, and Celia related all that had passed between her and Cranstoun, showing his letter, which she had been looking over just before she started from home.

Sydenham read it in silence. "It is his writing," he said at last: "one must believe one's eyes. Well, the frankness of that man's villainy is refreshing. Do you know what he expected, Celia?"

"No."

"Either that you would marry him, or buy him off: I don't think it mattered much to him which. And I verily believe the scoundrel thinks you will do the one or the other yet before the week is out. What a sealed book to such a rascal is an honorable heart!"

"But it is true—is it not?—that whether I write or he writes, the result will be the same to me."

"No: the fellow knows well enough that by turning informer he places you in a false position."

"How is that?"

"Had he suffered you to write, this Mr. Dunmore could not, for very shame, have demanded more than the original sum that Mr. Hartland received from your father's estate. But, getting the information from another, and having to pay heavily for it, he may possibly bring suit, in addition, for the mesne profits."

"I don't understand that term."

"It means the intermediate rents or profits that may have accrued from a property during the time it had been in the hands of a person to whom it did not belong: in this case the rents and profits of your father's property from the time it came into Mr. Hartland's hands up to the present day."

"That is terrible: then I or my guardian would have to repay all that he has paid out for my education and support. I shall be heavily in debt, besides losing all I have. How shall I ever be able to pay it?"

"I do not think any court in the United States would, under the circumstances, award more than the ten thousand dollars which the good management of your guardian has added, as your aunt informed me, to the thirty thousand originally put into his hands. At all events, dear child, do not vex yourself, in advance, about so uncertain a thing. Your affairs are in good hands. Don't let your thoughts dwell on them if you can possibly help it: better think of your school. Shall we ride?"

As Sydenham assisted her to mount, "By the way," he said, "what did you mean, that last day we rode together, by talking about parting with a favorite?"

"I cannot afford to keep Bess now."

"I don't know about that," said Sydenham, as they rode on. "I'm not sure that you can afford to part with her. You are right in wishing to husband your resources, but there is such a thing as false economy. Health, spirit, energy—these are now part of your stock in trade. It's a very wearing thing, Celia, to teach school day after day: the world underrates the importance and the labor of such work. We mustn't have you worn out."

"Ellinor's school hours are but five a day—limited to that on your recommendation, I think she told me."

"Yes: it is enough for pupil and teacher. Children, properly taught, can learn more in that time than in six or seven hours of daily lessons. But as to Bess, I've a proposal to make to you."

"I must support myself and pay all my own expenses, or I shall not be happy."

"Be sure that I respect that feeling. But which do you think will be preferable—to teach five hours a day and walk on foot, or to teach five hours and a half and have the advantage of a ride whenever you desire it?"

"The latter, certainly."

"I agree with you. Now, Celia, you must have given Lela, in the last two or three years, at least a hundred music-lessons."

"It has been a great pleasure to me."

"I don't doubt it; and I accepted the kindness," he added, smiling, "from Celia, the capitalist, thankfully and without scruple. Will the teacher let me talk to her very frankly?"

"Surely, Mr. Sydenham. You wish to speak to me on business: that is what I must learn now."

"Right. I have been thinking seriously of sending Lela to Philadelphia to prosecute her musical studies. But I dislike, more than I can tell you, to part with the dear child. I should so much prefer to have her taught here. She ought to have three lessons a week, partly in singing."

"If you think me capable, I shall be delighted to teach her."

"You may remember that, two or three years since, in Philadelphia, I was present, more than once, when Madame Schönbach was giving you a lesson: a friend wished to know my opinion of her system of teaching. I thought it admirable; and I have observed that you adopted it, faithfully and skillfully, in giving Lela lessons. I shall commit her musical education to you with entire confidence."

"How much I thank you!"

"I shall be the gainer. Probably you have not yet thought of your scale of prices."

"No. Mrs. Mowbray charges sixty cents—fifty cents only, I believe, to her youngest pupils; but I am quite inexperienced—"

"Celia, I have usually been thought a good judge in musical matters. You are a better musician, and have a much better system in teaching, than Mrs. Mowbray. Besides, you understand thorough-bass: she does not. And then her lessons, at sixty cents, are but three-quarters of an hour long. If you charge less than a dollar an hour, there can be but one good reason for it."

"What reason?"

"Because those who apply are too poor to be able to pay what your lessons are worth. Do as you please in their cases. I am not too poor to pay a just price. Indeed, there is a reason why I should pay more than they. I propose that you should give Lela her lessons at my house, and you will have to travel each time more than two miles."

"I shall greatly prefer it. Your Chickering is so much superior to Mr. Hartland's piano."

So it was arranged that Celia should give Lela three music-lessons a week, of an hour each, for a hundred and fifty dollars a year. "It will pay for Bess' keep," Sydenham remarked, "and leave something over for farriers' and saddlers' items. Depend upon it, the mare is a good investment. She may save you several doctors' bills. And on her back you can come to Rosebank and return in twenty minutes, instead of three-quarters of an hour, which you would have to spend on foot. You save time, and time is money."

Sydenham's delicate thoughtfulness for her welfare and comfort touched Celia to the heart. As they parted, her thought was: "Should I ever, but for the loss of fortune, have thoroughly known how good a man he is?"

Then the thought would obtrude itself: "How different the revelation in Evelyn's case!" But alas! alas! Though the eyes were opened, the heart was sick. Celia thrust back the thought as a disloyalty. Like the king of Israel when he learned the fate of his insurgent son, she still suffered love to cover a multitude of sins. By and by she might come to feel, as Sydenham had hinted, that the beautiful path of flowers she had been treading was barred in mercy. Not now. All she could do was to turn her thoughts resolutely to other things. There *was* comfort there.

As she rode home on the graceful little mare that was still to be hers, how marvelous the change a few short hours had wrought! Not in the external. She was still the daughter of an unmarried mother, and of a father who had led a life of deceit. She felt, as before, that her fortune—large for her, with simple tastes and living in a quiet village—was to go to another, leaving her almost penniless. Without, all was still the same. But within, a battle had been fought and won. The kingdom in the mind, that had been distracted by rebellious malcontent, was comparatively at peace. It had overcome its enemies and achieved independence.

It would have been a curious psychological inquiry how much of the victory which the young girl had that day obtained was due, as the greatest victories often are, to a petty incident.

> "Small sands the mountain, moments make the year,
> And trifles, life."

Let Wisdom smile and Age forget youthful weakness. It is none the less true that full half the grief with which Celia Pembroke encountered loss of name and fortune was lifted from her heart when she felt that, in giving up forty thousand dollars, she was not called upon to surrender, along with it, her petted favorite—her daily companion—her spirited little beauty, Bess.

Sydenham was a sagacious man.

CHAPTER XXXII.

WHAT THE LAW SAID.

SOME one has said that law is but the crystallization of natural justice, and Aristotle claimed for Jurisprudence that it is the most perfect branch of Ethics. To a certain extent, especially as regards the great legal maxims underlying all statutory provisions—the *leges legum*, to adopt Bacon's phrase—this is true. But many of the Common Law usages are essentially barbarous; and while the guards set up under that system to preserve the public rights of the subject have done much for human liberty, some of its rules touching private rights in social life and the regulating of property are much less liberal and equitable than the corresponding provisions under the Institutes of the Roman Law.

Both systems are, in our own country, gradually undergoing grave and wise modifications, dictated by that merciful and Christian spirit which is stealing over the world as it grows older and calmer, and which finds expression, from time to time, in amendments to the Statute Law of our several States.

This occurred strongly to Creighton as he looked up the various law-points in Celia's case. Ohio, he found, had enacted remedies for an injustice which older commonwealths have left unredressed. It was with a feeling of encouragement that, on the same afternoon on which Sydenham and Celia had been moralizing on Grangula's Mount, he sought an interview with Mr. Hartland the elder to report progress. The facts he had to state were these:

That an Ohio statute, passed in 1831 and re-enacted (with a mere verbal alteration) in the Code of 1854, provides, "*The issue of marriages deemed null in law shall nevertheless be legitimate.*"*

That an almost identical provision is found in the Missouri Code.† And that, although a Missouri circuit court decided, under that law, that the children of the second marriage could not inherit, the Supreme Court of the State reversed the decision.‡

That there had been no decision by the Supreme Court of Ohio on this point.

"My sister, Mrs. Wolfgang," suggested Hartland, "says Cranstoun told her that just such a case as Celia's had been decided adversely, not long since, in one of the counties of this State. Do you believe that?"

"It may be a mere blind or it may be true; probably the latter, for that would explain the grounds of Cranstoun's confidence. But it would be an endless task to look through the records of eighty counties in search of a decision made in one of them; nor is it important. Since a circuit court in Missouri decided against the rights of the children by the second marriage, one in Ohio may have fallen into the same error."

"But on what plea could a circuit court decide adversely?"

"Probably by construing the expression, 'deemed null in law,' as applicable only to marriages that are what the law calls *voidable*—that is, marriages which require a judicial sentence to establish their nullity."

"You think that a false construction?"

"Decidedly. I do not see how the language of the statute can, with any propriety, be so limited. I think the innocent child or children of the marriage *de facto*, though that marriage be deemed in law a nullity, come clearly within the letter and the spirit of the enactment."

Hartland sat for some time absorbed in thought. "Your opinion seems a logical deduction from the wording of the law," he said at last; "and I cannot help hoping, for Celia's sake, that you are right; yet I very much doubt whether

* Act of February 24, 1831, § xiii.

† "The issue of all marriages deemed null in law, or dissolved by divorce, shall be legitimate"

‡ *Lincecum* v. *Lincecum*, 3 *Mo. Rep.* 441. A case of bigamy, both wives being alive at the time of the husband's death. The children of the second marriage had sued, in a circuit court, for their share of the father's property, and had lost the suit. The case being carried to the Supreme Court of Missouri, the decision of the court below was reversed, and the right of the children to inherit affirmed. In giving judgment the court said: "Where a person is once clearly and positively legitimated, he ought not to be bastardized by implication or construction."

such a law is conducive to public morality. We are getting altogether too lax and lenient in our modern notions, Mr. Creighton. At this rate there will soon be no distinction between virtue and vice."

"We cannot punish crime until it is detected," replied Creighton. "Had Mr. Pembroke been detected and convicted, he would have been sentenced to hard labor in the penitentiary for one year at all events, and for six more at the option of the court."

"But if a man knew that after his death his wife and children might still suffer for his fault, it would be an additional motive to deter him from so heinous a crime as bigamy."

"Mrs. Pembroke and Miss Celia were as innocent in this matter as you and I, Mr. Hartland. Ought we to mete out punishment to the innocent by way of reforming the guilty? On the same principle we might enact that the widow and children of a bigamist like Pembroke should be condemned to years of imprisonment and hard labor. It is possible that such an enactment might occasionally exert a deterrent influence, but I think you would not recommend it."

"We shall not agree on such matters," said Mr. Hartland, coldly.

"Very true; and we are straying from the practical points at issue. On one of these points I think you may set your mind at rest. You are not at all likely to be held responsible for any reasonable sums which, having good cause to believe the property hers, you expended on your ward's behalf, nor can she be held to reimburse them."

"That is satisfactory."

Then they parted; Mr. Hartland somewhat nettled, as he always was when he came into contact with modern innovators who gave plausible reasons in support of their heresies, and with some misgivings also. "These sanguine world-reformers," he thought, "are not much to be trusted: their vagaries mislead them."

The next morning he called at Creighton's office. "You know," he said, "by reputation at all events, Mr. Marshall of Buffalo?"

"Joseph Marshall, who practiced law for some twenty years in this State?—one of the clearest-headed lawyers in it."

"The same, and a very intimate friend of mine. I should like, if you do not object, to obtain his opinion in this matter. The amount at issue is large, and my duty to my niece requires that I should neglect no reasonable precaution."

"You are quite right, Mr. Hartland. I do not know Mr. Marshall personally, but I shall be much pleased to have him associated with me in the case."

"Then, if you will be so good as to make out such notes of your own opinion as you may desire to have submitted to him, I shall start for Buffalo next Monday."

"With great pleasure." Then, after a pause: "Mr. Hartland, I begged you not to say anything to Miss Celia about the hopes I entertained to bring matters out all right; but if you see no objection, I think, now that I have substantial grounds to go upon, I ought to lay these before her."

"I have no objection," said the other, apparently with some hesitation.

Creighton noticed it: nevertheless the same afternoon he called to see the young lady. Mr. and Mrs. Hartland had driven out, and he found her just returned from school and alone.

They had met twice already since the day when Celia heard of her father's misconduct, and his manner had puzzled her. It had certainly changed. Formerly, in the days of her prosperity—for so in her thoughts she now regarded her past life—he had frequently spent his evenings with them; and his somewhat off-hand style of addressing her (strictly within the bounds of good-breeding though it was) had left an unpleasant feeling—a vague impression, as she had told Mowbray, that he thought her vain of her position as a village heiress.

All this seemed to have passed away, and within the last week he had treated her with marked respect—with a delicate reverence, she almost thought, for her misfortunes, but expressed in tone and manner, not in words.

Etymologists derive the term "lady" from two Gothic words, meaning bread-giver: "gentleman" has a less assured derivation, usually referred to birth rather than to disposition; yet I prefer to take it in the modern sense of our beautiful word *gentle;* so that the terms employed to designate those above the vulgar, and which ought to be restricted to Nature's *aristoi*, may both imply inherent nobility of character—in one sex that Charity, vicegerent of Deity, which dispenses earthly blessings; in the other, the same godlike attribute in a broader sense—that spirit, gentle and easy to be entreated, which Christianity has substituted for the stern, vengeance-dealing systems of an older world.

There are various qualities which mark the cultivated, well-bred man; yet not one perhaps is more characteristic than a gentle, deferential tone in addressing woman, especially in her season of sorrow. Celia felt this as Creighton spoke:

"I come, after consulting with your guardian, to talk a little law with you, Miss Celia. In a general way, I don't talk law with my younger clients, especially when I have hopes of success which may or may not be realized. But you have fortitude and a mind equal to adverse fortune, and with you I run no risk: you will not mistake probabilities for certainties."

Celia's color deepened: a wild hope sprung up in her breast, but she dismissed it, saying, "It is surely not probable—possible even—that there was no English wife living when mamma was married."

"Unfortunately, no; but that reminds me"—he took from a green bag a bundle of papers, selected one of these and handed it to Celia. "Will you have the kindness to look over these extracts, and to tell me if they correspond to what you read in your father's letters to Mr. Cranstoun?"

Celia read them carefully and said, "So far as I remember they correspond exactly."

"I did not doubt it. Cranstoun is not a man to commence, or even to threaten, a suit without some foundation. I grieve to think your father sinned, Miss Pembroke. I cannot remove from you the burden of that remembrance. Would to God I could!"

"But you spoke of hopes, Mr. Creighton—of probabilities?"

"Very important ones they are, but they regard yourself only; and I fear they will cause you less pleasure than your father's misconduct has caused you pain. You will forgive my speaking plainly to you?"

"I shall think you deal kindly with me," but the cheeks flushed.

Creighton colored slightly himself, saying in a low tone, "Miss Celia, you think yourself an illegitimate child?"

"I know it only too well," her eyes cast down. "I heard it," she added, shuddering, "from coarse and cruel tongues."

"What they said was false: you are mistaken. You are as legitimate as your aunt or uncle, or any inhabitant of Chiskauga."

Celia had not a word in reply, so astounded was she: and Creighton, adding, "You shall see the law," handed her another paper from the bundle, containing two lines only—lines almost of life and death to the poor girl. When she had read them, he said, "That was the law of Ohio at the time of your mother's marriage, and it is the law still. The marriage, at the time it took place, was null in law, but you see by that paper that you are nevertheless legitimate."

Creighton may have been right when he said that the joy would not be equal to the past sorrow. Yet it was a great joy, gushing over her heart, as if the breath of summer had penetrated, with sensible warmth, to its core. The badge of shame—a fancied letter B, which stung almost like the terrible A of old Puritan law,* the badge of shame which

* *General Laws and Liberties of Massachusetts Bay*, chap. xxviii., sec. 1: "A capital A of two inches long, cut out in cloth of a contrary colour to their cloaths," etc.

she had thought to wear through life—had suddenly dropped from her as by magic, yet the magician was a young lawyer, and his wand, two lines from a musty statute-book. A great mistake *he* made who applied to laws what Pope said of forms of government:

"Whate'er is best administered is best."

Laws, in their despotism, may save or destroy both soul and body. If the thirteenth section of that Act of 1831 had declared that "the issue of marriages deemed null in law shall be bastards," by what mode of administration would it have helped this poor guiltless orphan out of the pit of her grief?

Creighton sat watching Celia's countenance. It was a very interesting one, and—if love be dangerous—a somewhat dangerous one to watch. She had had, from early youth, a habit—very painful it had often been to her—of blushing at the touch of any emotion whether of joy or sorrow — at trifles, even, as at the unexpected sight of some girl-friend; and when deeply and suddenly moved the flush would overspread face and bosom.

Just then the changeful heaven of that countenance seemed suddenly overcast again, as if some cloud were crossing the sun of her new-found hope. It puzzled Creighton.

At last she looked up and said in low, eager tones: "Mr. Creighton, was mamma a legal wife?"

"I have looked carefully into that matter, knowing it would interest you, and I believe that during the three last years of her marriage she was. I will tell you why I think so. Kent, one of our best legal authorities, says that, by the Common Law, no peculiar ceremonies are requisite to the celebration of the marriage: the consent of the parties is all that is required.* And it is the opinion of a learned writer on the Domestic Relations that the marriage, if made at Common Law, without observing any statute regulations, would still be valid.† We have no statute, though I think we ought to have, providing that a woman who contracts a marriage in good faith, ignorant of a previous impediment, shall, as soon as the impediment is removed, become a legal wife; but this is the rule under the Spanish law, as it existed formerly in Florida and Texas;‡ and our State legislation tends in that direction. When the English wife died your father was free. Out of regard for your mother's feelings—mistaken regard, but doubtless most sincere—he did not renew, and cause your mother to renew, by the usual ceremony, the formal expression of that "consent of the parties" which undoubtedly suffices to legalize marriage. But that consent had been publicly given and recorded nine or ten years before, had never been withdrawn, and was substantially renewed by the continuance of your father and mother to live together as husband and wife until Mr. Pembroke's death. Thus the case seems made out. I must remind you, however, Miss Pembroke, that this is my opinion only, and that I may be mistaken, since I find no decision on the subject. But whether I am mistaken or not, the moral right of the case remains the same. And then, even if it should appear that the law fails to afford relief where justice cries aloud that it should, we must bear in mind—" He hesitated, as men who have been talking of worldly business often do when their thoughts stray off to a higher sphere.

"You promised to speak plainly to me," Celia said. "What must we bear in mind?"

"That your mother is now in a world which calumny cannot reach, and where legal injustice is unknown." He said it reverently and with emotion. Then, after a time, he added: "No law could have made her life more pure, nor her relations to your father more holy than they were. Do not, I entreat you, vex yourself without cause by imagining how, if the point had come up, legal technicalities might have caused it to be decided. It has no practical bearings on yourself or your future."

* Kent's *Commentaries*, vol. ii., p. 86.

† Reeve's *Domestic Relations*, pp. 196, 200, 290.

‡ 1 *Texas Rep.*, 621.

He paused to see whether the question of property would suggest itself. No. She was thinking of her mother, and of that untried phase of being far better than the earthly phase—of that world whose denizens serve God, not Mammon.

"I thank you from my heart," she said. "What you told me about my mother did me so much good."

"I have done nothing for you, as yet, Miss Pembroke, but I do hope to render you substantial service."

Still no sign that the question of heirship had crossed Celia's mind. It seemed left for Creighton to moot it. "Have you no curiosity," he said at last, "as to whether the fact of your legitimacy affects your property?"

"I thought that question was settled against me. Mr. Cranstoun said so."

"He told you also that you were an illegitimate child, but you see what that assertion was worth."

"Is it possible that I am still my father's rightful heir?"

"I think so, because the fact of legitimacy carries with it the right to inherit. But I am not sure that the courts will ultimately decide in your favor. Let me tell you exactly what the facts are."

"Did not Mr. Cranstoun say to Mrs. Wolfgang that it had already been decided somewhere against the children of the second marriage in just such a case as mine?"

"She says so; and such a decision may have been made."

"How, then, can there be any hope?"

"Because the decision spoken of is said to have been made in a county court only. But when county—or, as we call them, circuit—courts make blunders, we appeal to the Supreme Court of the State to correct these."

"But the Supreme Court may think it is not a blunder?"

"I see I was right in trusting you, Miss Pembroke. The Supreme Court may think so; and in that case your property will be lost."

The telltale blush showed that this did affect her. The new-found hope was about to die. Creighton came to its relief, adding: "But I feel convinced that our Supreme Court would declare such a decision to be contrary to law."

"Yet it is uncertain."

"Is any future event certain, except death? Then, too, law is proverbially uncertain. You do well to be prepared for the worst, yet I firmly believe we shall beat them."

As he took his leave he said: "You can afford to look with comparative indifference on the legal battle that is about to be fought in your behalf; for you will succeed in the world, Miss Pembroke, and will win the respect of the good, let it terminate as it will."

In pursuance of the purpose he had expressed to Creighton, Mr. Hartland set out for Buffalo, taking a Lake steamer at Cleveland. On board the boat, to his surprise, he met Nelson Tyler. The miller was on his way to Buffalo, to purchase a pair of burr-stones and some additional machinery for his mill. In conversing of Chiskauga matters, Mowbray's name came up, and the two did not differ materially in their estimate of the man.

When Mr. Hartland, soon after his arrival at Buffalo, called on Mr. Marshall, he found that that gentleman had almost withdrawn from the practice of law, and was residing at a pleasant country-seat a few miles out of town, where his time and thoughts were occupied in the collection and arrangement of a valuable cabinet of autographs—not of signatures, but of letters, more or less important, from most of the distinguished authors and statesmen of our own country since the days of the Pilgrims, and of European countries from a still older date. Hartland spent several days with his old friend, and had occasion to remark that never, in earlier years, when he had known him making ten or twelve thousand dollars annually from his practice, had the lawyer seemed so busily engaged as now, from morning often till late in the night, he was; sometimes in the delicate manipulation of old, creased, scarcely-legible letters of some great poet or philosopher; sometimes in mounting rare and valuable portraits and landscapes with which to illustrate some favorite work. It was a labor he loved—in the performance of which he seemed never to tire. Hartland marveled to see a man whom learned courts and dignified assemblies had once listened to with admiration, engrossed by such objects as these; and could not understand how, one day when a long, characteristic letter of Dr. Samuel Johnson, written near the close of the great lexicographer's life, unexpectedly reached his friend's hands, he should evince as much delight as a child just possessed of a new toy. He forgot that human character is far more interesting than insect life, and that it was ever a white day in his own calendar when some undescribed beetle or butterfly first blessed his sight. Men seldom comprehend the attractions of any hobby except their own.

It was a sacrifice to friendship which Hartland did not sufficiently appreciate when Mr. Marshall, with a sigh, locked the small fire-proof chamber that contained his precious manuscripts, and spent the greater part of two days among his law-books, studying Celia's case. In the end he came to nearly the same conclusions as Mr. Creighton, and wrote out an opinion endorsing the latter's views. This Mr. Hartland immediately despatched to Chiskauga, promising to follow it in a steamer which was advertised to leave Buffalo four days later; and in which the miller, having completed his purchases, had also engaged a berth.

CHAPTER XXXIII.

THE LAKE STEAMER.

"Roth, wie Blut,
Ist der Himmel;
Das ist nicht des Tages Glut!
Welch Getümmel!"
SCHILLER, *Lied von der Glocke.*

WE are living through a period of transition, and our young country exhibits the exuberance incident to such a state. In legislative hall or traveler's caravansary, in "silver palace car" or gorgeous steamer, we are wont to overlook the fitness of things, mistaking tinsel and glitter for appropriate enrichment, and often neglecting substantial comfort for worthless gauds.

Yet if there was extra gilding and carving and superfluity of mirrors and silk hangings in the stately "Queen of the Lakes," on which Hartland and the miller embarked, she was nevertheless a magnificent vessel, gracefully modeled and well appointed—a craft of which her genial captain might well be proud.

Full three hundred and fifty feet long, she had two decks stretching throughout her entire length. The lower of these was partially occupied, on either side, by the officers' berths, close to which rose the smoke-stacks, while the spacious forward deck and the open central space were crowded by a large number of steerage passengers, chiefly decent-looking German and Irish emigrants; a few of whom, however, had engaged bunks in the small, plain after cabin. Of the upper deck three-fourths was occupied by the main cabin for first-class passengers, handsome state-rooms being partitioned off on either side, and the after portion, which was appropriated to the ladies and their friends, was separated from the gentlemen's cabin by rich brocaded satin drapery. From the opposite end of this spacious room double doors opened on the upper forward deck, the favorite resort of the cabin passengers in fine weather.

Upon these two decks, on the present occasion, upward of four hundred passengers had found accommodation.

Captain Drake—for so the autocrat of this floating colony was named—had his wife and family on board, and had invited a number of friends on a pleasure-trip to Cleveland. A gay and thoughtless party they were; among them several young people of each sex, whom the captain, bent on the happiness of his guests, had apparently selected with special reference to their individual preferences, for they dropped naturally into couples, some secluding themselves in the ladies' cabin and looking over books or prints together; others, deep in conversation, promenading the forward deck.

The captain entertained them generously: champagne circulated freely at the upper end of the long dining-table. In the evening there was music. One young lady, of distinguished appearance, but somewhat inappropriately attired in an elaborate ball-dress, was a charming ballad-singer; and her rendering of the old song, "I'm sitting on the stile, Mary," called forth, from a good many eyes, the tribute of tears. Then there was an impromptu ball, two negro violinists composing the band. Captain Drake, his fifty-odd years forgotten, joined jovially in the dance, which was kept up till past midnight—in honor of May-day, the captain said, for they had left Buffalo on a warm, bright first of May.

Among the sober spectators of this gay scene were Thomas Hartland and Nelson Tyler; the latter cordially enjoying it, the former sitting unmoved, with a silent protest in his heart against the levities of fashionable life. Without waiting the termination of the dance, Hartland retired to his state-room. Having delayed to secure his passage until the day before the steamer started, he had been fain to put up with a somewhat undesirable berth, the upper one in a state-room alongside the wheel-house. As this room could have no door or window opening outside, it was lighted by a frame projecting from its roof and glazed, so that any one occupying the upper berth could, by raising himself, see, through the side-panes, what passed on the hurricane deck.

Hartland lay awake. At first, the sounds of merriment and music outside chased sleep away; and when these gradually ceased and the cabin was deserted, he still lay, he did not know how long, listening to the plash of the great wheel hard by, sinking at last into troubled and broken slumber.

In the dead of night he suddenly became conscious of the sound of footsteps overhead. Looking through the skylight, he discerned the figures of two men moving silently about, one of them having a lantern in his hand. Then he thought he heard their voices, speaking in eager, suppressed tones. Thoroughly roused, he donned a portion of his clothes and proceeded to the upper deck. A third man had joined the first two, and Hartland asked him what was the matter. In reply the latter pointed to one of the smoke-stacks, saying in a whisper, "Looks as if it might be fire." Hartland then perceived, dimly by the lantern-light, a slender line of light smoke or steam rising close to the starboard smoke-pipe, and he became aware that one of the two men whom he had first seen held a hose, of which he was directing the contents on this object of their suspicions. At first the stream of water seemed to quench the fire, if fire it was, but after a time, the smoke began to reappear and to drift aft, though still ascending only in feeble puffs. Hartland hesitated no longer, but returned at once to the cabin, where he roused the miller, and they awoke several other passengers, the doors of whose staterooms happened to be unlocked; making no noise, however, for they were both men of nerve and courage, and they knew the effect of a sudden alarm at night among so great a crowd.

Those who had been aroused hastened from the cabin and met the captain speeding up to the hurricane deck.

Still that ominous line of smoke! gradually increasing in volume, Hartland thought. A deathlike stillness over the boat, broken only by the dull, rushing sound of its huge wheels.

"These emigrants below ought to be warned," whispered Nelson Tyler to Hartland; and they both descended, moving slowly and quietly among the sleeping multitude that lay on the deck. They awoke the men gently, speaking in an undertone, and telling them it was better to be ready, though there was no immediate danger. As the officers, fearing disturbance, and confident, no doubt, that they could soon master the fire, had given no alarm, the news spread but gradually and without arousing any violent demonstration. With a low murmur the crowd arose.

Then the two mounted to the floor above. Men and women, their faces deadly pale, were creeping silently from the cabin, and soon the upper forward deck was nearly filled. They could dimly see, on the cabin roof, a line of men who had been organized to pass what few buckets they had from the side of the vessel. The crowd watched the result with feverish anxiety. No one spoke above his breath. All eyes were turned to that long, dark cylinder of smoke. It had doubled in volume, Hartland saw at a glance, since he first had sight of it; and the conviction flashed over him that the supply of water was quite insufficient to check the hidden flame. The horrors he had read of, about fires at sea, rose vividly to his mind, but he thrust them aside by a determined effort. He looked at Tyler. It was evident that the miller too realized the situation, yet he said but a word or two, and in a tone so low that Hartland overheard only Ellen's name: then a look of stern resolution passed over Tyler's face. Conscious of his own strength and skill in swimming, he was nerving himself for the struggle before him.

What a magnificent night it was!—clear, cloudless; starlight serene in its splendor, but no moon; the wind a moderate breeze, fresh and balmy, just stirring the lake surface into gentle ripples. Nature in her quietest, holiest aspect, shining with calm benignance from heaven, as if to give earnest of peace and protection to the creatures of earth.

Solemn the hush over that awestruck crowd! They felt what *might* happen, though most of them, not having noticed the gradual increase in that fatal smoke-column, were still buoyed up by hope. How character, unmasked, showed itself there! Some seemed self-absorbed; others had gathered into groups, the selfish instinct overcome by affection. Here a mother had brought her children together and was whispering to them that they mustn't be afraid. There a brother, his arm around a favorite sister, was speaking some low word of comfort and encouragement. Hartland distinguished among the rest the fair songstress of the preceding evening, half clad now, careless of appearance, mute with terror, a young man, lately her partner in that gay dance, by her side; bewildered he seemed, panic-stricken like herself: poor protector in a strait like that! She was not the only one who found out, in that terrible night, the difference between a companion fit to enliven hours of idleness, and a friend who will stand stoutly by and succor, through gloom of danger, when life is at stake.

Even a touch of the ludicrous mingled, as it will in the most tragic scenes. One gentleman had a silver-bound dressing-case strapped under his arm; another carried a hat-box, which he seemed to guard with scrupulous care. Tyler saw a young girl, who was standing near him, deliberately unclasp a pair of handsome earrings, then roll them carefully in her handkerchief, which she deposited in her pocket. And one old lady, walking distractedly up and down near the cabin door, kept eagerly asking the passers-out if they were sure they hadn't seen anything of her bundle. But all such frivolities were soon to cease.

How often, to the storm-tossed and bewildered mariner, has there shone, from watch-tower or pharos, a feeble ray, welcome as Hope herself, life-guide through night and tempest! But the hope, the safety of this waiting crowd was in merciful darkness.

A faint flicker of light! God in heaven! It had shot up along the edge of that large, dark smoke-pipe! For a moment it dimly showed the wan faces—a signal-fire, omen of coming fate.

Another! A shudder crept through the watchers—a long, low moan: they saw it all now. The fiery element, gathering power below, was slowly creeping upward upon them. The crowd glared around with the instinct of flight. Nothing but the waste of waters, with here and there a star reflected from their dark depths! And still, as dreary monotone, the rushing plash of those gigantic wheels!

Then there were eager inquiries for life-preservers. Not one, they were told, on the boat!* And the gilt glitter in that luxurious cabin—what a mockery now! The thousands squandered there might, wisely spent, have saved that night hundreds of human lives.

As it was, a portion of the passengers went in search of something to keep them afloat in case of the worst, returning with chairs, stools, pieces of board, and the like. Others, utterly unmanned and abandoning all exertion, gave way to wild bewailings.

A mother with several children, entreated Mr. Hartland to take charge of the youngest, a little girl.

"I am going below, madam," he replied, "where the crowd is dangerous, and where she would run great risk of being lost or crushed."

The mother submitted, kissing the child and taking it in her arms, and Hartland whispered to Tyler, "Let us go down. We may approach the shore before the flames gain head; and if we have to swim for it, the chance is better from the lower deck." So they descended.

Below, the forward deck was a mass of human beings. To them the danger was even more apparent than to those above. Flakes of flame already rose, here and there, from the deck near the smoke-stacks. Even the heat was beginning to be felt. But there was one favorable circumstance. The wind was westerly—a head wind, though veering a little on the starboard quarter—and flame and smoke were blown aft, leaving the forward half of the vessel clear.

Soon a larger fork of flame shot up, and there were screams faintly heard from the small after cabin. Some of the inmates, attempting to lower the yawl that hung astern, had been caught there by the drifting fire: their fate was sealed.

That last burst of flame must have shown itself on the upper deck, for there was a smothered cry from above, and then a voice—the captain's it seemed—shouting in loud tones to the pilot.

The alarm gained the crowd below, which swayed to and fro. Women and children shrieked in terror as the press came upon them. Men's voices rose—a hoarse murmur, like the gathering of a great wind. Tyler endeavored to make his way to the bow, but found that impossible: several stout Irish laborers turned threateningly upon him. "I'll risk my chance above," he said to Hartland, but the latter stayed below.

When the miller reached the upper deck a sheet of fire already rose nearly as high as the smoke-stacks, and the roof of the main cabin had caught. But he saw also in a moment a change that kept hope alive. The smoke and flames, instead of drifting aft, now blew dead to larboard. The captain's command to the pilot had been to port the helm and run the boat on shore.

But this change, bringing the mass of flame closer to the passengers, so that those nearest the cabin felt the hot breath on their cheeks, at first increased their alarm. They crowded fearfully toward the bow, and many must have been thrown into the water then and there, had not a voice called out, "Don't crowd: they're heading her for land." This assurance in a measure quieted the terror-stricken throng. There was the suppressed voice of lamentation, an appeal to Heaven for mercy here and there, but still no clamorous shout, no wild outcry. There could be seen, by that red glare, on some faces the calm of resignation, on others the stillness of despair.

Though the flames spread steadily, the engine continued to work, the wheels did their duty, and the pilot—noble fellow!—still kept his post, though smoke, mingled with thick sparks, swept in circling eddies around him.

Each minute was bearing these four hundred souls nearer and nearer to safety, and all eyes were now strained in the direction of the vessel's course. The blaze from that terrific bale-fire lighted up the lake waters far and wide, and—yes! was at last reflected on a low shore and trees. Some one near the bow cried out, "Land! land!" Others

* The law which now requires that all passenger steamers shall be fully supplied with these had not then passed.

caught and repeated the soul-stirring cry. And though the passengers in the rear of the crowd were already in perilous vicinity to the spreading flames, a faint shout of exultation went up.

But terrible and speedy came the reaction! The boat had been headed more and more to the left, and ere five minutes had elapsed — with a *thud* so heavy that she shuddered through all her timbers — the vessel struck a hidden sandbar, remaining fast, but before she settled swinging by the stern till her after cabin lay directly to windward. Thus the breeze, which had freshened, blew right from stern to bow.

Fearful was the result! In an instant the whole body of flame swept straight over the masses that had huddled together on the forward decks. At the same moment the huge smoke-stacks, loosened by the violent shock, fell, with a loud crash, down through the cabin, their fall being succeeded by a sudden and tremendous burst of surging fire.

No restraint now! No thought among that doomed multitude save one—escape from the most horrible of all deaths, to be burned alive! In the very extremity of despair they crowded recklessly on each other, sweeping irresistibly forward till the front ranks were borne sheer off the bow: then the next, then the next! Ere three minutes had elapsed the water swarmed with a struggling throng—men, women, children battling for their lives.

A few of the passengers in the rear rushed to the stairs, but they were in flames. No escape from that scene of horror, except by a leap of some twenty feet—from the upper guards down to the waves below, already covered with a floundering mass. But most of those who were left accepted the desperate alternative, flinging themselves over the side of the boat. Many fell flat and became senseless at once, sinking hopelessly to the bottom: others, dropping straight down, soon rose again to the surface. Now and then an expert swimmer, watching an opening in the living screen, dived down head foremost. Scarcely a score remained, the miller among them, on the extreme bow. Even at that appalling moment his attention was arrested by a brief episode in the scene of horror before him. A young mother—tall, graceful, with a look of refinement and a pale Madonna face, her arms around a baby asleep, it seemed, in their shelter—stood on the very edge of the deck where the rush of the headlong crowd had broken down the guards—alone! — her natural defender — who knows? — swept away by the human torrent, or perhaps, under the tyrant instinct of self-preservation, a deserter from her whom he had sworn to cherish and protect. All alone, to earthly seeming at least, though she might be communing even then with the Unseen, for her colorless face was calm as an angel's, and her large, dark eyes were raised with a gaze so eager it might well be penetrating the slight veil, and already distinguishing, beyond, guardian intelligences bending near, waiting to welcome into their radiant world one who had been the joy and the ornament of this.

As Tyler watched her, a tongue of flame swept so close he thought it must have caught her light drapery. A single look below, a plunge, and she committed herself and her babe to the waves and to Him who rules them.

Tyler rushed to the spot where she had stood, but mother and child had already sunk. For a brief space—moments only, though he thought of it afterward as a long, frightful dream — he gazed on the seething swarm of mortality beneath him—poor, frail mortality, stripped of all flaunting guise, and exhibiting, under overwhelming temptation, its most selfish instincts bared to their darkest phase.

The struggle to reach the various floating objects, and the ruthlessness with which a strong swimmer occasionally wrenched these from the grasp of some feeble old man or delicate woman —it was all horrible to behold. Then again, many swimmers, striking without support for shore, were caught in the despairing clutch of some drowning wretch, unconscious perhaps of what he did, and dragged down to a fate from which their strength and courage might have saved them. From the midst, however, shone forth examples of persistent self-devotion: husbands with but one thought, the safety of their wives; a son sustaining to the last an aged parent; but above all the maternal instinct asserted its victory over death. Tyler, even in those fleeting moments, caught sight, here and there among the crowd, of a woman with one hand clutching a friendly shoulder or a floating support, holding aloft in the other an infant all unconscious of impending fate. In one instance, even, a chubby little fellow, thus borne above the waters, clapped his tiny hands and laughed at the gay spectacle of the bright flames.

Meanwhile, the wind, veering a little to the south, and thus blowing fire and smoke somewhat to larboard, had left, on the starboard edge of the forward deck a narrow strip, on which, though the heat was intense, some ten or twelve persons still lingered beyond actual contact with the flames. But each moment the fire swept nearer and nearer, and Tyler felt that the last chance must now be risked. He dropped into the water, feet foremost, and disappeared.

While these things passed, Hartland, below with the steerage passengers, had witnessed similar scenes. Human nature, cultivated or uncultivated, is, as a general rule, in an extremity so dire, mastered by the same impulses. The difference inherent in race, however, was apparent. The sedate German, schooled to meet hardship and suffering with silent equanimity, and now standing mute and stolid—eyes fixed in despair—contrasted with the excitable Celt, voluble in his bewailings. Hartland, like Tyler, had kept himself aloof from the dense crowd, and so escaped being carried along by the frenzied fugitives when the flames first swept the forward deck. He was one of those men whose perceptions are quickened by imminence of danger. He noticed that the starboard wheel-house, which had not yet caught, afforded a temporary shelter from the drifting fire; and acting on a sudden conviction, he climbed over the guards on that side of the vessel, a little forward of the wheel, and let himself down till his feet rested on the projecting wale of the boat. Thus, holding on by the rail, he was able to maintain himself outside of the blazing current until only a few stragglers were left on deck.

There he remained some time, deliberately thinking over the situation. As a boy he had learned to swim, but for the last fifteen years he had been almost wholly out of practice. He called to mind the rules with which he had once been familiar, and the necessity of keeping the eyes open so as to elude the grasp of drowning men. As he held on there the risk from such a contingency was painfully brought to his notice. From time to time several of the passengers from the upper deck had slid down near him. At last one heavy body, from immediately above, dropped so close that it brushed his clothes and almost carried him down with it. He turned to see the fate of this man. After ten or fifteen seconds he saw him rise to the surface again, and with a start recognized Nelson Tyler. He was struggling violently, and Hartland observed that some one, as the stout miller rose, had clutched him by the left arm with the tenacity of despair. Both sank together, and Hartland saw them no more.

Several times he was about letting himself down, but held back because of the crowds that he saw rising to the surface and wrestling with death and with each other beneath him. At last he was warned that his time had come. Looking toward the bow, where several men, imitating his example, were holding on outside the bulwarks, but unprotected by the wheel-house, he saw the flames catch and terribly scorch their hands, the torture causing them to quit their grasp and fall back headlong into the waves. Still he watched, until, seeing a whole mass of bodies sink together, and thus leave an empty space just below him, he commended his soul to God, and, springing from his support, sank at once to the bottom.

After a brief space, when his eyes had cleared a little, he saw what it has sel dom been the lot of human being to witness. On the sand, there in the lower depths of the lake, lighted by the lurid glare of the burning boat, loomed up around him ghastly apparitions of persons drowned or drowning—men, women, small children too: some bodies standing upright as if alive; some with heads down and limbs floating; some kneeling or lying on the ground: here a muscular figure, arms flung out, fingers convulsively clenched, eyeballs glaring; there a slender woman in an attitude of repose, her features composed, and one arm still over the little boy stretched to his last rest by her side. Of every demeanor, in every posture they were—a subaqueous multitude! A momentary gaze took it all in, and then Hartland, smitten with horror, struck upward, away from that fearful assemblage, and reached the surface of the lake and the upper world once more.

There he found the water, not only around the bow, whence most of the passengers had been precipitated, but also between himself and the shore, so overspread with a motley throng that he resolved to avoid them, even at risk of considerably lengthening the distance. He swam toward the stern, where the surface was comparatively free, and after passing one or two hundred yards beyond, seeing no one now in the line of the land, which was distinctly visible, he struck out vigorously in that direction.

Then he swam on, but with gradually diminishing strength and courage, and a little nervous trembling.

He estimated the distance to the land at half a mile. It was, however, in reality, a quarter of a mile farther. But the air was balmy, and, though the wind blew, the waves were not sufficient to impede a stout swimmer. There are hundreds among us who can swim a much greater distance. Yes, if they start fair, mind and body unexhausted. But after such a terribly wearing scene of excitement as that—the man fifty-seven years old, too—will his strength hold out to reach the land?

PART X.

CHAPTER XXXIV.

FOR LIFE.

BETWEEN the detached sandbar on which the steamer had stranded and the land the lake was deep. The bottom was a smooth sand, and as one approached the low, level shore the water shoaled gradually. Hartland, with great exertion, had made about half the distance when a man—the first survivor he had seen—came up behind him, swimming strongly. As he ranged alongside, Hartland perceived, with equal pleasure and surprise, that it was the miller whom so lately he had seen go down in what seemed a death-struggle. Tyler called out to him: "Take it quietly, Mr. Hartland; don't swim so hard. You can't hold out so."

The other felt that the caution was timely. He became aware that in his eager efforts he had overtasked his strength. "You are right," he said. "I have been overdoing it: I must go more slowly."

"Can I assist you in any way?"

"Thank you, no. You'll need all the strength you have. Save yourself. Don't wait for me."

"Well," said the other, as he struck out in advance, "perhaps it's best. I may help you yet."

Left alone, Hartland proceeded more leisurely, seeking to husband his powers. But for a man of his years, unused to violent exertion, the distance was great—too great, he began to feel, for reasonable hope that he might reach the shore; for he felt now, at every stroke, the strain on his muscles. After a time, so painful was the effort that he could scarcely throw out his arms. Then a numbness crept over his limbs, gradually reaching his body. He was resolute, scorning all weakness that suffered the mind to usurp control over the will: he struggled, with Puritan hardihood, against the nervous helplessness that was invading his whole system; yet, even while he despised and sought to repulse all imaginative sensations, the fancy gained upon him that life was receding to the brain. He had no longer power to strike out. After a few random and convulsive movements, as if the body rebelled against the spell that was cast over it, he sank slowly to the bottom. An anxious sensation of distress, oppressing the breast, followed, becoming gradually more urgent and painful, until in his agony he instinctively struck for the upper air, which he reached almost immediately. A few deep inhalations, and a consciousness that he was now in comparatively shallow water, restored for a minute or two the exhausted powers, but after making a little way these soon failed again: he could no longer maintain his mouth above water, and, choking as a small wave broke over his face, he sank a second time. Strange, this time, was the transition! All pain, all anxiety was gone. The world seemed gradually sinking away. As he went down a sense of ease and comfort came over him, while a strange haze diffused around a yellow light. Then, as has happened to so many thus approaching the term of earthly things, the man's life passed in review before him. And there he argued, before the tribunal of his own conscience as never before, the question whether his conduct to wife and child had been marked by that love which is the fulfilling of the Law. Many allegations he made, numerous pleas he brought forward—urging the duty of discipline, setting out the saving efficacy of severity, pleading the example of Him who scourgeth every son whom He receiveth. In vain! He was too near the veil. The light from Beyond, where Love reigns evermore, shone through his filmy sophistry. His soul heard the verdict—against him! It heard more than the verdict. It heard those words, gentle yet terrible: "To him that hath shown mercy shall mercy be shown." Then it cried out, entreating for a little more time—a year—a single year only—in which to atone for the harsh, unloving past. So eager grew the longing that it drew forth, from life's inmost depths, the last residue of that reserve fund which Nature, in kind foresight, provides against a season of overwhelming exertion; and once more a spasmodic effort brought him to the surface—and to suffering again. Yet he breathed: he was still alive. How could it be, after that hour, so crowded with incidents, spent below? An hour? That protracted trial, the accusation, the defence, the pleas he had set forth, the arguments he had employed, the verdict, the bitter repentance, the prayer for respite to amend and repair the wrong,—it had all passed in less than a hundredth part of the time which, to his quickened consciousness, had seemed so long. Some twenty seconds only had he tarried below. A vague conviction of this stirred hope of life afresh, and a few feeble strokes carried him some yards nearer to the land. Then again that leaden sense of exhaustion! He gave it up. But this time, as his limbs sank beneath him, the feet just grazed the ground. It was like the touch of mother Earth to the Lybian giant, kindling a spark of life. A faltering step or two he made, and the water just mounted to his chin. Had he reached the land too late? He stretched out his arms toward it, but the body, powerless, refused to follow. Even then the tenacity of that stubborn spirit asserted itself. He dropped on his knees, digging his fingers into the sand and dragging himself along, till he was forced once again to rise and take breath. But with the light and the air came back excruciating pain. Then an overwhelming torpor crept over sense and frame. His limbs refused their office. Unable longer to maintain himself erect, he dropped on the sand. A brief respite of absolute rest there imparted a momentary courage. He crawled, under the water, a few yards farther. Then consciousness and volition gradually failed. As if by the inherent powers of the system uncontrolled by will, an automatic struggle was kept up—for a few seconds—no more! That was the last life-rally against fate. The temptation to lie there quiet, immovable—all care dismissed, all effort abandoned—was irresistible. But what was this?—a fearful reminiscence from the scene he had escaped? No. These bright sparks that flickered before his eyes were lambent and harmless. In his brain, too, there seemed an internal light—an irradiate globe, but genial and illuminating, not burning. Then came back again that wondrous atmosphere—that calm, effulgent, pale-yellow haze; and with it such a sense of exquisite enjoyment that all desire to return to the earth passed from the soul of the expiring man. A smile over the wan features, a slight quivering of the limbs, and then all cognizance of the world and its doings had departed; and the spirit was entranced on the verge of that unexplored phase of life to come, where the wicked cease from troubling and the weary are at rest.

What, meanwhile, had been the fate of our sturdy friend the miller? A more practiced swimmer than Hartland, and, though a few years older, a more powerful man, he was yet all but worn out when his feet first touched bottom. He had full two hundred yards still to go; and he fell three or four times while slowly and painfully wading toward shore.

The land once reached, and all motive for exertion gone, he dropped on the very edge of the water, lying there some five minutes or more without power to move. Then gradually he revived sufficiently to sit up and turn his gaze on the scene of horror he had left behind. The steamboat was now one sheet of flame from stem to stern. Little else than fire and smoke was visible except the lower portion of the wheel-house, where Tyler thought he could discern a small cluster of human beings still holding on; but of this he was not sure, the distance was so great. The boilers, he thought, could not have burst, for he had heard no loud explosion: now and then in the stillness slight detonations caught his ear, occurring, no doubt, as some barrel of inflammable matter was reached.

Then he looked to see the fate of his companions. Day was dawning and the wind seemed to have abated. His first impression was, that the lake had engulfed the whole of that gallant steamer's living freight, and that he alone was left to tell the tale of disaster. But as he scanned the water more narrowly he caught sight, here and there, of a swimmer making for the shore. Several of the heads, however, sank as he watched them. One had approached more nearly than the rest, but that, too, disappeared. Could it be Hartland's? He looked for it eagerly. It came in sight again, remaining stationary, as if the person had reached footing and paused to take breath ere he walked out. He was sure of it now: Thomas Hartland it was—stretching out his arms too, as if imploring help. Again the head sank, and again, but for a few seconds only, it came to the surface. At that moment, and before it went under to show itself no more, Tyler took rapid note of the direction in which it appeared—almost in a line from the spot on which he sat to the stern of the burning steamer.

"I must save him," was his next thought. But he was fain to rest there full five terrible minutes ere the vital forces rallied so that he could trust himself to the effort. Even then he staggered along like one drunk or just risen from sickness—once over a log submerged in about two feet of water. On that he sat down for a brief space to recover spirit and vigor. Precious moments he knew well, but he *must* rest. After a time he rose, bracing his nerves, and calling to mind that his friend could be now scarcely a hundred yards distant. After he had advanced, slowly and cautiously, until he supposed he must be in the vicinity of the body, he observed, some six or eight yards farther on, and a little off the line he had marked out to himself, a few air-bubbles, as if rising from below. He remembered to have heard that during the last efforts of a drowning person the pressure of water on the chest usually expels a portion of the air that still remains in the lungs, and greatly encouraged by the indication, he approached the spot. There, after a time, feeling around with his feet, he came upon the body. The touch gave him fresh courage.

But what to do next? He felt that if he attempted, in that depth of water, to drag the drowning man by the arm, his own head under water the while, he would but sacrifice his life without saving that of Hartland. In this strait, as the ripple broke over his shoulder, and something flapped lightly against his cheek, he was reminded that one of those stout Hibernians who had opposed his efforts to reach the bow of the boat had grasped the upper portion of his shirt sleeve and torn it half off. A bright thought! Tearing it off entirely and splitting it lengthwise in two, he knotted the pieces together, thus obtaining an impromptu bit of cordage, one end of which he managed to fasten around Hartland's left wrist. By this contrivance he was enabled to drag the body along without stooping. Buoyed up as it was, in a great measure, by the water, a slight pull sufficed to move it in shore. Yet even that small exertion exceeded Tyler's waning strength. At each step his limbs dragged more heavily: several times he stumbled from sheer weakness, and he was utterly spent by the time he reached the log where, on his way out, he had rested. Forgetting where it was, he fell over it as before, but not, as before, to rise again. There were less than six inches of water over his burly frame, yet he lay there helpless and insensible as the friend he had striven so hard to save.

* * * * *

Suddenly he found himself at home again, before his own dwelling; and strangely enough, without question in his mind as to how he came there. He heard Ellen's voice, and saw her issue from the house and cross to the well, a few steps off. She had an old-fashioned pitcher in her hand, the lower half blue, the upper white, with grapes and grape-leaves embossed over it—a legacy from his dead mother which the miller highly prized.

Beside the well stood Hiram Goddart, Tyler's principal hand in the mill, a good-looking, brisk young fellow, with a tin washbowl on a small bench before him, drying face and hands after his morning ablution.

"Good-day, Miss Ellen," he said, "I'm sorry to see you looking pale this mornin'. Are you ailin'?"

"Not ailing, thank you, Hiram, but I had uneasy dreams last night, and haven't got over them yet."

"You expect the old man here this evening?"

"Or to-morrow, some time."

"I'll be blithe to see him, Miss Ellen," blushing and hesitating. "I had a letter from Uncle Samuel yesterday: he's well-to-do, and has neither chick nor child to do for. He's willin', if I need it, to send me a thousand dollars or two to set me up in the world. I think your father likes me well enough. He'll have to go partly in debt to pay for that machinery he's buying; if I raise the two thousand, he might take me in, for a partner, like, in the millin' business. Then I wouldn't be a hirelin', and maybe—" Ellen's eyes glistened with tears, not of joy: her rustic lover's quick eye saw that, and his countenance fell. "You wouldn't let me ask the old man" —he said it despondingly—"if he would trust you to me? You'd be very lonely if—"

"Oh, Hiram," the girl cried, her sobs reaching Tyler's ears, "it's cruel of you to talk that way, and father gone, and only last week seven people killed when the rail-cars ran off the track. And then you know I've told you, as plainly as I could say it—"

"Yes, Miss Ellen, you needn't repeat it," said the poor fellow. "You never gave me no encouragement: I'll always say that." Then, taking the pitcher gently from her hand: "Let me fill it for you."

Ellen thanked him, voice and hands trembling. He drew a fresh bucketful and filled the pitcher. As she received it from him, it slipped through her hands and fell to the ground, breaking in pieces.

"How clumsy I am!" she said: "and father's favorite pitcher, that grandmother gave him! Oh dear! But don't wait, Hiram. I'll send Nancy with another. Breakfast will be ready in ten minutes."

With that she recrossed to the house, passing, Tyler thought, close to him. Then it first occurred to him as something strange that neither of them took notice of his presence—that they spoke of him as absent. And then the whole scene faded away: he shivered with cold; seemed to be lying out somewhere: felt hands turning him over, and heard a rough voice saying, "He's no that awfu' cauld. He'll aiblins come to. I dinna think he'll coup the cran yet."*

"He's a'maist deed, faither: he does na stir," said another voice.

"That's naithin', Tam. Nae doot he's sair forfoughten. A' droukit folk is, that's been lyin' a blink, wi' the water aboon them. And he tumbled ower just as we lap the fence o' Squire Doolittle's cornfield. He must ha' laid there four or five minutes or ever we gat at him and pou'd him out. I wonder what on airth the doited carle was aboot? Dinna ye mind, Tam, that he was wadin' in and staggerin' as if he was fou, when we first cam ower the hill and got sight o' him? He must ha' gane clean wud, the crazy cheel, to try it the second time, and he no able to stand. Hech, sirs!" he added, as a deep sigh, half groan, burst from Tyler, "whatten an ausome grane was that! He's waukin' up. Tam, help me turn him ower on his brisket: they say that's gude for them that's been drownin'."†

And when he had laid him face downward, the kind fellow took off a heavy frieze coat he wore and laid it over his patient. Then he put his hand on the region of the heart.

* A few words, here and there, in the way of glossary, may be acceptable: *Aiblins*, perhaps. *Coup the cran*, kick the bucket—die.

† *Sair forfoughten*, quite exhausted. *Droukit*, drenched. *Blink*, a little while. *Doited carle*, stupid fellow. *Fou*, drunk. *Wud*, mad. *Ausome grane*, awful groan. *Brisket*, breast.

"Is the breath in him yet?" asked the son.

"'Deed is it. He'll be speakin', belyve. He's a wee dozened yet; that's a'."* Then to Tam, as he called him: "My bairn, tak' aff that bit coatie o' yours and wrap his feet in't." Tom did as he was bid, starting, however, as he laid hold of one foot: it moved in his grasp. "The man's alive, daddie," he said, "sure enough: he can kick."

The father raised Tyler's head, placing his hand under the forehead. A little water came from the mouth: then the eyes opened. After a fruitless effort or two, the miller said: "Am I here yet?"

"'Deed an' ye are," replied the other. "Whar did ye think ye had gotten to? It's no very like the land o' the leal, here—d'ye think it is?—wi' this cauld soakit sand anaith ye, and you in thae screeded duds, and us twa in our sark sleeves." †

The words were not very intelligible to the miller, but he felt that this was real. "I'd like to sit up," he said, faintly. They assisted him, but he was so weak that but for Tom, who planted himself behind him and sustained his back, he must have fallen over again.

Then he took it all in: the sun risen; the lake, almost calm now; the steamer, still enveloped in flames; three or four stragglers crawling up the sand a little way off, and several men from the country hastening to their assistance. That brought back to his mind his own efforts to rescue Hartland.

"Mr. ——"

"My name's Alexander Cameron. Ye may ca' me Alick if ye like: maist folks do."

"You've saved my life, Mr. Cameron."

"Me and Tam, yes. It was easy done. There wasna' twa foot water where ye lay."

"There's another man there: I was trying to drag him out when I fell."

"An' that was what took ye into the water when ye were yinst out? Aweel, ye're a spunkie cheel, if ye are auld. So there's anither man in yonder? I'm thinkin' his parritch is cauld by this. A gude half hour he's been lyin' there. But if it'll ease yer mind ony, Tam and me'll try and howk him up. Can ye sit yer lane, d'ye think?" ‡

The miller entreated them not to mind him. After searching a few minutes, they dragged Hartland's body on shore and laid it out on the land, near to where Tyler was. Cameron examined it carefully. The veins of the head were swelled; the face was blue and livid; the tongue was visible between the lips, which were covered with white froth; not the slightest warmth over the heart or elsewhere. Even Tyler, who contrived to creep up to the body, thought the case desperate. They employed the usual means of restoration, however—cold water on the face, upward friction on the limbs and body, without obtaining the least sign of life. "They say sneeshin's gude for't," § said Cameron, taking from his pocket a small sheep's horn, or *mill* as he called it, containing snuff, and inserting a portion of the contents into the nostrils of the drowned man.

Ten minutes had elapsed in these fruitless endeavors, when a young fellow, clad in homespun, his small pocket-saddlebags indicating his profession, galloped toward them from an inland road.

"Od, but I'm fain to see ye, doctor," said Cameron: "here's some gear needs your reddin'. It's past me, ony way."‖

The young doctor, dismounting, examined the case with solemn and critical air, shook his head, and said,

"Do you know how long this patient has been under water, Alick?"

"A matter o' half an hour and mair."

"It's almost hopeless. There are cases on record of resuscitation after more than half an hour's immersion, but they are rare."

"I gied him some sneeshin', doctor. Was that a' right?"

"Quite right. It stimulates the in-

* *Belyve*, by and by. *Dozened*, stupefied.

† *Land o' the leal*, land of the faithful—heaven. *Screeded duds*, torn rags. *Sark sleeves*, shirt sleeves.

‡ *Yinst*, once. *Parritch*, porridge. *Howk up*, dig up. *Yer lane*, by yourself.

§ *Sneeshin*, snuff.

‖ *Fain*, glad. *Some gear needs your reddin'*, a job that needs your care.

terior surface of the nostrils, and tends to excite circulation."

"It was wasted on the puir bodie: he'll never need bicker* nor sneeshin-mill mair."

In the mean time the doctor had been feeling Tyler's pulse as he lay listening to their conversation. "Alick," he said, "ye'd better be attending to the living. This man's made a narrow escape of it, and he ought to be in a warm bed this very minute, instead of here on the wet sand. Take my horse, if he can sit him, get him home as fast as ye can, and—ye've got some brandy or whisky in the house?"—

"Oo, ay: we aye keep a sma' drappie: ye never ken when it may be needed."

"Well, it's badly needed now. The man's chilled through."

Tyler declined the offer of the horse, but on receiving from the doctor the assurance that he would not leave Hartland until every means of restoration had been exhausted, he consented to go. Alick made him put on the frieze coat, and he and Tom supported him, one on each side.

It was hardly three-quarters of a mile to the Scotchman's cabin, but the miller's sufferings during that short journey were terrible. It seemed to him as if a hundred needles were pricking him from head to foot. His head swam: he was forced to sit down and rest a dozen times on the route. When they came to the squire's fence, Cameron and his son had to lift him over. The field had been recently ploughed. The Scotchman looked at it doubtingly.

"He's unco silly," he said to Tom, "and this bit bawk's hard to win through. We maun jist carry him."†

And, in spite of Tyler's remonstrance, the stout farmer and his son picked him up between them.

"He's a buirdly‡ carle," said Cameron, quite out of breath, as they set him down on the other side of the field. "I'se warrant him to weigh gude fourteen stane. What's your callin', stranger?"

"I'm a miller. Nelson Tyler is my name. I live at Chiskauga: it's a village near the Indiana line."

"Tyler? That's a gude Scotch name—a'maist as gude as Cameron. Aweel, we'll hae ye hame in a jiffy, and I'll gar Grannie pit on some het water, and we'll hap ye up and rub ye weel. Ye're feckless the noo, but the mistress has some auld Ferintosh in the aumbry that'll set ye up; and we'll hae ye hale and hearty the morn." Then, after a pause: "We'd best be steerin', gin ye think ye can hirple on. They bare feet o' yours 'll be gettin' cauld."§

Tyler could not help looking down disconsolately at his own forlorn condition: his drawers were the only nether garment he had saved. Cameron understood the look.

"Ye left yer breeks on that burnin' boat, did ye? But never fash yere thoom about that, man: there was mair tint at Sherra-moor. I hae a pair o' shoon and some orra-duds at hame: they're maybe a thought ower tight for ye, but ye're welcome to them till ye can do better."‖

The miller thanked him warmly, and as the rest of the way lay over level pasture-field, he contrived to walk, though at each step the leaden weights that seemed to clog his heels grew heavier. By the time he reached the spacious double cabin a feeling of stupor and utter helplessness came over him, and ere a chair could be brought he had sunk on the floor.

They carried him to the fire, and "the mistress," as Alick called his hale, stout, red-cheeked wife (who bore her forty-odd years as if they scarcely numbered thirty), bustled about, and soon had a warm bed ready, in which Tyler was

* *Bicker*, wooden dish.

† *Unco silly*, very weak. *Bawk*, ploughed land.

‡ *Buirdly*, bulky, broad-built.

§ *Gar*, make. *Feckless the noo*, exhausted just at present. *Auld Ferintosh in the aumbry*, old whisky in the pantry; so called because a certain Forbes was allowed, in 1690, to distill whisky on his barony of *Ferintosh* in Cromartyshire, free of duty. *Steerin'* stirring, moving. *Hirple*, to walk lamely or with difficulty.

‖ *Mair tint at Sherra-moor*, more lost at (the battle of) Sheriff Moor (an action disastrous to the Scottish arms, fought in 1715). *Orra-duds*, spare clothing.

laid. "Grannie" was greatly exercised just at first, rushing about the house without any definite purpose, exclaiming, "The Lord's sake! Gude guide us! That bangs a'!"' But she soon resumed her usual equanimity, put a large kettle on to boil, and was ready, with her experience of threescore-and-ten, to prescribe various infallible remedies for the exhausted man; chief among them a warm potent potion, sweetened with brown sugar — a Scotchman despises white sugar when whisky is concerned— and of this palatable mixture the "Ferintosh" which Tyler's host had promised him formed a chief ingredient.

The miller's sensations, as he lay there dream-haunted and bewildered, were of a singular character. The sheets, as he touched them, seemed as thick as the coarsest sailcloth, the blankets like inch boards. His own body appeared to him to have stretched out to gigantic proportions. He felt as if he were eight or ten feet long, and as if it were impossible that the bed on which he lay should contain him. Then there was a sinking down, down, as if to some depth impossible to reach. He thought the man who had dragged him to the bottom of the lake ere he could get free of the boat had again clutched his arm. He started in terror, struggling to free himself, and rolled over on the cabin floor. When they came to lift him up he stared wildly round him, muttering, "I couldn't help it: it was his life or mine."

After they had covered him up again, and, at Grannie's instigation, put some bottles of warm water to his feet, he fell into a troubled doze, which lasted an hour or two.

When he woke, he saw, lying on a bed opposite to him, a stout, portly, ruddy-faced man, in full dress, with a shining black satin waistcoat and a massive silver watch-chain. The miller rubbed his eyes, wondering if that could possibly be the same gourmand he remembered to have seen only the day before at dinner on shipboard, stuffing himself with delicacies till one wondered where he found room to stow them away, and calling for an additional bottle of champagne when the captain's supply was exhausted. The very same! That expanse of satin waistcoat was unmistakable. But how could he ever have come here—in all that toggery too?

"Is it possible"—he said to his host, who had come to ask if he felt better—"is it possible that fellow with the watch-chain got off from the boat?"

"'Deed did he."

"And swam ashore with all his clothes on?"

"Hoot na! He couldna soom, buskit that gait.* There was a bit coble gaed out to the steamboat—"

"A coble?"

"That's a fishin'-boat, ye ken—"

"It brought off some of the passengers?"

"A matter o' twenty o' them, they say. They grippet on to the big wheel, and bided there till the boat took them awa'; yon chiel amang the lave. It's a wonder to me how siccan cattle as that hae a' the luck: the Lord aboon, He kens the gowk was na worth savin'. And there's anither o' them; that Dutch body, sittin' by the chimlie-lug."†

The man to whom he referred was a Jewish-featured German, some fifty or sixty years old, sitting on a rocking-chair by the fire, bemoaning his fate. "Ach, mine Gott!" he repeated: "mine gelt ischt all gone! Gott im Himmel! Was soll ich thun? Verdammter Zufall! Every thaler ischt gone!"

Cameron went up to him. "Auld man," he said, with some asperity, "you've been grainin' aboot that siller ye've lost till I'm sick and tired hearin' ye. Ye seem to hae clean forgotten that yer life's been saved the day, when hundreds o' better men have gone to Davie's locker; and deil hae me if I think ye've said a be-thankit for it yet."

"Mine life!" rocking himself violently to and fro. "Was ischt mine life goot for if mine gelt ischt all lost and gone?"

"No muckle, I'll agree; but then

* *Couldna soom, buskit that gait*, could not swim, dressed up that fashion.

† *Amang the lave*, among the rest. *Chimlie-lug*, fireside (literally, chimney-ear).

they say we should a' be thankfu' for sma' favors. Was ye yer lane? Had ye nae wife?"

"Ach, ya! But mine gelt ischt all gone. Mine wife ischt all gone too."

"Won't somebody kill that d—d Dutchman?" roared out Satin Waistcoat from his bed.

"Ye may come an' kill him yersel', for a' me," said Alick, coolly, "but I dinna think he's worth it: a man that'll set up his money for an idol, as thae pagan Jews did that gowden calf in the wilderness, and then let the mistress come in ahint a'—like Lot's wife when she turned to a pillar o' saut—may gang his ain gait for onything I care."*

Amid such talk the day passed. Many dropped in before evening; some from the wreck—others to hear the particulars of so terrible an accident. It appeared that a boat which had put out early in the morning had picked up twenty-one persons — one woman among them— chiefly those who had saved themselves by clinging to the lower portion of the starboard wheel; of which number, strange to say, was a child not more than seven or eight years old—the son of an English emigrant, it appeared. Father, mother and four children were among the lost, and the poor little orphan, but a few hours before member of a cheerful, thriving family, now stood in this Western cabin a solitary estray, without relative or friend. Grannie took him on her knee. "Hae, there's a piece," she said, handing him a large slice of bread and butter: "dinna greet, my bonny dawtie: yer faither and yer mither's forsook ye, but the Lord 'll tak ye up."

Six persons only, besides Tyler, saved themselves by swimming — in all but twenty-eight survivors out of four hundred and twenty souls. The captain was found among the dead, his arm around his wife. Not a few perished, as had nearly been the miller's fate, in shallow water. Many more would doubtless have reached the shore by swimming but for the fatal encumbrance of clothes. All appeared to have retained their shirts, the greater number their drawers, and many bodies washed on shore were of persons, like him of the watch-chain, fully dressed. Pity they had not followed the example—recorded by Saint Pierre in his world-renowned story—of the sailor on the deck of the Saint Géran, "tout nu et nerveux comme Hercule," who, though he failed like Paul to rescue Virginia, yet, by the wise precaution he took, succeeded in saving his own life.

The young physician, who called late in the afternoon, brought word that though he had persisted for several hours in his endeavors to save Hartland, they had been ineffectual, and that arrangements were already being made for his interment.

An hour before sunset a four-horse wagon, with several chairs and one or two feather-beds, drove up to the cabin. It had been sent by the innkeeper of a village some five or six miles distant, in case any of the survivors chose to return with it to his hotel. The miller decided to go, in spite of Cameron's hospitable invitation, kindly pressed, to remain with him a day or two.

Satin Waistcoat went also, of course. He pulled out a purse, apparently well filled, and came toward his host to pay for breakfast and dinner. "Put up yer siller," said the latter, a little sharply. "We're no bien to brag o'. But I dinna keep a public, to be seekin' pay for a meal's vittals; and naither am I a beggarman, to need an aumos.† Ye're welcome to what ye've had."

When they were taking leave, Tyler asked Cameron what he intended to do with the little orphan.

"Oo, we'll jist let him rin with the bairns, and gie him a bite and a sup till better turns up."

"Suppose I were to take him and make a miller of him?"

"Ye hae a rale leal Scotch heart, Mr. Tyler, anaith that broad brisket o' yours. I'm unco glad me and Tam pou'd ye out. It'll be the makin' o' the bairn."

* *Ahint*, behind. *Saut*, salt.

† *We're no bien to brag o'*, we're not rich to boast of. *Aumos*, alms.

"The Lord be thankit!" said Grannie. "I kenned weel He would haud till His word."

"Will you come and spend a week or two at the mill this summer or fall," said Tyler to Cameron, "and bring Tom with you? Maybe he'd like to be a miller too. I'd give him the best kind of a chance."

"I'm no misdoubtin' ye would, and Tam's gleg at the uptak.* But I canna weel spare him frae the farm. Ony way, I'se come and see ye the first chance."

"I won't say a word about these trowsers and the hat and the jacket you made me take."

"Ye'd best no, or we'll hae a quarrel. But I'll tell ye what: we'll mak a niffer,† and ye'll gie Willie here—that's what the wean ca's himsel'—ye'll gie him a pair o' Sunday breeks and a blue Scotch bonnet wi' a tassel to't. Wad ye like that, Willie?"

Willie did not quite understand the kindness that was intended him, but when Tyler, laughing, asked him, "Would you like to go in that wagon, Willie, and sit beside the driver and see the horses?" the little fellow clapped his hands, and then gave one of them to Tyler.

So, with many thanks to the mistress and to Grannie, and a hearty shake of the hand from Tam, they bade good-bye to the hospitable Scotchman.

CHAPTER XXXV.

THE BODY THAT WAS TOO LONG FOR THE BOOT.

EITHER Grannie's prescription warm and strong, or her son's dry humor, or else perhaps the excitement of the day, fed by constant news touching the fate of his fellow-sufferers, had, at the moment Tyler left Cameron's log cabin, caused the miller almost to forget his aches and pains. But these were grievously recalled on the journey, brief as it was, over a rough wagon-road to the village tavern. Though he had lain down on one of the feather-beds, each jolt of that springless wagon was torture. He grew weaker, mile by mile. The landlord and a stable-boy had to carry him up stairs to bed, on which he sank, body and mind utterly exhausted, and scarcely conscious where he was or how he came there.

A doctor was sent for, who shook his head and spoke a little doubtingly of the case, prescribing nourishing food, given often and in small quantities, with occasional stimulants. Mounting his horse, he said to the landlord: "The man would do well enough, and might be up to-morrow, if he had twenty years less on his shoulders. But age tells. I can ride Speckleback"—patting his neck—"as far in a day, for all his fifteen years, as I could when he was a seven-year-old; but when patients are plentiful and far apart, and I put him through his fifty miles before night, then I have to ride the filly for two or three days till his old legs supple again. He's a stout fellow for his age, that lodger of yours, but even if there's no funeral, he isn't likely to be up for a week. You may bring him through by good nursing: that's the main thing."

Tyler remained for several days, sunk in a strange sort of lethargy—a dreamy state, the past and the present inextricably mixed; his mind sometimes engaged with dim and shadowy reproductions of the horrors he had passed through, sometimes visited by peaceful visions similar to those that soothed Hartland's dying moments. But there was once in each twenty-four hours a sort of lucid interval, in which the patient took note of things around him and was comparatively clear-headed. This occurred from two to three o'clock each morning, lasting, at first, about an hour. Except during these intervals he could not eat. While they lasted the chief thing Tyler noticed was the appearance of a woman at the foot of his bed: she might be of any age above sixty—parchment-faced, with snow-white hair and cap, silent, and, except that her fingers knitted rapidly and mechanically, absolutely immovable—no change in the cold, impassive face, the gray eyes fixed on him

* *Gleg at the uptak*, quick at learning.
† *Niffer*, exchange, swap.

Tyler rubbed his own eyes, but there it was still. Could it be an apparition—his grandmother, who, he recollected to have heard, was a celebrated knitter? If so, it must have been a ghost of the ministering kind, for it glided slowly to the fire, stirred something that had been set to simmer there in a small pot, and brought the sick man, by and by, a glass—not of nectar, unless nectar be a beverage much resembling warm egg-nog with whisky in it. It did not say anything to him, however, merely signing to him to drink what it presented: then, after setting the empty tumbler on a small table at the bed-head, it resumed its station and its knitting, and the gray eyes watched him with stony gaze as before. Then the old crone was mixed up in his dreams; sometimes extending a hand to help him out of the water—sometimes telling him that she would meet him soon in the next world.

Gradually the intermittent periods of lucidity became longer—two, three, four hours. He was coming back to life, and the figure at the foot of the bed emerged from its ghostly phase—feeling his pulse, dropping, now and then, a word or two as to his wants: in short, settling down into a careful, flesh-and-blood nurse, albeit singularly taciturn.

On the fourth day a slight fever supervened. That abated, however, and on the sixth Tyler sat up, with a feeling of returning health and a keen sense that the sunshine had never before looked half so bright.

He had replenished his wardrobe from a ready-made clothing store in the village, the owner giving him credit without scruple. "I know by your face you'll pay me," he said; "but even if you didn't, it wouldn't break me; and we must all lend a helping hand in a case like this."

He was two hours in dressing, compelled to rest every few minutes during the process. When nearly dressed he happened to cast his eyes on a looking-glass set on a chest of drawers. Startled, he turned round to see who had entered his room. No one there! Yet when he looked again in the glass there still it stood—a feeble, wan-faced old creature, with hollow, staring eyes, and hair silver white. A second time he turned perplexed, wondering whether his senses were beginning to wander again. At last, after a third look in the mirror, it flashed upon him—*that was* NELSON TYLER!

What we call *Time* in this world may not exist in the next under any phase which corresponds to our present perceptions of it. These perceptions, even here, are sometimes revolutionized. That hour of twenty seconds spent by Hartland beneath the lake waters in self-trial and condemnation was as truly an hour to him as if the long hand of the clock had marked its sixty minutes. And so even physical effects that are usually the result of years may be produced in days. That terrible week had been ten years in Tyler's life. He was ten years nearer death at its close than he had been at its commencement. His hair, but slightly sprinkled with gray on that bright May-day morning when the "Queen of the Lakes" swept gracefully from her moorings in the harbor of Buffalo, was, on this seventh of May, colorless as the snow when it falls from heaven. The rush of circumstance had put forward the hands of life's dial. Would his own child recognize him under his advanced years?

In a buggy which the landlord loaned him he ventured out, taking Willie—who had been thriving under the buxom landlady's care—with him, and driving slowly to the scene of disaster. What a sight met his eyes! A wide trench, some one hundred and fifty or two hundred feet long, had been dug along the bank, and contained—so they told him—three hundred and seventy bodies that had been washed ashore, or dragged up from the sand-bar on which the steamer stranded by friends and relatives in search of their dead. These bodies had been enclosed in rough poplar boxes, the lids loosely tacked on, so that the corpse within could be readily inspected. Upon each lid had been chalked the name when there was any clew to it, but in the great majority of cases only a few words designating sex, probable age and apparent nativity of the deceased.

A crowd was assembled around this hideous trench: the greater number mere spectators, drawn thither by the curiosity which any great tragedy arouses, but a good many were engaged in examining the rude lettering on the boxes, and some in the ghastly duty of inspecting their contents, urged, perhaps, by hope of recognizing, in some decaying form, a brother, a father, perhaps a sister or wife.

Some of these searchers, however, seemed to be young lawyers or other agents, who had accepted the revolting office—an office not without danger also, for Tyler's perceptions, sensitive through sickness, detected a faint odor, indicating that in a portion of that encoffined mass decomposition had already begun.

Two men, who appeared to have been thus employed, came from the crowd and stopped to take a last look at the scene near Tyler's buggy.

"Catch me undertaking such a job again!" said the younger of the two to his companion. "If it hadn't been for that chloride of lime, or soda, or whatever it is, I think I should have fainted before I got through that awful pit. I don't believe the stench will be out of my nostrils for a week. And we have to give it up at last."

"We found one of the two," replied the other; "and that's better luck than most of them had."

"I say, Jack," rejoined the first speaker, "did you hear the dreadful stories they were telling about the plunder of the dead bodies — watches, jewelry, money they suppose too; and one young girl who had her earrings torn off."

"It may be exaggerated," replied the other, "but no doubt it is partly true. A great crowd always draws pickpockets; and they probably concluded that the dead would miss their rings and watches and pocket-books less than the living, and would be very sure not to prosecute them for the theft."

"I suppose that is their cold-blooded way of looking at it, but it's very horrible."

"I came across a more horrible thing just before I left home."

"Did you?"

"I was standing in our savings bank last Saturday afternoon when a crowd of depositors came in; one widow among them, over fifty, and four children to feed by taking in plain sewing. She had put a fifty-dollar note—the savings, she told me afterward, of nearly two years—into her bank-book, and held that over her shoulder in the press. Some villain picked it out. These wrecker-thieves are honorable gentlemen compared to him, if they do look Death in the face and go on picking and stealing still. You ought to have seen that poor creature's agony. Money saved, twenty-five cents at a time, through two whole years, to be laid by against a rainy day, and gone in a single moment, no doubt to pamper drunken riot or worse debauchery. It's very shocking to think of, the tearing rings out of the ears of a young creature that's dead, but it's a venial crime compared to tearing the heartstrings of a poor, old, overtasked, hardworking mother that's living and can feel the torture."

"You always were a queer creature, Jack, but I can't help thinking of the bleeding ears for all that."

"Don't let's talk about it, Ned. I want to get out of this. Let's hunt up the two men that hired that hack along with us, and see if we can't get off to-night."

Tyler had seen and heard enough. He returned to the tavern a good deal fatigued, but a quiet night's rest did much for him. He was up, though a little late, to breakfast.

As he passed out with Willie to go to his room, the two men whose conversation he had listened to on the lake shore were paying their bills at the office counter. Tyler stopped to look at them. The face of the elder seemed familiar, but he tasked his memory in vain to discover who he was or where he had met him. They passed up stairs to look after their baggage, and Tyler noticed a four-horse carriage at the door. "Are they going in that hack?" he asked his host.

"Yes, to Cleveland, where they take the railroad. Why couldn't you go with them?"

"I have no money to pay you my bill."

"Don't let that stop you, Mr. Tyler. I'll not be harder on you than the tailor was. Send me ten dollars when you get home, if you have it to spare."

"And the old woman that nursed me?"

"I guess she ought to have a V. So you can make it fifteen."

"I'll send you twenty the day I get home. Give the old woman half. She earned it."

Just then the two men came down, the younger first. "Mr. Morris," said the landlord, "couldn't you give this man a seat in your hack?"

"Very sorry, but we're full already—four of us, and that's all it holds."

"Who wants a seat?" said the other as he came forward—"anybody from the wreck?"

"Yes, this old man here: he swam ashore, and then went back into the water to try and save a friend of his. That time he'd have been drowned, sure enough, if it hadn't been for Scotch Alick. He's been a week getting over it, as it was."

"Old gentleman," said he whom his companion had called Jack, turning to Tyler, "you shall have my seat, and heartily welcome too: I'll get up beside the driver."

Tyler wrung his hand in thanks: "I've this little fellow, but he can sit on my knee."

"Any baggage?"

"Out in the lake, yes," smiling; "but we won't wait for it."

It was just as much as the miller could do to climb into his seat, the landlord helping him.

"Hand me up that youngster, landlord," said Jack; "I know he wants to see the horses, and my knees are stronger than his grandfather's."

"That's not my grandfather," said Willie as soon as he was seated.

"Your father, is it? He's old to have such a son as you."

"Father and mother are both drowned, and Bessy and Liz—Jem and Harry too."

"Good Heavens!" said kind-hearted Jack; "and who's that old gentleman?"

"Don't know. He's goin' to make a miller of me."

Jack looked at the child's sad, earnest eyes and kissed him, his own eyes moist: then he turned, and, after scrutinizing Tyler's face, said to Morris: "Ned, hand me up one of those printed handbills." He looked it over carefully; then to himself: "No, it can't be; but it's a singular coincidence."

"Mr. Morris," said one of the occupants of the hack, "what sort of luck had you and Mr. Alston?"

"Got one body and sent it home, but couldn't find a trace of the other, though we must have opened at least fifty of those infernal boxes. It may have been washed ashore some distance off."

"Then probably the coroners didn't have a quarrel over it."

"How do you mean?"

"Didn't you hear about that? The bodies came on shore close to the county line; and there were two rival coroners, each anxious to have the honor, or rather the profit, of holding a few hundred inquests. Finally, I think, they agreed to divide the spoils."

"Well," said Morris, "if a man's in business he must look out for custom. It's three dollars a body, and the county can afford to pay it. These coroners don't make fortunes: it isn't every day they have such a windfall as this. I wish one of them had made his three dollars off that miller's body, so we could have taken it home to his daughter. No doubt it would have been a comfort to the girl. Are you worse, old gentleman?" turning to Tyler, who had sunk back as if exhausted, his eyes closed.

"No, it's nothing," rousing himself; "but is that gentleman's name, beside the driver, Mr. Alston?"

"Jack Alston, yes; and a right good fellow too, if he has odd notions sometimes. From Mount Sharon: do you know him?"

"Mr. Alston," said Tyler in a feeble

voice. without replying to Morris, "will you let me see that handbill you were reading?"

It was handed to him. The reading of it seemed to produce a strange impression. They saw him struggle for composure. At last he said quietly to Morris, "I think it's just as well the coroner didn't hold an inquest on that miller you're looking after."

"Why? Do you know anything about the body?"

"Yes."

"Then, in the name of Goodness, let us know where it is. We've had such a time after it. Driver!" raising his voice, "stop: we must go back again."

"No, you needn't: you've got the body here."

"What?" said the other, confounded —"in the boot under the driver, or strapped on behind?"

Tyler, weak as he was, couldn't help laughing: "The miller was six feet and over: it would have been hard to get the box into the boot, I think."

"For God's sake, stranger, tell us what all this means, at once."

"It isn't every man that has a chance to see his dead body advertised, and ten dollars reward offered for it—"

"By the Lord Harry!" broke in Jack, "if it isn't the burly miller here in the body among us! Give us your hand, old fellow. I had some suspicion about it when this youngster here told me you intended to make a miller of him. But then the white hair! How could they make such a mistake?"

"No mistake, Mr. Alston;" shaking his head sadly; "but *I* made a mistake myself, yesterday, when I first got up from a sick bed and looked in the glass. I didn't know it was Nelson Tyler."

"No wonder I didn't find it out, then. Well, I've heard of such things before, but I never believed them. Do you mean to say that your hair was only 'sprinkled with gray,' as the handbill says, one week ago?"

"The day we left Buffalo, yes—if that's only a week since. It seems to me like six months."

"Mr. Tyler," said Alston, "what was it that the landlord said about your going back into the water, after you had saved yourself, to help a friend? Who was it you tried to save?"

"Thomas Hartland of Chiskauga; but I didn't make it out. I contrived to get the body along till the water was about two feet deep, and then fell down senseless myself. You would have got my body, slick enough, along with Mr. Hartland's, if it hadn't been for a stout Scotchman and his son who dragged me out."

"You're a noble fellow, Nelson Tyler," said Alston, warmly: "first, to risk your life, and all but lose it, for a friend; and then to adopt an orphan that hadn't a soul left to take care of him. But how did you expect to pay your way and his back to Chiskauga?"

"To tell you the truth, I didn't see my path very clearly; but in our country you can always find somebody to help in a case like this. I felt sure the railroad people would put us through free."

"That reminds me," said Mr. Morris, taking out his pocket-pook and selecting from it two half-eagles, "that I owe this gentleman a debt." He handed the money to Tyler, adding with the utmost gravity, "The reward for finding that body, Mr. Tyler, that was too long to get into the boot, you know."

They had a good laugh over this, and quite a merry time, all things considered, till they reached Cleveland, whence, the same afternoon, they proceeded by rail on their return to Chiskauga.

CHAPTER XXXVI.

ONE OF NATURE'S WONDERS.

WHILE Tyler lay in lethargic sleep and penniless—off the line of telegraphic communication, too — at that country tavern, he had neither spirit nor means to send speedy news of his condition to his daughter. But ere he left Cleveland he telegraphed to a friend at the Riverdale railroad station nearest to Chiskauga, asking him ,to ride over and inform Ellen that her father was on his way home.

The tidings came like a message from heaven to the desolate girl. The terrible suspense—worse than the worst certainty—which she had been enduring for the last five days had worn on mind and body till she seemed more fit to occupy a sick bed than to go about as she still did, wearied and wan, attending mechanically to her daily duties.

The poor child had her own personal griefs and anxieties in addition to those which regarded her father's fate. She had fallen, alas ! into pitiless hands.

The ancients were wont to picture the Harpies as rapacious birds with human heads, who snatched from some hungry man the untasted meal, destroying or befouling what was intended for nourishment and comfort. More cruel are the Harpies of humankind—filching or defiling the holier food of the mind and heart, decrying good name, bedaubing fair fame and murdering reputation. Venial in the comparison, and of motive less shameful, is even the base offence of the robber-incendiary. He may hope to clutch from the burning edifice valuable spoil, and that edifice may, ere long, be rebuilt stronger, fairer, more stately than before ; but the backbiter has not even the poor excuse of plunder, and the ruins of a blasted reputation may be eternal — beyond reach of restoration even by the slanderer himself, should late repentance seek to repair the desolation he had wrought.

But Amos Cranstoun and Catherine Wolfgang thought of none of these things. The one stung by jealousy, the other by envy, they sought to gratify these evil passions, reckless on whose head their defamations fell. Neither specially disliked Ellen Tyler, yet, as events turned, she was their chief victim. They felt that Mowbray and Celia could be most effectually reached and punished by imputations on the chastity of the miller's innocent and simple-hearted child.

Day by day she was made to feel, sometimes by intangible trifles, sometimes by ruder demonstrations, the spreading of the subtle influence. On May-day there was a pic-nic, numerously attended, on Grangula's Mount, and to this the invitation had been of a general character. Ellen went. By Celia, Leoline and others she was treated with their wonted kindness, but on the part of several of her usual companions she met averted looks, a few rudely and pointedly avoiding her. On one occasion, when she had seated herself on a bench on which six or eight young girls of her acquaintance had already taken seats, they rose in a body and left it.

She returned home heart-broken ; and when, two days later, there was superadded a week of torturing suspense in regard to her father's fate, the unhappy girl, looking forward to desertion by all earthly aid and hope, was, for the time, crushed beneath her load of sorrow.

One star—was it of bane or of blessing ?—shone through the darkness that was enshrouding her. She met Mowbray twice during that terrible week. He spoke to her gently, kindly, soothingly—spoke, at last, of marriage. Ellen burst into tears, faltering out Celia's name.

"Do not let us speak of her," said Mowbray, coloring. "She has— Everything is over between us for ever—for ever, dear Ellen! It was her doing: perhaps she likes somebody else better: at all events, I was glad to be honorably released. Don't you know why? I have felt lately—you must have felt it too—that for months I have loved you far better than her—far better than any one else in all this world. It would have been wrong for me to marry her, loving you best. Now I am free, and you will be my little wife—will you not, dear, dear Ellen ?"

It was not in a nature like Ellen's to make any answer but one to this. Child-like, faithful-hearted, inexperienced, tender, she saw in Evelyn Mowbray more than her love : he was her hero also, her ideal of all goodness, nobility, generosity. To another it might have occurred that Mowbray's conduct to Celia showed inconstancy, and laid him open to the charge of mercenary motive. Not one light cloud of suspicion rested on the heaven of her simple faith. Celia's position, if she had lost much money, seemed to Ellen still far above her own, and it was Celia's own doing. Didn't Mr. Mowbray say so?

But the glamour which indued the image of clay with the vestments of a god owed its power of charming to something more. Mowbray *had* taken a fancy to this pretty, warm-hearted, bright-eyed girl. Celia had deeply wounded his vanity, and Ellen's look of love mingled with reverence was balm to the wound. He had not lied to her when he said that he preferred her to her rival and to every one else: he certainly did—just then. Truth lent force to his words and warmth to his tones. Ellen knew that she was loved—that she was preferred to a young lady, beautiful, refined, accomplished. Her vanity, like his, was flattered, and became the ally of her love.

Could she say aught but yes when he offered her the first place in his heart, and a shelter in his arms from the revilings of a merciless world?

One only condition she attached to her consent—that her father, when he returned (not *if* he returned) should say yes also.

He *did* return when hope was almost gone; but alas! alas! how worn, how pale, how changed! Ellen's tearful joy when the old man took her once more in his arms was most touching to see. She supported him into the house, set him in the wonted easy-chair; then sank at his feet, burying her face in her hands and laughing and crying alternately, without power of control.

When her first wild emotions had somewhat subsided, she stood, with swimming eyes and an aching heart, gazing—oh so piteously!—at that wasted form. "Father, father!" she cried, "how terrible it must have been! Poor white hair!" putting it back from his forehead and kissing him fervently again and again. Then she knelt down, laid her clasped hands on his knees, and looked up in his face: "You must rest now, father dear, and I must nurse you. Hiram can mind the mill: he's been quite attentive since you went away. You must be very quiet: you mustn't be anxious, nor trouble yourself about anything except getting well." Then sadly, in a low tone: "I've been a trouble to you, father: I've done what I ought not to have done: you've been anxious and sorry about me. Dear, kind father, you mustn't be anxious, you mustn't ever be sorry about me, any more. They may say what they please and promise what they please: I'll stay with you and take care of you, as mother would have done if she hadn't gone to heaven. I'll never leave you—never, father dear—as long as you need me—as long as you want me to stay." Then she took the white, thin hands in both hers, stroked them and laid her face on them.

The old man, wholly overcome, looked at his daughter with dim eyes, thinking, the while, of that pathetic old story that tells us of the Hebrew widow and the Moabitess, her daughter-in-law. The words seemed to sound in his ears: "Whither thou goest, I will go; and where thou lodgest, I will lodge. The Lord do so to me, and more also, if aught but death part me and thee." He gently drew his hands from hers, laid them on her bowed head and said: "You are your mother's own child, Nell — the dearest blessing God has given me. May He bless you as I do, and lead and protect you when I am gone!"

The next day, when a quiet night's rest had a little recruited the miller's strength, and when both were calmer, he related to the wondering and excited girl the tragical scenes through which he had passed; omitting, however, that vision of home which appeared to him while he lay under water insensible. As he concluded his narrative, Hiram Goddart came in to take his orders for the day. When these were given and the young man had departed, Tyler said to Ellen: "Has Hiram heard from his uncle Samuel since I left?"

"Yes"—a little embarrassed: "did he tell you he expected a letter?"

"No. Any news from the old man?"

"The letter came on May-day, I believe; at least Hiram told me of it next morning. He did not show it to me, but I think it must have been in reply to something he had written about a partnership with you in the mill; for he said the uncle offered him one or two thousand dollars to set him up in the world."

The miller started, shuddered, turned pale.

"Poor father!" said Ellen; "how you must have suffered! You have these pains still?"

"Not much, my child: it has passed. Did Hiram say anything about a partnership?"

"I think he did. Oh yes—now I remember: he said you might perhaps want money to help pay for that new machinery. Was that all lost, father?"

"Yes, Nell: nothing but the old man's come back to you; and he's good for nothing but to give trouble now."

Ellen put her hand on his mouth: "I know you love me, father dear," the tears rising to her eyes, "and that you don't want me to cry. Then you mustn't say such cruel things as that."

"Well, I won't. I used to tend you when you was little and your mother ailin', and I never thought it a trouble. So you shall fetch me a pitcher of water, dear Nellie, fresh from the well."

Ellen brought it, and when she had poured out a glass, her father asked, "What's come of that blue and white pitcher?"

"Oh, father, I'm *so* sorry!"

"It's broken?"

"Yes. It was the very same morning Hiram spoke to me about his uncle's letter." Then, looking at her father: "You *are* suffering still from those aches you told me of. I see it in your face."

"Just for a moment, Nell: never mind it. So you and he were at the well together, were you?"

Ellen blushed: "Why, how did you know that, father?"

"It wasn't difficult to guess. You generally fetch a pitcher of water for breakfast; and that's about the time Hiram mostly comes to wash by the well."

"Yes, he was wiping his face and hands when he told me about the letter."

"You see. That must have been just about the time I got on shore. I wonder if you had been dreaming about steamboat accidents."

"No, but I had had bad dreams about you, and kept thinking of the seven people that were killed on the railroad when the cars ran off the track."

"And maybe Hiram kept thinking that if anything did happen you'd be very lonely—"

"He had no business to tell you all that. I don't thank him for it!" a little pettishly.

"Don't blame the lad for nothing, Nell. He never said the first word about it, good or bad. But my Scotch aunt Jessie used to sing me a song that Burns or somebody wrote: it began—

> 'Wilt thou be my dearie?
> When sorrow wrings thy gentle heart,
> Wilt thou let me cheer thee?'

And I remember that was the way I felt about your mother when I was courtin' her, one time when her father was ill. I think Hiram must have been saying something about some other partnership besides the millin' business that morning?"

Again that telltale blush: "Father, you must be a witch. How could you guess all that?"

"You think I never heard that, when young people meet by the well, they do, now and then, talk of such things? How do you know I never did it myself?"

"But then nothing can ever come of it. Hiram's as good as he can be: you never had a more faithful hand; only I couldn't love him. I told him it couldn't be. And you don't want me to marry him, do you?"

"You love your old father, Nell, and you're bent on taking care of him. D'ye think he would ever ask you to marry anybody you couldn't love?"

Tyler had many kisses from his daughter that morning, but none more fervent than the one she gave him as he said that. Yet she could not make up her mind to tell him, just then, that Mowbray had asked her to be his wife. "By and by," she thought, "when he is stronger."

"Nelly," said Tyler, "you've your housework to do and that orphan Willie to look to; and I'm a'most as much worn out tellin' you that long story as if I'd gone through it all again. Leave me to rest, child: maybe I'll get a nap."

Yet he was not thinking of napping. When Ellen left him his mind was in a tumult. As he recalled and arranged the wonders that had just come to light, he sank into a long, solemn reverie.

He had looked upon it as a dream. Nothing more natural, considering whither his thoughts had strayed off, even while he was dragging Hartland's body through the water, feeling step by step more like dying himself than saving another. Yet he had never, in his life, dreamed anything so vividly. No occurrence in the actual world had ever seemed to him more real. The Scotchman's voice and the cold wet sand appeared to him, at the first moment, more like a vision than that from which they recalled him. And thus—actuated, however, by curiosity rather than by any belief that the scene had been truly enacted at the well-side—he had cautiously questioned Ellen.

The result overcame him with wonder and with fear. The coincidences were too many and too exact to be casual. First, there was the correspondence as to time—the morning after May-day, probably at the same hour, for the miller was wont to breakfast about sunrise; then the various details of the conversation—Hiram telling the girl of the letter from Uncle Samuel, and the sum named in it, "one or two thousand dollars;" the proposal about a partnership, never broached by the lad before; then—still more unlike the fortuitous—Hiram's suggestion that the money might help to pay for the new machinery; then his suit to Ellen and his allusion to her being left alone; finally a pitcher broken at that very time, and that pitcher the same he had seen in the trance—his mother's bequest. Common sense told him this could not all be chance. What was it, then?

The man felt awestricken, as in the presence of a Superior Power. The next world came near to his senses, as never before, though that might have been due, in part, to his late narrow escape from death. New and strange thoughts crowded upon him. He had never intended to doubt that the soul had a separate existence and that it survived the body: he would have been shocked if any one had suspected that he lacked belief in that article of the Christian creed. Yet he had received the doctrine, as the common mind receives that and a hundred more, passively—with sluggish acquiescence only. No living conviction of its truth had come home to him. If he had been hard pressed as to his reasons for faith in that tenet, he might have been very much puzzled to find them.

Very much puzzled ten days before, but not after that morning on the lake shore. For then he had seen, he had heard—if perceptions indicate sight and hearing—what till then it had not entered into his heart to conceive. While his body lay insensible under the waters—soon to return, it seemed, to the earth as it was—his spirit, love-called,* had hied away, it would appear, leaving its earth-clog behind, yet connected with it perchance by some invisible, attenuated chord, which still permitted return to its home of clay, so long as the fine, spiritual catenation was not finally severed. The soul had in the twinkling of an eye, overswept one or two hundred miles of space to visit home and child, and take note of the cherished one's well-being.

Such—not in its detail, but in its general outline—was the theory upon which Tyler, after an hour of profound meditation, settled down. He accepted the strange phenomenon it had been his lot to witness as establishing the soul's separate and independent action, and affording proof past all denial of its immortality. But an untutored mind, suddenly brought into contact with the new and the wonderful, is apt to run to extreme; and thus the miller, alarmed into superstition, interpreted his vision not

* "Si forte fu l'affettuoso grido."
DANTE, *Inferno*, canto 5.

only as evidence of another world, but as an omen foreshadowing his own approaching entrance into it. "Many external circumstances," says an able naturalist,* "appear to be received in almost all countries as ominous."

But when an omen is taken to indicate death, the tendency of the belief itself often is to work out its own fulfillment. Whether the miller's death was hastened by his presentiment, or whether his mind was disabused by communication with those who held more enlightened opinions, will appear in the future chapters of this story.

In the mean time his love for Ellen caused him scrupulously to conceal from her what agitated his own mind. But, like Mary at the Master's feet, he laid up these things in his heart.

CHAPTER XXXVII.

UNDER THE DEPTHS.

DR. MEYRAC sat by Mrs. Hartland's sick bed counting her pulse, one rainy evening several weeks after the shipwreck. Celia had gone down to see to the preparation of a nourishing soup. The voice of the patient, as she addressed her physician, was faint and low:

"You will tell me the truth, doctor. What are the chances that I shall live?"

He did not immediately reply; and when he did the question he asked seemed irrelevant:

"Is it that madame has great anxiety about the affairs? I heard say that Mr. Hartland lose by one railroad."

"You suppose I wish to make a will? No; I am not thinking about property: Ethan attends to that; but I wish you to tell me—"

"I am very pleased. Now I will answer madame's question. According the symptoms, you ought to recover; but I see you sink, sink, all the days. There is some wrong. I can cure de body, but I have no medicine for cure de mind. Madame's mind is not at ease."

The agitation that caused a sudden flush over Alice's pale, thin face attested the sagacity of the observation.

"I pray madame not to imagine I vould inquire: it is not at all my affair; but I vould offer one advice."

"Speak to me frankly, doctor: I ask it as a favor."

"You are too good. Vell den. Someting oppress you. It weighs on your mind day and night. You rest not: you sleep not. But I cannot cure nobody visout sleep. You must change dat."

"How can I change it?"

"See! If you shut it up, it vill oppress you more and more: maybe it vill be too strong for my tisanes, and you will go to die. The body must be help, and dere is a vay to help it. You are not one Catholique, or I vould tell you send for your confessor; but it is just as good. Find some sage friend dat you love, and say it all. It vill be much relief: vat you call disburden. Ven one is ill, it must never too much load down eeder de stomach or de mind."

Celia entered, and soon after the doctor took his leave, she accompanying him to the door. "Mademoiselle Celie," he said, in French, "try to amuse our good friend. Read to her, sing to her. Don't let her feed on her own fancies: they are not wholesome. Too much care will kill a cat."

In the course of the evening, Celia, mindful of the doctor's injunction, proposed reading something. "What shall it be?" she asked.

"Have you not been translating recently portions of Madame Roland's autobiography?"

"Yes."

"I once dipped into it, and I think it would have interested me intensely, but you know how imperfectly I understand French."

When Celia fetched her manuscript and began to read, she was amazed at the emotion exhibited by her auditor at certain passages—this among them:

"Roland was of a dominating character, and twenty years older than I. One of these two superiorities might have been well enough: both together were too much."

* Brande, who succeeded Sir Humphrey Davy as professor in the Royal Institution.

And again: "It was Roland's desire, at the commencement of our marriage, that I should see as little as possible of my intimate female friends. I conformed to his wishes, and did not renew my intimacy with them till he had acquired sufficient confidence in me to be no longer jealous of their love. That was a mistake. Marriage is grave and austere—"

Celia started: that sigh from the sick bed seemed to come from the very depths of the heart; but she proceeded:

"Marriage is grave and austere; and if a woman with strong affections is deprived of the solace of friendship for those of her own sex, a necessary aliment is cut short and she is exposed thereby. How numerous the corollaries from that truth!"

The invalid clasped her hands, pressing them tightly over her heart, but she said nothing; and Celia went on reading:

"If we lived in solitude, I had many weary hours of sadness and suffering. If we went into society, I attracted the affection of persons, some of whom, I perceived, might have interested me too much. So I devoted myself wholly to work with my husband; but that, too, had its evils."

"Dear Madame Roland!" was all the comment Alice made. Celia, fearing over-excitement in her aunt's feeble state, said:

"I translated only passages that struck me here and there. Here is one other: 'In default of happiness, one can often obtain peace, and that replaces it.'"

Celia laid her manuscript aside as Ethan entered. He noticed, with apprehension, the hectic flush on his mother's cheeks. Fever was rising, but she urged her son and niece to retire. "You have both your day's work to do to-morrow," she said, "and need rest: Nancy can stay with me."

"Housework is as hard as keeping school," said Celia. "Let me stay with you to-night, mother—please!"

Mrs. Hartland had two hours' troubled sleep in the early part of the night—more than she had been able to obtain for several days and nights past. As soon as she stirred, Celia sprang from the lounge where she had dropped into a light nap, and was by her side. The cheeks betrayed high fever.

"Does it still rain?" Alice asked.

Celia threw back the shutters, and moonlight from a cloudless sky filled the room. "It is a brilliant night," she said.

"That storm oppressed me. Put out the lamp, dear child. I want the moonlight."

Celia sat down beside the bed. Her aunt tossed about, occasionally moaning. The forehead was burning hot, and the girl began to fear delirium. But after a time Alice took her niece's hand and seemed to be thinking of her, for she pressed it several times, shuddering a little now and then. When half an hour elapsed, she startled her niece by saying,

"Dr. Meyrac thinks I shall die, but I must tell you something before I go. I knew how I had sinned, but, Celia, Celia, I never thought I should do wrong to you."

"Wrong to me, mother?"

"I did not see that I was doing wrong. It's all clear now. Surely in the next world all will be clear."

"Do you mean that you have loved me and indulged me too much. What else have you ever done?"

"I want to tell you about the days when your dear mother and I went to school together. We lived in Arch street, next door to a rich merchant; and his eldest son— Ah, Celia, what a noble, generous, handsome boy he was! He was just your mother's age—three years older than I. I don't remember when I first knew him, but he went to school with us more than three years; and never did brother treat sister more gently, more kindly, than he treated me. His name was Frank."

"Is he alive still, auntie?"

"I think I must have been a precocious child: I know I was a foolish one. It wasn't love I felt for Frank: it was worship. At school I contrived always to sit so that I could see him, yet I scarcely ever dared to look. If he was in the same room with me anywhere, it was happiness enough for me. I seemed to feel it if at any time he was going to pass our window, and I always looked up just in time. But if anybody had guessed all this, I think I should have died. One day I was terribly frightened. We had got together with a number of children, and one of them proposed that all the boys' names should be written on scraps of paper, folded up and put into a hat. Each girl was to draw one. We thought it was rather wicked, but when it came to the point none of us refused to try our chance. I drew two—one accidentally folded within the other. The first I glanced at was the name I had hidden in my heart: I crushed it, unobserved, in my hand, and showed them the other, which contained the name of a rude boy whom I could never abide. I know I should have fainted on the spot if I had been obliged to show Frank's name. Yet I could not make up my mind to destroy the scrap it was written on. I had a small bead-purse, lined. I ripped open the lining, slid the precious memento inside and carefully sewed it up again."

"Did he die, mother dear?"

"He went to a higher school—afterward to college. I didn't see him for sixteen years: then I was a wife and he a widower. Oh you mustn't despise me, Celia. I was a wife, and I am a widow now, yet I have that little bead-purse still."

For some time she was unable to proceed, covering her face with her hands, her frame shaking with sobs. Celia sought to soothe her, kissed her tenderly, and could not restrain her own tears. With a strong effort, Alice at last mastered her emotion so as to proceed. But she evidently spoke under high feverish excitement, and as if she felt she *must* go through with it:

"Maybe I had some excuse for marrying. He had married some years before. I knew it would be an awful thing to go on loving a married man. And, besides, it was not a man I had loved—only a boy; and I thought it would be so different when I saw him again. Then Mr. Hartland was such a moral, upright person. Everybody respected him, and so did I. I never chose my seat in church so that I could see him, to be sure; nor ever particularly noticed whether he was in the room or not; and I never knew or cared when he passed our window. But I had got it into my head that if a woman married a good man, she wouldn't be able to help loving him afterward. Dear child, whatever you do, never marry a man you don't care for, no matter how good he is, in hopes that you *may* love him by and by. And if you care for your own soul, Celia, never marry one man as long as you love another."

"I shall never marry anybody, dear auntie—never!"

"That's bad, too. And you don't know. If that boy I worshiped so had turned out a worthless man, I think I should never have connected the two, or kept caring for him. But when he was there for years daily before my eyes—daily doing good—the very embodiment of all that is kind and generous and faithful—the idol of hundreds besides myself — the benefactor of the whole neighborhood — your own best, noblest friend, too—"

"Gracious Heaven!"

"Yes, you have guessed it—Frank Sydenham. Sometimes I watched him from behind the curtains as he rode past our windows. But he never saw it. Thank God that he has no cause to despise me! I had to tell you, Celia, for I haven't come to the worst thing I was guilty of—the wrong I did you."

"You are exhausting yourself, dear mother—"

"It must be told, and better at once. I saw that Mr. Sydenham loved you, Celia—indeed, how could he help it?—and I didn't wish him to marry you. It was very, very wicked in me; but that was one of the reasons why I wanted so much that you should marry Mowbray."

Celia was so amazed at this disclosure that, for the time, she could not utter a single word. Alice proceeded desperately, as a convict might in his last confession:

"I did think I'd hide it from you,

darling, and let you believe your aunt was a good woman. But I couldn't bear to put it off. In heaven—but I dare say I sha'n't go there after all I've done — at any rate, I couldn't bear to think that you should hear it there first; so I *had* to tell you here."

Celia still sat like one stunned, her mind bewildered with the strange ideas—unwholesome fancies Dr. Meyrac might well call them—that had just been thrust upon her; and her aunt added:

"I don't expect to live, my child, and I'm sure I don't wish it. But whether I live or die, I want you not to think worse of me than I deserve. If I live, I shall never feel again as I have done. I can't tell you how much this sickness has changed all my thoughts and wishes. Whether I am here to see it, or whether I witness it (if spirits are permitted to look back) from the other side, it will be a happiness to me to see you Frank Sydenham's wife. I hope and pray you may be."

"Dear mother, don't I know there's nothing you think would make me happy that you wouldn't be glad of? But for Mr. Sydenham's sake and for mine, please, please don't talk so. Such a thing never for one moment crossed his thoughts."

"His lips, you mean. Of course not, so long as he knew you were engaged to Mowbray."

"Pray, pray don't! I do believe Lela doesn't love her father much better than I do; but my love for him is just like hers—"

At this point, however, conscience checked her. She remembered the day—was it only seven or eight months ago?—when she was sitting in that arm-chair before Sydenham's parlor fire. Had she really told him then that he never seemed to her like a father, and never would? Had he kissed her? Only on the forehead, and only as any kind old gentleman might. But was he so old, after all? She was getting confused, so she came back to what she did know.

"I haven't a heart to give to Mr. Sydenham if he asked for it. They say Evelyn is engaged to Ellen Tyler: I dare say it's true; but, mother, mother, I love him still!"

Celia laid her head on the pillow beside her aunt's. Alice put her arms round the girl's neck, kissed her fervently, and wept silently and long. "My own child, my own darling!" she said at last. "Ah, if my little Lizzie had only lived! My heart would never have strayed from home then."

After that they were long silent. Then an intuition came to Celia. "They would tell her if they knew all," she thought; then to her aunt: "You think more of Ethan and his welfare than of anything else, don't you, mother?"

"Of you and Ethan. I have nobody else to care for now."

"But you may have, by and by."

Her aunt looked up, troubled, but her brow cleared when Celia asked: "Did it ever occur to you that Ethan might have taken a fancy to some one in Chiskauga?"

"Has he?" with a look of surprise.

"It isn't settled, I think. She feared that she was getting blind, and accepted him conditionally only."

"Miss Ethelridge, is it?"

"Ellie — yes. Such a noble, warm-hearted girl, mother: so much—oh so much — better than I shall ever be. Ethan's heart is in it, and he would marry her, if she were blind, to-morrow."

"But a blind wife—a blind mother of a household, Celia?"

"I know; but perhaps she might have a dear, good mother-in-law staying with her. You will never see your little Lizzie again, auntie, till you see her in heaven, but you may see your grand-children."

The look that came over Alice's face was something beautiful to see. After a pause she said, in a low voice, "Perhaps I may recover. Celia dear, what was that last extract you read me from Madame Roland's diary?"

Celia went to the window and read by the bright moonlight: "In default of happiness one can often obtain peace, and that replaces it."

Toward morning Alice slept tranquilly several hours, and awoke free from fever. Then she sent for Ethan, and had a long talk with him. From that day they dated her convalescence.

It was an imprudent thing in Alice Hartland to speak as she did to her niece, especially as, by Ethan's advice, they had begged Mr. Sydenham to act as Celia's guardian, and he had consented and been appointed. The girl was not at all disposed to imagine people in love with her. But this new relation brought Sydenham and her a good deal together. Then, too, she visited Rosebank thrice a week to give Leoline music-lessons. So that, even if she had desired to avoid him, she could not well do so without appearing unfriendly or ungrateful. She did not really desire to avoid him, but she was no longer at ease with him as formerly; and when she became conscious of this it provoked and annoyed her. If she had not been too busy to be sentimental, it might have made her unhappy.

She had neglected the school somewhat during her aunt's illness, but as soon as Alice was able to sit up and walk about a little, she returned to her teaching, resolved to make up for lost time. Some of the pupils, she found, had been taken from school by their parents. Was the poison working? Was she to be a clog, instead of an aid, to Ellinor? Her dream of usefulness began to fade.

For a moment the thought crossed her that she ought to withdraw from the partnership. But Ellinor's waning sight! And then the indignation against injustice which lurks in the mildest natures woke up a little too. Ought Mrs. Wolfgang and her abettors to succeed in their base plot? "They ought not, and they shall not," she thought, "if I can help it." She was getting pugnacious. That is wholesome—in moderation.

The same evening (Mrs. Clymer having gone out) Leoline and her father urged Celia so cordially to take tea with them, after her lesson was over, that she could not well refuse. She spoke of the pupils they had lost.

"I shouldn't wonder," said Sydenham, "if you have been setting that down to your account." Celia looked embarrassed. "I thought so," pursued Sydenham. "There *is* a cabal formed—not against you individually, but against the Chiskauga Institute. Poor Ellinor Ethelridge has her full share of the abuse. They have been inventing and circulating all kinds of scandalous stories about her past life."

"Who, papa?" asked Leoline.

"Cranstoun and Mrs. Wolfgang, and their set—all whom they can influence or delude."

"If it really would shield Ellie from their malice—" Celia began, but Leoline gave her such a look that she stopped, half inclined to laugh.

"If you do—if you do!" said Leoline, shaking her finger at her. "What! Give it up, and let these wretches have it all their own way!"

"We must fight the battle through, Celia," Sydenham said—"not for your sake and Ellinor's only: for the sake of the place. I never let such things go."

"That's my darling papa," said Leoline, kissing him. "And, Celia, if you desert us, I'll disown you."

"She will not desert us," said her father, smiling.

"I'm afraid," said Celia, "that what somebody calls 'the old Adam' within me was a good deal stirred up when I thought of Mr. Cranstoun and Mrs. Wolfgang enjoying their triumph."

"I declare I begin to have hopes of you, Celia." Of course it was Leoline who said this; and she added: "I once heard some one say to papa (I hope it's not wicked to repeat it) that we 'need a little of the devil in us to keep the devil out.' But it's only a tiny bit of the old Adam that's in you, my dear—of Adam when he was so old he had almost forgotten about Paradise—nothing worse, you good girl. It's only creatures like me that have a touch of the old Serpent. Then, perhaps *he* wasn't so very bad, after all. Milton gives him rather a fine character."

Celia laughed, and that did her good: "If you had been a man, Lela, what a soldier you'd have made! You would have led your men anywhere."

"I don't know about that. I never was tried with that 'villainous saltpetre.' It must be a nervous sort of thing to stand to be shot at."

"It needs as much courage to be slandered without flinching," said her father. "The best way to avoid cowardice in danger is to think of others, not of one's self. These children that are under your care will be the sufferers, Celia, if you give way. Cranstoun and his set are making war on them."

"What motive can he have?"

"Two, probably. A certain young lady wouldn't have him: that cuts deep. Then Creighton is in his way—has already carried off, probably, half his law-practice. So he connects *his* name with the scandal he spreads about Miss Ethelridge. They were friends, you know, before either of them came to Chiskauga."

"What a world!" said Celia.

"I dare say it's all right enough," said Leoline. "What would be the use of that organ of combativeness if everything went just straight? Let's divide forces, papa. If you'll manage that sneaking rascal, Cranstoun, I'll undertake Mrs. Wolfgang."

"Gently, my child. I'm afraid you'll turn out like the 'beau sabreur.' Murat, with his white plume, was splendid at the head of a cavalry charge, but when it came to military tactics—"

"Well, papa, you be Napoleon. I won't charge till you bid me."

"Keep a good heart," said Sydenham to Celia. "We are too strong for them. And from what Creighton told me, you may not need to remain schoolmistress unless you like."

"But I do like, in any event."

Sydenham smiled, well pleased, and Celia blushed. "What a ridiculous habit it is!" she thought.

"And by the way," added Sydenham, "all that lecture of mine on Grangula's Mount went for nothing, it seems. I have to congratulate you, Celia—no, not you, the people of Ohio—that they had sense and justice enough to pass and maintain in force a law under which you are your father's legitimate child."

"That must be gall and wormwood to Mrs. Wolfgang," said Leoline. "It will be no fight at all. Their ammunition's giving out."

"Not so fast, Mademoiselle Murat," smiling. "We mustn't underrate our opponents' strength. I haven't made up my mind just what ought to be done, Celia, but, depend upon it, we shall see you and Ellinor through."

Then they had music, and Celia rode home by moonlight. She left Rosebank, as she almost always did after a talk with Sydenham, in good heart. There was something contagious, too, in that daring spirit of Leoline's.

When Celia reached home, she found that Ellinor had been spending the evening with Mrs. Hartland, and that Ethan's lady-love was in a fair way to become a special favorite with her possible mother-in-law. "If you had searched the world over," Alice said to Ethan, as he returned from escorting Ellinor home, "I don't think you could have pleased me better."

How happy the good fellow went to bed! After he was gone, Alice looked so much better and more cheerful than usual that Celia, after putting her arms round her neck and kissing her, was tempted to venture a saucy question: "Auntie, you've got over thinking you were so terribly wicked, haven't you?"

Alice winced a little, yet she could not help smiling, and Celia went on: "Do you think it would have been behaving so very much better to take a stand against Evelyn, so that Mr. Sydenham might have had a chance by and by?"

"Ah! you think he might have had a chance?"

"No, I don't, but you do. Mother dear, *would* it have been the virtuous thing and the kind thing to run down Mowbray, and tell me I ought to be ashamed of myself to love such a man as that, when there were so many better ones in the world, and then to have given me a hint that I had better take Mr. Sydenham instead?"

"For shame, Celia! You've been talking with Leoline, one can see."

"Not about you, mother. There's another thing I want to know"—in a graver tone, a slight shade of sadness coming over the April sky of that tell-tale face—

"Well, dear?"

"I've been with you daily, years and years. You kept away from Mr. Sydenham. You devoted yourself to my uncle. You labored with him as Madame Roland did with her husband. I think you gave up dear friends, too, for his sake. What more could you do?"

"I don't know," hesitating. "Yes, I could have kept from thinking about Mr. Sydenham at all."

"I wish you'd tell me how to set about such a thing, auntie." The tone was light, but the soft eyes glistened. "Right in the midst of our lessons I keep thinking of a man that's not half so good as Mr. Sydenham, in spite of all I can do."

"Poor child!"

"*You* kept thinking Mr. Sydenham was a man in a thousand—so he is—that he did ever so much good to this village, to all the neighborhood. So he does: I don't believe Pope's 'Man of Ross' was a bit better. Why shouldn't

you think what was true? Then maybe you thought—don't be angry, mother dear—maybe you did think, sometimes, that if you had been his wife—"

Alice turned deadly pale.

"Well, I won't, mother. But how *could* you help it? And it was true, too. Then you *did* the right thing. You never neglected one duty: you never said one complaining word. You did more than praying not to be led into temptation: you kept out of it. My uncle's dead and gone, and I shall never think of him but kindly. Yet if I had been in your place, auntie, I could never, never have made him the wife you did. You never crossed a wish of his. And I dare say he knows now what a hard time you had of it!"

Alice wept so long that Celia blamed herself bitterly for the agitation she had caused. Yet when it was over, and her aunt had had a night's rest, she was all the better for her niece's downright words. Her mind gradually resumed its tone. And—let the truth be told even if the widow's character suffer thereby—before another month had elapsed there came over her a calm, subdued cheerfulness, such as, during all her married life, that pale face had never worn.

PART XI.

CHAPTER XXXVIII.

WHAT THE CAPTAIN SAW ON THE SNOW.

"When deep sleep falleth upon men; in slumberings upon the bed; then God openeth the ears of men and sealeth their instruction."—JOB xxxiii. 14.

"YOU will come to see him, Mr. Harper?"

"Surely, my child. I did purpose to call on Betty Carson this morning, but that will do later."

"It will be such a kindness to us! I don't know what to think of father's state."

It was Ellen Tyler who spoke. They were sitting, on a bright, fresh morning, toward the end of May, on Harper's woodbine-shaded porch.

"What are the symptoms, Ellen?"

"I'm afraid you'll hardly believe me, sir, they are so strange. I suppose he must have dreams at night about that awful boat-burning. Anyhow, we can't let him sleep without locking the door: he told us to do it himself. The reason was, he had got up two or three times in the middle of the night and rushed out into the yard, as if the house was on fire. Last night I heard a noise in his room: he had raised the window and was trying to undo the shutters. When I ran in and did my best to wake him, he cried out: 'Quick, quick, Nelly! Don't you see the flames?' Oh, Mr. Harper, only think if he had jumped out! You know our house stands on the edge of the steep bank, and he would have gone down, eighteen or twenty feet, into the mill-race. I never was so frightened in all my life."

"I am glad you came to me, dear child."

"I wouldn't have troubled you indeed, sir, if I had thought I could manage it myself. Preacher Larrabee sometimes comes to see father, though we don't belong to his church; but he's at Mount Sharon this week. 'Seems to me father has something on his mind that vexes him; and then—oh I'm sure he thinks he's going to die. You're such a good man, Mr. Harper, and I know you can do him good."

He smiled and laid his hand kindly on her head. "Wait here," he said: "I'll go with you."

In an adjoining paddock was Trooper comfortably browsing. His master enticed him, with a tempting ear of corn, into the stable, harnessed him to the ancient gig and drove round to the front gate.

"Come, my child," he called to Ellen.

"Mr. Harper," the girl said as she came up, "let me walk home. I'd rather father should think you came to see him accidentally."

"What's that you've been buying in the village?"

"Some stuff to make a soft cushion for father's arm-chair."

"Get in, then. I picked you up returning home. I'll tell him so."

The good man was quite unprepared for the sad change in Tyler's appearance, but evincing no surprise, he conversed a while on commonplaces, and then said: "Your daughter tells me you haven't quite got over that terrible accident. You must have passed through scenes such as few men have witnessed."

"That's a truer word than you think for, Mr. Harper. Nelly dear, I want to have a good talk with the minister, and maybe he'll stay and take a bite of dinner with us. Nell brags on her strawberries, Mr. Harper—Hovey seedlings, I think she calls them: her sparrowgrass is pretty much over, but her peas are in their prime—"

"Strawberries and peas are too great a temptation. I'll stay and see what sort of gardener Nelly is."

"Now, Nell," said her father, "put your best foot foremost;" and the girl, delighted, ran off on her mission. "I didn't want the lassie to hear what I've got to tell: she has trouble enough already. I've had a call, Mr. Harper."

"A call?"

"A notice that I'm not long for this world."

"Tell me about it."

Tyler related the story of his escape, the vision he had during his trance beneath the waters of Lake Erie, and the numerous and minute coincidences between what he dreamed and what actually happened at the time in his mill-yard at home. Then he added: "I dare say you can't believe it, Mr. Harper, and I won't think a bit hard of it if you say so. Sometimes I think I don't more than half believe it myself."

"A single year ago," replied the minister, "I might have acted the Sadducee in such a matter: but I have had a strange experience since. Last autumn my Methodist friend, Mr. Larrabee—and he is a pious and truthful man—told me a story just as wonderful as that. But you said that you had had some notice that you were soon to die. How was that?"

"Wasn't that vision notice enough?"

"I must tell you Mr. Larrabee's story, Tyler, and then you can judge for yourself."

He did; and afterward, at Tyler's earnest request, wrote it out for him, as follows:

THE METHODIST PREACHER'S STORY.

During the early years of the present century, Captain John Pintard, then a young, unmarried man, was master and part owner of a small schooner belonging to Shrewsbury, New Jersey, and trading between New York and Virginia.

On one occasion, during the month of January, returning from Norfolk laden with oysters, the vessel was driven on shore, by stress of weather, between Cape May and Great Egg Harbor. The captain and crew succeeded, by strenuous exertions, in reaching the land, much exhausted, however, by exposure, especially the captain, who had been at the helm for nearly twelve consecutive hours. By this time it was quite dark.

The spot where they got on shore being only about forty miles from where Captain Pintard lived, he was familiar with the neighborhood, and knew that there was a tavern about a mile distant. He pointed out the direction to his men, and through a dismal tempest of snow and sleet they commenced their journey toward it.

The captain took the lead, but thoroughly chilled as well as exhausted by his long vigil and exposure to the bitter cold, he had not proceeded far before he felt creeping over him that overpowering torpor which to the wintry traveler has so often been the precursor of death. He knew his danger and sought to shake off the lethargic feeling. In vain. He threw himself on the snow, and bade his men hurry on to the tavern and send back assistance. At first the brave fellows refused to do so. Two of them sought to drag him along, but after a time, warned by approaching drowsiness in themselves, they became convinced that his safety as well as theirs required that for the time he should be abandoned.

His sensations when they left him he ever after described as soothing and pleasurable. He felt as one enjoying the luxury of a comfortable bed, and was soon wholly insensible to cold and tempest.

The next thing he remembered was that he seemed to be getting over the fence on the back part of the lot on which stood his mother's house. He saw the door open and his mother, sister and aunt Nancy come out toward the well. The aunt went in front, carrying a lantern; his mother followed with a pail in her hand, and as she approached the well, a sudden gust of wind blew off her hood. "What a terrible night!" he then heard her say: "it blows a hurricane. Pray God my poor boy be not out in it!"

"Oh no," replied the aunt: "even if he was off the coast, he must have seen it coming on and made for some harbor."

The captain was very anxious to speak to them and assure them of his safety, but the first attempt failed, and before he could renew it, mother, sister, aunt and his paternal home all faded away, and he felt sudden and excruciating pain. Next he became sensible of voices around him. At last he distinguished the words, "He's comin' to: rub away, boys! Captain John's good for many a year yet." He recognized the voice as that of a pilot with whom he was well acquainted. "Can I be at the old tavern?" he thought. After a time he opened his eyes, and they met those of the pilot looking at him. This latter was a jovial old fellow, but somewhat profane withal: the captain and he had often been boon companions.

"Halloa, Captain John!" he cried. "Come back, eh?" The reviving man tried to speak, but could not. "I say, old fellow," continued the other, "been on a cruise down below? Seen Old Davy there? What's the news from hell anyhow, Captain John?"

A second strenuous effort to articulate was more successful than the first, and the captain, catching his old companion's tone, replied: "I heard there was a great demand for pilots there."

The retort caused a roar of laughter from all present, and none joined in it more heartily than the object of the joke.

The men, it seems, having safely reached the tavern, had instantly despatched aid to bring in the inanimate body of the captain. The usual restoratives had been employed for some time in vain—at last successfully. After a few hours' sleep the sufferer was comparatively well. When he awoke next morning, the strange dream he had had during his trance recurred to his memory with all the vividness of a real occurrence. He could scarcely persuade himself he had not actually been at home and seen his relatives and heard their conversation.

Pondering over this matter, his impatience became so great that he bade his first mate look to the condition of the schooner; and then, hiring a conveyance, he set out for his mother's house to have his doubts solved.

The old lady's joy at sight of her son was great, and to the bad news he brought she replied cheerily: "God will give you the means to buy another schooner. He didn't forsake you when you lay in that trance on the snow."

"Mother," said the captain, "did you go out to the well, last night, late?"

"Yes, my son. Why do you ask?"

"Tell me what happened, but try to remember everything you said and did, no matter whether it was important or not. Was any one with you?"

The old lady reflected: "Yes, Nancy was with me, and your sister. It was pitch-dark, and Nancy carried a lantern. I remember, too, the wind was very strong and blew off my hood. I thought I should have lost it."

"Did you say anything, mother?"

"Yes. I prayed God you might not be out in such a fearful night."

"And I," said Nancy, "told her I was sure you must have seen it come on and made for some port or other."

The captain sat deep in thought. "I've been very wicked, mother," he said at last. "My first word, when I woke from that trance, was a profane jest. But I did not know, then, *how* merciful He had been. He showed me last night that I had an immortal soul. While my body lay on the snow He brought my spirit here, home to you. I saw you and Aunt Nancy and sister come out to the well: I saw your hood blow off: I heard every word you said. I have been a wicked, careless sinner: I've never sought religion, as you wished me to do; but, with God's help, mother, I will."

His mother, a devout Methodist, was delighted. Her son kept his word. He became a noted member of the Methodist Church, and a constant frequenter of prayer and exhortation meetings. At these latter it was frequently his habit to relate, as the most remarkable incident in his religious experience, the story of his trance on the wintry snow and his spirit's visit to the maternal home.

When Mr. Harper had told the miller the above story, in substance as here set down, the latter asked: "But do you think it can be depended on? It must be nearly fifty years since it happened."

"I like to follow up such things," said Mr. Harper. "Last winter, as I was going to New York, Mr. Larrabee gave me a letter that put me on the track. Captain Pintard, I found, had been dead a good many years, but his widow, Mrs. Phœbe Pintard, a hale, hearty old dame, confirmed to me all the main incidents. I found a niece, also, Mrs. Maria Douglass, of Middletown, New Jersey, who had heard the particulars, more than once, from her uncle himself; and she, after reading the story just as I have it, allowed me to use her name in attestation of its truth."

This set Nelson Tyler to thinking. "How long did the captain live after that vision?" he asked.

"Over thirty years."

A deep sigh of relief attested the miller's satisfaction. That little fact outweighed, with him, the longest philosophical argument. "But it's all very strange," he said at last.

"Very strange, yes. We are fearfully and wonderfully made. Yet I see nothing unlikely in it. Skeptics and scoffers are increasing among us, and God may choose this method of helping our unbelief. You were very near death, Mr. Tyler. Your spirit may have been asserting its independent existence a little in advance, and borrowing of the near Future one of the faculties to which it is born heir. I do think you have been favored by witnessing one of those experimental proofs—rare and precious—that confirm to us the soul's immortality—one of those inestimable phenomena, the character of which enables us to solve, by crucial test, the divine problem of a world to come."*

* I agree with good Mr. Harper as to the importance and the need of such experimental proof. Many excellent persons, pious and strictly nursed in faith, have been overtaken by Giant Despair and led captive to Doubting Castle. In the rectory of Epworth, occupied a century and a half ago by Samuel Wesley, father of John, the founder of Methodism, there occurred at that time certain strange physical disturbances which the family found it impossible to refer except to an ultra-mundane source. Emily, the eldest sister of John, narrating these in a letter to her brother, wrote: "I am so far from being superstitious that I was too much inclined to infidelity; so that I heartily rejoice at having such an opportunity of convincing myself past doubt or scruple of the existence of some beings besides those we see."—*Memoirs of the Wesley Family*," by ADAM CLARKE, LL.D., F. A. S., vol. i., p. 270.

"It set me thinking about that more than I had ever done before," said the miller.

Ellen came to announce dinner. The sight of the peas and strawberries proved a pleasant diversion from the greater mysteries of Nature they had been contemplating; and when the good pastor remounted his gig his young hostess said to herself, "How much more cheerful father is! I haven't seen him look so like himself since the day he came back from that awful journey."

In the evening, all motive for concealment being now done away, the miller related to his wondering daughter both his own experience and that of the Jersey captain. As in the father's case, so in Ellen's—the effect was to quicken religious sentiment and bring home more vivid convictions touching the reality of a future state.

Up to this time, Nelson Tyler, though he usually attended divine service, had not been a "professor," but on the week following he and Ellen joined Mr. Harper's church.

Mr. Harper, meanwhile, revolving in his mind what he had just heard, drove slowly back to Chiskauga and stopped at Betty Carson's door.

Betty was a little out of sorts. A new washerwoman, Nance Coombs, had taken off some of her customers. This was due to the exertions of Mrs. Wolfgang, who had resented the tone Betty assumed in defence of Celia and her parents. The villagers were beginning to take sides on the Pembroke and Ethelridge controversy, and the contest promised to wax warm. Betty spoke to Mr. Harper of the great kindness Mr. and Mrs. Pembroke had shown her. "And then I was always such a favorite with little Miss Celia: she was a jewel of a baby, sir. And Mr. Pembroke, he set store by me. One day he made me write my name to a paper of his—for a witness, I think he said."

"Why, Betty," said Harper, smiling, "I knew you could read, but I didn't suppose you could write too."

"Just me name, sir. He was a rale

kind man—was my husband—afore he took to drink. He was a good scribe, too; and he used to set me a copy—*Betty Carson*—till I could write it most as nice as himself."

Mr. Harper did not think of asking Betty what sort of paper it was she witnessed.

CHAPTER XXXIX.

THE MITE.

THERE was a *Mite* at Mrs. Hartland's.

When a village has two clergymen, it is fortunate if they happen to be friends. As the Methodists of our little village did not feel able to support a resident pastor, Mr. Larrabee preached on alternate Sundays at Mount Sharon (the county-seat) and at Chiskauga. He and Mr. Harper being on the best terms, their respective congregations were wont to act in harmony.

There was a ladies' sewing society, for example, composed of Presbyterians, Methodists, and persons who were neither, the members of which had several times helped to eke out Mr. Larrabee's scanty salary by contributions, in labor or in money, to the comfort of his family. Just at this time, the Presbyterians having purchased a cabinet organ, on which a hundred dollars was still due, the society held weekly "Mites," as they were called, at which each person contributed ten cents or more toward the liquidation of the deficiency. Mr. Harper, Mr. Larrabee, Mr. Hartland while he lived, Mr. Sydenham and others had a standing invitation to these meetings, and while the ladies plied their needles one or other of these gentlemen often read or spoke to them.

About six weeks after Hartland's death his widow offered the society the use of her spacious parlors during the afternoon for one of its weekly assemblies, and Sydenham agreed to attend. He found some fifty or sixty ladies. But Ellinor and Celia, busy at school, were not of the number: they were working, just then, under considerable discouragement, nearly one-fourth of their pupils having been withdrawn.

Sydenham read to the society from the life of Oberlin, the Alsatian philanthropist and benevolent pastor of Ban de-la-Roche. Adverting to the effects of his fifty years' labor of love among a primitive people, he reminded his auditors how, by public instruction, whole communities may advance in civilization. Then, in few words, he took occasion to commend the Chiskauga Institute. It was managed, he remarked, by two ladies of rare qualifications and admirable judgment, and ought to have a hearty and united support. "I have visited schools and colleges," he went on, "in many of our States, and in most of the kingdoms of Europe, and I know that this institution compares favorably with the best of its class. Few villages in any country are as fortunate as we in the matter of teachers. I have heard with regret," he added, after a pause, "that idle or ill-disposed persons among us have circulated mischievous stories regarding these teachers—stories that are either irrelevant or without any foundation whatever. So far as these tend to impair the usefulness of public functionaries, it is a war against the best interests of the place—an unprincipled war, too. One of these young ladies has spent her entire life among us. Blameless you well know that life to have been. Against her it is alleged that she is an illegitimate child, and as such should not be countenanced. If that were the fact, it would be a most cruel injustice to visit such a misfortune on the innocent. But it is not true. Miss Pembroke is as strictly legitimate as any one to whom I have now the pleasure of speaking.

"As to the other lady in question, I happen to know that of which we must charitably suppose her detractors to be ignorant. The reverse of fortune which caused Miss Ethelridge to seek a home among us resulted from no misconduct of hers. The manner in which she has borne it, the courage and ability with which she has maintained herself, and the good she has done us, are above all praise: they entitle her to esteem and honor. Her conduct ought to obtain for her—*will* obtain for her among all just and well-disposed persons — protection and encouragement. I should not," he subjoined in a quieter tone, "have taken up your time with these remarks if I did not feel that the reports to which I have alluded are an injury not only to those who disgrace themselves by retailing them, but to all of us and to our children. Will you allow me to recommend, ladies, that you meet them with a demand for proof, which you will find is not forthcoming?"

Sydenham left soon after speaking, and the circle gradually thinned till fifteen or twenty only remained; among them, Mrs. Wolfgang, Mrs. Creighton, Leoline, and our friend Norah, who had joined the society on Leoline's invitation, and who proved to be as deft at needlework as skillful in butter-making.

The ladies naturally dropped into talk on what Mr. Sydenham had been saying. At first the opinions expressed were favorable. That roused Mrs. Wolfgang, whose countenance had been gradually darkening at each successive commendation of the school and its teachers. "For her part," she broke out at last, "she thought there ought to be a line drawn between morality and immorality. What did they know about Miss Ethelridge, except that Mr. Creighton had been acquainted with her before she turned up here? *She* knew, for the postmaster had told her, that letters in Mr. Creighton's handwriting had come to the lady year after year. Was she engaged to him? She ought to be. But it didn't look like it: she went about with other men. Was that to be called decent behavior? She held her head high enough, as any hussy might. What of that? She had relations, no doubt, yet not one of them took the least notice of her: she never heard of a letter coming to her in a lady's handwriting. It was all very well for Mr. Sydenham to say there was nothing wrong. If there was nothing wrong, why didn't he let them know all about it? A bad sign when things won't bear the light! And if he didn't know any more about her than he seemed to know about Celia Pembroke, she (Mrs. Wolfgang) wouldn't give much for his opinion. *She* knew, if Mr. Sydenham didn't, that the girl's mother never was legally married: she had seen letters from the father to Mr. Cranstoun, confessing it. Wasn't that proof? Others might send their children to the daughter of a kept mistress if they liked: she had too much self-respect, and too much regard to the morals and the reputation of her poor innocent girls, to trust them in the hands of any such creature. 'Like father, like son,' was a good old proverb, and it applied just as much to daughters as to sons. Then, too, what were they to think of an offence so scandalous that it needed downright lies to support it? If the child of a man's mistress wasn't a bastard, she'd like to know what a bastard was?"

Leoline, our readers may remember, had said to Celia, as they were returning from Grangula's Mount after the public speaking, that if she was "hard put to it" she thought she could make a speech herself. She *was* hard put to it now. While Mrs. Wolfgang was abusing Celia and Ellinor she had sat still, choking down her indignation, calling to mind her father's warning to Mademoiselle Murat, taking stitches each long enough for two, and curbing with all her might her eagerness to retort. She would have succeeded—for the girl, with all her impulsive warmth, had a good deal of self-control when occasion called for it—she would have succeeded in keeping silence, but for the last hit, the imputation against her father. That was the drop too much. She started involuntarily to her feet, dropping her needle and crushing in her left hand the garment she had been sewing.

"Mrs. Wolfgang," she burst forth, "you called papa a liar." Then she stopped, trembling from head to foot and struggling desperately for composure. "You called him so because he said dear Celia was a legitimate child. Yesterday I asked papa to show me the law. I saw it: I read it. It said that even if a marriage is not legal, the children shall be legitimate. Mrs. Pembroke's marriage was not legal, but Celia Pembroke *is* legitimate. The law of the land—the authority next to God's—says she is. Who knows best—the law or Mrs. Wolfgang? Who is the liar now, and what is the liar's portion?" Here she checked herself. "That mayn't be just. Perhaps she knows no better: it may be sheer ignorance, but ignorant people ought to hold their tongues. And this is the woman that wants somebody to tell her all about Miss Ethelridge from the time she was a baby in long clothes, so that *her* wisdom may enlighten us, and we may get to know whether it's quite safe and proper for us to countenance our teacher! *She* wants to sit in judgment on Ellinor Ethelridge, and settle who may write letters to her and who may not! Why, nobody can look for an instant at the two faces without seeing which is the scold and which the Christian and the lady. I want to know what good Mrs. Wolfgang has ever done among us to entitle her to be judge and ruler? Has she lifted her finger to help on the education of the place? Has she entered the walls of the school she's been trying to ruin? Never since I've been a pupil there. What *has* she ever done for Chiskauga? Nothing that I know of, except to backbite the best people in it, and set her neighbors by the ears. Christ tells us that the peace-makers shall be called the children of God: I wonder whose child Mrs. Wolfgang ought to be called? I know I'd as soon have a viper in my house. No wonder good Madame Meyrac turned her out of doors. Poor Celia, poor Ellinor!—to fall into such merciless hands as hers!"

Here Leoline broke down for a moment, bursting into tears. But she dashed them indignantly away, and turned from Mrs. Wolfgang to the other members: "I'm ashamed of myself, and I'm *so* glad papa wasn't here to hear me! I know I oughtn't to have spoken as I did before ladies so much older than I. I hope you'll forgive me. I never *could* stand injustice and cruelty; but I'm very, very sorry I spoke at all: I wish somebody else had done it."

Before she could say more, Mrs. Creighton crossed over, took her in her arms and kissed her. "You're a brave, generous girl," the old lady said; "but when you've been a few years longer in the world, you'll find out that it's not a bit worth while to vex and agitate one's self so about bitter tongues. Get your hat and parasol and come with me. You're a darling, if you did 'speak out in meeting,' like the old woman that didn't intend it."

For the moment Mrs. Wolfgang had been fairly cowed into silence by Leoline's impetuous charge upon her, but as they went out her voice was heard—in an undertone, however—denouncing the insolence of upstart misses.

CHAPTER XL.

THROUGH A KEYHOLE.

When Norah returned from the Mite, she had just time to prepare supper before Terence came in from the farm. At table she told him all that had passed, and she observed that it made him very grave. When the dishes were washed and the children out at play, Terence said, "An' couldn't I tell Mister Sydenham mor'n he knows about Miss Ethelridge?"

"An' how did ye come to know anything about a lady like that?"

"Sure, an' wasn't I Cap'n Halloran's groom in the ould country, and didn't she come to his rooms, and didn't I see her there?"

"Did she know ye, Teddy, when ye took Derry and Cathy to school?"

"Sorra bit. I guess she'd a knowed me fast enough when I was behind the bar, and didn't wear no burd nor mustashes. But me that's a rough fellow now, with me face all hairy, and a farmer's coat on—that's another thing. Ye ought to ha' seen me in them days, in the captain's curricle, wi' them black-legged bays, and a heap finer dress than the captain's own. I wouldn't have had to coort ye nothin' like as hard as I did. Ye'd have took to me right off, Norah, and jist dropped into me arms."

"I expec' ye thought, them times, wi' the lace on yer coat and on yer hat, and yer shiny, white-top boots, that it was the girls' place to ask you and not you them. Set ye up! I niver could abide impudence, and I wouldn't have had sich a stuck-up fellow to save him. But what did ye know about Miss Ethelridge?"

"It isn't Miss Ethelridge—it's Miss Talbot."

"Well, Miss Talbot, then. Was it good or bad ye knowed about her?"

"It was bad I knowed o' the master, and good I knowed about her. She's a trump—she is. The captain wanted to have his wicked will of her, but she was too many for him."

"I'd tell Mr. Sydenham about it ef I was you, Teddy."

"I'll do it, this blessed night. Haven't ye got some butter for Miss Leoline?"

"An' isn't there two pounds and a half good, that I churned jist afore I went to that Mite?"

It was put up with scrupulous care, Pennsylvania-fashion, in a snow-white napkin, the produce of Norah's own spinning and weaving and bleaching in her maiden days. With the basket on his arm Terence trudged to Rosebank.

When Sydenham admitted him to his study he was somewhat embarrassed:

"I dunno' ef it's the right thing for me to be troublin' ye, Mister Sydenham. But I hearn they were speaking ill o' the schoolmistress, and—and I knowed somethin' about her myself in the ould country."

"Get yourself a chair, Terence. I take an interest in anything that relates to Miss Ethelridge."

"Thankee, sir; that's just what Norah tould me."

"What did you know of her?"

"Ye see, Mister Sydenham, me ould faither had a shealin' and a bit garden-spot on Squire Halloran's place: that was in Connaught. The squire, he had lots and lots of land, and he had a son that was a cap'n in the army. He was a wild young man, was master; but I didn't never think he'd have been half as bad as he got to be ef it hadn't been for a divil of a black-coated Frenchman that put him up to all sorts o' tricks. The fellow was the cap'n's jintleman, that waited on him and dressed him; and I was the groom. I hated that Frenchman. His name was Vealmong, but I think they spelled it Vileman; and he was jist right named at that."

"Were you staying in London?"

"Near St. James'—yes. I think it was through the Frenchman somehow—on a race-course maybe—that the cap'n got acquainted with a jintleman that cut a great dash and was a'most as wild as master was — Sir Charles Cunningem, they called him. One day me and the master went to his house and took two ladies a-drivin' in the Park: one of them was Lady Cunningem, and the other was Miss Talbot: I think she was a cousin to Sir Charles. I had a good look at them thin; and though it was mor'n a year and a half after that, I knowed Miss Talbot in a minnit when the cap'n brought her one evenin' to his rooms."

"Miss Talbot?"

"That's Miss Ethelridge. She looked bewildered-like, as if she didn't know where she was or what she was doin'; and master, he hurried her into the parlor a'most afore we had time to see her. Then he came out and sent the Frenchman off on an errand. Thinks I, there's some rascality on hand; and I slipped into the cap'n's bed-room, that was next to the parlor, wi' a door between. I locked the door — the lock went very easy—for fear he might come in on me, and I got sight o' them through the keyhole. I ain't no eavesdropper, Mister Sydenham, nor niver was: I'd scorn sich a meanness; but I knowed it wasn't fair play they was after, and I knowed that Vealmong must be at the bottom of it; an' sure enough he was. An' I kep' a-thinkin' a young thing like that ought to have a chance, ef so be they had set some of their divil's traps for her."

"You're a good fellow, Terence."

"Sure, an' ef it had been me own sister wouldn't I have gone down on me knees to anybody that would 'ave gi'n her a helpin' hand?"

"But what happened?"

"It was sort o' curious, Mister Sydenham. I niver jist understood it. Seemed she wasn't herself at first: she looked stupid-like. It came across me maybe he'd had her somewhere to get soda water or ice cream, or somethin', and drugged it: there wasn't no wickedness that Frenchman couldn't put a man up to. Any way, for a while she didn't hardly look able to speak. The cap'n, he put his hands up to her, but she kep' him off all she could. At last, says she: 'Cap'n Halloran, ef ye keep me from goin' back to me cousin's, I'll alarm the house!' Says he, 'Me sarvants is too well trained for that: they niver come till I ring the bell!' With that she made a spring at the bell-rope, but the cap'n, he was too quick for her. He got her be the hands and forced her back."

"Is such villainy possible?" broke in Sydenham.

"Indade, an' it is," resumed the other: "it's every word as true as the blessed Gospel. The cap'n, he says to her then, 'Ye can niver go home no more. Ye came here wi' me alone and o' yer own accord.'"

"'O' me own accord?' says she. 'O' me own accord? How dar' ye say that?'

"'Me sarvants saw ye come in,' says he, as cool as ye like: 'I can get them to witness that no force was used. Ye're disgraced for ever. Ye've played me fast and loose, Miss Talbot, long enough: ye're in me power now. But I'm a jintleman. I'll send for another clergyman, ef ye'll promise not for to go to insult him, like ye did the last I got ye.' The poor thing sunk down on a sofa, and I couldn't hear what she said. But it sort o' stirred him up, and says he: 'It's yer only chance to go from here an honest woman.' With that she sprung up and looked all round her like a wild thing. 'Ye needn't look,' says he: 'the door's locked.' And thin he sprung to the chamber door and tried it. 'Lucky!' said he: 'that's locked too.' She ran to the window, but he snapped the spring over it, and that was so high it was out of her reach. Then she seemed like she gi'n it up, walkin' away, slow and desperate-like, to the fire-place. There, on the mantelpiece, bless the luck! was lyin' a dirk—the prettiest little thing ye ever seed, Mr. Sydenham—"

"Thank God!" his auditor ejaculated.

"It was in a blue velvet sheath, and when the cap'n went on some o' his wild sprees o' nights he mostly took it along. She had it in her hand in a moment: I seed the blade flash in the light. Then she was as quiet as if she'd bin in her own drawin'-room. It was grand to see, Mr. Sydenham. The cap'n, he was a-goin' up to her, but I think she scared him—and he wasn't no coward, naither. She didn't say a single word, but she raised her arm as steady as if it had been a fan she was holdin'; and I guess he saw in her eyes what would come next. Anyhow, he started back, and says he: 'For God's sake, Miss Talbot!' She jist lowered the dirk a little, and says she, soft-like, as if she'd been a-speakin' to some nice young man at a party: 'For *your* sake, Cap'n Halloran. I don't think yer soul's ready to appear afore its Maker; but it might ha' bin there by this ef ye'd come one step nearer. Ye expect a life o' pleasure, I suppose, and ye wouldn't like to have it cut short to-night. Take care!' Mr. Sydenham, I never heerd soft words cut so since me mother bore me. Thin I saw her touch the point of the dirk, and there was blood on her finger when she drew it away. But she sort o' laughed, and she said to him, jist as easy as if she'd been talkin' uv his white vest: 'It's lucky the gallants, now-a-days, don't wear no shirts o' mail anaith their doublets. Nothin' less'll turn that edge.' Ye better believe, Mr. Sydenham, she had made him feel it was dead earnest."

"Well?" cried Sydenham, as Terence paused in his story.

"I saw the cap'n was a'most at his wits' end. He walked back and forth, and I heard him cussin' to hisself. One time, when he came close to the door I was at, he said somethin' about taming wild birds in a cage. Then he made for the other door to unlock it. And didn't I make tracks for the street door, to be ready for him? When he came along, says he: 'Teddy, don't let nobody in but Vealmong, ef ye vally yer place.' Then he turned as he was goin' out and says he to me: 'That poor lady in the parlor is clane out of her mind. I'm goin' for the doctor. Nobody must go near her or say a word to her. She's dangerous when she gits in them fits.'

"I waited till I knowed he must be out o' sight, and thin I jist quietly unlocked the bed-room door. She was standin' a-gazin' at the fire; and says I, 'Miss Talbot, ef so be ye want to go to yer own folks, it's me that'll help ye away.' Oh, Mr. Sydenham, I niver was so beshamed in all me life. The poor, sweet cratur went down on her knees to me, that wasn't nothin' mor'n a sarvant, and jined her hands, and the tears was in her eyes; and when she said, 'God bless ye!' I 'most cried meself. But it wasn't no time for cryin', for the cap'n, he might come back any minit. So I took her down the back stairs and let her out at the sarvants' door, and says I: 'An' is it a cab ye'd be needin', miss?' for I wanted to see her safe out of his sight. But says she, 'Ye mustn't go for a cab. Ye may be missed, and I don't want nobody to lose his place for me. I'll find my way.' She made me take a sovereign from her, and I watched her all the way down the street; but she didn't take the road to Sir Charles', and I hearn she never got there."

"Did the captain," asked Sydenham, "suspect that you had let Miss Talbot out?"

"Jist at first—yes. He axed, as mad as fire, 'Who went and unlocked that bed-room door?'

"'The Divil, he knows,' says I. And sure that wasn't no lie, Mr. Sydenham, for there's not a bit o' doubt he was helpin' the cap'n and knowed all about it. But master, he looked hard at me, and says he, 'I'm thinkin' there's somebody else knows it, forbye the Divil.'

"'True for you, cap'n,' says I; 'for the lady must ha' knowed it too. Maybe she pried the door open wi' a knife or somethin'?' The cap'n, he gin a look at the mantel, and there was no dirk there; and thin he went to the door and shot the bolt, and looked at it keerfully.

"'By God,' said he, 'it's true! She's the divil.'

"Now ye see, Mr. Sydenham, jist as soon as I'd let the lady out, I went up to the bed-room, an' I took a strong, sharp knife, and I dented and scratched the door-bolt till a man would ha' sworn somebody had been tamperin' wi' the thing. And that was the way the cap'n, he got chated. But two days after, when I hearn the poor young cratur was lost, I couldn't nohow keep me tongue in me head afore that Vealmong, an' I tould him to his face it was him that was the head divil o' the whole villainy. An' he was hoppin' mad, and got the cap'n to pay me off. But the black varmint did me a good turn, for all, for I might ha' stayed in the ould country an' slaved till me fingers was worn to the stumps an' me bones was old and stiff, and niver had no sich lovely place to live in, nor no sich nice jintleman to work for as jist yerself, Mr. Sydenham."

"You've been to Blarney Castle, haven't you, Terence?" asked Sydenham, smiling.

"An' is it at the Blarney-stone ye think I larnt to tell the truth, Mr. Sydenham? Sure, I niver was in county Cork, at all, at all. An', Mr. Sydenham, don't ye think yerself that's a lovely place, wi' the graveyard quite convanient, and all the white marble shinin' through the trees up there, and the waterfall singin' a'most like the sea, and the creek for Derry to sail his boat on? And thin, doesn't the whole country-side know what a jintleman ye are, Mr. Sydenham, and all that ye've done for them as needs it, Mr. Sydenham — let alone them as doesn't? That's naither new nor strange."

"Well, you shall have it your own way," said Sydenham, laughing. "I'm glad you like the place, and I'm well satisfied with the way you manage it. As for Norah's butter, it can't be surpassed."

"Thin, if ye're continted, so is me and Norah; and I hope we'll live long to serve yer honor and Miss Leoline."

"It would have been a pity and a shame," thought Sydenham, as Terence took his leave, "if that fine young fellow had died in a prison." Then his thoughts reverted to the strange story he had heard. Poor Ellinor! Brave Ellinor!

Later in the evening, another visitor came — Mr. Harper—to see Sydenham as Celia's guardian. He had been to Dr. Meyrac's, where he met Ethan, and where they had been talking over Celia's fortunes, and speaking of the possibility that Mr. Pembroke might have made a will, which had been suppressed. Then Ethan had said the only chance of getting at it was to find one or other of the subscribing witnesses. As Harper walked home, Betty Carson's story about signing a paper for Mr. Pembroke came suddenly to his mind: so he continued his walk to Rosebank and laid the matter before Sydenham.

"I am greatly indebted to you," said the latter. "This may be important. I shall see Creighton about it to-morrow morning."

He did so. Creighton proposed that they should go to Betty's at once. She told them, word for word, what she had told Harper.

"Did Mr. Pembroke say anything else, except that he wished you to witness the paper?" asked Creighton.

"Not as I remember, sir."

"You don't know what sort of paper it was?"

"No, sir; only the sheets was long. I can't write nothin' forbye me name; nor I can't read writin'."

"Who was in the room at the time?—Mrs. Pembroke?"

"No, sir. It was in Mr. Pembroke's room up stairs. Mrs. Pembroke was givin' Miss Celia a lesson in the parlor below. There was nobody but us and Mr. Cranstoun in the room."

"How did you happen to be there?"

"Mr. Cranstoun met me at the front door, and says he: 'Betty, Mr. Pembroke wants to see ye about the starchin' of them shirts o' his'n!' So I went up."

"Did Mr. Cranstoun know you could write your name?"

"Yes, sir. He axed me wance to sign a note along wi' Matthew—that's me husband that was—and says I, 'I can sign me name, and I guess it's all right, Mr. Cranstoun, but I can't read a word of it.' It wasn't all right, though, Mr Creighton, for I had that note to pay twice."

"Did Cranstoun witness that paper of Mr. Pembroke's, too?"

"Yes, sir."

"Did Mr. Pembroke keep the paper and put it away?"

Betty considered a little: "Now I think of it, sir, we heerd Mrs. Pembroke on the stairs sayin' somethin' to Miss Celia: and Mr. Cranstoun, he looked at Mr. Pembroke, and says Mr. Pembroke, hasty-like, 'Take it, Cranstoun;' and he grabbed it and put it under his coat, and buttoned his coat up; and I remember I wondered what it could be that Mrs. Pembroke wasn't to see."

"When was this?"

"Well, sir, it was in winter—I expect three or four weeks afore Mr. Pembroke died."

"Was he ill at that time?"

"Not to say very ill, sir, but he was confined to his room, and his wife was desperate uneasy about him."

"Now, Betty, I want you to consider. Do you think it was Mr. Pembroke's will that you witnessed?"

"Well, now," said Betty, with a start, "in course it was. And wasn't I stupid not to think of that before? Yes, Mr. Creighton, sure enough, an' it was his will he had made; and he didn't want his wife to see it, for fear she'd think he was goin' to die right off. Sich a good, considerate man as he was!"

"But did he *say* it was his will?"

"I guess he must have, Mr. Creighton. What else could it be, and he sick and soon to die? It was his will, sure, and nothin' less. I could a'most take my Bible oath on that."

That was all they could get. After they left the house, "It's no use," said Creighton to Sydenham. "It's a lost ball. It would be the easiest thing in the world to persuade that old woman that Mr. Pembroke told her it was his will she was asked to witness. I'd only have to suggest just what he was likely to say, and repeat that three or four days, and stick to it that I was quite sure he must have told her, because it was his duty to tell her, and because he wasn't a man to neglect his duty. I haven't any doubt she would swear to it conscientiously. But it would be a lie. He didn't tell her. One could see that by her surprise when I suggested it. The idea never had been in her mind before."

"But you have no doubt it was the will?"

"Not any. Observe the facts. Cranstoun selects Betty because he knows that, though she can sign her name, she cannot read manuscript. He watches her arrival, meets her as she comes in, makes an excuse to get her to Mr. Pembroke's room. When they hear Mrs. Pembroke coming, the husband bids Cranstoun take the paper, and he conceals it. I am satisfied it was the will, and equally satisfied that we shall never be able to prove that a will was made at all. Cranstoun has burned it long ago—unless, indeed," he added after a pause, "the rascal may have laid it by as a card which, some day or other, if the game goes against him, he may play with the chance of winning a trick."

They walked on for some time in silence, when Mr. Creighton suddenly stopped and turned to his companion: "No, Mr. Sydenham: that will wasn't burnt. Cranstoun was sure to preserve it—to be used, in case of accident, in the event that Miss Pembroke accepted him—as no doubt the scoundrel dared to presume she would—as her husband. But, so far as we are concerned, it might as well have been burnt years ago, for I don't see the smallest chance of getting at it."

So that hope died out.

CHAPTER XLI.

THE MILLER'S DAUGHTER.

"Hear, Father—hear and aid!
If I have loved too well, if I have shed,
In my vain fondness, o'er a human head,
Gifts on Thy shrine, O God, more fitly laid—

"If I have sought to live
But in one light, and made a mortal eye
The lonely star of my idolatry—
Thou, that art Love, oh pity and forgive!"

HEMANS.

AN unwonted excitement pervaded Chiskauga. News had arrived, early one morning, that Tyler's mill, dwelling-house and all the outbuildings were burnt to the ground; that the miller and his foreman Goddart had perished in the flames; and that they didn't know what had become of the daughter. Various corrections gradually modified this report, until, by midday, the most incorrigible newsmongers were fain to admit that it was the mill only that was burnt, and that nobody was hurt except Hiram Goddart, whose hands had been somewhat scorched in a fruitless attempt to drag out part of the personal property.

Even this last version of the story, however, needed correction. The miller had, indeed, received no personal injury at the fire; yet before two days had passed his daughter began to fear that worse had befallen him.

She slept in the room next to her father's, and, still anxious about him, her sleep, on the night of the fire, had been unquiet and easily disturbed. A flickering light shining through her chamber window had awakened her. She went out as quietly as possible, roused Goddart, who alarmed the other hands; and by great exertions they succeeded, within half an hour, in checking the flames. It was for the moment only, however: they soon broke out afresh, and spread so fast that it became evident the building (a weatherboarded frame, with shingle roof) must go.

Then Ellen bethought her of her father. Since the attempt he had made, one night, to escape from his bed-room, they had secured both the windows by stout bars outside, across the Venetian shutters, besides locking the outside door. There was a second door, communicating with Ellen's room, so that he could knock in case he wanted anything during the night, but that also she locked when she retired to rest.

When she unlocked this door on her return from the fire, she was terribly frightened. The glass in both the windows was shattered, a chair broken to fragments lay on the floor, and beside it her father, apparently insensible. Approaching with the candle, she perceived stains of blood on the floor. Then she came very near fainting, but love overcame fear; and when, with trembling hands and tear-dimmed eyes, she had examined his condition, she became satisfied that the blood came only from his hands, which had been cut in several places, apparently by the glass, in his vain endeavors to force the windows. The door also bore the marks of heavy blows, dealt with the stout wooden chair, which had evidently gone to pieces in his hands.

She dragged a mattress from the bed, and contrived to place him on it. When she had sprinkled water on his face he revived, and his first words were: "You can't swim, Nell, but I can save you: I was once a capital swimmer. Come!" and he tried to rise, but fell back powerless.

"Father dear," said Ellen, "you are at home. This is your own room. See!"

"But the fire, Nelly, the fire! D'ye think I can't see through these cursed shutters, if they are barred? The boat *is* on fire. Don't I hear the flames crackling? Quick!"

"Father, father, hear what I tell you. There's no steamboat. The mill's on fire—that's true; but the wind's north-east, and Hiram says there's no more chance of the fire catching this house than if it were a mile off. I'm afraid the mill's gone, past saving: I'm very sorry for that. But you're safe, father, and we've a house still over our heads. God be thanked for that!"

If he had been able to rise, she couldn't have kept him there, but his desperate exertions to escape by door or window had completely exhausted him. Gradually, by dint of iteration, she appeased him: and when Goddart soon after came in and reported that the mill could not be saved, it seemed to relieve him, and the delusion gradually vanished.

"So ye won't get burnt nor drowned, my little Nell. Let the gear go! Kiss me, my child."

The wounds on his hands were slight; and when Ellen had dressed them, and they had lifted him to bed again, he sank into a heavy sleep.

It had been a great shock. The good that Harper did had been undone. At a time when the miller's mind had been slowly regaining its tone, all the horrors of that dreadful night on Lake Erie had come back on him in full force. And with these came back the fancy that God had sent him a premonition of death. The logic of Preacher Larrabee's story was clear, indeed, but nerves already shattered and terribly shaken by a second agitation beclouded logical deductions. The father, tender of his daughter's feelings, succeeded, however, in concealing from her this superstitious relapse.

Well did Ellen merit the old man's regardful care. Weak in her judgments because of inexperience and imperfect culture, the girl had a strength such as few strong men have, deep-rooted in her affections — a dangerous strength in a world like this. Imprudence to any extent she might commit, but one act of deliberate selfishness, never.

Her love for Mowbray was an idolatry, but because it was not a selfish idolatry, so neither was it exclusive. Never since her tiny arms were first stretched to the proud father in infant recognition had she loved that father as now—all the more warmly and devotedly because of the warmth and devotion of her love for another. The angel that had stirred the depths of that young heart was of the holiest in Heaven's host. Duty was more sacred now, gratitude more tender, good-will to all men felt with livelier glow. The waters from that mystic fount, motionless till the angel came, now irrigated with freshening influence all her life's little domain.

When a fortnight had passed, and the miller was still unable to sit up more than two or three hours each day, vigil and anxiety began to tell on the poor girl.

"Ellen," the father said one day, "you'll be sick yourself if you wait on me so much. You need the fresh air. Take Joe: he's quiet to ride, and we don't need him now. Willie can stay by me, if you're uneasy about leaving me alone."

When she came to see how he was

before she set out on her ride, she kissed him, saying: "I promise you never to do anything to make you sorry again. You know I won't. Don't you, father?"

"I know you're an old man's darling, Nell, and as good as gold. I'd let you do anything—anything in this world that I thought would make you happy. But to keep company with a young man that —that never asked you to marry him—*that* would make you miserable, Nelly—miserable, mayhap, as long as you live. That's all I'm afraid of: I want you never to do that."

"I never will." And there she stopped, on the very point of telling him that Mowbray and she were engaged. But, as once before, she put it off with the thought, "When he's better and stronger." And she only repeated, "I never, never will."

"I know you won't, Nelly. God for ever bless and protect you, dear child!"

Thenceforth Ellen usually rode out two or three afternoons in the week. Of course, Mowbray got to know it, and of course he sought to meet his promised wife.

To Mowbray's questions, repeated each time they met, as to her father's condition, she returned desponding answers. His brow clouded—Ellen thought from sympathy. One day he said, "Ellen dear, have you ever told your father that we're engaged?"

"I was afraid, he's so weak."

"But we couldn't marry without telling him."

"Marry?"

"Isn't a girl that's past nineteen old enough to marry?"

"How can we be married and father so ill?"

"I don't see what's to prevent it. He might be ill for months or years."

"You wouldn't like, Mr. Mowbray—"

"Evelyn, dear Ellen."

"Evelyn"—hesitating and blushing—"you wouldn't like your wife to spend half her time nursing a sick father."

He would have controlled his countenance had he been able. Ellen read its expression and added, "You see it wouldn't do."

"Why couldn't we have a careful nurse for him? You could go and see him when you chose."

"Oh, Evelyn, how can you?"—voice trembling and tears springing to her eyes. "God himself couldn't love me if I forsook father."

"The Bible says a man shall leave father and mother and cleave to his wife."

"Oh don't, don't! He has nothing left but me. It's fourteen years since mother died: he has never said one angry word to me since then, not even—" it flashed over her that it wouldn't do to talk of that. "I've often vexed him, poor father! I've been thoughtless and careless, and he's been so good! I think he always felt I had no mother, and couldn't bear to thwart me or deny me anything. If you only knew, Evelyn! I'm sure the Bible never meant that a girl like me, that used 'most to forget her mother was gone—he nursed and petted and loved me so — it never could mean that I was to go and leave him on his sick bed now. And he's so weak and helpless! If you were to see him, Evelyn! His hair's as white as snow. He's *such* an old man now!"

She said it plaintively, dreamily—pausing. Then, with sudden impulse, "I won't leave him!" Mowbray started, and something in his face made her add, "Dear, dear Evelyn, I can't."

"Of course you must do as you please, Ellen."

"As I please? You think I don't love you?"

"Not as well as you love your father, it seems."

Ellen wept like a child. Mowbray tried to soothe her: "I know you love me, dear Ellen: I didn't mean that I doubted your love." He would have been a wretch if he had doubted it under the look of those sad, reproachful eyes.

All she said, as Mowbray assisted her in mounting her horse, was: "He would die if I were to leave him."

During the long summer afternoons Tyler usually lay in a lethargic state. Very, very mournful thoughts filled the silent hours that Ellen spent by his bedside. Never for a moment did she repent her resolution. "He shall not die if I can save him:" that was her one thought as to her father. Yet she made to herself a sort of reproach, pitying and excusing her lover.

"It's not his fault"—such were the thoughts that swept over her solitude—"it's very natural he should feel put out about it. What have I ever done for him except to love him?—and I couldn't help that. He makes all the sacrifices. Don't I know I'm no fit match for him? Couldn't he marry the best lady in the land? Then we're so much poorer now than when he asked me: all the machinery burnt on the boat, the mill gone too; yet he never said the first word about it. And then that talk of the village! When others left me and insulted me, he was always the same. And now, the only thing he ever asked me I *had* to refuse him. Poor Evelyn! I know he must think I don't care for him as he cares for me. If he could only look into my heart!"

Then she began to think, could she ever do anything—make any sacrifice—for him to prove her love? She was romantic in her way, this simple miller's daughter; and she felt that if her father no longer needed her it would be nothing to risk her life or lose it for Evelyn; but how could *he* ever know that? It was only in novels that lovers had a chance to give their lives for one another.

He had seemed to wish that she should tell her father of their engagement. She *could* do that, at least. So one day she did, adding, "I can live without him as long as I've you, father; and may God forsake me if I leave you till I see that you don't need me! I told him I never would. But if you—if you go to mother and I am left here—I shall want to die too unless I'm his wife. I love him so, and he's so good, father — you don't know."

It was another shock, though he strove to conceal that from his daughter. Still, he received the news with mixed feelings. The presentiment of death had been gaining on him; and who was to protect the orphan when he was gone? He gazed on that sweet, sad face—felt that the heart of love and trust that spoke from it was in the keeping of another past recalling; and the thought came to him: "Nobody but a mean coward would injure her; and the proud peat, with all his uppish ways, is no coward. And then he *has* made up his mind to marry the miller's daughter. Anybody might be proud of Nelly. Maybe he will." So the kind old man, thinking how soon he might be where he could never show earthly kindness more, could not find it in his heart to say no to his child's love.

One only condition he attached to his consent: "It's best you should both have time to know your own minds. You're not twenty yet, Nell. In a little more than a year you'll be of age. By that time either this useless father of yours will be well again and able to spare you, or else—"

Ellen would not let him go on. She had been touched to the heart by his prompt consent: it was a load taken off her mind; and it was with a gush of joy and gratitude she said:

"You're going to get well, father: I'm sure you are. But come what will, I take God to witness that I will not marry Evelyn Mowbray till I am twenty-one years old. And if I ever do marry him, I'll come and see you every day: he said I might."

No concealment from her father now: it lightened Ellen's heart; but her father's, alas!—though the girl knew it not—was loaded down with one grief the more. How could he have confidence in Mowbray?

Accumulating burdens were becoming too much for the old man's waning strength. Before the fatal journey to Buffalo he had fortitude, courage to meet any reverse of fortune. He had escaped from that burning horror—one of seven who had made their own way to shore. But he had escaped, as soldiers often do from the dangers of a hundred fields, to return home broken-down, unmanned, health and hope and energy gone.

The lethargic symptoms increased. An hour or two a day was as much as he could bear to sit up. Ellen became thoroughly alarmed, and rode into town for Dr. Meyrac. When the girl, on their way back, related to him the particulars of the shipwreck, the effect on her father and the relapse on the night the mill was burnt, he looked grave, but merely said that it was a very remarkable case —such as he had read of, but never met with before.

Alone with the miller, the latter said, "I shall not live long, doctor."

"That may be. Yet I find not any disease pronounced. De nerves are shaken: de forces are feeble. If you have not hope to live, it may arrive that you vill die. All the same, you may yet survive. The courage is there for much;" meaning, probably, that courage had much to do with his patient's chance of recovery.

The miller briefly related to him his trance and its correspondence with realities at home. The man of science smiled with good-natured incredulity: "It is hazard only. Dere are dreams very singular, but dey prove not anything. Let not discourage yourself for dat."

Harper's view of the matter had done much more to quiet the miller's mind than Meyrac's skepticism did. Chance? He knew that couldn't be so. Then he brooded, more and more, over the idea of a death-warning. The needed courage that Meyrac had spoken of failed.

Ten days later his mind began to wander. He was haunted by the recollection of the man who had clung to him as he first rose to the surface. He appeared to re-enact the scene, struggling desperately, striking out his clenched fist, as if at an opponent; and then, drooping despondingly, he muttered, "What could I do? Is it murder to strike a man that's just going to strangle you?" After a time he sank into a comatose state, lasting many hours. And when at last he came to his senses, his feebleness was extreme.

Another day the over-excited brain seemed to reproduce the scene of his exertions to rescue Hartland. He imitated the dragging of a heavy weight till he was bathed in perspiration: then fell into a heavy sleep that continued all the night through. From each of these attacks he awoke with diminished strength. The lucid intervals, too, became shorter and less frequent.

But, except during the moments when fancy recalled the dangers he had passed, he did not seem to suffer much. The coma into which he constantly relapsed became more and more deep. They scarcely knew when he passed away. Ellen sat, for the last two hours, his hand in hers, and not a movement—not the slightest convulsive twitch—gave intimation of pain or struggle. Half an hour before it was all over she heard him say, in a tone that awed her—so solemn, so utterly different was it from his usual manner—"Deal with *me*, O God! as Thou wilt, but let that man love her: let him cherish her." Then the very last, low words of all—two only: "Dear Nell!"

No need to speak of the orphan's desolation. For days after her father's death one wish was uppermost—that she had died with him. Even her lover was half forgotten.

It was two weeks before she saw him; and the first time they met nothing of moment occurred. He spoke kindly and sympathizingly, doing what he could to comfort her, and evincing deep regret that there had ever been any difficulty between her father and himself.

At their next interview she told him that she had informed her father of their engagement, and that he had acquiesced. He expressed pleasure at this.

Then they talked of the future. "How forlorn you must be," he said to her, "all alone there, with nobody to care for you!"

"Hiram's as kind and attentive as he can be. He seems to guess all I need before I ask him. And then I've little Willie to care for."

"That mustn't go on, Ellen," a little sharply. "Of course we must let some weeks or months pass, but sorrow can't call back those that are gone; and if we could now know your father's wish, I'm sure it would be that you should be happy, and have some one who had a right to protect you as soon as possible."

Then she had to tell him of the solemn promise she had made to her father on his deathbed.

He rebelled at once. How cruel, in its results, is often the affection, even the self-sacrifice, of weak, fond parents! All the strength of the young Widow Mowbray's love, inconsolable under bereavement, had centred blindly in her boy. His very faults so much resembled those of the husband she had idolized throughout their few short years of marriage that she could scarcely find it in her heart to reprove them. In her little household everything had given way to him. In all things the child and his will and his caprices had taken precedence. They were poor: she had to do much of her own work, but if the little sluggard lay in bed two hours after the breakfast-hour, he was never disturbed; and when at last he sauntered carelessly down, she broke off whatever she was about, to see that he had a warm, comfortable meal. In the same way she saved him, year after year, every exertion, every annoyance, at expense of double exertion and double annoyance to herself. When he grew to manhood, and expenses necessarily increased, it was she who must be stinted that he might dress like a gentleman, wear fresh, delicate kid gloves to balls and parties and smoke the highest-priced Havana cigars. When the young man began to long—as youth, ever since Virgil's days, has always longed—for a horse, their scanty capital had to be encroached on to build a stable; and it was the mother, not the son, who undertook additional labor—labor beyond her strength—to pay bills for oats and corn that the idle fellow might spend half his days in pleasure rides.

Selfishness is a weed needing little culture, and Mrs. Mowbray had unconsciously nursed its growth for twenty-four years in her son Evelyn. He grew up utterly impatient of contradiction, and feeling it as an injury—almost as an insult—when another's comfort, or will, or sense of duty even, crossed his own good pleasure. Who can calculate the effects, springing from devoted kindness, yet tending from sin down to crime, of such a training?

"Nonsense, Ellen!" Mowbray broke out when she had made her confession. "How old are you?"

"In less than three months I shall be twenty."

"And you mean to say you've gone and promised not to marry for nearly fifteen months?"

"Yes," though the poor child had hardly courage to say it.

"Then you did a very foolish thing: that's all I can say."

"Oh, Evelyn, think! If your mother had been dying, and she had asked you not to marry me till you were twenty-five, what would you have done?"

"Mother never would have been so silly. She knows how unhappy it would have made me; and she never crosses me."

"Father didn't want to make you unhappy, Evelyn."

"Then what did he make you promise that for?"

Ellen was not ready with an answer.

"It *would* make me unhappy if you were to keep your promise, Ellen; and if your father didn't want that, then it would be wrong in you—"

"Don't say that, dear Evelyn."

"Why not? Why does it make me unhappy to wait? Because I love you so dearly. What would it signify to me whether it was fifteen days or fifteen months if I didn't care for you? If you cared—"

He was looking at Ellen as he said this, and her eyes, brimful of sorrow and of love, would not let him go on in that strain. So he said, "Don't you think your father wanted me to love you dearly, Ellen?"

"Evelyn, Evelyn! But I never told you. Half an hour before—before he went to mother and left me alone—that was his dying prayer. The very, very last word on his lips was my name. And you want me to disobey him?"

Was she listening to hear those last words of the dying repeated again? She looked up to heaven, and the expression that lighted her face overawed the man, self-indulgent and impassive to spiritual influence as he was.

"If father had not wished you well, Evelyn," she went on after a time, "would he have let me marry you? I don't know why he made me promise as I did. I never can know now, except that I'm sure it was out of his love for me. I only know that I did make that promise, and that God heard me call His name to witness that I would keep it. And then, Evelyn—"

"Well, dear?" the tone getting impatient again.

"I think father can hear and see us now. When he was lying hundreds of miles away, all but drowned, his spirit saw everything I did and heard all I said, one morning at the well, to Hiram Goddart."

"What did you say to him?"

"He spoke of proposing a partnership in the mill. When father came home he told me the very words."

Mowbray laughed incredulously. Then his brow darkened: "Did your father hear Hiram propose a partnership to his daughter too?"

"You're cruel, Evelyn, and Hiram's as good as he can be. He couldn't help loving me, any more than I can help loving you."

"If you think me cruel, and Hiram Goddart the best man that ever was, I suppose you can't help that either?"

They were sitting on a mossy bank, under the deep forest shade, Mowbray's arm around her waist. He withdrew it. The action, as much as the harsh words, overcame her. She shuddered, as one stricken with ague, and when she could speak for weeping, she said, "I don't know what I'm saying, Mr. Mowbray. I didn't mean you were cruel: when others were cruel, you've always been kind. And all I meant about Hiram was that he is kind and good. Surely, surely you know that I love nobody but you."

"Why do you call me Mr. Mowbray, if you love me?"

"Did I call you so? I think it must have been because I didn't know if you would ever be more to me than that."

"Ellen, whatever I ask you, you refuse me. Are you going to break off our engagement and marry Hiram?"

That was the drop too much. With an uncontrollable impulse she threw her arms round his neck and hid her face in his bosom, her frame convulsed with sobs.

"If you knew, Evelyn," she faltered out at last—"if you only knew how it breaks my heart to refuse you anything! But see! Father mustn't be angry with me, up there in heaven—he and mother. I think it won't be long till I see them there; and I *must* be able to tell the old man—him that never spoke one unkind word to me—that I didn't break my word to him—what I promised him when he was dying. Oh, Evelyn, I must, I must! You're good, Evelyn: you're so good—so good to me! You don't want me, when I die, to be thinking that the first word to them will have to be that I lied to father just before he left me, with a prayer to God for me on his lips."

He did not reply, but he soothed and caressed her, as she lay in his arms, till the sobs gradually ceased and she recovered, in a measure, her tranquillity.

After a time she spoke again: "You said *if* I cared for you, Evelyn. I know I've never done anything for you. If I only knew—if I could find out—what a poor orphan like me could do to show you what sort of love it is I have for you!"

It was a perilous state of feeling. Ellen did not know that such affection as hers once prompted Arria to suicide; and is not suicide a sin?

"That promise I gave to father," she pursued: "it's the only thing. Ask me anything else, Evelyn—anything. There's nothing I would deny you but that."

"Nothing?" A base, coward thought just glanced through his mind as he said it—so base that the man, selfish as he was, shrank from it as from a serpent. Vice had still its "frightful mien" to him.

"No, Evelyn, nothing." Sweetly, calmly said. No dream of evil. Purity itself in that trusting smile. No inkling of wrong in those loving, guileless eyes. How sharp the rebuke so unconsciously given!

Had the girl been less generous, less faithful, more given to thinking of evil, her danger would have been much less than it was then.

In their after meetings Mowbray did not again bring up the subject of Ellen's promise, nor further insist on marriage before the time her father had set.

I know it is the world's way, when some poor young creature strays from the path of peace, to settle it that she sins at the prompting of selfish, incontinent passion. Alas! that happens sometimes. But far, far more frequently the temptation is one in which selfishness has no part. Sometimes it is abject poverty that rules: dishonor is incurred to prolong the life of helpless father or mother or to win bread for orphaned infancy left to a sister's care.

Sometimes—and this sad truth almost eludes attention—the motive is traceable to romantic self-sacrifice, wild eagerness to prove the reality of a love arrested, perhaps, for the time, in its placid, legitimate course. Few men conceive of such a sacrifice. It is often made for men when they know it not. God forgive the sacrilegious traitors who know and accept it, bringing to ruin those the latchet of whose shoes they are not worthy to unloose! If such obtain Divine mercy at the last, what wretch, blackened with a thousand crimes, but may hope for pardon too?

PART XII.

CHAPTER XLII.

THE ABDUCTION.

"Magnetism has been made, by turns, a trade, a pastime; a science, a philosophy, a religion: a lover's go-between and a physician's guide."—DELAAGE.

IN the study at Rosebank, on a Saturday afternoon, some ten days after Tyler's death.

"Is it possible, Mr. Creighton?" said Sydenham. "It sounds more like some coincidence invented to help out the plot of a novel than an incident in real life. What a strange chance!"

"*Is* there such a thing as chance?" replied Creighton. "We are wonderfully made: are we not also wonderfully led sometimes? What so strange as truth and God's economy! But are you sure as to the name?"

"Terence pronounced it Cunningem, and called him Sir Charles."

"It must be the same," Creighton said, referring to a paper before him: "'*Charles Conynghame, Baronet.*'"

"So that scoundrel Cranstoun could not keep to the truth even about so simple a matter as a name. Dunmore, he told Celia, the guardian's name was."

"He was afraid we might forestall him—writing first, or by the same post as himself."

"The suit is in Sir Charles' own name?"

"Yes. He takes Miss Ellinor's death, it seems, for granted."

"So, then, she is the heir?"

"As against him, certainly; but if my view of the law in the case—and Mr. Marshall's too, by the way—be correct, Miss Celia is co-heir, and the sisters will divide equally."

"The sisters! I can scarcely realize it."

"Mr. Cranstoun, however, would say your ward was excluded from the succession."

"Celia will be delighted."

"That's a great deal to say for any one, Mr. Sydenham."

"So it is, but you will find I am right."

Creighton's face flushed with pleasure: "It does one good to meet with a nature so noble as that."

"Did you know that Ellinor's name was Talbot?"

"No. And she never told me her guardian's name—only the general incidents of her story. I knew her only as Miss Ethelridge. Good that Terence peeped through that keyhole: how else should we have known what a heroine the young lady is? And then his deposition as to her identity is the very thing. But first I must see her, to make sure there's no mistake."

That same Saturday morning Celia entered Ellinor's room in riding equipment. "Another French scholar," she said—"Ellen Tyler. I've just been to see the poor girl. What suffering there is in this world!"

"Occupation is the surest alleviation. I'm glad she is coming to us."

"How does the list of scholars stand now?" asked Celia as Ellinor set down Ellen's name. "Is it up to what it was when I joined you?"

"Not quite, I see: five less—that's all. Good Mr. Sydenham's kind word at the Mite was help in time of need."

"And Lela's, the darling! But I've something more to tell you, Ellie. I've had *such* a time with dear auntie! I never saw her so near being downright angry with me before. I shall have to give up, I'm afraid, and you must help me."

"I wish I had been there to see."

"You needn't laugh. I had got aunt persuaded to let me pay Mr. Hartland a hundred dollars a year for my board, and eighty more for Bess. Now that it is her own house she rebels, and says if I won't accept my board and Bess' keep from my mother's sister, she'll never forgive me as long as she lives."

"She is in good circumstances, and

you owe her that kindness. You must agree to it, dear child."

"On one condition. I'll be a good girl if you will too. See here, Ellie! I wanted to help you in the school, and I've been nothing but a millstone about your neck."

"Indeed! I'd like to have a few more such. I had no idea millstones were such pleasant wear."

"It's serious, Ellie: don't put me out. Suppose Bess and I stay with auntie for nothing. Mr. Sydenham pays me a hundred and fifty dollars a year for Leoline's lessons; and I can't, with any propriety, spend more than that on dress and knickknacks."

"So you want to violate our articles of partnership, and make me take all the profits?"

"What a darling you are to guess it so nicely! Precisely, my dear: that's just it."

"You know, Celia—you *know* I can't do that."

"Indeed I don't. But I'll tell you what I do know. If you stand out against me, I'll stand out against auntie—I will. So you may take your choice. Then I want to whisper something in your ear."

"Be reasonable, Celia—"

"Certainly, if you will only listen. 'Strike, but hear!'"

"Well?"

Celia whispered: "It's all in the family, my dear. Ethan will be auntie's heir. If I don't pay auntie, Ethan will lose a hundred and eighty dollars a year. That's all the same as if Mrs. Ethan lost it: 'they twain shall be one flesh, you know. I'd be getting paid twice, Ellie: is that what you call reason? Then how are you going to buy that furniture? Ethan tells me his secrets sometimes."

"You are too bad!" But Ellinor took the laughing girl in her arms and caressed her and kissed her and called her pet names, till neither could refrain from tears. What they both cried for I don't exactly know.

After a while Celia said: "There are two sisters, Ellie—at least they made an agreement they were to be sisters. I think the elder will be married soon. I don't believe the younger will ever marry—not for many years, at all events; and she has more than enough to live on comfortably. Now do you think it's just the sisterly thing for these two to keep such strict accounts that the elder can't have what she needs for wedding-things and to do a little toward house-furnishing, because the younger may possibly need some money ten years hence?"

"Ten years, Celia? You're going to make him wait that length of time?"

"Whom?"

A knock at the door and Nelly came in: "Mr. Creighton, Miss Ellinor, for to see ye."

"In a minute or two, Nelly, please tell him." Then, when the girl had gone: "If you don't know, Celia, or if Nelly did not stumble on the answer, then I can't pretend to guess. Wait for me, won't you, dear?"

In quarter of an hour she returned pale and agitated.

"What has Mr. Creighton been telling you? Bad news, Ellie?"

"No." Then, after a pause, "I ought to be glad."

"And yet you're sorry. You'll tell me all about it, won't you?"

"Yes, dear. I promised you I would, some day." She drew Celia to the sofa, retaining her hand.

"After mother's death I had a guardian—a rich man, not a good one—Sir Charles Conynghame. Mr. Creighton came this morning to know from me if that *was* his name. I don't know why: not from idle curiosity, he said, and that he would tell me more to-morrow. He had heard the name, it seems, from a man who once saved me—saved me I mustn't think from what—at my utmost need: a brave, good young fellow, the father of little Derry and Kathleen. Strange that I didn't know him again when he brought them to school!"

"Terence, the Irishman, who manages Mr. Sydenham's farm?"

"Yes; but I must go back to my story." Her gaze, as she paused, seemed exploring some mysterious distance. Celia knew, as she looked at those eyes, how sad the recollections must be.

"How happy you were, Celia," Ellinor said at last, "to have had such a mother! Mine — but I dare say I was wayward and disobedient and hard to manage, or perhaps mamma was soured by some cross or grief. It's terrible to say, but I don't remember one really happy day at home. I *had* happy days, but they were spent with Cousin Constance. She was ten years older than I; and my idea of angels in heaven was that they must be like her. One childhood's recollection, standing out from all the rest, is my being dressed out in my first white silk frock—just seven years old then — for Constance's wedding. 'She's Lady Conynghame now,' my nurse whispered to me as the bridegroom placed the ring on her finger."

"She married your guardian, then?"

"Her husband afterward became my guardian—yes. I remember, when the marriage was over, I put my arms round the bride and told her, crying bitterly the while, what nurse had said, and asked her if she wasn't my cousin Constance any more. She smiled, then cried a little herself — which I thought was very strange on her wedding-day—and said she was my own very cousin Constance, and always would be till she died, and that there was nobody in all the world she loved as well as me. I suppose her husband didn't quite like that, but he took me up kindly and kissed me, and told me mamma had agreed that I should come and see Cousin Constance whenever I liked. 'Didn't you, Mrs. Talbot?' he said, appealing to her, and she assented."

"Mrs. Talbot?"

"Ah! I forgot. Mamma, who liked show and station, gave me three baptismal names—Mary Ellinor Ethelridge: Ethelridge was her maiden name. Constance always called me Ellie, and I only brought two of my four names with me to democratic America."

"Had Lady Conyinghame children?"

"None—except me, she used to say. Mamma died when I was twelve years old, making Sir Charles her executor and leaving me in his care, the property to go to him in case I died unmarried and without a will. I should have been perfectly happy with my cousin, only that, as I grew older, I saw that she was not happy. She had been over-persuaded to the marriage. Sir Charles was rich, indulgent, good-natured in a general way, but without any feeling deserving the name of love. He became a gambler, too, keeping dissipated company, and risking hundreds, if not thousands, on his favorite horses. Constance behaved admirably to him. He was proud of her, and grudged her nothing as long as the money lasted. But what sympathy, what companionship could there be? Some Frenchman talks of people who think themselves entitled to rank and fortune because they've 'taken the trouble of being born!'* Well, my dear, Sir Charles was one of these."

"Poor Constance!"

"And if you had known, Celia, what a noble, loving darling she was! To me friend, sister, mother—teacher, too, and guardian. If I know anything, if I'm good for anything, it was her doing. I don't think one human being ever owed more to another than I to her. When I lost her—"

"She died?"

"When I was seventeen. We had been a year in Paris. The fashionable dissipation into which she was forced wore upon her, but far more her husband's increasing dissipation. Titled swindlers, professional gamblers, jockeys and stable-boys were his companions. He seemed to become daily more reckless, and was often embarrassed for money. Once, I remember, we had bailiffs in the house. But I think another grief wore on Constance's spirits more than all the rest. In some way—perhaps from himself, when flushed with wine—she must have come to know that he was using the money which as executor had been placed in his hands."

* "Noblesse, fortune, un rang, des places; tout cela rend si fier! Qu' avez vous fait pour tant de biens? Vous vous êtes donné la peine de naitre, et rien de plus."—BEAUMARCHAIS, *Le Mariage de Figaro*, Acte V., Scène 3.

"Your property, Ellie?"

"Yes. Some eight or ten thousand pounds—I don't know the exact sum. On her deathbed, when delirious with fever, Constance spoke, in frenzied words which I shall remember to my dying day, of some terrible dishonor—some breach of trust of which her husband had been guilty. Suddenly she took me in her arms, lamenting over me in terms oh so pitiful!—then crying as if her very heart would break. Later I knew what it meant. I'm sure it hastened her death. Next morning—ah, Celia, I was never an orphan till then!"

Celia had taken Ellinor in her arms, and when a burst of grief, controlled up to that moment, had subsided, she asked her, "Had you to remain in Sir Charles' house?"

"What could I do? When we returned to London, his widowed sister, Mrs. Beaumont—hard, haughty, aristocratic in the worst sense—came to keep house for him. To her I was an encumbrance, and no day passed in which she did not make me feel it. I was far worse than alone. If a fervent longing could have brought death, I should soon have been with my lost darling again."

"You were spared to do good here, and for me to love you, Ellie."

"God overrules all, but in those days I had not learned to realize that. I fell into a weak, nervous state. The physician recommended exercise. To avoid driving out with Mrs. Beaumont, whom I hated, I went regularly to a noted riding-school not far off."

There she stopped. Celia guessed the reason. "If it pains you to go on, dear—" she began.

"I'm a coward: that's the truth. I linger over details, because the rest—Never mind, I want you to know it all."

"Well, Ellie?"

"The style of people who frequented our house after dear Conny's death changed much for the worse. Among them was one whom we had known while Constance was alive, and who had seemed to me, at first, better than most of the others. He was Sir Charles' intimate friend—Captain Halloran, of the Guards. He was handsome, and I think may once have been good. I liked to talk to him more than he deserved: even then I used to be conscious that I did. Yet there was something genial and pleasant enough about him, except now and then when a certain look came over his face: I can't describe it, but it gave me the idea of a reckless, self-indulgent man. At other times I felt in his society quiet, satisfied, and, strange to say, often very drowsy."

"As I do, sometimes, near you, Ellie."

"Yes, dear. Once or twice in the evening I had to leave the drawing-room after talking with him, for I was actually afraid I should go to sleep. Yet it was some time before it occurred to me that he had anything to do with it: I thought it was only nervous weakness. One morning, when he called to see me, and when I pleaded my engagement at the riding-school as excuse for cutting short the visit, he begged so hard to accompany me that I yielded, though till then I had never allowed any one but a servant to attend me. During the lesson he remained in a small gallery overlooking the riding-arena, and to which gentlemen accompanying young ladies to the school were admitted. Once or twice during the hour I rode a sleepy fit came over me, so that the riding-master noticed it and asked me if I had not been up very late the night before. In returning home the unaccountable feeling so gained on me that I must have walked some distance in an unconscious state. The thundering rap which announced our return awoke me on the doorstep."

"What a wonderful thing!"

"When I thought it over, it recalled to me a discussion I had heard, a few evenings before, between Captain Halloran and several other gentlemen, but to which, at the time, I had paid little attention. They had spoken of human magnetism and its strange effects, and now it suddenly occurred to me that my drowsiness might be due to magnetic influence."

"Did you avoid him?"

"I never allowed him to go with me to the riding-school again; and I tried to keep away from him as much as I could. But I found that a difficult thing to do. Several times, when he sat down by me and began to talk, I resolved, as soon as common politeness permitted, to rise and leave him. But when I tried to rise I felt that I had lost the power. It seemed to me as if he were telling me to sit still, and that I *had* to obey him. I felt, too, a sort of fascination, partly painful, partly pleasurable, in yielding to this mysterious authority."

"Poor Ellie!"

"I had a sense of danger, too; and had it been possible I would have left the house for some other where the captain could not reach me; for in his absence he was comparatively indifferent to me, and I had self-control enough left earnestly to desire that I might never see him again. But Sir Charles was the only relative I knew anything about—the only person, indeed, on whom I had any claim."

"Did Captain Halloran make love to you, Ellie?"

"About a year and a half after Lady Conynghame's death he proposed to me. With a strong effort I managed to refuse him; and very glad I was of it after he was gone. But he persisted, coming almost every evening, usually to dinner. Mrs. Beaumont, I saw, encouraged him. One day, when I felt that I grievously needed help, I asked him how he knew that Sir Charles would consent. Then it came out about my property. The captain said my guardian had squandered every penny of it, and of course would resist my marriage with any one. Then he professed that he cared nothing about the money: his father would 'come down handsomely,' he said, in case of marriage. But on my guardian's account it must be a private marriage—by special license. 'I have it here,' he said, taking a paper from his pocket. I've often wondered, Celia dear, how the poor little birds feel when the serpent's eye is on them and they can't even move a wing. When I read that license, it seemed to me like the fiat of doom. If I had had anybody to sustain me, I could have escaped. But everything seemed crumbling around me, life valueless, and nothing worth striving for or striving against. I had, indeed, misgivings about my suitor, yet I felt a sense of protection, a soothing of nerves, when I was near him. All the other *habitués* of the house were repulsive to me. Captain Halloran saw his advantage and pressed it, assuming my consent. I felt that I was giving up, half by attraction and half in despair."

"You agreed to marry him? Poor darling!"

"When it came to the point, and he told me, one afternoon, that he had a carriage a square off to take me to his aunt's, where the clergyman awaited us, I repented and flatly refused to go. To my surprise, he said it should be just as I pleased; he would wait my time and pleasure; he would speak to his servant and dismiss the carriage. How long he stayed after his return to the drawing-room I never knew, nor when nor how I left the house. I first awoke to a sense of my situation (as I had done in returning from the riding-school) at the loud rat-tat-at of a fashionable knock. I heard the captain swearing at his servant for making such a noise, and he looked uneasily at me. But I had presence of mind enough to express no surprise, and followed him submissively into the house, with one resolve on which I strove to concentrate my will—namely, not to suffer that stupor to return."

"Was the clergyman there?"

"A man with a hateful countenance, but scrupulously dressed in canonical robes. Then there was what *seemed*, at least, a lady, over-dressed, very condescending, and to whom the captain introduced me, calling her aunt: several younger ladies also, and a baronet, a friend of the captain, whom I had often met at our house. When the 'aunt' kissed me I shuddered. You will think me superstitious, I know, dear—"

"Perhaps not, Ellie."

"It came to me, I cannot tell how—I suppose a Swedenborgian would say my interior sight was opened—it came to me, not in words I think, but flashing over my mind as if I had heard some one whisper: 'No aunt, no clergyman: all false!' I turned suddenly to the woman, who spoke to me in what she meant for an affectionate style, introducing to me two of the young ladies dressed in white, who were to act, she said, as my bridesmaids. They also addressed to me some civil commonplaces. But something in the tone and manners of all three made me think they were not persons of position, accustomed to good society. The captain beckoned to the clergyman, who began the ceremony, speaking with a slight foreign accent, I thought. I let it go on till it came to the question whether I took this man to be my husband; and then to Halloran's utter astonishment—for I know he thought me still entranced—I answered with all the energy I could muster, 'No, I do not.'"

"Brave darling! But what a terrible plot!"

"These things don't happen in novels only, Celia. The wonder is, that the strange control which animal magnetism gives is not more frequently abused. There was a pause when I came out with that unlooked-for denial, and I felt that Captain Halloran was exerting his utmost influence to throw me again into a somnambulic state. But either some mysterious guardian influence interposed, or my excited indignation enabled me to resist, for I succeeded in resisting.

"'Go on,' said the captain to the clergyman: 'it was a mistake. Ask the question again.' But before he had time to proceed I turned to the young baronet. 'Sir George,' said I, 'a man of honor will not stand by and permit this.'

"'D—n it, Tom, this won't do,' said he to the captain: 'an elopement's all well enough, but a gentleman can't refuse a lady protection when she asks it.'

"The captain turned white to the very lips with anger, but he choked it down and only said, 'You know she came here willingly, George.'

"Maybe,' the other replied; 'but a lady has the right to change her mind. Where do you wish to go to, Miss Talbot?'

"'Home,' I said, 'to Sir Charles'."

"'You hear?' said Sir George to the captain: 'it can't go on.'

"'Sir George,' cried Halloran, 'you shall answer for this.'

"'All right, my good fellow,' said Sir George, coolly. 'But will you take her home, or shall I?'

"The captain, I saw, was furious, but after some hesitation he said that if the carriage was still in waiting, and if I insisted, he would escort me. With that he left the room. I expressed my gratitude to Sir George, and begged that he would see me safe out of the house. This, on the captain's return, he did, waiting till he heard the order given to the coachman: 'To Sir Charles Conynghame's.' Then I felt comparatively at ease again, having made up my mind to disclose the whole to my guardian, and to ask that Captain Halloran be forbidden the house. This threw me off my guard, particularly as the captain spoke in the most submissive terms, saying that he saw now that my aversion to him was unconquerable, and that it was useless to press his suit farther. As he said this I felt—and hated myself for feeling—that in spite of his gross misconduct, I had no aversion to him. On the contrary, I felt again that inexplicable attraction, and found myself seeking excuses for his behavior. It occurred to me that perhaps, in trance, I might have actually consented to leave Sir Charles' house; and then, as to the marriage, had I not seen the special license? This revulsion of feeling was dangerous—the more so, as we were in a coupé, single-seated, and I had no choice but to let the captain sit by me. He had lowered the blinds, which I was glad of, for I feared to be recognized as we drove along. Gradually that subtle influence began to steal over me again. The way seemed very long, but such was the fascination that I did not care how long it was. I felt as if I could go on so for ever. The last thing I remember was the thought that, though I was again sinking into trance, the knocking at Sir Charles' door would awake me."

"Did it?" asked Celia, eagerly.

"Alas, dear child! we never arrived there. When I awoke to partial consciousness we were ascending the stairs of a house that was unknown to me. It seemed to be divided into apartments after the foreign fashion. The door had been opened by Halloran's groom, whom I recognized; and in the passage I caught a momentary glimpse of a face—that of a servant in black—which I felt sure was the same repulsive countenance that belonged to the person who assumed to marry us. Then the whole base plot lay bare before me, and I knew that I had been brought, in trance, to Captain Halloran's private apartments."

"Good Heavens!" exclaimed Celia. "What *did* you do?"

Then Ellinor narrated to her friend the substance of the scene with which our readers are already familiar, ending with her escape, by Terence's aid, into the street.

"And then?" asked Celia, breathlessly.

"I hurried, I knew not whither, passing through street after street, and when darkness came on I found myself in a part of the city quite different from any I had ever seen—the streets narrow and dingy, the houses poor and dirty. It must have been some disreputable region, for, to my terror, I was several times accosted in a shocking manner by vulgar men, from whom I had the greatest difficulty in escaping. The bystanders offered me no aid: indeed, my alarm seemed to afford them amusement. Or perhaps it was my dress, so utterly out of place there. One ruffian, after talking to me in the most revolting terms, attempted by force to thrust me into a horrible-looking house. My screams brought a policeman to the spot. At first *he* seemed disposed to treat me with indignity also. But when I explained to him that I had lost my way, he became more respectful and offered to take me to the nearest stand for coaches. On the way a desperate resolve took possession of me. What explanation to my relatives was now possible? I *could* not face my guardian and that insolent sister of his.

'Anywhere, anywhere,
Out of the world!'

—these were the terrible lines that beat themselves into my brain. Yet I struggled for control as long as I was with the policeman, entering a cab, and, when he asked where the man should drive to, giving my guardian's address, in Grafton street, Piccadilly. Soon after, however, I stopped the cabman, asked which was the nearest of the bridges, and bade him drive there. He hesitated, muttering something about his fare. But when I produced a sovereign and insisted, he turned. I shuddered fearfully when I found he had obeyed my order. I seemed to hear the rebuke: 'You fear the face of man and affront the presence of God!' I had my hand on the cab window to lower it and call the driver. But Despair prevailed, ever recalling, with frighful iteration, the lines:

'Mad from life's history,
Glad to death's mystery
Swift to be hurled—
Anywhere, anywhere,
Out of the world!'

I was beside myself. I felt as if I were pursued by the Furies. Oh forgive me, darling!"

Celia could not reply for weeping.

"It's cruel, dear child," Ellinor resumed, "to grieve you so, but the rest is soon told. In the very act of springing from the bridge a friendly hand held me back. I turned, indignant at first, but when I met Mr. Creighton's honest, manly face, and heard a few words of gentle expostulation, the evil spirit was exorcised. Yet I was scarcely 'clothed in my right mind.' The remaining events of that night are phantasmagorial. I know we were roughly repulsed from several doors where Mr. Creighton sought to obtain a room for me. At last I found myself in bed. Toward morning I sank into a sort of stupor, from which a knock at my chamber door aroused me. I had lain down in my clothes, so I rose and unlocked the door. It was Mr. Creighton. He begged me, though it was early morning, to come with him at once, as he had secured a lodging for me. As he hurried me into the street, I found that we were leaving a hotel, and I turned for an explanation, asking him where I had passed the night. He is one of God's noblemen, Celia, with the true instincts of God's nobility. I shall never forget how he spoke to me—with such delicate forbearance, with such tender regard for my feelings. 'Forgive me, young lady,' he said: 'it was an absolute necessity, since the alternative was that we should remain all night in the street. I *had* to give you my room.' Then, when he saw how dreadfully embarrassed I was, he added: 'You are too weak now to tell me by what terrible cruelty or injustice you were brought to despair, and perhaps you may never think me worthy to know. But to-morrow I shall call to ask if I can take a message to your friends or serve you in any way.' All the rest of his conduct was of a piece with this. When he found I was resolved never to see my relatives again, but to maintain myself by needlework, and that I positively refused to accept money from him, he refrained from visiting me except at considerable intervals; and when, after several weeks, he was obliged to leave London, he told me he had written about me to his uncle, an old Quaker gentleman, who would visit London in a month or two. I told you the rest. When Mr. Creighton took leave I don't think I said one grateful word, but I know Elizabeth Browning's glorious lines were in my heart:

> '*Thee* I do not thank at all:
> I but thank God, who made thee what thou art—
> So wholly godlike.'

I don't know which I venerate most—Mr. Creighton, young as he is, or that saint-like old man, Uncle Williams, as I used to call him. They did far more than to save me from suicide: they reconciled me to life in a world where such honor and loving-kindness are to be found."

Celia took the weeping girl in her arms and kissed her again and again. "They were as kind to me as to you," she said: "they sent me a sister."

CHAPTER XLIII.

EVENTS THICKEN.

> " So we grew together,
> Like to a double cherry, seeming parted."
> *Midsummer Night's Dream.*

AFTER a time, when the two girls had become quieter, Celia fell into a reverie. When she looked up and saw Ellinor's eyes on her with that wonderful look of love they sometimes wore, she said, "I keep thinking — but that's foolish and ungrateful too — if you only *were* my real, real sister."

"Ah, that reminds me — I've something to tell you, Celia. It's almost as strange as that dismal story of mine, but it's not gloomy. Last evening I picked up a little book — a wonderful book, Celia; you must read it—Isaac Taylor's *Physical Theory of Another Life.* Constance had once given me a copy of it, and it brought her forcibly to my mind. When I went to sleep, thinking of her, there came to me such a vivid dream. I can scarcely yet believe that I didn't actually see my darling standing beside the bed."

"She appeared to you?"

"As in very life, Celia, except that she seemed idealized, etherealized. How beautiful she was!"

"Did she say anything?"

"Not at first, but above her head—it seemed in letters of light — were the words: 'Bring forth the blind people that have eyes.' (I found the text this morning in Isaiah.) Then I saw in the distance, but gradually enlarging or approaching (I couldn't tell which), two figures—you, Celia, and, strange to say! myself. I — or rather my 'double'—seemed groping as if to touch you. Then I thought Constance turned, raised her hands as in blessing over us, and I heard, in a tone that went to my heart, the word 'SISTER!' With a start I awoke, and it was long before I could convince myself that Constance wasn't there."

"What could it mean, Ellie?" hesitatingly.

Ellinor smiled: "That I shall be blind, and that you will be to me a sister and a blessing."

"And you smile?"

"Constance smiled when she turned and blessed us, though I *had* to grope for you, dear child."

"But I'm not your real sister; so maybe you won't be really blind."

"As God wills."

"And if God does will it, I'll try to be 'eyes to the blind;' but, at all events, you must be my real cousin—my cousin Ethan's wife, Ellie dear. I don't think he would live if you were to refuse him."

Supper was late that evening at Dr. Meyrac's. They were waiting for Ethan Hartland, who had been invited to join them, but had first to go on business to Mount Sharon.

When they were seated, and Ethan had been telling them the news from the county-seat, Ellinor suddenly exclaimed,

"Who put out the lamp? Or was it the oil that failed? But in a single moment—how strange!"

No one replied. They all turned, in amazement, to Miss Ethelridge. She was not in the habit of jesting, and the look on her face was of unmistakable surprise.

"What did you say?" Ethan began, after a pause. Ellinor looked at him—at least her eyes, bright with intelligence, were directed, inquiringly, to his face. Was it possible? His very heart stood still at the thought.

"Ellinor, dear child," said Dr. Meyrac in French, "I would see you a moment in my study." He went up to her and took her hand: "Shall I conduct you?"

Ellinor's mind was in a maze, but she assented. "What is it, doctor?" she asked as he led her off.

"Is she ill, mamma?" said Lucille Meyrac.

"Alas, my child! It is as your father has feared. But how very, very sudden! And without the least pain, for she evidently thought not of it."

"Blind, mamma?" And the girl turned pale as a sheet.

"I remember that your father once told me of just such a case—in some town of the provinces. But I was incredulous. It is rare: it usually occurs by degrees."

"Is it paralysis of the optic nerve?" Ethan forced himself to ask.

"Yes. Poor dear mignonne!"

Then they were silent. After a time the doctor and Ellinor returned, and he assisted her to her seat. Ethan's bitter grief gave way to wonder and admiration. Not a trace of sorrow on that placid face. Could she not see him?—for the brilliant eyes turned to his, he actually thought, as if to discover how he bore it. But he knew now. It had come in very deed! How glad he was she didn't see his tears! *Did* she not see them?—for she said, in a tone that sank into his heart of hearts, "Do not grieve, dear friend. It is a relief to me that it is all over."

Dr. Meyrac was often abrupt, and now and then somewhat despotic, but he was a man of instinctive delicacy. He had found out how it stood with Ethan and Ellinor, and he so contrived it that when supper was cleared away they were left alone. "It is he who must be her physician henceforth, my dear Elise," he whispered to his wife. "See to it that no one intrudes on them."

Nor must we. When, at the end of an hour, Ethan rose to go, Ellinor said: "To-morrow evening, dear, dear Ethan. Cannot you wait for my decision till to-morrow?"

He kissed her fervently and tore himself away, without trusting his voice to answer.

Immediately after breakfast next morning, Creighton called at Mrs. Hartland's and sent up his card to Celia. She came down at once, but with her hat and shawl.

"You were going out, Miss Pembroke?"

"To see poor Ellie. You have heard—"

"Yes. But I have something to tell you that you ought to know before you go. It relates to her."

The evening before, Ethan had, with difficulty, persuaded Celia not to see Ellinor that night. When she came down to meet Creighton she had been nervously impatient, and, almost unconsciously, had remained standing. But his words recalled her. Laying aside hat and shawl, she seated herself. "I'm afraid I've been very rude, Mr. Creighton," she said, blushing a little: "I shall be most happy to hear what you have to say."

Our readers know what it was. Celia felt as if she were dreaming. She scarcely took it in at first. She asked him again and again if he was sure, *quite* sure; and when the details he gave her, including Terence's testimony, left no longer a doubt on her mind, she suddenly recalled all that Creighton had done, and for whom.

Tears started to her eyes, and she gave him both her hands: "I know what a good man you are, Mr. Creighton: she told me yesterday. And you saved my sister's life."

Creighton blushed like a girl, but he turned it off, asking, "Will you tell her, or shall I?" As Celia hesitated, he added: "It will come best from you." Then, smiling, "You are not sorry now that I detained you, Miss Pembroke?"

All the way home Creighton kept thinking of the look she gave him in reply. But gratitude is not love.

And what were Celia's thoughts as she sped toward Dr. Meyrac's? They were mingled still, for a time, with incredulity. Sudden, unlooked-for joy, like some unexpected stroke of misfortune, often comes before us, for the moment, as incredible. Celia seemed to herself almost as walking in trance, and she half feared to wake and behold it a dream. Had the news been that her lawsuit was gained and a certain forty thousand dollars still her own, she would have received it joyfully, of course, but calmly, and she would have believed in it at once. But this was something beyond her wildest anticipations—like some gift in a fairy tale. Would it vanish away?

No. That mysterious being whom she had heard of as her father's first wife had been Ellie's mother. Never one happy day at home, Ellinor had said. Ah! that explained her father's flight. But he must have loved Ellie. She thought of him taking his first-born in his arms, kissing her, weeping over her, perhaps, before he left; grieving after her, too, no doubt, even when a second daughter came. How strange it all was!

Another apology she found for her father's conduct. Though he had abandoned his little daughter, still she remained at first, as he knew, with her mother; and afterward, as he must also have known, in the care of one who was far more than that mother had ever been to her. She was well provided for, too. He had given the mother and child half his fortune.

A new train of thought! That forty thousand dollars would not go to profligate Sir Charles Conynghame now. Eliot Creighton had come that morning specially to talk to her on that branch of the subject. But at first, when he saw her wild joy at the discovery of a sister, he could not find it in his heart to speak to her of money. And afterward that look of Celia's, which he carried home with him, put it out of his head. A poor head for a lawyer, it must have been: he was ashamed to think of it when he got home. But Celia threaded her legal way without his aid. Creighton had already told her that the guardian was heir-at-law only in case the ward could not be found. Ellinor was the heir. The sole heir? Never mind: time enough to think of that by and by, for just then she reached Dr. Meyrac's garden gate.

At the first moment when she opened the blind girl's chamber door, and saw the large resplendent eyes fixed on her with all their wonted love, the arms stretched out in welcome and the face calm—yes, actually with a smile on it!—she was bewildered. But when she sat down beside her, and Ellinor put one arm round her and passed the other slowly, gently over her face, with a slight start as she detected the tears—then the reality burst on Celia at once. Never, never again to see the sun or the spring flowers or the face of a friend!

Morning and night, the glorious break of day and the peace-breathing twilight, all one changeless blank now! Over the whole fair external world the blackness of darkness for ever! She had been told of it the evening before: she had lain awake half the night thinking of it; but—

"Because things seen are greater than things heard"—

she had never felt it, it had never become part of her consciousness, till now. She had come to tell her sister the incredible secret, but even that, for the moment, passed from her mind. "Ellie, Ellie!" was all she could say; but the blind can detect sobs as well as tears; and no words could have told half as much as that warm embrace.

After the first gust of grief, however, Celia struggled bravely for composure. Ellinor's silent caresses, too, produced their usual soothing effect. Then, with returning tranquillity, came back to her also the astounding, the rapturous news. The long swell after the tempest was there still, but the sun broke out on it.

—The sun, warm and cheering. Her heart overflowed under its glow. "Ellie," she said, and the blind girl started: she felt that there was joy in the tone—"dear Ellie, you don't *know* what I've got to tell you. It would have made me—it *has* made me—oh so glad!"

"Then it will make me glad, too, dear child. Tell it me."

"I have a right to take care of you now. Till you're married, Ellie, nobody—nobody in all the world—will have the same right."

"What is it, Celia?—what is it?" The eyes turned eagerly, restlessly, to Celia's face, as if, for the first time, the soul within were impatient of the darkness.

"Your mother thought herself a widow. She was not. Your father—our father, Ellie! think!—*our* father came to this country and changed his name from Talbot to Pembroke."

"To Pembroke!" Celia feared, for a moment, that Ellinor would faint, she grew so deadly pale: the conflicting emotions of the last twenty-four hours had sorely tried her nerves. But the color gradually returned to her cheeks, the sightless eyes lighted up, and a look came over her face such as Celia had never seen there before. It awed her. It seemed to her the expression of heavenly joy.

"God is good!" Ellinor said in a low tone—"oh how good! In man's hands that's terrible! but in His—" Then her lips moved as in prayer.

Yet after a time there was a sudden revulsion. She came back to this lower world again, all the feelings of her impulsive nature breaking over the bounds within which she had schooled them to abide. Her joy was exultant. Triumph was the expression Celia now read in her face. Ellinor took the astonished girl in her arms, kissed her passionately again and again, laughing and crying over her the while. "Sister!" she repeated—"sister! my own, my own!"

Then the current of her excited feelings changed once more. "Constance knew it," she said, humbly: "she knew all that awaited me. Really blind, Celia; and this my real, real sister!" Gradually the wild excitement subsided, and she added: "God has given you your wish, dear child, and we shall be *so* happy!"

The first day of blindness! Yet it was said from the very heart.

When they had sat together a little space in silence, Ellinor resumed: "I think you know I would never tell you anything but the very truth."

"I don't believe in what I see and feel more than I do in your word."

"I'm very glad of that. Then see, dear! In the last few hours two things have happened to me. I have become blind—I dare say for life; and I've found out that the very girl I would have chosen out of all the world—out of all the world, Celia—is my own, actual sister. Do you think that I would take back my sight on condition that I should remain all my life blind to what you've told me just now? I've gained far more than I've lost. As God is my witness, I do most religiously believe it."

"Oh, Ellie, how *can* you talk so?"

A knock at the door, and Dr. Meyrac came in: "I think my patient had better keep out of church this morning, Mademoiselle Célie. We must have her a little accustomed to her new phase of life before she goes into public."

They assented, and then they told him the news. He was much surprised, of course, but he received it quietly, with French politeness: "I know not which of the two is the more fortunate. You are worthy of each other, my dear young ladies."

Then the business aspect of the affair struck him: "Ah, it is charming. That good-for-nothing of a Cranstoun is checkmated."

For the first time that day Celia saw a painful expression cross her sister's face, but Ellinor said nothing until the doctor, after inviting Celia to dinner, left the room. Then she took Celia's hand: "Sister, I see what good Dr. Meyrac means. It is to Sir Charles Conynghame that Cranstoun has written. If suit is commenced, it will be in Sir Charles' name."

"It has been commenced."

"Ah! Then my name can be used to arrest or defeat it; but it will be a mere form. We know well enough—Mr. Creighton is convinced—that—that father made a will, witnessed by Cranstoun, leaving his American property to your mother and you."

"He thinks so—that's all: there's no proof of it."

"Of course it's so. He knew—or he thought—that I was provided for. We *must* respect his wishes, Celia."

"Sister Ellie, you can't always have your own way, even if—" She commenced the sentence playfully, but broke off with a deep sigh.

"Even if I *am* blind. Well, dear?"

Celia sat lost in thought for a brief space; then she looked up: "There's nobody you respect more than Eliot Creighton."

"Nobody."

"You didn't hear his election-speech: I did. That man wouldn't swerve one hair's breadth from the right for favor of man or woman."

"He's the very soul of honor."

"Well, Ellie darling, there's one thing —only one — that we two sha'n't agree about. Let us refer it to him and abide his decision."

After some further talk, in which Celia stood her ground resolutely, her sister assented; and it was agreed that after dinner they would visit Mrs. Creighton. "I can't see my way," Ellinor said, "but I shall be love-led."

They found mother and son at home. Mrs. Creighton was a charming old lady —charming and handsome too — with bright, tender eyes undimmed by her fifty years. It was touching to see her reception of the blind girl. If she had been her own daughter, she could not have folded her in her arms with warmer tokens of affection. And she was delighted when the sisters — each setting forth the rights of the other—submitted their difference to her son as referee.

"Wise girls!" she said. "You're too romantic, both of you, to be trusted. I haven't quite made up my mind which of you two I like best; and I'm not sure that Eliot has. So I think you may trust him."

Ellinor thought she knew very well which was the favorite, but she did not say so. And it was on her lips to reply, "Mr. Creighton might be trusted to arbitrate between his best friend and his worst enemy," but neither did she make that remark. She quietly awaited Creighton's answer.

"I dare say mother's right"—he hesitated a moment, just a little bit abashed, then suddenly closed the sentence—"in what she says about romance. The matter ought to be decided at once, and I'm afraid it can't be without help. You honor me very highly, young ladies; and, since you wish it, I'll do my best."

He sent them his decision that evening. It read as follows:

"OPINION

in the Case of Ellinor Ethelridge Talbot and Celia Pembroke.

"Proof that Miss Talbot lives and establishing her identity, sent to Sir Charles Conynghame, will probably induce him to withdraw his suit. If not, the identity can be established and he will certainly be defeated.

"Then the law of Ohio will regulate the case. I believe that, by that law, Miss Talbot and Miss Pembroke are equal heirs. But as there has been no decision in point by the Supreme Court, I may be mistaken. Miss Talbot might possibly be declared sole heir.

"I do not doubt that the late Frederick Pembroke (or Talbot) left a will, but it will probably never be found; and meanwhile the legal effect is the same as if it did not exist. That will did probably, but not certainly, make Miss Pembroke sole heir of the American property.

"Under these uncertainties, I think the matter ought to be decided according to what we may reasonably conclude to have been the wish of said Frederick Pembroke (or Talbot).

"But it was evidently his intention to leave half his property to each of his daughters. My opinion is, therefore, that each sister should take half of the American property, and that if any portion of the property now held by Sir Charles Conynghame as executor of the late Mrs. Talbot and guardian of her daughter should hereafter be recovered, that also should be equally divided between the sisters aforesaid.

"(Signed) ELIOT CREIGHTON."

Sydenham, who had called to see Ellinor, was at Dr. Meyrac's when this document arrived. It was submitted to him as Celia's guardian, and he heartily approved it.

So that affair, as such differences always can be between reasonable people, was settled at once.

And this opinion of Creighton helped Ellinor to decide in another matter more important than money. Ethan came for his answer. Celia had half won his cause in the course of the day. "We frail mortals are never satisfied," she had said to Ellinor: "prosperity spoils us—the more we get the more we long for. I found a sister: now I want a brother too."

Ellinor had been arguing herself into the conviction that to one of moderate means like Ethan a blind wife would be a pecuniary burden such as he ought not to bear. That scruple was removed: she would not come to him empty-handed; and whereas her lover's fate, till then, had been trembling in the balance, now the scale on which she had piled her doubts and scruples kicked the beam.

Thus in the course of twenty-four hours Mary Ellinor Ethelridge Talbot lost her sight, found a sister, acquired twenty thousand dollars and became an affianced bride.

Which may we fittingly do—rejoice or condole with her?

CHAPTER XLIV.

GOING HOME.

"So Ann still lov'd: it was her doom
 To love in shame and sorrow:
Charles came no more; but, 'He will come,'
 She said, 'to-morrow.'
Oh yet for her deep bliss remained;
 She dreamed he came and kissed her;
And in that hour the angels gained
 Another sister."
EBENEZER ELLIOTT.

SUMMER passed and part of autumn. During that time two items of news only broke the even tenor of events in our quiet village. First: a report came that an uncle of Mowbray, who had avoided all intercourse with him and his mother, was dead and had left Evelyn a fortune which rumor estimated at a quarter of a million of dollars. Second: Creighton had started for London: gossipry said to see about another fortune in the hands of a rich English nobleman, who, as Terence O'Reilly had found out, was Miss Ethelridge's cousin.

Up to the time when Mowbray went on a five or six weeks' visit to New York, on the business alluded to, he and Ellen had met every few days. It excited no remark, for their engagement had become public, and such was the habit of the place.

When Mowbray returned, it was known that he had been put in possession of the uncle's legacy—not quite as large as was reported, but a comfortable fortune—a hundred and eighty thousand dollars, besides a handsome dwelling, richly furnished, in Philadelphia.

Then village gossips alleged that the meetings between the lovers became less and less frequent; but this might have been because Mowbray was busy selling their house, furniture and other possessions. Early in October his mother and he left Chiskauga: it was said to return no more.

The evening before they went an incident happened which Mowbray was never able to explain. He had been to take leave of a friend who lived beyond Mrs. Hartland's house, a mile out of town, and he was returning about ten o'clock. There was a new moon, but the sky was clouded. Just as he was crossing a street running west, that had been opened half a mile from town, but was not yet built up, he heard what seemed a rifle-shot close by, and for a moment he thought he was hit. But, removing his hat and touching himself all over, he found he was mistaken. The shot, he thought, had come from behind a board fence to a grain-field on the right of the cross street; but when he went up to it there was no one to be seen in the field. He did imagine, for a moment, that he could distinguish a figure gliding along at some distance close to the fence, but a second look dissipated that impression: he could see nothing stirring.

When he reached home he went straight to his room, having some packing still to do. As he deposited his hat on a table he started. Two holes, evidently from a good-sized rifle ball, right through the hat, about two inches below the crown! He sank on a chair. "I thought I felt something graze my hair," he said, half aloud. Conscience suggested a name, but a little reflection caused him to reject it. "She refused him," was his thought; "and then these country fellows might knock a man down in open daylight, but they're not assassins." It was an hour before he resumed his packing, and by that time he had resolved not to say a word to any one about it.

On the second morning after the departure of the Mowbrays, Hiram Goddart called at Rosebank much excited. Ellen Tyler, he said, who had seemed dreadfully depressed the day before, had not spent the night at home. She had been present at supper, though she scarcely touched anything, and had put Willie carefully to bed, but her own bed had evidently been unoccupied: she must have wandered out, no one knew whither. He had inquired at the village, and she had not been heard of there. What added to his alarm was that the night had been pitch dark, and after midnight there had been several hours of heavy rain. This had now ceased, but the morning was raw and gusty.

When Mr. Sydenham asked Goddart whether Chewauna creek was high, the poor fellow fairly broke down: "Surely you don't think, Mr. Sydenham—" There he stopped.

"No, Hiram — not that. But the banks are steep and rocky, and she might have lost her way in the rain and darkness."

It was agreed that Hiram should follow the line of the creek, and that Sydenham should explore the various roads and by-paths leading from the mill. At Leoline's earnest instance her father permitted her to accompany him.

Two or three hours were spent in fruitless search. At last Sydenham bethought him that a few weeks before, when following an obscure bridle-path, he had caught sight, in the distance, of Ellen and Mowbray seated under a forest tree. Why it occurred to him that she might have wandered to that spot I cannot tell; but there, in truth, they found her. Insensible, it appeared, stretched out on the wet grass; her clothing drenched, for she wore a light cape only over her usual dress; her face deadly pale; the eyes closed; her hands cold as ice. Outwearied with a struggle she seemed, and sunk to rest at last. Beautiful in their calm, innocent expression were the sweet child-features, but there were traces of tears on the wan cheeks.

Leoline sprang from her saddle, knelt

down and chafed the cold hands, a gust of mingled sorrow and indignation filling her eyes the while. Mowbray was one of the men whom she could not endure.

Sydenham had taken the precaution to bring with him a blanket and a small flask of wine. He handed these to her: "Are you afraid to stay here, my child, till I ride home for the carriage?"

"Afraid, papa? Don't think about me. But how can you manage to get a carriage here?"

"We are only quarter of a mile from the road: I'll bring two or three of the men, and we'll rig up a litter. If she revives, give her some of the wine."

Leoline took off a thick sack which she wore, and contrived to substitute it for the thin cape that was soaked through. Then she wrapped Ellen up as warmly as she could in the blanket. But the poor girl seemed chilled through, and it was a long time before any symptoms of returning animation showed themselves. Soon after that Sydenham returned, and with him Mr. Harper. Ellen was a favorite of the good man. He had heard in the village vague rumors about her disappearance, and had come to Rosebank seeking more certain tidings.

The movement of the litter seemed gradually to revive the sufferer. When they had lifted her into the carriage, Mr. Harper, who had been walking with Sydenham, came to the door. "Ellen, my child," he said, "I promised your father the day before he died that if you ever needed help I would stand in his stead. I'm going to take you home to my little place."

Ellen was very, very feeble, but she contrived to take the kind old man's hand: "Oh, Mr. Harper, not to your house. I can't, indeed I can't—I don't deserve it."

"You felt, last night, as if you couldn't trust in God. That was wrong. But we can't always do right. We can't always trust in God when there's not a gleam of light in the darkness." Then he entered the carriage, arranged her pillows, sat down opposite to her and bade them drive on. "You need very careful nursing, Ellen, and good old Barbara is an excellent nurse." She was about to remonstrate further, but he stopped her: "When we get home: you mustn't talk now." She obeyed him as a little child might, but she wept long and silently.

Barbara had been in Mr. Harper's service fifteen years during the life of his wife and twelve years since her death. She was at heart a kind soul, though a little stiff in some of her notions, and her reverence for her master was unbounded. She received the poor girl without question, and was unwearied in her endeavors to counteract the chill and prostration caused by that cruel night of storm.

In the course of the day Hannah Clymer came to aid in nursing the invalid. Dr. Meyrac, in his report to Harper, spoke somewhat doubtfully: "There is to fear *fluxion de poitrine*—vat we call pneumonie—but it may not come: in two, tree days one shall know for sure. She seems very triste. Is it that the poor child grieves? Has that nothing-worth perhaps deserted her?"

"I fear that he has, doctor."

"It is pity—that complicates the case: visout it the pronostic would be favorable. But if the heart sinks, who can tell? Seek to keep the heart up, Monsieur Harper. You may be better doctor than me."

In the evening Mr. Harper sat with the patient while Barbara was preparing tea, and Ellen said to him: "I hope you'll not be troubled with me long, Mr. Harper."

"For your sake, Ellen, I do hope you will speedily recover; and if I could see you more cheerful, I should feel sure of it."

She lay quite still for some minutes; then, hesitatingly: "Mr. Harper, is it wicked to wish to die?"

"We must all die, but it is our duty to wait God's good time."

"I think God wishes me to die. When people are bad they kill them; and perhaps if I die, God will think that was punishment enough and let me be with father and mother. It would be *so* good of Him if He would! That's all I care about now."

Harper took one of her hands in both his: "Why do you wish to die, dear child?"

"I am *such* a great sinner. People will never pardon me here. I don't think there ever was a better man than you, Mr. Harper, but I've disgraced myself, and even you can't forgive me: I know that. But I think father will. Nobody was ever so kind to me as father. I would tell him everything. Mother too. I was such a little girl when she left me with father, and she won't expect much from me, maybe."

In spite of his best efforts, the tears were rising to the old man's eyes. Barbara came in with tea, and Harper, fearing over-excitement, pursued the subject no farther at that time.

Harper pondered over Ellen's words, wondering what their exact meaning might be. When Meyrac called next day, he told him what she had said. "Ah what child!" was the doctor's comment: "poor little simpleton! That has no self-esteem. One must sustain it." And after a brief visit to his patient he took a hasty leave. In the course of the day, Celia, Leoline, Ellinor, Mrs. Hartland and Mrs. Creighton came to see Ellen. Harper wondered whether Dr. Meyrac had begged them to call.

In the evening the patient asked to sit up: she seemed to suffer much when lying down. She had some fever and a hacking cough. She was quiet, but it was the quiet of resignation, Harper thought, not of hope. He sought to encourage her: "You see, Ellen, that the people you esteem most all come to visit you and interest themselves about you."

"Yes"—it was said sadly, despondingly—"they are all kind and good; and I'm very glad I shall not live to disgrace them." Then, looking up earnestly in that tender face: "Mr. Harper, I heard that you can read Hebrew and Greek, and know all about what the Bible says and what God thinks."

"It is true, my child, that I have spent most of my life in studying the Scriptures in the original tongues; but God's thoughts are not as ours: His ways are past finding out."

"I'm very sorry for that."

"Why are you sorry for it, Ellen?"

"I'm so much afraid God won't let me go to father by and by, when I die; and I wanted so much to know, and I thought maybe you could tell me."

"Perhaps I can. There are some things that God *has* told us. Why are you afraid you will never be in heaven with your father?"

"Because father was such a good man—and—" she buried her face in her hands and he saw the tears trickle over her fingers: at last, in a low tone that went to his heart, she sobbed out, "and oh, Mr. Harper, I'm not a good woman!"

Harper looked at her as Christ, when he sojourned on earth, may have looked on some humble Judean penitent. Ere he could reply she interrupted him, speaking hastily, as if fearing her courage might give way: "I joined your church, and I know I ought to tell you. I promised father before he died that I wouldn't marry Mr. Mowbray till I was twenty-one—not for a year yet: we've been engaged five months. He wanted me to marry him sooner — this year. But I couldn't lie to father—and he just dead too—could I?"

"No: you did quite right to refuse him."

"Do you think so, Mr. Harper?"

"Yes, and God thinks so too."

"Does He?" with a pleased smile: in a few moments it faded: "But Evelyn was angry: he thought I didn't love him, and that made me very, very sorry, for he had been as kind and good to me as he could be. Then I thought what a poor thing I was compared to him, and what could I ever do for him? And I told him if he would only let me keep my promise to father, there wasn't anything else in the world I would refuse him; but Mr. Harper—" a feeling of oppression had been gradually gaining on the poor girl: she couldn't say another word. Harper was startled and fearful of what was coming; and, after he had bathed her throbbing temples and she had gradually revived, "Don't talk any more," he said: "it exhausts you."

But though face and neck were flushing scarlet, and though her respiration was becoming hurried and painful, she went on: "I didn't mean — I never intended—maybe you won't believe me—" and she looked up at him—such an imploring look!

He understood it all now! The first impulse was to reprove the offender—to show up before her the enormity of her fault — but that suppliant look! His heart was not proof against it; and afterward, when he thought it over, he took himself to task for this; but just then he couldn't help saying, "Say no more, my child. I do most religiously believe you. You have a right to be believed. You wouldn't tell a lie and break your promise to your dead father: if you had, you might have been that bad man's wife to-day."

"Oh, please, please, Mr. Harper, don't call him a bad man. I'm not a bit better than he is."

"What did he say to you before he went?"

Ellen hesitated: "I haven't seen him for three weeks." The sigh and the look—so utterly hopeless both—aroused in Harper as much anger as that indulgent heart of his was capable of feeling.

"He forsook you without a word!" he broke forth, but seeing how much pain he gave her, he checked his indignation, saying gently: "Are you sorry for what you have done, my child?"

"I'm very sorry for it when I think of God: I'm sure it must have made Him angry, and I don't know as He'll ever forgive me. Yes, I'm very, very sorry: it was *so* wrong; only—I'm afraid that's wicked too—I'm not sorry Evelyn found out that I told him the truth about putting off the marriage. He knows now that it wasn't because I didn't care for him. He knows that I do love him; and I can't help being glad of that."

It was a new revelation to the warm-hearted, guileless minister. He looked at the girl with dimmed eyes, wondering, the while, whether that passage about Jonathan's love "passing the love of woman" was not a mistranslation. His voice had a wonderful tenderness in its tones when he said, "You are glad you made him know that you love him, even though he deserts you without a single farewell?"

"Oh, Mr. Harper, how can I help forgiving him that? He is so rich now. He will have a great, fine house, with carriages and horses and servants: then fashionable people, that know so much, will all come to see him. And I know so little: I can scarcely speak French even. He would be ashamed of me if I was his wife."

"You have forgiven him everything, then?"

"I love him. Oh yes: I couldn't go and leave him for ever and not forgive him. I should never be happy, even with father, if I did that."

No complaint of death—not a spark of resentment toward the author of all her sufferings: loving still. Ellen had never read Goldsmith's two celebrated stanzas: she only acted them out. Her feeling was that she had "stooped to folly," and that she *had* to die.*

The kind old man's heart yearned toward her: he couldn't help it. "My poor child," he said, "you asked me if I could tell you whether God would forgive you and suffer you to be with your father, if you died—"

"*When* I die. Don't be sorry for that, Mr. Harper: I'm glad. You know I mustn't bring shame on your church and Miss Celia's school; and maybe they won't think so hard of me when I'm dead. Then, if I can only get to go to father, I'll be a great deal happier than if I had to stay here. Do you really think God will let me?"

"I'll tell you what Jesus Christ once did and said, and then you can judge: that's better than to take my word for it. It was when he was preaching in a city of Galilee, probably Nain. He was invited to dine with a man named Simon, one of those called Pharisees, who

* The sentiment, as expressed in a German translation (Lessing's, I believe) beginning—

"Lässt sich ein liebes Kind bethören"—

is more tender and delicate than the original.

thought themselves saints or godly men—better than all others: the people thought them so too. In those days men did not sit at meals: they lay on couches, with their feet uncovered. While they were at table a woman came in: most persons believe it was Mary Magdalene, but I don't think that was her name. This woman—" he hesitated—"you have done very wrong, Ellen, but this woman was a far more grievous sinner than you've ever been. All the city knew of her evil doings. Decent people would not associate with her. No doubt Simon thought she would never be forgiven, and he was shocked when he saw her come into the house and stand behind the couch where Jesus reclined. She wept, thinking of her sins; she kissed Jesus' feet, and anointed them with precious ointment and wiped them with her long hair. It was all she could do to show her love."

Ellen had been gazing at the narrator, her soul in her eyes. She must, no doubt, have read that chapter of Luke before, but how little common iterances—set words repeated week by week—come home, especially to the young and the happy! The story was all new and strange to her as Harper related it. When he stopped, struck by her eager, pleading look, she said, "Oh, go on, Mr. Harper: please go on. *Did* Christ forgive her?"

"You shall hear the very words," he said, taking a Bible from the table beside him. Then he read to her how Simon thought Jesus could not be the Christ or he would have known what sort of woman this was; how Jesus, divining Simon's thought, told him the parable of the two debtors; and how Simon had to admit the likelihood that when both these men were frankly forgiven their debts, he to whom most was forgiven would love the most. Then came the comparison between the cold reception given to his guest by the self-installed saint and the humble, tender regard of the self-accusing sinner. And finally the words—how few how simple! yet embodying the very essence of all that Jesus came to teach and to die for—"I say unto thee, her sins, which are many, are forgiven; for she loved much."

To the last that look of eager, doubtful inquiry! Then, when the gracious words came, such a deep sigh of relief! Her head drooped, her eyes filled with tears of joy and gratitude: her lips moved—

"The voiceless prayer,
Unheard by all save Mercy's ear;
And which, if Mercy did not hear,
Oh God would not be what this bright
And glorious universe of His—
This world of wisdom, goodness, light,
And endless love—proclaims He is!"

"And you forgive me, too?" were the first words Ellen was able to utter.

"I, dear child! A sinner like me! I forgive you with all my heart and soul. Dare I condemn when my Saviour proclaims forgiveness?"

Ellen never directly reverted to the subject afterward, but from that time her quiet wish for death was unmixed with despondency. The words of consolation had allayed grief and fear. Herself forgiving, she readily believed in forgiveness. Her sufferings thenceforth were physical only.

But these were great. At times, next day, she seemed unable to endure a recumbent position. Fever and cough had both increased, so had the feeling of oppression: there were great thirst, much lassitude, and no appetite whatever—a settled, stinging pain also on the chest. Meyrac employed the test of auscultation. It was, he then told Harper, a severe attack of pneumonia, caused by exposure. He bled Ellen—with some misgivings indeed, for he had lost, under similar treatment, one or two patients lately by this disease, and his professional faith in the theory about the congested lung that must needs be unloaded by use of the lancet was beginning to be shaken.

Hannah Clymer, relieved on alternate nights by Norah, spent most of her time by Ellen's bedside, and ere many days had passed she came to feel as if the life of some dear child of her own was at stake. So gentle and uncomplaining—such a calm cheerfulness even. Entire oblivion of her wrongs, utter forgetfulness of self; no "See how a Christian can die !" about her. Yet, if the graces of our religion give title, a Christian indeed, in whom was neither bitterness nor guile. There was, no doubt, scant cultivation of the intellect, small scope of thought, little knowledge of the world and its wondrous economy: lack of strength, too, to hold firm, and of prudence or stern principle to restrain. For all her twenty summers, there was much of the child about her. Yet of such is the kingdom of heaven. There was faith, hope — above all, love. She had given up this world, the heart failing in the struggle through it: her thoughts and wishes were already in the next—to her not a shadowy object of belief, but an assured reality, close at hand. To Mrs. Clymer she loved to speak, as any child might, of going to see her father and mother, just as if she were from home for the time, but was soon to return to the shelter of the dear familiar arms.

On one occasion only her thoughts seemed to revert vividly to the past. As the disease ran its course the torturing pain diminished, giving those around her hopes of her recovery—false hopes, for next day there was very high fever, running at last into delirium. Then the sufferer appeared to be greatly excited, addressing her lover as if present; now reasoning with him about the sacred promise made to her father; anon showing wild joy and conversing as if he had returned to leave her no more. But when the delirium passed off, though she was weak to utter helplessness, yet she was quite calm; and then all her allusions, breathing a sweet, trustful tenderness, were to her parents and to the welcome that was coming. It was her last thought, if one might judge from the smile that spoke from the quiet lips after the soul that gave it birth was gone—after the spiritual body, emerging to higher life, and awaking from the brief transition-slumber among rejoicing friends, had been ushered into its new home—there where there is "no more death nor sorrow nor crying, neither any more pain; for the former things have passed away."

PART XIII.

CHAPTER XLV.

MR. HARPER SPEAKS HIS MIND.

" Indignant scorn confest I feel, to see
That sovereign sin, that hag Hypocrisy,
So dupe the witless world and simple thee."

ONE evening, three days before Ellen's death, Barbara had come to Mr. Harper, alarmed: "There's a man been prowling around the house, evenings, a'most ever since that poor girl came here, Mr. Harper. I don't like his looks nor his ways. Just afore I closed the shutters to-night there was his face at the window."

"Of Ellen's room?"

"Yes, sir."

"You know, Barbara, that I've never locked an outside door, nor fastened down a window, in the fifteen years I've been here; and what harm has come of it?"

"I know, sir. But then the pitcher may go to the well ninety-nine times, and get broken at last."

"Is he about still?"

"In the front yard he was, sir, a minute ago."

"Bring me my hat and cane."

Under a shady kolreuteria,* with its masses of bright brown seed-vessels sheen in the silver moonlight, leaning with his back against the front gate, and looking, it seemed, intently at the house, Mr. Harper found a man in working jacket of fustian, with a slouched hat. As he approached him, the other took off his hat, saying: "I ask your pardon, Mr. Harper, but I wanted to know how Miss Ellen is to-night."

Harper could not remember where he had seen the speaker before, but the tone was civil, and he replied: "I am sorry to say she is no better—worse indeed: I'm afraid we shall lose her."

The moonlight fell distinctly on a handsome face, with something of a dissolute look over it. The face darkened—with anger, Harper thought, as much as sorrow—and the fellow muttered what sounded very like a curse. But if it was a curse, he restrained himself instantly, and said with emotion, for his voice trembled: "I worked for her father, and they always treated me well. There never was a better girl." Then, abruptly, "Do you believe in hell?"

Harper looked at him in astonishment; and the man, as if he felt there needed apology, added, "I hope you'll excuse me, Mr. Harper. I didn't mean to ask an uncivil question of a good man like you, that took poor Miss Ellen in and cared for her. But they say you've no end of learnin', and I thought you'd be likely to know whether there is hell-fire or not."

He spoke like a man in earnest, and he had touched on Mr. Harper's vulnerable point. The latter replied: "It is an important question. I'm very sorry all of us cannot read the Word of God in the Hebrew and Greek. The translators were men, and some of them indifferent scholars. In our Authorized Version the Hebrew word *sheol* is usually translated 'hell;' but the Hebrews really meant by it a vast pit, a common grave underground — nothing more. The Jews seemed to have thought that our rewards and punishments were on earth, not hereafter."

"But you don't think that's so, Mr. Harper, do you?"

"No: I only tell you what the Jews believed. In the New Testament *hades* means the state of the dead in general—a sort of intermediate existence: we do wrong to translate it 'hell.' There is another Greek word, *gehenna*, that was

* One of the handsomest and most meritorious of ornamental shade trees, growing to the height of thirty or forty feet, introduced into England from China a century ago, and less in use among us than it deserves. In summer its long blossoms cover it like a yellow cloud. Then succeeds a profusion of large seed-vessels—at first red, then yellow, and lastly of a rich brown. It blooms at three or four years old. The villagers, because they had a habit of planting it at their front gates, usually called it the *gate tree.*

used in Christ's day, and sometimes by Christ himself, to typify a place or state of punishment. Yet it was, in fact, the name of a deep valley or gorge near Jerusalem, into which the dead bodies of criminals and the carcases of animals were cast."

"Then you don't believe there's a lake of fire that bad men are thrown into when they die?"

"In God's Word, correctly translated, I find nothing to prove that."

"I'm sorry for it: there are some of us that need hell-fire. But you think bad men will be punished in the next world, don't you, Mr. Harper?"

"Undoubtedly: the Bible declares that they will, and nothing can be more certain; yet in regard to the actual condition of the dead, either before or after the resurrection, the Scriptures teach us very little. But why are you sorry there is no proof that there is a hell of burning flames?"

The man—it was our old acquaintance, Cassiday—hesitated: "I won't tell you a lie. I was thinking of John Mowbray. There ought to be just such a place for him."

"You mustn't talk so. God alone sees what ought to be. But what do you know about John Mowbray?"

"That he's an infernal scoundrel. I oughtn't to talk so before you, Mr. Harper, and I didn't intend to. But I'll tell you what I do know about him: The evening before he left, when I was out in the country a mile beyond the Widow Hartland's, I passed a house where a young man lives that Mowbray was intimate with. The window was open, and the two were laughin' and talkin'. I thought one of them used Miss Ellen's name, and I couldn't help stoppin' a moment. I'm not over-particular, Mr. Harper, but when I heard that boastful liar speaking of a virtuous young lady that he had been engaged to as if she was—well, as no man that's a gentleman, or a gentleman's son, has a right to talk—if I had had him just then by the throat, may-happen he'd have found out, by this, whether you're right about a burnin' hell or not."

"That would have been murder."

"I know that's an ugly word; and I suppose it would be hard to get such a thing out of a man's head afterward: maybe it's best when a fellow misses his chance and can't do all he's a mind to. But I wonder what God takes care of a blackguard like that for, and sends him cartloads of money, as if he were the pick of the earth?"

Before Harper could reply to a difficulty that millions have tried in vain to solve, Cassiday had swung the gate violently open: then, recollecting himself, he closed it gently, again took off his hat to Mr. Harper, and strode down the sidewalk toward the village, as if the avenger of blood were behind him.

"A strange man!" thought Harper—"not altogether evil." Then his thoughts reverted to Mowbray. The good man didn't like to feel as he felt just then toward him.

Ellen's funeral was numerously attended. The body was laid, as she had earnestly requested, beside her father's. The services were simple, and affected many to tears: there were two mourners who seemed unable to restrain themselves — Hiram Goddart, good, kind-hearted young fellow, and Willie, who had been a special favorite of Ellen's. He felt, poor little stray! as if he had lost a second mother.

Ellen, who had no near relatives, had not, in her last days, forgotten these two who now so bitterly wept her loss. In the will which, at Harper's instance, she had executed, she left all the mill property, burdened only with a few small legacies, to Hiram Goddart, on condition that he should adopt the little orphan and care for him, in all respects, as though he were his own son. Religiously, as if it had been a behest from Heaven, did Goddart carry out the last wishes of the girl he had so hopelessly loved.

During the day of the funeral, and for several days thereafter, all Chiskauga was busy talking about Ellen and Mowbray. While some spoke kindly of the unfortunate and forsaken orphan, much was said that was uncharitable and unjust; and of this a good deal came to Barbara's ears. She repeated it to Mr. Harper, and he was greatly moved thereby.

The funeral was on a Monday, and in the course of the week it became generally bruited about that on the next Sunday Mr. Harper would preach Ellen Tyler's funeral sermon. That was not strictly true, yet the spirit had moved him, and he did resolve to speak on a topic which had been strongly brought to his mind by Ellen's fate and the village comments thereon.

Harper's church, built in the simplest Early English Gothic, of warm gray freestone, had a quaint old air about it, not common in Western villages. When the hour came, curiosity had attracted an overflowing audience. Seats, aisles were all filled—every foot of standing-room occupied.

The preacher took a brief survey of the difference in spirit between the Christian system of ethics and the morality of all preceding creeds. He reviewed the gradual advance from stern severity and the retaliating code to a rule under which mercy tempers justice, and love is the fulfilling of the law. And he proceeded to show that the master-principles of that gentle religion which was promulgated in Judea at a period so remote that fifty generations have since risen and perished, are still far in advance not of the practice only, but of the laws and the avowed sentiment, of the present age. Then he went on as follows:

"We are, to this day, in many of our common feelings, far more heathen or Jewish than Christian. Draco's thought was of avenging justice; Judaism spoke of the offended dignity of the law; Christianity tells us of the joy in heaven over one sinner that repenteth, greater than over ninety-and-nine just persons. Little of that virtuous indignation against evil-doers, so easily put on, do we hear from the lips of Jesus; and when he did express it, it was chiefly directed against the Scribes and Pharisees, hypocrites, who devoured widows' houses, and then, standing up in the same temple as a humble, repentant brother, were wont to say: 'God, I thank Thee that I am not as other men are, or even as this Publican.'

"What a world will this be, dear friends, when we shall judge not, lest we in turn be judged; when we shall estimate at its actual wickedness that besetting tempter of the social circle, scarcely second in mischief to the demon of intemperance; hydra of many names: now, as mere tittle-tattle, indulged in to enliven the inanity of some dull tea-table; now, as street-corner scandal, raked forth to relish the twaddle of loafing idleness; and anon reaching the grade of serpent-tongued slander, deliberately employed to blast and to destroy.

"Against calumny, in its avowed shape, both law and public opinion are arrayed, but as to the petty species of backbiting, no whit less heinous, the sinners against charity and truth are often found in Society's most respected circles. 'They meant no harm; they were only talking: it was but a jest.' Ay! miserable jest, paltry small-talk to the idle tale-bearers; but bitter earnest, often deadly defamation, to the down-trodden victim! How many of earth's best and purest have been hunted to death by ribald tongues!

"There is another consideration worthy of remark in connection with this meanest among human vices. The cruel are cowardly, and the defamer is no exception to the rule. In dealing with one class of offences especially he is wont to pass by arrogant trespass, while he breaks the bruised reed and crushes the weary soul, already brought nigh to perishing."

He paused. The tall, spare form was drawn up to its full height, the mild eyes lit up, and he "spoke as one having authority:"

"There is a terrible wrong daily perpetrated in society; often veiled under a garb of light; usually sustained by public opinion, vaunting itself as the argus-eyed; seldom exposed, because it needs courage to expose it, yet not the less a wrong, cruel, flagrant, dastardly, iniquitous in principle, demoralizing in result.

"The iniquity consists in this. There are two culprits arraigned before the bar of Public Opinion—their offence mutual, their culpability unequal; still more unequal their power to endure the world's condemnation. The one, by nature the stronger and hardier, in most cases the tempter and the hypocrite, ofttimes the forsworn: the other, of a sex sensitively alive to public reproach, usually more sinned against than sinning; too often deceived by a loyal, unsuspicious nature; sometimes betrayed by a warm and a lonely heart.

"And now, how deals the world as between these two offenders? In what measure do we apportion to each respectively the anathemas of our resentment? If the stronger animal, in the face of deceit detected or perjury laid bare, brave it out, do we indignantly spurn from our presence the shameless transgressor? And if the deceived one, rudely awakened from a feverish dream, return, contrite and in misery, to the home whence she strayed, does Society, rejoicing over her repentance, receive her with glad jubilee, saying: 'This, my daughter, was dead and is alive again: she was lost and is found?'

"Must I give the answer? A true-hearted poet, Bryan Procter, shall give it for me, in some of the noblest lines the present century has produced. Two pictures he places before us:

WITHOUT.

The winds are bitter, the skies are wild,
  From the roof comes plunging the drowning rain:
Without, in tatters, the world's poor child
  Sobbeth aloud her grief, her pain.
No one heareth her, no one heedeth her;
  But Hunger, her friend, with his bony hand,
Grasps her throat, whispering huskily,
  'What dost thou in a Christian land?'

WITHIN.

The skies are wild and the blast is cold,
  Yet riot and luxury brawl within:
Slaves are waiting, in silver and gold,
  Waiting the nod of a child of sin.
The fire is crackling, wine is bubbling
  Up in each glass, to its beaded brim:
The jesters are laughing, the parasites quaffing,
  'Happiness!' 'Honor!' and all for him!

WITHOUT.

She who is slain in the winter weather,
  Ah! she once had a village fame—
Listened to love on the moonlit heather;
  Had gentleness, vanity, maiden shame.
Now her allies are the tempest howling;
  Prodigals' curses, self-disdain;
Poverty, misery. Well, no matter:
  There is an end unto every pain.

The harlot's fame is her doom to-day,
  Disdain, despair: by to-morrow's light
The rugged boards and the pauper's pall;
  And so she'll be given to dusky night.
Without a tear or a human sigh
  She's gone, poor life and its fever o'er!
So let her in calm oblivion lie,
  While the world runs merry, as heretofore.

WITHIN.

He who yon lordly feast enjoyeth,
  He who doth rest on his couch of down—
He it was who threw the forsaken
  Under the feet of the trampling town.
Liar, betrayer, false as cruel;
  What is the doom for his dastard sin?
His peers they scorn, high dames they shun him?—
  Unbar yon palace and gaze within!

There—yet his deeds are all trumpet-sounded—
  There upon silken seats recline
Maidens as fair as the summer morning,
  Waiting him rise from the rosy wine.
Mothers all proffer their stainless daughters;
  Men of high honor salute him 'friend!'
Skies! oh where are your cleansing waters?
  World! oh where do thy wonders end?

"Is this justice? Is it morality? Is it Christianity?"

The congregation sat in breathless silence. Harper himself felt as Moses may have done on Mount Horeb when he was bidden to put his shoes from off his feet, for the place whereon he stood was holy ground. His voice had a touching solemnity as he continued:

"Once, in the olden time and on a memorable occasion, a question of somewhat similar import was asked.

"It was in the temple at Jerusalem. She whose recent offence, proved beyond denial, was doubtless then the common talk of the day—she was there, in the midst. And there also were the notables of the nation, who walked in long robes and loved greetings in the markets; to whom were assigned the highest seats in synagogues and the chief rooms at feasts; representatives of the rank and respectability of the Jewish metropolis; the Scribes, men of learning, doctors in the law; the Pharisees, exclusives of their day, conformists in every outward observance, devotees to every formal ceremonial. They were all there to tempt Him of whom their officers (sent to take Him, but returning overawed) had declared: 'Never man spake like this man.' They set out their case, and they asked Him: 'What sayest Thou?'

"They were there to tempt Him. He had preached to them the novel doctrine of mercy, unknown to Jewish law. He had inculcated forgiveness of a brother's sin, even to seventy times seven. He had spoken to them the parable of the lost sheep, of the missing piece of silver, and, more forcible yet, of the prodigal son. And they were there tempting Him to deny, in practice, the great lessons He had taught in theory.

"Cunningly was the case selected and the question put. They knew well that the transgression of her who stood before them, shrinking from every eye, was punishable, by a code unchanged through fifteen hundred years, with a terrible death—by stoning; nay, that its very suspicion entailed social excommunication. Would He adhere to His integrity against venerable law—against united public opinion? Shrewdly had they calculated the dilemma and the risk.

"For a time, Jesus, as if He heard them not, withheld His reply; and His questioners, now secure of victory—one can imagine their triumphant tones—asked Him again: 'What sayest Thou?'

"They spoke to One who knew, in all its mysteries, the human heart; and from its inmost recesses He summoned an ally against legal cruelty and social wrong. They who tempted Him looked, perhaps, for evasion: they may have expected to extort a condemnation of the trembling culprit. But that glance, those soul-searching words, are not addressed to her. The lightning falls upon them—'HE THAT IS WITHOUT SIN AMONG YOU, LET HIM FIRST CAST A STONE AT HER.'

"The discomfiture is complete. Conscience-routed, these goodly exemplars of learning and virtue slink away, one by one, even to the last. The woman and her Christian Judge are left together, alone.

"How changed, now, the voice that carried dismay to the self-righteous heart! 'Woman, where are those thine accusers? Hath no man condemned thee?' 'No man, Lord.' 'Neither do I condemn thee. Go and sin no more.'"

Again the speaker paused. When he resumed, there was, in the simple dignity of his manner, a touch of generous indignation which awed his congregation the more because, in the good man's teaching, it was so rare. They felt that he was speaking under the sense of a holy mission:

"Ye who lay on others' shoulders burdens grievous to be borne, and take measure of your own purity according to the fiery zeal with which you crusade against frailty in your neighbors—ye who, for a pretence, make long prayers and pay frequent tithes, yet neglect the weightier matters of the law, justice and mercy—Scribes and Pharisees of our modern day, stand forth and answer! Have you ever read that story? Has its holy lesson ever come home to your hearts? Never! never! Else had you read therein the rebuke of your own barbarity—the conviction of your own heathenism. Inflexible judges you may be, unflinching censors—CHRISTIANS you are not! Christ spake comfort where you persecute: Christ rescued where you destroy.

"Say, if you can, why judgment should not be pronounced against you. Is the voice of immaculate virtue so clamorous that it *will* be heard? Do you feel that you are subjects of an especial mission—champions, yourselves free from all stain, and called upon by Heaven itself to vindicate the cause of offended purity? Then show the chivalry of champions—the bravery of virtue. Let not your coward blows fall ostentatiously on the weak, incapable of defence. Assault the strong: strike at him who, in return, can defy and resent. Make war not on unresisting repentance, but on brazen-browed guilt: on the liar who deceived—on the perjurer, repaying trust with treachery, who first swears fidelity and protection, and then, recreant to his oath, apostate to his manhood, flings aside his victim to misery and to scorn.

"You will not? Then learn to know yourselves. Claiming to be guardians of virtue, you are but aiders and abettors of vice. Through you, tolerators of perfidy! the villain, whose betters sleep in the penitentiary, walks the world undenounced, scot-free. You acquit *him* without a trial, and to his victim, condemned in advance, *all* trial is refused. I do not plead for the impenitent: repentance must come before forgiveness; but this I say: by your example the returning wanderer—even if her heart be chastened and purified by life's cruelest lesson, even though she pray, with tears, to re-enter wisdom's pleasant paths, sinning no more—is thrust back, unpitied—is shut out, unheard. In soul and spirit, despite her errors, she may be faithful-hearted as any of her sex—one who might yet be restored, a grace and a blessing to society. Yet, without quest or discrimination, you deny her entrance at every door save that of the abandoned: she is driven forth to perdition. In league with her destroyer, it is you who hunt her down, until at last—oh, the unspeakable secrets of that prison-house!—there is left to the lost one but the fearful choice between infamy and starvation!"

As he ended a feeling seemed to cross the speaker that he had been carried away by the impulse of the moment beyond the bounds of charity. For he added quietly, in his usual gentle tone:

"If in denouncing the self-righteous Phariseeism of the day I have been betrayed into unseemly warmth, let me stand excused. I assume to judge the offence, not the offenders. The men, like the murderers of Jesus, should be forgiven, 'for they know not what they do.'"

When the congregation, dismissed, were returning to their homes, most of them conversed in low and hesitating tones, as men are wont to do when they have been listening, impressed by some startling doctrine which they lack alike argument to confute and courage to accept and to act upon.

Ultimately, however, truth prevailed. Ellen's offence was of rare occurrence among these simple people, and public opinion on the subject had not crystallized as rigidly as in older communities. Harper's stirring appeal to that still, small voice so often overborne by prejudice had great effect: the sad fate of the culprit, too, induced gentle judgment: so that, except by Mrs. Wolfgang, Cranstoun and their incorrigible set, the girl was seldom mentioned in Chiskauga thenceforth, except kindly and charitably, as "poor Ellen!"

One of Mr. Harper's congregation went home heartsick—heartsick! Yet in the end the sickness was unto healing, not unto death. Celia had clung to her love for Mowbray so long as that love could frame excuse for his shortcomings. But eyes and heart were both opened, at last, to the enormity of his offence. She saw, as if clouds had been lifted from the future and the truth let in, that, as Sydenham had expressed it, her way had been barred in mercy. The blow that threatened to deprive her of fortune and reputable name had saved her from marriage with an unprincipled traitor. She was, indeed, very heart-lonely: his image, all unworthy as he was, haunted her still; but she had weathered the breakers on which a life's happiness might have been wrecked.

CHAPTER XLVI.

IN LONDON AND CHISKAUGA.

"Blind people that have eyes."
ISAIAH xliii. 8.

MR. WILLIAMS, intimately acquainted with our minister to England, had furnished his nephew with a letter of introduction; and the minister, who happened to have met Sir Charles Conynghame in society, gave Creighton a note to that gentleman, endorsing the bearer's character and standing. The house whither the Directory led the young lawyer was in a narrow street of plain, small dwellings, situated, however, in a fashionable neighborhood.

The furniture of the parlor into which, after giving a servant his card and the minister's letter, Creighton was ushered, had once been handsome, but was now a good deal the worse for wear.

The hour was early for London, but the master of the house, attired in a rich dressing-gown, soon made his appearance. His manner was coldly polite.

"You are a lawyer from America, I believe, sir?"

"Yes."

"May I ask what procures me the honor of this visit?"

"More than eight years since a ward of yours, Miss Mary Ellinor Ethelridge Talbot, suddenly disappeared from your house. She is now living in a village in one of our Western States—the State of Ohio—and she has employed me professionally to confer with you in regard to her property in your hands."

"A very unlikely story, sir."

"True, Sir Charles; but you are no doubt familiar with the French proverb: 'Le vrai n'est pas toujours le vraisemblable'—Things that seem to us unlikely are sometimes the exact truth."

"You expect me to believe that Miss Talbot, after withholding from me, for eight or nine years, all knowledge of her existence, has suddenly turned up in the wilds of America?"

"Precisely, except that you are slightly in error on a point of geography. The wilds of America are about a thousand miles west of Chiskauga, where Miss Talbot resides."

"I can imagine but one motive for such conduct, and that might invalidate your client's testimony."

"What motive?"

"A disreputable life."

"Out again, Sir Charles. With this very handsome little dagger"—handing him one with a smile—"on the afternoon of the seventeenth of May, 1848, Miss Talbot effectually defended her honor against a very disreputable and very constant guest of yours, Captain Halloran of the Guards. You will observe that the Halloran crest is on the blade."

"Pardon me, Mr.—" referring to the letter in his hand—"Mr. Creighton; but Yankee ingenuity has never been disputed. The dirk is very nicely gotten up, including the gilt H on the sheath—quite a capital piece of workmanship. But I think an English court of law would hardly believe that a young lady who had voluntarily eloped with an officer would defend herself, the same afternoon, against him, using his own dagger."

"We are losing time, Sir Charles, fencing with blunt foils. It would no doubt be tedious to you to go over with me these documents," taking a package from his pocket: "perhaps you will kindly refer me to your lawyers?"

"Messrs. Ashhurst & Morris, Old Jewry."

"I shall have the honor of proving, to the satisfaction of these gentlemen, that Miss Talbot, deceived by shameful artifice and promise of immediate marriage, was conducted to a house of equivocal character—was introduced, by Captain Halloran, to the mistress of that house as to his aunt; that, after the exhibition of what purported to be a special license, an attempt was made to perform the ceremony, the individual who personated the clergyman being the captain's valet; that one of the habitués of your house, Sir George Percival, was present—"

"Ah!"

"I think the two young gentlemen afterward had a duel in consequence of what passed. We shall prove that Miss Talbot refused to let the ceremony proceed, appealing to Sir George; that, in consequence of his remonstrance, Captain Halloran promised to comply with Miss Talbot's demand to be driven home, instead of which he conveyed her to his own private apartments; that when he attempted insult the young lady, snatching from his parlor mantelpiece the dagger which I had the honor of showing you—"

"For which you have Miss Talbot's testimony."

"I beg your pardon—the deposition of an honest, brisk young Irish fellow, Halloran's groom."

"The captain admitted his groom as witness of such an interview? *Credat Judæus!*"

"I do not ask you to believe that: the captain supposed the interview to be without witness. But I need not proceed with details into the truth of which your lawyers will inquire. Miss Talbot escaped on the evening of her abduction, supported herself for months by needlework, and was rescued from poverty and approaching blindness by an old Quaker gentleman, my uncle. He procured her a passage to America, where she remained for some time as governess in my aunt's family. She is now the principal of a successful seminary for young ladies in the same village in which I myself live, and is engaged to be married to a most respectable young gentleman in good circumstances."

Sir Charles, as his visitor proceeded calmly with these details, had gradually become very grave. Creighton's easy, assured manner alarmed him.

"I can say nothing in regard to your extraordinary story, Mr. Creighton, until my lawyers report to me."

"Of course not, Sir Charles. I wish you good-morning."

The senior partner of the law-firm proved to be an honest and judicious man. Creighton liked him, and disclosed to him frankly the extent of his powers. Ellinor had authorized him to compound the matter with her guardian on any terms he (Creighton) saw fit to accept.

"I don't mind telling you, Mr. Ashhurst," he said, "that Miss Talbot is extremely unwilling to institute legal proceedings against Sir Charles. Lady Conynghame was the dearest friend of her youth—a second mother to her. She prefers to take a portion only of what is due to her, if necessary to avoid litigation."

"You honor me by such plain dealing, Mr. Creighton, and you shall have no cause to repent it. I have begged Sir Charles, again and again, to transfer his law business to some other firm—it is very unpleasant to act for so reckless a spendthrift—but his father was very kind to me in early life, and the son clings to me still. If he has, as I fear, squandered Miss Talbot's property, his conduct is unpardonable. But his affairs are in terrible disorder; and he has great difficulty in extracting from the ruins of an excellent property a decent support. Leave these papers with me; and if, as I see no reason to doubt, your case is satisfactorily made out, I will tell you, on my honor, what I think Sir Charles *can* do, and whether he is willing to do it."

Creighton left with him Sir George Percival's address (in London, as good luck would have it); Terence's deposition; his own affidavit, detailing the attempt to commit suicide; that of the woman with whom Ellinor had boarded as seamstress; that of Mr. Williams and of his sister; and finally Mr. Williams' letter recommending Miss Ethelridge to Mr. Sydenham.

A week afterward, Mr. Ashhurst said to him, on returning the documents: "You have worked up your case most creditably, Mr. Creighton. It is clear as noonday. Ah! I mustn't forget to return you the dirk—*spolia opima*—that brave young lady's property by right of war. By the way, I sought out the maker, Rodgers, and he showed me, on his books for 1846, the order Halloran gave for that very dagger, the Halloran crest to be enameled on the blade."

"What will Sir Charles do?"

"Withdraw at once the suit against Miss Pembroke; and as to your client, I'm really ashamed to tell you—"

"I'm sure you've done your best, Mr. Ashhurst."

"Indeed I have; and that best is that Sir Charles proposes to pay you, against a receipt in full, three thousand pounds—little more than one-fourth of what he legally owes Miss Talbot; but to raise it he will have to resort to the Jews and submit to ruinously usurious terms."

"Three thousand pounds only?"

"I believe, on my soul, it is the best he can do."

"Your word suffices, Mr. Ashhurst. I accept on behalf of my client."

"The money shall be paid to you within three days."

Creighton was greatly pleased. Formerly he had liked London as a residence, but just at present he pined for home.

Meanwhile, Celia and Ellinor continued their school. The latter, notwithstanding her infirmity, could give lessons, as usual, in English literature, in history, mathematics, French and other branches—even in botany and mineralogy. She continued—what had always been her habit—to take the senior class out once a week into the forest. She could still distinguish most of the wild flowers by their odor; and when at a loss she caused one or other of her pupils minutely to describe the specimen, which her accurate knowledge of botany almost always enabled her to classify. It was her wont also, when they reached some eminence commanding an extensive prospect, to require of each in succession a word-painting of some portion of the landscape, or perhaps of a gorgeous sunset, or of some picturesque effect of light and shade from flitting clouds.

Two excellent results were thus obtained: the girls acquired a habit of exact observation, and a facility in describing what they observed. The practice awoke artistic taste and a love of natural beauty; and as the pupils perceived the pleasure it gave their teacher, their affection for her added zest to the exercise; so that it became at last one of their favorite amusements.

After a time, too, Ellinor, greatly to her surprise, found that, in some strange manner for which she could never account, new powers came to herself. She could walk unattended throughout the streets of the village, without risk of injury or danger of losing her way. When some months had passed there was developed a faculty even more wonderful than this.

It happened, one afternoon, that a letter arrived from Creighton, stating the result of his negotiations with Sir Charles Conynghame. Ethan, who had been out all day, attending to some surveying for Mr. Sydenham, was returning about five o'clock on horseback. As he rode slowly down the main street of the village, he observed Ellinor on the sidewalk at a little distance. She was approaching a ladder that had been carelessly left standing against one of the houses. Ethan instinctively checked his horse, and was about to call out to her in warning, but, as she came within three or four feet of the ladder, she turned out so quietly and naturally to avoid it that he was half tempted to believe she had recovered her sight. Nor was that all. There were two horsemen a little in advance of him. She suffered them to pass, and then deliberately crossed to where her lover, still fixed in astonishment, had remained. Coming up close to his bridle-rein, she laid a hand on his horse's neck and said: "Have you heard the news, dear Ethan? A letter from Mr. Creighton: he will be at home in a few days."

"Good God!" he exclaimed, startled out of all self-possession, "is it possible that you see, Ellie darling?"

"No: I shall never see again; but God is very good to me. Without sight, I can feel my way to you."*

Ellinor was on her way to fulfill an engagement to tea at Mrs. Hartland's. In the evening they all walked down to the lake to visit Mrs. Creighton and ascertain whether she too had a letter from her son.

The genial old lady was in high spirits, with a long letter on the table before her. Ellinor expressed her entire satisfaction with the settlement that had been made, and asked if Creighton's letter to his mother contained any further news.

* Ellinor's case is not an isolated one. A friend of the author, a physician in good practice in Philadelphia, has had two blind patients with similar powers. Driving in his coupé one day in a crowded street of the city, he saw one of these, an elderly man, after avoiding an obstacle on the pavement, step down into the street and come up to the side of his carriage to ask a question. When the doctor inquired how he knew it was he, and how he could thus find his way, he could give no explanation except that it "came to him." This man had what have been called mediumistic powers, but he had never exercised them professionally.

"Yes, an article that may interest Celia: he met, in London, her old friend Miss Ballantyne, now Mrs. Stanhope, on her bridal tour."

Elizabeth Ballantyne, a connexion of Mr. Hartland, and formerly a resident of Chiskauga, had left the village two years before on a visit to Columbus, and they had recently heard of her marriage to a gentleman of wealth and position, some twenty-five or thirty years her senior.

"I should so much like to know how Lizzie and her husband get on," said Celia to Mrs. Creighton.

"Quite as well as could be expected, Eliot says, considering the disparity between twenty-three years and fifty."

"That *considering* must be a terrible drawback, I think," Ethan said. "I have no faith in such matches. I'm sorry for Lizzie."

"Yet she may have married for love," rejoined Mrs. Creighton. "I saw a newspaper paragraph the other day—whether true or not, of course one can't tell—about General Changarnier. I think it was while he was commander-in-chief of the army of Paris, under the Presidency of Louis Napoleon. He had been invited (so the story ran) to a large dinner-party, at which the subject of marriage between young girls and old men—so common in France—came up. The general, himself a bachelor of some fifty-five winters, took strong ground against the custom, saying he thought it a scandalous thing for a man advanced in life to seek in marriage an inexperienced creature of less than half his years, just entering the world. A young lady, wealthy and well connected, recently come out, and who had been observed to listen with eager eyes and changing color, suddenly complained of illness and was compelled to leave the dinner-table."

"She might," broke in Ethan, "have been enamored of his rank or of his African renown."

"Perhaps. Yet that was a remarkable mode of showing such a species of affection. And she might have really loved him—if not exactly for himself, at least, like Desdemona, 'for the dangers he had passed.' At all events, the circumstance excited remarks which came to the general's ears. Explanations followed which opened his eyes—or his heart. The young lady, who had fainted after she left the room, revived, and is now Mrs. General Changarnier."

"I haven't a bit of faith," said Ethan, "in a man marrying for pity, or because a young lady's secret has leaked out."

"Yet that will happen, sometimes; and then the vanity of fifty-five is very apt to be flattered by the love of twenty-one."

"A vanity-prompted match is worst of all."

"That's true enough, Mr. Hartland. All I meant to say, as possibly applying to Celia's friend, is, that young ladies are wayward, and will sometimes fancy old men."

Mrs. Hartland did not intend to look at Celia, and very surely Celia did not intend to blush. Yet both things happened; and though Mrs. Creighton was too well bred to betray that she noticed it, she certainly did.

There was a somewhat awkward pause. To make matters worse, just at that moment Sydenham entered, and Celia, to her utter discomfiture, felt her blush deepen. She could have pommeled herself from sheer mortification at being so silly, and at feeling embarrassed, as she did, in replying to Sydenham's greeting. Mrs. Hartland evidently shared her embarrassment, and Mrs. Creighton looked so grave that Sydenham said, involuntarily, "No bad news, I hope, from your son?"

The question seemed to recall her from some uneasy train of thought. "Only good news," she said, smiling. "He has arranged the business of these young ladies, and I trust we shall see him in a few days."

This led to a business talk in connection with the compromise Creighton had effected, and with which Sydenham was much pleased. As no further allusion was made by any one to the Stanhopes or to General Changarnier, the rest of the evening passed off tranquilly. Sydenham accompanied the Hartland party home.

A week later, one chilly autumn evening, Mrs. Creighton's little parlor looked cheerful by the bright firelight. Two hours before, her son had arrived, bringing with him, on a visit from Philadelphia, his sister Harriet Clifford, a young widow without children; but she was up stairs, unpacking her trunk.

Eliot had wheeled a sofa toward the fire, and was seated beside his mother, his arm round her waist.

He passed a hand caressingly over the soft, smooth bands of the gray-streaked hair: "I wonder if you'll ever seem old to me, mother? It won't do for you to be a grandmother till you get one or two respectable wrinkles."

"If I thought that was the only obstacle, I'd try to be grave and thoughtful, so as to qualify myself."

"But you think there may be other obstacles?"

"Perhaps. Harry, poor child! thinks there never was such a man as her husband—unless, maybe, her brother; and her brother—"

"You don't think his chances of marrying are good, either?"

The mother hesitated: "I wonder if anybody's son, twenty-six years of age, ever chose his old mother for confidante before?"

"Can't say. Everybody is not as wise as your son, mother dear, nor as lucky. They might not get the exact truth in return for their confidence—as I shall." He tried to say it lightly, but the mother detected his deep emotion. How willingly she would have suffered it all for him! But each must bear his own burden; and then, after all, what did she really know?

"I feel sure she is not engaged, and, for aught I can tell, there may be no chance that she will be; but you are right about getting the exact truth from me." And she told him the Changarnier episode.

Of the elements that make up the passion of jealousy there was, in Creighton's nature, but one—if indeed it be one—its sorrow. Terribly grieved and disappointed he was. He felt, as thousands have felt in ages past, as thousands in ages to come will feel, that there was no more cheering sunshine for him in this life—that his path henceforth was in the cold gray twilight. Then it came over him that he *couldn't* give her up. Shakespeare, interpreter of every human emotion, had truly interpreted his:

> "For where thou art, there is the world itself,
> With every several pleasure in the world;
> And where thou art not, desolation."

He did not doubt his fate: bold and self-reliant in worldly affairs, he was diffident, as true love is till one blessed word is spoken. But not for that was his esteem, his friendship for Sydenham one jot the less. "She could not have made a worthier choice," he said to his mother, sadly, not bitterly.

"I'm not sure that she has—"

Harriet, who came in at the moment, overheard the words: "Done what, mother? Gone and engaged herself? In trouble, poor brother?" going up to him and kissing him. Then, to her mother: "Would she have done for a daughter-in-law?"

Eliot could hardly help smiling, despite his heavy heart. His looks expressed his surprise.

"Eliot dear," she went on, "if any one has a sister that he cares for, and that he considers a good judge of her sex, and if he wishes to keep her in the dark, he shouldn't talk to her a dozen times in the course of a three-days' journey about one particular young lady that he hopes she will like. But you haven't answered my question, mother."

"Eliot and I seldom disagree in matters of taste. Whether she will do for a sister-in-law I can't tell. Have you made up your mind that anything mortal is worthy of that brother of yours? I hope you've kept up your music lately: before Eliot marries you ought to have St. Cecilia's power. You know

> 'She drew an angel down.'"

"But if the angels are all of one sex, mother, that wouldn't help matters."

"I don't believe they are."

"Neither does brother, I know. *Is* she angelic?"

"No," replied her mother. "She's a good, lovable mortal, very pretty, too,

> 'Not too fair and good
> For human nature's daily food.'

I used to think her somewhat weak of purpose, and a little sentimental in her ways, but when she believed her money to be lost, and since, she has shown character and force."

"She has a noble spirit," Eliot put in: "any man might be proud of such a wife."

"I think St. Celia will do," said Harriet. "May I hear how it stands, brother?"

"Tell her, mother." And Harriet heard all about the telltale blush and the French general.

"You did very well," she said to her brother, "to admit me as a confidante. I'm little more than a girl yet"—with a sigh—"and girls get to learn each other's secrets. Don't imagine I have the least intention of prying into your lady-love's. But I want to tell you what happened to me a few weeks ago. I have a very dear friend, some eighteen years old, who has just such a trick of blushing as your Celia has."

"*My* Celia!"

"Never mind: it was a slip of the tongue; and who knows but it may all come right some day? Lucy—that's the young girl's name—asked me one day if I could give her any idea how she might cure herself of a weakness so annoying. 'I can't tell you,' she said to me, 'how often these foolish cheeks of mine give false notions of my feelings: people will put silly things in girls' heads, and then if I blush when something recalls the idle nonsense, it's set down to a serious fancy or a hidden passion, when nothing is farther from my thoughts.' Now, Eliot, may not Lucy's case be this young lady's also?"

Creighton began to think that possibly it might. "Would you mind, mother," he said, "if I left you for half an hour or so? I hate to do it this first night, but I suppose I ought to report progress, just in a few words, to these young ladies."

"Of course you ought. Take an hour or more: Harry and I have hardly had a chance for chat yet. And, Eliot, I think you had better go first to Mrs. Hartland's. Ellinor is very often there in the evenings."

Ellinor was there, and Sydenham was not; yet it was an hour and a half before Creighton returned home. And though he lay awake that night for two hours, thinking over his reception, he could not make up his mind whether he ought to hope or despair.

PART XIV.

CHAPTER XLVII.

A FRUITLESS RIDE, AND OTHER MATTERS.

"Le bonheur tient aux affections plus qu' aux événemens."—MADAME ROLAND.

"WHO is Dr. Rowe?" said Ellinor: they were speaking French, and it was in Meyrac's parlor, after tea.

"I think Monsieur le Docteur must have heard of him," Creighton replied.

"Is it the philanthropist," asked Meyrac, "who has done so much for the benevolent institutions of New England and for the education of deaf-mutes and of the blind?"

"The same. I made his acquaintance a few days since, in passing through Boston."

"I should have been enchanted to be of the party."

"His conversation would have interested you. I asked him which he considered the greater loss — sight or hearing."

"That does interest me. Well?"

"His reply surprised me. 'There is no comparison,' he said; adding that he had sometimes half doubted whether, under favorable social conditions, loss of sight was a misfortune at all. 'I knew a lady,' he went on to say, 'the head of a family with several children, who became blind a good many years ago. She was a somewhat nervous, anxious creature before her loss: now she is cheerful, tranquil.' Dr. Rowe thought her husband really loved her better, admired her more, than he had ever done; and the relation between mother and children was beautiful."

"Yet we must not generalize too hastily," Ellinor put in.

"I do not think Dr. Rowe did. I suggested that probably this was a bright, lively, affectionate household. He admitted that it was, and that with other surroundings the result might have been very different. 'The blind,' he said, 'live more in the world of the affections than we do, and that is the highest world, after all. Their pleasures are more strictly social than ours: they miss love more, and they enjoy it more. Blindness, to a convict in solitary confinement, might become an intolerable affliction, far heavier than loss of hearing. But in cheerful society it is natural that the deaf, daily witnessing the outward signs of thoughts and emotions that escape them, should be fretful or impatient, for the tender voice, the accent of affection, cannot be interpreted through the fingers.' The doctor added that it was his firm belief, founded on years of daily observation, that the inmates of a well-conducted blind asylum were happier and better satisfied with their lot than the average of persons without its walls."

"As to that," said Meyrac, "I agree with him. Yet if the regulations outside of the asylum were as wise as those within it, that might alter the case."

"And then," added Ellinor, "it cannot be denied that in losing sight we lose much power of usefulness."

"That depends," said Creighton. "Are you sure that children would not be better taught if instruction came more by conversation and less through books? By the way," he added, taking a volume from his pocket. "I've brought a little book for your acceptance, Miss Ellinor. You know of Francis Huber?"

"The naturalist, who wrote so much on the domestic economy of the bees?"

"The blind man who, fifty years ago, dictated to his wife, Maria Aimée—well named!—a book that is still considered the best authority on the subject. Some of his eulogists assert—but I dare say that's exaggerated—that nothing of importance has been added to the natural history of the bee since his time."

"You were thinking of a blind friend, Mr. Creighton: that's like you. Does the volume contain the result of Huber's observations?"

"No—the memoir of his life by his

friend, Monsieur de Candolle; and with such a pretty love-story in it!"

"May not one hear that?" asked Lucille Meyrac.

"Certainly, mademoiselle. When Huber was little more than a boy, he and the daughter of a Swiss magistrate, named Lullin, fell in love with each other. Even then he had commenced his researches; and blindness was brought on, while he was still quite young, from intenseness and minuteness of observation. The prudent father, thinking no doubt, like you, Miss Ellinor, that the youth's usefulness was hopelessly impaired, forbade the match."

"Ah, what unhappiness!" said Lucille.

"The noble girl declared that she would have submitted to her parents' will if the man of her choice could have done without her. As it was, she refused many brilliant offers, waited till she was her own mistress at twenty-five, then married her first love, shared his enthusiasm and his labors for forty years, and aided to make her husband one of the celebrated men of his day. 'As long as she lived,' he said in his old age, 'I was not sensible of the misfortune of being blind.'"

"But that is altogether charming," exclaimed Lucille. "Shall I read it to you when you have leisure, Mademoiselle Éléonore?"

"Dear child, yes: I shall be delighted."

Just then Ethan joined their party, and Ellinor told him of Creighton's gift.

Meanwhile, Lucille, who had taken up the book, smiled brightly at something that met her eye.

"I'm curious to know what that is," said Creighton.

"May I read, mamma?"

"Certainly, my child, if Monsieur Creighton desires it." So Lucille read: "Huber was habitually cheerful. When any one spoke to him on subjects which interested his heart, his noble figure became strikingly animated, and the vivacity of his countenance seemed, by a mysterious magic, even to light up his eyes, which had been so long condemned to blindness."

"I know who is just like him," the girl added.

Ethan's looks showed that he knew it too. How late he stayed that night I don't know, nor did Dr. Meyrac: on such occasions he always trusted Ellinor to lock up the house.

Next morning, Ethan called on Creighton to ask if he would act as "groomsman" in a ceremony to be performed that day three weeks.

"Most willingly; but you take me by surprise."

"We did not intend to marry till next spring, when our cottage on the lake will be ready; but mother told us that if we wished to make her happy, we would have the marriage at once and spend the winter with her. Last evening I got Ellinor's consent."

"An excellent arrangement, I think."

"I want your aid in settling all her property upon her."

"Ah? That is right: I'll attend to it with pleasure. If we lived a dozen miles farther west—just over the Indiana line—it would be unnecessary: the State laws there anticipate such intention as yours. Marriage in Indiana, since the year 1853, conveys to the husband no property, either real or personal, of the bride. But as to that matter, we, this side of the line, are still, like Simon the Sorcerer, 'in the gall of bitterness'—or, which is pretty much the same thing, in the bonds of the common law."

"I thought that had been modified some ten years ago."

"Slightly: so that the husband's interest in the real estate of the wife cannot be taken for his debts, nor conveyed nor encumbered without the wife's concurrence; and one or two other similar items. But a husband in Ohio becomes the absolute owner of his wife's personal property, even so far that if both unite in selling her land, the money received for it is his, and if he buys other land with it, that too is his, and descends to his heirs. As to the wife's real estate, he cannot, indeed, sell it without her concurrence; but, except in case of desertion or failure to provide for his family, he has the control of it, and the rents and profits are his while the marriage lasts."

"Twelve miles of longitude make all that difference!"

"Even so; yet an Indiana lawyer told me, the other day, that he did not believe one vote in twenty of their people could now be had to change the law back again."

"Well, one Ohio wife shall have the same rights as if she were an Indianian."

"The wonder is, Mr. Hartland, that any man can omit such an act of common justice without feeling self-condemned as a tyrant."

After paying all law-expenses (including a fee of one thousand dollars, which they had the greatest difficulty in getting Creighton to accept, his charge being five hundred dollars only) each of the sisters had about twenty-six thousand dollars, invested so as to bring in nearly eighteen hundred a year. They were rich!—far richer, they both felt, than either had ever been in her life before. They would not have been poor if they had lost it all.

After Ethan had looked over the statement of Ellinor's property, and was about to go, Creighton felt tempted to inquire who was to be bridemaid, but he refrained: it would be the bride's sister, of course. The thought made him grave.

The marriage was quite private and simple. The bridegroom was more self-possessed than his groomsman, and Celia showed evident emotion; probably because, as soon as breakfast was over, she was to part with her sister on a ten-days' tour to Niagara and the Canadas. Dr. Meyrac gave the bride away. When the carriage which conveyed the two to the station had driven off, he said to his wife: "But it is astonishing! One reads of such things—"

"What things, my friend?"

"That face of young Hartland's. I wish I were sure that any of us will have such moments by and by in heaven as he is having now in that fiacre."

"But, Alphonse, has not the good God—"

"Without doubt. It may be that it is all well arranged. Yet one likes to be certain, my dear. In waiting let us hope." And he took his hat and cane to visit a patient.

The next day was Saturday, with a bright November sun cheating one into the belief that winter was yet afar off. Mrs. Creighton and her daughter sat in the afternoon sewing.

The girl dropped her work on her knee: "So Eliot's gone out riding with Miss Pembroke?"

"Yes."

"How much does that mean in this part of the country, mother?"

"Not much if it happen but occasionally; only that the girl thinks well of her cavalier, and has no objections to become better acquainted with him."

"That's something; but of course she thinks well of brother, and who wouldn't want to be better acquainted with him? Still, you think she might say yes to somebody else next week?"

"Certainly, and no one would think strange of it."

"Well, that's sensible; and she looks like a sensible girl and a nice girl enough: then twenty-six thousand dollars is a convenience for a young lawyer—"

"For Goodness' sake, Harry, don't say that before your brother: he's crazy enough on that subject already."

"He's a noble fellow, and I won't plague him. But I can't see why the male animal, when he accepts without scruple a maiden's 'priceless affections'—with a life's devotion thrown in—should shy off at a little yellow dross. Then she ought to be very grateful to him for the skill and care he has shown in recovering her property, to say nothing of saving her sister's life."

"Worse and worse, Harry! Do pray be careful. If there's one thing Eliot has a horror of, it's marrying a woman who should accept him out of gratitude. He's haunted by that idea."

"Yet gratitude, like pity, is akin to love."

"Or to friendship. Mr. Sydenham is a charming man, very handsome, I think, and doesn't look a day over thirty-five years old—hardly that. And the girl may have no heart to give."

Harriet took up her work with a sigh. "I won't think anything more about it," she said, resolutely; but I don't believe she kept her word. It was a scarlet sacque she was making, and thoughts must have been worked in with the stitches, for she never after took it out to wear without thinking of Eliot and Celia.

A little later the brother returned. He said not a word beyond commonplaces till after tea. Then he asked his sister: "You'll stay with us this winter, Harry? Or is somebody with a heartache waiting for you in Philadelphia?"

"Nothing of the sort."

"Then you can stay. I must work hard now, and I will."

"I wonder if I could guess what put it in your head to ask me, just this minute, about staying?"

"Don't you believe that I like to have you with us?"

"Indeed I do: you're a jewel of a brother. I wish I were a certain young lady that I wot of, or else that she knew, as well as I do, what a jewel of a husband you'd make."

"A girl may think that a young fellow would make a creditable husband, and yet fancy some one else and marry him."

"No doubt. Will you give me a penny for my thoughts?"

"A silver penny, if I had it—copper's too base: ah! here's a tiny three-cent piece."

"You were thinking that if a man's ladye-love refuses him, what's best for him, and what he ought to turn to, is hard work; and that's quite true. Then you were thinking, besides, that if a man works hard all day, and hasn't a nice wife to come home to for comfort in the evenings, the next most comforting things are a nice mother and sister. The mother might see that the tea was warm and strong and the omelettes up to the Paris notch; and the sister, that no button was off and no stocking undarned. I think I'll stay."

"You're a clairvoyante, Harry, and a dear girl besides," with a kiss.

"Poor brother!" giving him two in return.

"What did she say, Eliot dear?" asked his mother in a low voice.

"I'm ashamed to tell you. I think it's the nature of women to think better of us men than we deserve. She said: 'You're as good as you can be, Mr. Creighton. I honor you, and I feel the honor you have done me. I owe you, for saving Ellie from death, a debt of gratitude that a lifetime couldn't pay. But I think far too highly of you to offer what you ought not to accept—what I know you would refuse—a divided heart.'"

"She's a good child, brother. It's hard for a girl that's not engaged to let a man into such a secret. She *does* honor and trust you, or she wouldn't have done it. I'll stay and get better acquainted with her."

"It's no business of ours," said Mrs. Creighton, "and I'll try to put it out of my head; but I *should* like to know just how Mr. Sydenham feels toward her."

"As if any one she cared for could help loving her!" said poor Eliot, with a deep sigh.

"So you've made up your mind," said Harriet, "that it's Mr. Sydenham?"

"If you had seen her blush when she could hardly get that little mare of hers, Bess, past the lane that turns off to Rosebank, you wouldn't ask that."

"Ah, well! it can't be helped. There's a wide, wide gap between a wife and a sister, or even between a wife and a mother, Eliot; but yet—"

"Don't, Harry. I must get such fancies out of my head. I must work, work!" The mother's eyes filled with tears, but she said nothing. He went on: "Help me to think of that, mother. And help me to remember how many millions never dreamed of such love as is mine already, here by this fireside."

Happy they who can turn from what

they have lost to what they still enjoy! It *was* a bright, blithe fireside, and the little group gathered around it loved each other, in a quiet way, very dearly. To any one who was himself of genial temperament there was a charming home-atmosphere, redolent of peace and harmony, about that pretty cottage and its inmates. Alas! that such oases are found but here and there amid the social bleakness of this lower world!

Early next morning Harriet Clifford met Celia Pembroke on her way to the Chiskauga Institute. She turned and they walked on together. "Miss Pembroke," she said, "I taught school for eighteen months when I was a girl younger than you. Let me help with your sister's classes till she returns. I want something to do."

"I shall be delighted. I was just wondering how we should manage. We have more pupils than ever before. While Ellie and I were dependent for support on our teaching, the numbers fell off. Now that we are both—thanks to your brother—in easy circumstances, scholars pour in."

"The way of the world, Miss Pembroke. By the way, since we're to teach together, hadn't we better be Celia and Harry to each other? You needn't adopt the final *y*, if you don't like it. I've been thinking myself of spelling it with an *ie*, like Mattie, so as to avoid the imputation of trenching on the masculine prerogative."

Celia laughed and assented. The two took to each other from the first, and Mrs. Clifford proved an excellent teacher.

That afternoon Celia had a music-lesson to give at Rosebank, but when she rode up she found Leoline's pony, Bucksfoot, saddled and bridled at the door, and Leoline herself came out.

"Papa suggested that we might not have many more such splendid afternoons before winter sets in, and that we had better make the most of it."

"I believe your father has intuitions, Lela: I *did* want a ride—that's the truth."

Leoline, as our readers may have observed, was sometimes troubled with a restless desire to see her friends happy. She called to mind her father's advice not to interfere in Celia's love-matters, but after they had chatted some time about other things, she didn't think she was disobeying his injunction by saying, somewhat abruptly, "I wonder, Celia dear, if you'll ever marry?"

"I do not think I ever shall."

"That's what I was afraid of. But you won't do for an old maid. I'd make a much better one?"

"Why?"

"Well, I don't exactly know. I'm not a girl that's nearly so apt as you to—"

"To take a fancy to a handsome face?"

"I wasn't going to be so rude as to say that, though maybe it's true enough: falling in love isn't much in my way. You'd make such a good wife, Celia—far better than hard-hearted I. Papa said so yesterday."

"He said I'd make a better wife than you?"

"Not exactly: he's too polite a papa for that. But he said you'd make an admirable wife, and of course he knows I wouldn't."

"But I'm not inclined to fall in love with handsome faces, or any faces, now."

Leoline looked grave; then, after a pause, "I'm very sorry for that," she said, thoughtfully.

"Sorry that I'm getting to be a little more like you? You ought to be glad. You would never have made such a mistake as—"

"Never mind about that, my dear. I once heard papa say it was one of the failings that 'lean to virtue's side' to think better of others than they deserve. I like you all the better for it; but I can't be glad to think of you as an old maid."

"Why not?"

"Because, as I told you papa said, you'd make somebody *such* a good wife. And then wife and mother—that's woman's vocation, you know."

"But if you don't take to that vocation, why should I?"

"Oh, I'm different. It's a pity I don't take to it, but how can I help that?"

"I think I know one who might get you out of that difficulty, if you'd let him — some one I once heard you admire."

"Naughty creature! but you're mistaken: that wouldn't work: I told you it wouldn't, from the first. I'm a hopeless subject in that line, Celia, but you're not."

"Suppose nobody wants me."

"That's not a supposable case. I can suppose that you don't want them, and it makes me sorry to think of it."

"Lela darling"—her eyes moistening a little—"let me tell you something. I hope you'll never, never have such an experience as I've had. I know it was sent in mercy. I feel—oh so thankfully!—all I've escaped. I hope I shall never see him as long as I live; but yet, for all that—"

"It's I that have been a naughty girl, Celia. Papa told me not to meddle with your love-affairs, and I didn't intend to do it. But now I've gone and made you think of things that—that it's not the least worth while—"

"It is not your doing, Lela, it's mine. I can't help thinking about them: some day I hope I shall be able to help it."

"And some day I hope you'll be somebody's pet and make him *so* happy. And till that time comes I'll let your heart alone. It has been plagued enough already, without my blundering. Let's have a good gallop, Celia."

CHAPTER XLVIII.

AS FAR AS THE STORY GOES.

WINTER passed. Of those in whom our readers take interest no one died—no one had been married. Ethan and Ellinor were established at Mrs. Hartland's. If Dr. Rowe had visited them, his doubts as to whether, in a genial home, blindness was always a misfortune, might have been strengthened.

Ellinor had intended to continue her labors at the Chiskauga Institute, but a conversation with Dr. Meyrac modified her plans.

"You have done nobly, so far, Madame Hartland," he said; "but a married woman, when she can afford it, should husband her strength and her thoughts for home necessities and home duties: the next generation may benefit thereby. Permit me to suggest that you gradually withdraw from the school, and let Madame Clifford, if she will, take your place."

Much to Ethan's satisfaction, Ellinor followed this advice; only retaining, for the present, the senior classes in English and French literature, and, when the weather permitted, continuing those weekly excursions to the woods which her pupils had come to regard as a pleasure and a privilege.

Celia spent a good deal of her time at Rosebank; sometimes remaining there, at Leoline's urgent invitation, for the night. She felt the less scruple in so doing because her aunt had now a daughter as well as a son to gladden her fireside, and seemed contented and happy beyond what her niece had ever believed she could be. Those fancies about Sydenham, of which Meyrac (though of course he could not have deciphered them) had detected the unwholesome tendency, were gradually fading out: a grandchild or two, Celia felt convinced, would dissipate them altogether. Now and then the widow took herself to task—for Alice was given to self-accusation—because she could not help feeling the death of her husband to be a welcome relief. He was so good a man, she thought, and she, as his relict, ought to be mourning his loss. He *had* been just, upright, a faithful provider, a man who intended, no doubt, to make his wife comfortable; but good?—how about that simple, homely virtue? Musselmen buy birds in the market and set them free, under the beautiful superstition that the souls of these liberated captives will one day bear witness to their kindness before the throne of God; but if Hartland had lived in Mecca, he would have regarded such ransom as money thrown away. Like the Pharisees in Jesus' day, he had failed to "learn what that meaneth: 'I will have mercy and not sacrifice.'" Can there be goodness without mercy? Is a domestic martinet a good man? Harshness, exaction of implicit obedience, severity in household rule—are these the qualities that fit a human soul for a high place in another world, where love is supreme? If in that world we "know even as we are known," Thomas Hartland had already found out that the widowed partner he had left behind ought to rejoice, not to lament, that Death had freed her from tyranny.

Celia was a frequent visitor also, during the early part of winter, at Mrs. Creighton's. Harriet Clifford and she had become fast friends, and she intended her visits to the cottage on the lake in pure kindness. When she refused Creighton she earnestly felt that she valued no one more highly as a friend. Besides, she was deeply grateful to him for all he had done for her sister and herself; and, though she had resolved never to marry him, yet on every account she wished, as much as possible, to take off the edge of her refusal, and to show him that she liked his company. Must she make a stranger of an excellent and agreeable man merely because she could not give him her hand?

All this was very well intended, and indeed generous, on Celia's part, yet I don't think it was very wise. It is a pretty theory enough that a young girl, free in every respect but one—namely, that she has no heart to give in marriage—should cultivate the friendship of a man a few years older than herself, and deeply in love with her, after she had refused to be his wife. Yet in practice, somehow, it doesn't work. Unless she thinks that by and by she may change her mind—when Celia refused Creighton she had no such idea—she may be doing a cruel thing.

That was the last thing the girl dreamed of doing or meant to do. She saw that when she entered Mrs. Creighton's parlor the son's eyes lighted up. The evenings were pleasant to her: they seemed even more pleasant to him, and Celia liked to give pleasure. Then they talked of Europe, of London and its wonders, of Paris and its attractions, of Eliot's student-life in Göttingen, of a visit he had paid to Rome and to Naples. Sometimes they branched off to other subjects, literary, artistic, scientific. Creighton was thoroughly well read, of sprightly intellect and comprehensive mind. He had been a shrewd observer and he was an excellent talker: Celia liked to listen to him. Surely there was no harm in all that—great good, indeed.

And then it was not as if he could mistake her motive. Forewarned, forearmed. She had told him in plain terms that she wished his friendship, and that she did not wish, because she could not return, his love. It was quite safe. There was no inkling of flirtation about it. Why couldn't he have her for a friend and some one else for a wife?—Leoline, perhaps: she wished he would.

Ah, Celia! I think you couldn't have helped knowing that you were not a disagreeable person. And you surely didn't need to be told that Creighton thought you particularly attractive. These long talks the poor fellow had with you about France and Germany and Italy—were they just the likely thing, do you think, to turn his thoughts to Leoline as a wife? You didn't calculate all that matter well.

One good came of it, however. Creighton threw himself, heart and soul, into his profession. He worked up his law cases with untiring industry. One or two important ones were thrown into his hands. He electrified the court and his brethren of the profession by several brilliant efforts, resulting in unlooked-for success. How much midnight oil he burned—for Chiskauga had no gas—I am not able to say; but he grew nervous-looking and pale. Gradually he attracted to himself the best half of Cranstoun's practice. He was spoken of as a rising man.

An unexpected event still further

brightened his business prospects. Amos Cranstoun, disappointed on every side, foiled alike in his plot against Celia and in his intrigues against the Institute, seeing a profitable practice melt from him day by day, sold out his Chiskauga possessions in disgust and emigrated to Texas.

He persuaded Cassiday to join him. Ever since Ellen Tyler's death the latter had been restless and unsettled. Once or twice he had relapsed into his old habits of intemperance; and Ethan, highly though he prized him as groom, had told him that the next time it happened he should be dismissed. Cassiday preferred, as others in higher places and similar circumstances have done, to resign his office.

"What did I tell ye, Teddy?" said Norah to her husband when she heard of their departure. "Didn't it answer best to let the spalpeen go?"

"But God hasn't drownded him, as ye thought He would."

"An' hasn't He sint him off on wan o' them steamboats down the Mississippi, an' isn't that the next thing to it?"

The same evening Norah had a letter, out of which, when she opened it, dropped a hundred-dollar note. When she had recovered from her amazement she and Terence read:

"MISTRESS NORAH O'REILLY:

"It was very good in you to nurse Miss Ellen Tyler when she lay sick. She and the old man were both very kind to me. I don't care about livin' here, now she's gone. I planted some flowers on her grave, and I want you to keep them in order and water them, and to set out some more when they're gone. The note that's in this letter will help pay for your trouble. I'll send you seventy dollars more from Texas just as soon as I can spare it. B. C."

Terence was the first who spoke: "Ef God gets him drownded on the way down, ye'll lose yer seventy dollars, Norah."

His wife did not answer: she was fairly crying. "God forgi' me!" she sobbed out at last.

"An' is it cryin' ye are, acushla? He was niver worth it. But I expec' it's a true sayin' for all, that the Divil isn't not half as black as he's painted. I'm mighty glad I didn't go after the fellow wi' a shillalah, any how."

One pleasant day early in March, Ellinor being somewhat indisposed, Celia had taken her place in the weekly excursion to the forest. On the way they met Leoline and Creighton on horseback. She mentioned this to Harriet Clifford on her return.

"Leoline is a charming girl," said Harriet—"bright, outspoken, and a young person of much character, who improves greatly on acquaintance. I like her. Mamma told me of her 'speaking out in meeting.' There isn't one girl in a hundred would have had courage to do it."

This set Celia a-thinking. For several weeks past she had been visited with qualms about the discretion of her visits to the lake cottage, and she had made these less frequent, usually timing them when she thought Creighton was likely to be absent. When he visited her, which might be once a week on the average, the symptoms made her uneasy: he was getting thinner, and she noticed a restless, nervous, unsettled look that was anything but habitual to him.

"You work too hard," she said to him one day.

"Hard work is wholesome for me," was the reply, but she did not like the bitter smile with which he said it.

After the encounter above mentioned, and Harriet's comments in connection with it, Celia scarcely visited the Creightons for six or eight weeks. Then conscience upbraided her for treating good friends so coldly. With all her love for her sister, she missed their society, thinking of them often and uneasily. She was not satisfied with herself.

"You are working too hard, Celia dear," Harriet said to her one day after school was over.

Celia had it on the tip of her tongue to say that hard work was good for her, but she remembered the spiritless smile with which Creighton had made the same reply, and merely said, "Not harder than you, Harriet: one feels languid the first warm days in spring. I'll come and have some music with you to-night: that will brighten me up."

She came. In the course of the evening Mrs. Creighton begged for the ballad, "When stars are in the quiet sky." Celia had sung it once or twice in the early days of their acquaintance; and now, for the first time, the request embarrassed her. With self-chidings for being so silly, she sat down to the piano at once. There was some uncertainty in her voice at first, but Mrs. Creighton thought and said that she outdid herself. Creighton said nothing, and his conversation, that evening, was less interesting than usual. Celia was grave and evidently out of spirits, though she did her best to conceal it. After a time Ethan dropped in, and she went home with him.

Next day, on her return from school, Celia found a letter on her table. She knew the handwriting, and locked her door before she opened the suspicious-looking missive. Her color came and went as she read:

"To Miss Celia Pembroke:

"I write because I would not have a hasty answer, and because I want to say what I have to say, calmly.

"It can't go on, Miss Pembroke. As God is my witness, I have done my best. A hundred times I've taken myself to task. Heaven help me! I think I've done little else (except what I've been driven to) than take myself to task all this last winter. You can say nothing to me in the way of reproach that I have not said to myself. I know I ought to be able to go on with my work in peace, but I cannot: the doubts, the uncertainties of my position thrust themselves into my office-hours. I ought to submit to the inevitable—and when I know it *is* the inevitable I suppose I shall learn to submit to it—but I need not submit to the tortures of suspense: they darken my life.

"I know that all you said about wishing me for a friend, and then all your visits to mother's house, were as kindly meant as they could be. I enjoyed your visits far too much; and when you discontinued them lately I felt miserable. But don't you see that there must be an end of this? I would be an ungrateful wretch if I did not value your friendship: priceless it would be to me if I cared for you less. But, Celia (let me speak to you this once—Eliot to Celia), even if I could keep on working near you, it would never do for me to stay here and be only your friend. If you knew just how I feel toward you—how day by day and week by week the yearning grows—you would not wish me to stay on such condition. If I did, and you married here, how would you like, each time you saw me, to feel that I loved you as no man ought to love another's wife? Do you think I would ever subject you to such an indignity? That's one of the things I *can* help—and I will.

"Don't vex yourself about it if I have to go. It's not your fault that I had to love you. It may be my fault, but it is certainly not yours, if you have no heart to give in return for mine.

"*Have* you none to give? I thought I could leave Chiskauga with the answer I had from you six months ago about that. But I felt last night—no matter why—that I couldn't go without asking—not the same question I asked then—not whether you would be my wife now—but only, just as I have put it, whether you have a heart to give that *might*, some day, when past regrets shall have faded, possibly turn to me.

"I cannot go without trying the sole chance that remains. But if you have to dismiss me, I ask only four words: '*There is no hope.*' Absolve me, I entreat, from the impertinence of desiring to know *why* there is none. I want the bare fact—that which regards my own fate only, not any one else's.

"If it must be, we shall leave Chiskauga in three or four weeks. And if I must hear, some day, of your marrying a man worthier and happier than I shall ever be, oh be sure, Celia—be sure—that your sister herself will have no good wishes for your welfare, heartier, warmer, than mine.

"ELIOT CREIGHTON.

"CHISKAUGA, *May* 2, 1857.

"P. S. My present income from my profession, if you care anything about knowing, somewhat exceeds two thousand a year."

Abrupt enough: not much of a love-letter—not a fine sentence or impassioned period in it. Yet it awoke to consciousness some fruitful thoughts that had been lying, half dormant, in the girl's heart. It was one of Celia's idiosyncrasies that odd scraps of poetry, floating like driftwood on the Mississippi, were apt to lodge and accumulate in the nooks and corners of her brain; now sinking out of memory, anon coming to the surface when some strong influence, as just now, stirred the depths. The scrap which emerged on the present occasion was a stray stanza, translated from some German sonnet or other, the rest of which had been swept down the Lethean stream. The waif had haunted her several times, especially during the latter part of the winter:

"'Now tell me how Love cometh?'
'It comes unsought, unsent.'
'And tell me how Love goeth?'
'That was not Love that went.'"

Had that young dream of hers been of something other than love? Was it but a fancy, built on the shifting sands of Impulse, which, when the winds rose and the waters beat against it, ought to be overthrown?

The dream was fading away — no mistake as to that. Nor did it seem less certain to the girl's awakened sense that the fancy had never been founded on esteem. Could she ever have respected as husband a youth idle of habit, infirm of purpose, selfish to the mother who loved and indulged him? And then, if that terrible tragedy had happened after their marriage, could she have lived, as wife, with Ellen's betrayer? She shrank appalled from the thought.

If Love, once the heart's inmate, cannot go, this had been but its worthless similitude. The sooner the thing was out of her sight—ten feet underground—the better.

In after time—because the heart, if it be genial, waxes charitable with years—there was a certain reaction: then news of his well-being came to be grateful; but not now. She wished no news about him: she was sure of that after she had read Creighton's letter.

That night she lay awake she knew not how long. Next day her school-hours were invaded, as Creighton's office-hours had been, by vagrant doubts. In the afternoon, after giving Leoline her music-lesson, she had a long, solitary gallop in the woods: then she slackened rein and let Bess walk lazily back. By the time she reached home she had decided that she must have a talk with Creighton. Ere she went to rest she wrote and burned up several notes. Next morning, before breakfast, she indited and sent to one whose heart was beginning to wax sick with "hope deferred," the following:

"TO ELIOT CREIGHTON, ESQ.:

"I have taken time, as you wished, to think over your letter, and I am not willing to dismiss you, as you phrase it, with four words. Can you spare time to ride out this fine morning?

"CELIA PEMBROKE.

"*Saturday.*"

Almost before breakfast was over Creighton's horse was at the door. While they traversed the village little passed between them. As they rode by Harper's modest dwelling, Celia said, "I'm sorry you missed that sermon after Ellen's death."

"Good Mr. Harper wrote it out at my suggestion; and I have not read so powerful an appeal for many a day. Your sex is often adored, but seldom fairly treated. Flattery, Courtesy, Indulgence are gay courtiers, but grave, sober-eyed Justice is worth them all."

Celia had concluded, the day before,

that it was good for a wife to be proud of her husband. The thought came to her again.

"Which road do you prefer?" Creighton asked.

"Shall we ride to Grangula's Mount?" Then, with a smile, she added, "I have pleasant associations with it."

Creighton ought, in common civility, to have expressed his assent, but he did not. Perhaps, too, it was his part to allude the first to the letter he had written, but that also he neglected. He spoke, instead, of Ellinor, saying how much pleasure it gave him to see her so bright and contented. "It was but the other day," he added, "your sister said to me that she had never known what happiness was till she became blind."

"A sentiment I met with in Madame Roland's autobiography may explain that, I think."

"And the sentiment was—?"

"That happiness depends not so much on events as on the affections."

"It is one of the foundation-truths of the world. Every year stamps it more and more on one's heart."

"On some hearts."

They were getting didactic. Conversation flagged till, arrived at the Mount, Creighton, to use the language of the country, had "hitched their horses to a swinging limb" and they had seated themselves in the shade.

"Mr. Creighton," Celia then said, her voice somewhat unsteady, "I am perfectly sure that if I married a worthy man, no one would congratulate me more sincerely than you. But when you wrote that were you thinking of any one in particular?"

The usually self-possessed Creighton reddened with embarrassment, and Celia, despite the guard she thought she had set on that silly habit of hers, blushed over face and neck.

"I pained you, Miss Pembroke," he broke forth when he saw her emotion: "I had no right—"

"I think you *had* a right," she tried to say quietly. "I wished to tell you—" There she stopped, and, after a moment's hesitation, abruptly and very irrelevantly, it seemed, she added: "Harriet tells me you've been reading *Sir Charles Grandison* lately."

He could not imagine what this was leading to, but he answered, instinctively, "Yes."

"Have you come to the episode about Sir Charles' ward?"

"Emily Jervois?" Then it flashed on him — her hopeless love for her guardian!

"Her case is not mine. I never was in love"—she said it with a nervous sort of smile—"I never was in love with either of my guardians."

"Thank God!" He did not intend to say it aloud. The tone of his voice went to Celia's heart: it revealed to her all he had been suffering, and she added, very earnestly,

"I have been weak and foolish, Mr. Creighton, but I solemnly assure you that I never loved Mr. Sydenham except as his daughter might; and he, as surely, never dreamed of me as a wife. When I spoke six months ago of a divided heart—"

"It was Mowbray!"

"It couldn't have been what we ought to call love, yet it *would* come back for months in spite of pride, in spite of reason. Could I say yes to you while it haunted me?"

"And now, Celia, now?"

"Evelyn Mowbray would be less dead to me if he were in his grave."

It was all told. And then Celia Pembroke found out, for the first time in her life, what Love's words are like. All that Creighton had garnered and guarded in his heart for long months, that happy heart poured out now—a revelation of which she had never even dreamed. On the grass at her feet, both her hands in his, those wonderful gray eyes on hers, she felt that this was her first love. It quenched all lingering recollections of that other feeble counterfeit, as the sun puts out the faintest star. She had had visions, as girlhood will, of a fair world, but this that was opening upon her outshone her brightest dreams. Grangula's Mount was hallowed in her memory for evermore.

When the first wild waves of emotion had subsided, and on the long swell of satisfied affection that succeeded something like conversation was possible, Creighton said: "Celia darling, what helped you to find out, at last, how it stood in that dear heart of yours?"

"There was a short sentence in your letter about leaving us in three or four weeks."

"I hated to write that. It seemed so like an appeal to your pity."

"Did it? Perhaps we might both have been much to be pitied if you had gone: at all events, I discovered when that alternative came suddenly before me, that *I* should be. I wanted to know if I really, really loved you; and when I found out that I couldn't let you go—"

A sudden interruption prevented the conclusion of the sentence; not that any impertinent intruders showed themselves: it would have been quite awkward if they had.

When Celia recovered herself—all to the bright bloom that *would* linger—she said:

"Now it is my turn, Eliot—"

"Is it?"

"Don't be foolish—my turn to ask questions."

"Ah!"

"The other evening, when you felt that you couldn't go without interrogating your fate—'no matter why' you wrote me—"

"You want to know about the *why?*"

"Yes."

"Yesterday I should have been ashamed to tell you. If there's one creature I despise more than another, it's a man who presumes on a woman's favor. But that evening when you sung to us, it was like Nourmahal's song in Lalla Rookh."

"The air with the 'deep magic' in it that the dark sorceress taught her? You must have a powerful imagination."

"I wonder who taught you such an expression of that exquisite fancy of Bulwer's. There *was* sorcery in it, I'm certain. I never felt its beauty before. *Did* you think of me, Celia?—*did* you care for me a little while you were singing?"

"Yes."

"I thought so. It was the first time I had thought it."

"You did not use to care for me."

"When?"

"When you first came here."

"I was drawn to you the very first evening we sang together. But you were an heiress then, and I was a poor, briefless lawyer. You were engaged, too, and I had no business to care for you as I did. It provoked me."

"I thought there was something wrong—that I had displeased, disgusted you, perhaps—"

"I *was* disgusted, but it was with myself for my own folly: that was all."

"It seems to me so strange now that there ever was a time—"

"The future, Celia!—the bright, happy future! Let the past go."

"I thought my fate a cruel one. How little I knew about it!"

I don't believe either of them ever knew how long they sat there under that magnificent elm. In after years they made an annual pic-nic pilgrimage to the spot on a certain anniversary.

As they mounted their horses at last and turned toward home, Creighton asked: "Celia, what made you say you had pleasant associations with Grangula's Mount?"

"Because it was here I first got an idea what sort of man Eliot Creighton was. By the way, saucy Leoline, who had been admiring you that day, told me, as we were riding home, that you would never fancy her, but that I was just the sort of person you would be sure to fall in love with."

"Sagacious girl!"

"I wish she could find somebody worthy of her—"

"No hurry, Celia. Far better she should enjoy in that pleasant house of her father's a few years of beautiful girlhood, fancy free."

"She's only three years younger than I."

"But three years of innocent gladness, three years to lay in a stock of strength and health and spirit and experience against the realities of life! And then I think you're more than three years older than Miss Sydenham. You've crowded two or three years into the last twelvemonth."

"I feel as if I had. I think I must be about twenty-five—only two years younger than you. Lela seems to me a mere girl in comparison, but such a dear, brave, spirited darling."

"I like her so much."

"Hadn't you a nice time with her that day we met you in the woods, lover-like, on horseback together?"

"You can't make me believe you were jealous."

"I think it rather opened my eyes. But any one might love Lela. Don't you wish, as somebody has it, that you had 'another heart to shrine her in'?"

'One God and one heart, Celia. That's Nature's creed and Love's."

"Forgive me, Eliot."

"For an innocent pleasantry? Soame Jenyns believed that part of our happiness in heaven would spring from an exquisite perception of the mirthful. I dare say he's right."

"Shall you find excuse for every foolish thing I say or do?"

"If anything you ever say or do needs excuse—yes."

"Now I think of it, there's one thing I did that was rather shocking."

"Pray, what was that?"

"I pretty much asked you to have me—and this is not leap year."

"You asked me to have you?"

"Didn't I? Your modest prayer was —don't you remember?—not by any means that I should agree to be"—she blushed a little—"to be Mrs. Eliot Creighton, but only that I should be so good as to let you know whether I had a heart to give which, some day or other—in five or six years, I suppose—that would be a reasonable time for the fading of past regrets—might possibly turn to the humble suitor who would wait just as long as my ladyship pleased. And now, as the children say, I've gone and done it—"

"That's shocking, is it? Don't I know why you did it? From pity. You saw I was getting ghostly—quite lackadaisical and hatchet-faced."

"You mustn't joke about that. You *are* looking pale and thin, and it's my fault: I knew it was that day you told me hard work was wholesome for you. I've repented of that. The bad child won't do so any more."

But lovers' talk, unmatched in its proper place, will seldom bear retailing.

The sixteenth of June was their wedding-day. Mr. Harper was asked to officiate: a great pleasure it was to the kind old man, for both Celia and Creighton were favorites of his: he thought he had half persuaded the latter to study Hebrew.

The morning before the wedding Celia found, on her toilet-table, a deed to herself of the Hartland dwelling-house and its appurtenances, signed by her aunt and cousin—a very pretty marriage-gift: plenty of room for her new mother and sister-in-law—and then Bess would remain in her old stall. She had scarcely recovered from her surprise when, descending to the parlor, she espied, standing there, a semi-grand Steinway, with a kind note from Sydenham lying on it. She tried the tone and could not restrain an exclamation of delight.

"When you return from your wedding-trip you will find me at Ethan's," her aunt said to her during breakfast.

For Ethan had found out that his wife and her mother-in-law were unwilling to be separated. And like a good fellow, as he was, he had modified his building plan, interposing between the ground floor and the French attic a second story.

Mrs. Wolfgang was disgusted with the arrangement, declined to visit her sister-in-law, and changed her residence to Mount Sharon: report said, because she had matrimonial designs on a rich old bachelor, clerk of the court there. I have not heard that she succeeded. If he finally escape the snare, the husband-market of California is still open; and Leoline may some day be gratified by the intelligence that the Rocky Mountains are interposed between herself and the object of her special aversion. I don't think the widow will go to Texas, as she once thought of doing; for by the last accounts from thence the Chiskauga public learned that Cranstoun had lost his property and Cassiday his life in the Great War. Some time, however, before the Mississippi was closed by Confederate batteries, a letter reached Norah, postmarked Austin, Texas: it contained seventy dollars, but not a word of explanation.

If any reader of ours, traveling in Western Ohio, should happen, some summer day, to look in upon Chiskauga, and if, as he ought, he visit its picturesque cemetery, entering it by the eastern gateway, he will find, on the left as he passes up, a neatly-fenced burial-spot, marked by a white marble slab bearing a name not unfamiliar to him; and planted around it he will see choice flowers fresh and carefully tended. Which is happier now—the young girl whose earthly burial-place was beneath these flowers, or a man, young and handsome still, owner of a marble-fronted, richly-appointed dwelling on Arch street; prosperous, all the world says, and envied by all who are struggling for similar prosperity? He married well some time since—this young man—for he was accepted in due form by a stylish-looking person about his own age, boasting good family connections, who dresses becomingly, enters a drawing-room gracefully, receives her guests with ease and dignity, and is satisfied, on the whole, that she married him; for she finds that twelve thousand a year, carefully managed, does tolerably well. The villa she got him to rent last summer at Newport was rather small, to be sure, and she has to be a little careful about evening-parties—they are so frightfully expensive now-a-days. Nor has she been to Europe yet; but they expect to rent their house in Philadelphia, furnished, next summer, and then they can afford to go. Meanwhile, she contrives, by well-ordered economy, to keep a brougham and never to neglect an evening at the opera. It's not amiss, take it all together, she thinks. Her husband (though his poor mother knows better) still inclines to believe that his wife loves him, and it may be a year or two before he is undeceived.

It is to be taken into account, however, that if that fashionable husband were to be brought face to face with an evil deed of his that would not usually be called murder—if he stood beside that village grave and read, cut on the pure marble, a simple name—his cheek might blanch, and his heart, all selfish as it is, might sink within him. But then he is not obliged, that I know of, to visit Chiskauga at all; or even if business should take him there, he need not enter the village graveyard. The world he lives in is another world, having no connection with that in which he was once doomed to vegetate. Old things have passed away: he has left his youthful follies behind.

It would be an unheard-of thing—yet how often is truth unheard of, and how infinitely, sometimes, does human conception of the strange fall short of the truth!—it would be a strange, unheard-of thing to say that Ellen Tyler is far, far happier to-day than he, the falsely-styled favorite of fortune, by whom she was cheated and betrayed.

Yet, withal, the man is not worse than hundreds of others on whom Society smiles—children of this world, who look upon riches as little less than a passport to heaven. Let him make the most of the cumber and trouble he idolizes. Let him smother, if he can, under glitter and gauds, ugly recollections of lying and cruelty. Let him robe conscience in purple and fine linen. He has chosen his part. Of all such it may be said, as in the olden time it was of the self-seekers who "loved to pray standing in the synagogues and in the corners of the streets:" "Verily I say unto you, They have their reward."

What of the humble, sequestered future of the two sisters and the husbands of their choice? They had escaped life's worst perils, but they were still young and inexperienced. All earthly seas, even beyond the breakers, are visited by storms; and Goethe has wisely said:

"All beginning is hard, but hardest is household beginning."*

Yet, through error and trial, through storm and sunshine, they have enjoyed a liberal portion of happiness. Many hours they have spent when life was "lovely and pleasant," and when husband and wife felt they had little left to desire except that one day—in death undivided—they might pass together to those regions where skies are brighter and pleasures are higher than are skies and pleasures, at their best and brightest, here below.

* The line here paraphrased occurs in that charming pastoral, *Herman and Dorothea*, reading in the original:

"Aller Anfang ist schwer, am schwersten der Anfang der Wirthschaft."

www.ingramcontent.com/pod-product-compliance
Lightning Source LLC
LaVergne TN
LVHW010228110826
845151LV00004B/1227

* 9 7 8 1 4 2 5 5 2 5 7 0 5 *